Black Arrow

Arthur C. Eastly

Enjoy
Art Eastly

4th Floor Press, Inc.
www.4thfloorpress.com
www.black-arrow.ca

Library and Archives Canada Cataloguing in Publication

Eastly, Arthur C., 1936-
Black arrow / by Arthur C. Eastly.

Issued also in electronic format.
ISBN 978-1-897530-31-3

I. Title.

PS8609.A768B53 2012 C813'.6 C2012-906405-X

Published by 4th Floor Press, Inc.
www.4thfloorpress.com
www.black-arrow.ca
www.wheatgrasspublishing.ca
1st Printing 2012
Printed in Canada
Cover Art by J. Scot Paisley

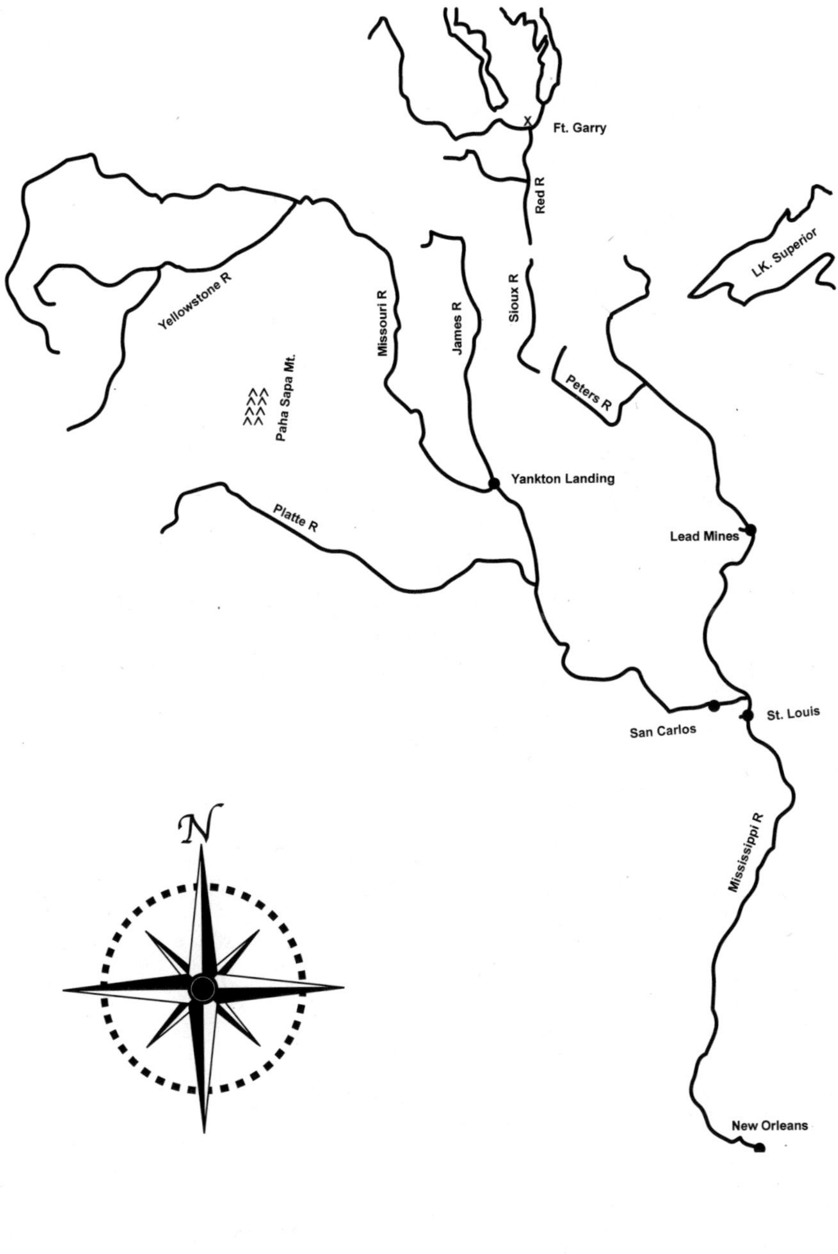
Ft. Garry
Red R
LK. Superior
Sioux R
James R
Missouri R
Yellowstone R
Paha Sapa Mt.
Peters R
Yankton Landing
Platte R
Lead Mines
St. Louis
San Carlos
Mississippi R
New Orleans
N

Chapter 1

Carrying the long gun in the crook of my left arm, I walked out of camp, away from the trees, to a small knoll where I stood staring at the western horizon, thinking of what lay ahead.

At sunrise, the long trip west to the mountains would begin with little knowledge of the route or troubles we might encounter; I was worried and a little scared. Likely, my mind was creating worse situations than would happen; at least I was trying to convince myself of that. Despite my careful planning, now I faced the reality of venturing into a new and unknown wilderness to trap and trade. The trip was based on only a few words, describing a mountain area with many beaver, told to me in the spring at a Mandan Indian village I visited. Every day of travel would take us farther from the familiar, away from people we knew and with just two men to accompany me. Very good men, mind, but still I was scared and nervously fidgeted with the French-made Charleville long gun which was waiting for cleaning. With a forty-five inch barrel, it was the most accurate long gun available on the frontier in 1800, the only gun that could outdistance Indian bows with acceptable accuracy.

My best friend, Rene Beauchamp, watched me from camp where he sat beside an oak tree chewing on a willow twig to clean his teeth. As always, Rene's trade musket was close at hand. A gun good enough for hunting, provided you got close to an animal, except the accuracy was erratic. A worse problem was their habit of exploding, causing serious injuries. Rene compensated by charging his musket with a smaller amount of black powder to reduce its power; so far his musket functioned properly.

Thinking of that gun brought my promise to mind. When our trading made a little extra money, fulfilling my promise to Rene of a new Charleville long gun would be top of the list. Last spring, after finishing our first year as free traders, all our furs went to buy trade goods. Rene suggested accepting the Bay's offer of an advance against future fur deliveries. I refused to go into debt to the Company. After five years clerking for the Bay and observing all the schemes used to get furs from trappers as cheaply as possible, I didn't trust the way they did business.

Chiding myself that the Charleville wouldn't get cleaned if I kept reminiscing, I walked back to camp, opened my cleaning bag and got started.

∞

Rene watched, wondering what James Richardson was thinking about and his mind wandered back to the days when he first came to know Richardson. Rene's mother was a Cree Indian. Rene considered himself a Cree and loved the free life; hunting and moving around as the seasons dictated. He thought like an Indian. The white men called him Métis because his father was French. Richardson wasn't like that; he only saw a man and if you were honest and strong he treated you like a man. He treated Indians the same way, with respect and honesty.

Rene remembered back five summers when French voyageurs arrived at the Company's trading post, at the forks where the Assiniboine and Red Rivers meet, bringing large freight canoes weighed down with supplies after paddling all the way from Montreal in the east. Along with supplies, they brought young men being sent west to join the staff at the Company's fur trading posts. One amongst the group of new arrivals stood out. His name was James Angus Richardson, a big mouthful, until Rene overheard men refer to him as Jar. It was some time before Rene understood where that came from. They were calling him by his initials, JAR. Over time, Jar became so accustomed to it, he often needed to pause to recall his real name.

Rene soon realized that Richardson was different. He dressed and looked much the same as the other young men except for his large size and serious, no nonsense attitude. Jar read the white man's writing and worked with numbers, so he was assigned as Chief Clerk to assist Fort Garry's Factor in the daily routine of the Fort. He kept accounts and records, with letter writing added on. Other new recruits went further west to help man the Bay Company's widespread network of eighty-seven outlying Posts.

Despite being referred to as a Fort, Garry was really just an odd collection of scattered log buildings which were fast becoming a company distribution center. Local people talked often of Bay plans to build a large Fort nearby as a station for an Inland Governor to oversee the widespread operations farther west.

Supplies arrived at Garry in flat-bottomed skiffs from the York Factory on the west side of Hudson's Bay and in freight canoes from Montreal. Fort Garry's Factor was responsible for allocating those supplies to trading posts all across the Saskatchewan River country.

In similar fashion, furs from trading posts came down the rivers each spring to Garry where they were sorted for quality and repacked before being sent on to London through Hudson's Bay or Montreal.

As summer turned into fall, Rene observed Jar leave the Fort to return later with geese, ducks or grouse. Jar carried no weapon, causing Rene to wonder how the boy obtained the birds. The next time Jar went into the bush Rene followed and watched him place a round stone in a leather pouch at the end of a long string, whirl it around his head and throw it at a goose with great accuracy. Jar got four geese and Rene casually intercepted him on the trail back to the Fort and helped carry the birds.

Rene didn't know what this strange, silent weapon was until the next trip into the bush when Jar explained the sling to him and showed him the leather pouch that held the stone. After a demonstration, Rene practiced with the sling. That was the beginning of their friendship.

Jar's steady supply of fresh birds for the table pleased the Factor. In late fall Rene was hired to hunt for a winter supply of meat, the Factor sent Jar along to help, giving him the loan of a company musket. In the methodical culture of the company, a careful record was kept of everything issued. It was expected that each load of powder would be accounted for with game or a good explanation.

Rene's deeper insight into the nature of his new friend began on that first hunting trip. Richardson produced a bow and arrows; a bow different from anything Rene ever saw before. It was six feet tall, reaching well above Rene's head and used arrows longer than a man's arm. It was a bow which took a strong man to draw the length of an arrow, which Jar did with ease, displaying his great strength.

It was a bountiful hunt. Each time the bow brought down an animal Jar removed the correct amount of powder from the company supply, along with a lead ball and placed it in a separate pouch. They proved to be a successful hunting team, bringing in buffalo, deer and elk on a regular basis. The Factor, happy with the results, willingly released Jar from his clerking duties to hunt.

As supplies of powder, shot and other small items accumulated, Rene sold them for Jar. Over time it became obvious the boy was slowly building his wealth for some definite purpose.

Late in the fall when the snows started, they sat together in the storehouse where Rene demonstrated the method of making the long, narrow snowshoes necessary for walking through bush in deep snow. They prepared clothing for the cold weather that was coming, including Voyageur-style hooded capotes made from blankets and Cree-style knee-high, bush moccasins for deep snow. Hunting would continue all winter whenever the weather cooperated. Even so, unless you were very lucky it was impossible to find game when the weather turned bad and the animals settled into good cover to wait for better days. They were always out searching on good days; often with no success. In late winter, game usually became scarce and often people at the fort went through a time of hunger before the spring brought relief.

During Jar's first fall at Garry, in 1795, the snow came early, piling into deep drifts, driven by strong winds. When the Factor held his Christmas Ball in December, the snow was deep. Many people struggled into the fort; still attendance at the three day party was lower than expected. The Factor was unhappy. It was his largest celebration of the year and everyone was expected to put in an appearance. Jar and Rene watched as everyone ate huge amounts and the meat supply disappeared rapidly. They knew hunting would be necessary early in the New Year to supplement the dwindling supply from the fall hunt. Clear, crisp days for most of January provided them an opportunity to bring in a number of animals. Each time they were forced to travel farther from the fort to find game.

February brought days with longer daylight while the temperature dropped to thirty below as they set off once again through deep snow, each driving a dog team. Nineteen days later they returned with a butchered moose on one sled and two deer on the other; the last meat of the winter.

At every opportunity, they went out searching for scarce game in the severe weather. Often, they went hungry for days at a time and Jar commented about the careless waste of food at the Christmas Ball, insisting if the food had been properly husbanded at the time, little hunger would exist later in the winter. Those discussions shaped both their attitudes toward food preparations for future winters. Jar learned fast. By spring, he was expert at preparing winter camps with shelter from the constant winds, having learned all the little things it takes to survive in cold weather.

Shortly after spring came, canoes from posts in the west started arriving with furs. A report of canoes approaching brought everyone down to the river to see old friends and help with unloading. Many shot off their muskets, accompanied with much yelling and laughter. As Chief Clerk, Jar was responsible to count and record what each post brought so the records from the traders could be verified. All went well the first few weeks until Athabasca trader, George Sampson, arrived with his canoes and crew. Sampson was stocky, five foot seven inches tall with strong arms, a beard he rarely trimmed and a liking for fur hats and Bay Company boots. A wide, bulbous nose and small pinkish eyes gave his chubby face a bovine appearance. Employed by the Bay for over twenty years, Sampson was a burly man with a reputation for drinking excessively, bullying his men and abusing the young Cree women around his post. Sampson elbowed and hard shouldered his way through life with a habit of causing trouble. He would never be promoted; he knew it and took his anger out on everyone around him, excepting only the Factors.

Year after year, Fort Garry men carefully stayed out of Sampson's way, avoiding him each time he arrived. This being Jar's first spring at Garry, he didn't know Sampson or who he was and knew nothing of his reputation. In any case, there was a job to do.

Sampson waded to shore, looked up at the gathered people and climbed the riverbank straight toward Jar, who was standing beside the wooden box containing his records. Jar saw Sampson coming and something in the man's attitude alerted him. As Sampson got near, he extended his right arm to push Richardson aside, growling, "Out of my way, boy."

Jar slapped the arm aside with his hand. Sampson stopped in surprise, his face turned red and he shouted angrily. "No man slaps George Sampson and gets away with it!" Following the shout, Sampson swung a mighty roundhouse right at Jar's head, meant to lay him unconscious on the ground. Rene saw this happening and immediately started moving closer to his young friend, his hand loosening the belt knife in its sheath. Rene didn't intend to interfere in a fair fight, but if Sampson attempted to injure or maim the boy, his knife would put an end to it. Everyone, including the Factor, watched Sampson; all being sure Jar would take a beating through no fault of his own. In the end, Rene wasn't needed.

Jar stepped to his right so the roundhouse blow went over his left shoulder. He landed a hard left punch to the side of Sampson's rib cage, knocking the wind from his lungs and causing him to bend over. Shifting left, Jar swung a hard right uppercut to Sampson's large nose, snapping his head back. Blood spurted as Sampson tumbled down the riverbank, rolling face down into the water where he lay still. Everyone watching was surprised and no one moved for several seconds. They all stared in disbelief at Richardson standing calmly, looking down from the top of the riverbank.

Jar pointed and called to the men near the water. "Ye men best gie him a haun afore he drowns." With the spell broken, two of Sampson's men rushed to pull him from the river. The crowd of traders, Indians and Métis excitedly discussed the fight, looking at Jar, appraising him in a new light. There were many comments about how lucky the boy was. Finally, a Métis man everyone referred to as Old Joe, who was standing with a small group of men, commented. The Factor was close enough to overhear him. "Sampson lucky, not boy. Beauchamp ready stick knife in ribs."

Sampson's nose was broken and cracked ribs caused him to favor his right side. By morning both eyes were swollen and black. Rene grinned to himself remembering the fight. In retelling, the story grew, convincing everyone that Jar was best left alone. Those who would go against him could expect nothing but misery. Fur traders were a rough lot and fighting was common. Still, no one wanted to tangle with the man who so easily beat George Sampson.

Rene's second surprise came during the summer with the arrival of the company-issued Jamaican rum on the northern skiffs. Every Bay man received a gallon of 180 over-proof rum as part of his yearly pay. The men drank to relieve the boredom, poor quality food and harsh living conditions. A gallon of rum was poured into a wooden barrel which was filled with water to make a year's worth of drinkable rum. Most men used up their allotment before spring came, with no new supply available until the boats arrived from York Factory in midsummer.

While Richardson enjoyed a mug of ale, he didn't care for liquor. Rene watched with interest to see what Jar would do with his gallon jug. When it was put up for sale the following April, five men banded together to buy the jug. More gold and silver coins were added to Jar's hoard. Each April for four years, Jar sold his jug, taking advantage of competition to get the highest price possible.

Every winter to follow was similar until Richardson's contract with the Company was fulfilled. That day, Jar told Rene of his plan to go south and become a free trader; Rene quickly asked to go along. Jar agreed and promised when the company was up and running Rene would have a one quarter interest. Rene's protests that it was all Jar's money and should be Jar's company fell on deaf ears.

Rene's musings of the past were interrupted by the sounds of a horse and both men stood up to watch, taking positions on opposite sides of the camp among the stacks of supplies. Soon, they saw the animal coming through the trees. The rider was Andre Troyes, the son of Rene's oldest sister and the third member of their party.

Rene stirred up the fire, adding a few sticks of wood so they could cook meat. Filling the pot with water, he set it on a flat stone beside the coals to heat for making tea. Each man speared his meat on a sharpened stick, propped it over the fire to cook and sat down to wait.

Rene was the oldest of the group at thirty-eight. Andre was twenty-four and Richardson had turned twenty earlier in the summer. Richardson had signed a contract with the Bay in Glasgow when he was fourteen and served out his five years before leaving the employ of the Company the year before.

The Factor was furious when Richardson had refused to renew his contract, flying into one of his not infrequent rages; shouting threats, shaking his fist in front of Jar's face and promising to send men to hunt him down if he traded in the Company's territory. Those threats were still out there, hanging over their heads like a big axe.

In the summer of 1799, Jar led his small caravan away from Fort Garry, following the Red River south, to trade for furs with the Sioux and Mandan Indians living along the Missouri River. After some searching, Jar established a home base on Peters River, which was north of the Missouri and flowed from the west into the Mississippi. East of the Mississippi was territory claimed by the recently formed United States of America, south of the Missouri, the land was Spanish and to the north, the Hudson Bay Company held title to all the lands west of the Great Lakes and north to the Arctic Ocean; a grant from the King of England. According to a copy of the grant, which Jar had access to as Clerk, the Bay's title was to all the lands draining into Hudson's Bay. To the south, the title extended to the headwaters of the Red River which flowed north. The Company chose to ignore this detail and claimed all the territory north of the Missouri River.

Legally, where Jar chose to settle was outside the areas the three parties claimed or were entitled to. That fact meant little in the vast wilderness of forest, grass, lakes and rivers. When the Factor at Fort Garry became aware of their activities, he was likely to take action.

Jar traded carefully for furs with his limited supply of trade goods while Rene and Andre trapped beaver during the first winter. In late spring, they returned to Fort Garry, knowing the Factor would be gone north to York Factory for the Governor's annual meetings.

Negotiating hard and haggling with the men left to run the post, Jar obtained the best value in goods for their furs, including the bare necessities such as salt, tea, powder, lead and as large a volume of trade goods as possible. Iron kettles, awls, thread, needles, arrow heads, hatchets and knives along with other assorted items were obtained. It was a larger stock of trade goods than the summer before. Only one luxury was allowed. Three heavy wool Bay blankets to make into warm winter coats. It cost three beaver for each of the best blankets and their snow white color made for good camouflage during the winter.

While waiting for the meat to cook, I began writing in my logbook as Rene and Andre watched. Neither could read and the words meant nothing to them. They understood the maps I drew when traveling and were familiar with the compass used to take readings to draw maps. Rene and Andre didn't need a compass; both could find their way except in the worst of storms and only a fool traveled in bad weather. A wise traveler settled in good shelter and sat out a bad storm.

Writing in the log every day kept track of the date. It wasn't important to the way I was living, I just liked to know. Changing of the seasons was all that really mattered. Starting with the date, seventh of August, 1800, I glanced at the thermometer to note the temperature and added a brief description of the weather. Lastly, I noted that all our preparations were done and in the morning we would leave Peters River to find our way west to the mountains and spend the coming winter trapping and trading for furs. 'We know not what dangers await us.'

Carefully wrapped in oiled cloth to keep it dry, the book went back into the saddlebag along with my compass and thermometer. I leaned against a large cottonwood and turned my head to look around, listening carefully for unusual sounds. A magpie hopped around at the edge of camp looking for discarded food. Birds sang, leaves rustled in the breeze and nothing seemed out of place.

As the sun sank toward the western horizon, it was growing dim under the trees where our camp was located. Andre moved to add a few small sticks to the fire, causing my thoughts to turn to my two companions.

Rene and Andre were slim, wiry men with the black hair of their Cree ancestors, equally at home in the woodlands or out on the prairie. The western prairie, that great expanse of grass that seemed to go on forever, was a natural place to them. They fit in like the buffalo, antelope, wolves and birds, knowing instinctively what to do and how to find food or shelter from a storm. Both were constantly alert and sensitive to any changes around them. On foot they moved silently and with ease, having the ability to disappear into their surroundings, which was critical when hunting or potential danger was nearby.

After five years of traveling with Rene, striving hard to be like him, I gradually improved to the point that Rene occasionally commented, "You like Indian." It was a compliment and few white men in the area could match me. Still I would never be as accomplished as my companions. It was natural behavior to them, while I needed to think all the time; where to step, being careful not to brush tree branches or make noise in other ways.

Both men started eating their meat while mine stayed to cook longer. Finally picking up the stick and shaving off thin slices with my hunting knife, I slowly chewed. It was still juicy with the red color gone, just the way I liked it.

With the rising sun barely showing itself, giving the underside of the scattered clouds a pinkish tinge we rode out of camp leading six packhorses loaded with supplies. Putting the rising sun behind us, we started west to the mountains. Our plan was to travel west for several days before turning slightly south to cross the Missouri at a point well upstream from Yankton Landing. From our Sioux friends we knew of a crossing where the horses would be able to ford the river, especially if no recent rains had occurred upstream.

Spring runoff from the mountains was over now, allowing the water level in the Missouri to fall. Crossing the river was the first major problem we expected to encounter and could cause a delay of several days if the water level rose due to rain. We might lose a horse with everything it carried. All this we discussed repeatedly and still I worried. I was financing the enterprise with money it took six years of hard work and frugal living to accumulate and there was no appeal in the idea of starting over again. My mind gnawed on the problem like a dog chewing on a bone and would, until we were safely across the river.

At midday we stopped to give the horses a rest, having travelled nine or ten miles. The trees were thinning out and soon we would be into open, wide grasslands. Rene set the teapot on the edge of a small fire to heat while we chewed on venison jerky, listening to crickets sing in the warm, dry grass. Later, while sipping tea in the shade, Andre pointed out the many fluffy white clouds drifting high across the deep blue sky and commented, “Weather good, no rain comes.”

All afternoon I rode in the middle, leading the packhorses, carrying the long gun crosswise on my saddle. Andre and Rene were out ahead, one on each side of me, about a hundred paces away. While the Sioux were mostly friendly, this was Indian country. We were wary of the Arikara who were troublemakers and often not even friendly to other Sioux. The Arikara lived some distance away across the Missouri and south of the Yankton Sioux. However, Indians moved around freely, often showing up unexpectedly.

It was big country, appearing flat and wide open, which could easily deceive a traveler. There were countless places where an enemy could lay in wait; hollows, folds in the landscape, ravines and stream beds. The two Cree were constantly alert, their natural instincts probing for anything that might indicate danger. Suddenly, Rene waved his arm and pointed to the northwest. We changed to the indicated direction, purposely varying the route of travel. If you made a mistake out here you might never get another chance. Coming over a slight rise, I saw the reason for the change. There was an area of low, marshy wetland ahead. Our previous route pointed at the south end of the marsh. Now the new direction would take us around the north side.

Packhorses loaded with trade goods would be a temptation to anyone who saw them. We hoped to slip quietly across the country without attracting attention. Our planned route would avoid all populated areas that we were familiar with until we got into new, unknown country south of the Missouri. We had no knowledge of what was on the other side of the river.

Well short of sundown, we came to a small lake with willows crowding the shoreline and a good campsite in a clump of poplar trees. After the horses were watered and picketed in plain view in the tall grass, Rene suggested, "Jar and Andre go scout. Look for sign of people. Rene start fire, cook meat."

We went in opposite directions along the lake and returned. I reported. "The only sign is o' deer coming to slake thair thirst." Andre shrugged. Around bites of meat, I asked, "Rene, dae ye think we huv come twenty mile tae day?"

Rene chewed slowly, thinking about it. "Rene think more than twenty."

I waved my knife. "Maybe so. It wid be a guid first day. Anither day 'n the packhorses wull be toughened up tae the trip."

Andre lit his pipe and shortly afterwards Rene did the same. My father's pipe was in my leather bag. I didn't smoke it every day.

Just before dark we brought the horses close and left the fire to burn down. I suggested, "Andre, ye stand first guard, then Rene. I wull tak the last shift." Always an early riser, I liked to watch the stars and see the night darkness give way to a new day. We would stand guard because if the horses were stolen there would be no way to continue west unless the trade goods were abandoned.

Nine days after starting, we crossed the James River and changed our direction of travel to the southwest to shorten the time to the Missouri. West of the James, the land was very dry with water much harder to find. Unless it rained, water for the horses could become a problem. The grass was brown on the high ground and the horses stirred up dust with every step, even at a steady walk.

Hour after hour, I swayed gently in the Indian-style saddle made from wood and rawhide. My horse was an even gaited animal so the riding was easy, making the long days more boring than tiring. There was plenty of time to observe the country, noting landmarks.

Soon after the midday halt on the twelfth day, the Missouri River valley became visible in the distance. It was too late in the day to attempt crossing and avoiding the valley overnight would reduce the chances of meeting other travelers. We walked the horses into a small, sheltered valley where spring water trickled from a ledge of rock. It was a good site, providing a well sheltered camp. A blackened ring of rocks indicated this was a known place used many times by other people.

Twelve days of slow travel in ninety degree heat, with the last two short of water, was hard on all of us. The horses would benefit from extra rest and be in better shape for the day ahead. After the horses were watered and picketed on grass and the camp organized, Rene climbed the slope to settle down under a clump of brush to keep watch. As unlikely as it was that anyone was in the area, we didn't want a surprise.

Watching, Rene spotted a coyote trotting along their back trail. He smiled. Trust that wily old trickster to come snooping around. Coyotes were the most adaptable animals on the plains and in many ways, the smartest. Anywhere you went you found old coyote, on the plains, in brush country, the mountains, it didn't matter. Coyotes found a way to fit in and adapt to any local food available. The large grey wolves roaming the grasslands were the only enemy who could cope with coyotes; even so, the coyotes found a way to get along with wolves. Many Cree stories of wily coyotes were passed down through the generations. As a young boy, Rene had listened to the stories and observed their ways.

After cleaning the long gun I went up the slope to take over. Rene slid down from the top of the bluff before standing up so he didn't skyline himself to any observer. He explained about the coyote before making his way back to camp. Andre was busy preparing a stew, slicing buffalo meat into cubes and dropping them into the iron kettle with water, wild onions, salt and corn. The kettle steamed and bubbled over the fire. Dinner would be a change from the roasted meat of the past days.

After carefully checking all around to get familiar with the terrain in every direction, I opened the log to start a description of the day's travels, estimating the distance and sketching a map of the route. These sketches were for use in drawing a larger map showing the entire trip, with all the streams, lakes and natural landmarks. I also kept a record of various animals, birds and plants seen along the way.

Now deep into buffalo country, so far seeing only small groups of animals, we were yet to encounter one of the big herds. Yesterday,

Andre had used his bow to bring down a buffalo cow for fresh meat which would last for a few days. When you were living on just meat it was surprising how much three men could eat in a day. Using a bow instead of a long gun was preferable because it was quiet. Noise carried a long way in that wide open country when the wind wasn't blowing. Besides, the bow saved on powder which might be scarce before we returned in the spring.

Slowly scanning the horizon, a small herd of buffalo was raising dust in the west. They were heading south to the river. I watched and carefully noted where the trail was. Everything on the plains needed water and in some areas it dictated how you could travel. This was the time of day when people lit cooking fires and I watched for any sign of smoke.

On our back trail a large group of antelope, in fact several groups, moved slowly across the land. Antelope possess excellent eyesight and can outrun everything else on the grassland. If there were men out there, the antelope would disappear so quickly it left you wondering if your eyes were playing tricks on you. They were the fastest animals on the plains and very difficult to hunt.

Chapter 2

Daylight was upon us. I arose from my place on guard and stirred what remained of the coals to start a fire before calling just loud enough to reach across the camp. "Be ye lazy lads aimin' to sleep the day away then?" Rene was awake, just lying there. Andre was never one to hurry from his blanket of a morning. Soon both came to the fire to start meat cooking with good water to drink.

Slipping out of the small valley, I rode a circle around looking for any sign of travelers, while Andre and Rene loaded the horses. There was nothing to be seen. We lined out to the west to where buffalo had traveled the night before and followed along their well-used trail, which was always the best way to enter a deep valley like the one ahead. Buffalo have front legs that are shorter than their hind legs. As a result, they never go straight down a steep slope because they would fall over from the massive weight carried in their shoulders. A buffalo trail always angles across a slope, slowly winding its way down, making easy travel for the horses. This was a route used by the big herds with several trails running parallel to each other to accommodate the large number of animals. From the description the Sioux had given us, it would lead to the Missouri at a place where the buffalo regularly crossed.

Andre led the packhorses with Rene off to the right, higher up the slope, while my horse was on the lowest trail. The valley this side of the river was covered in a dense growth of large trees; oak, cottonwood and a mixture of others I couldn't put names to, with clumps of low growing brush. Off towards the river there were willows.

Almost at the bottom of the slope, my nose picked up a hint of wood smoke on the slight breeze. Turning in the saddle, I pointed to my nose, giving the sign for fire and Rene nodded. After several minutes with no further smell of smoke it seemed like my nose must have been playing tricks so I started forward. Coming out on the flat ground I turned to the side to wait as the pack train arrived. Suddenly, a scream came from east of us.

My right leg went up over the horse's neck and I dropped to the ground, as did the others. All of us were on the ground, ready to defend ourselves, almost before the sound died away. The horses were stopped at the edge of a grove of large oak trees which were widely spaced with very little underbrush. A quick scan of the area revealed no threat as we rushed the horses into the shelter of the trees. While I tethered the horses, Andre and Rene scouted in opposite directions to check the area around us.

Going on our way as silently as possible to avoid getting involved was a temptation, but the thought was quickly discarded. Someone was in trouble and it wasn't our way to not offer help when it was needed. Besides, we were leaving a horse trail easy enough for anyone to follow. If there was to be trouble it was better to deal with it now when we wouldn't be surprised.

With my bow and long gun in hand we started away from the horses, moving through the trees, spread out some twenty paces apart. The forest started to change to cottonwoods with clumps of low growing brush. Fallen branches shed from the self-pruning cottonwoods made walking difficult. A man needed to be careful where he stepped to avoid the sound of a snapping branch, instantly alerting anyone nearby.

The scream came again and it was close, probably no more than two hundred paces away. With no way to know what we were facing, we moved cautiously and silently through the trees, staying low and moving from tree to tree; constantly alert for any sound. Gradually, a clearing in the forest began to show in front of us. Carefully, I eased closer, making only the slightest sound in the dry grass, until only one large tree stood in my way. Crouching down on one knee behind the tree provided a good view of the clearing.

It was a small Indian camp, probably one family. It appeared they had camped there for the night and were attacked by other Indians. An older, white haired man was lying on the ground, his head smashed in from a tomahawk blow. Two warriors holding burning brands from the fire were standing over a man lying on the ground with an arrow through his left shoulder. A third sorted the family's belongings, while two more were holding a young woman by the arms. No doubt they had plans for her later on.

All this my eyes took in quickly before my head turned to locate my companions. They were nowhere in sight. I put my attention back on the scene in front of me. Rene and Andre would find the best positions to be effective. There was no need to worry about them; they would do whatever was necessary.

Taking three arrows from the leather quiver on my back, I notched one, holding the other two in my left hand, which gripped the bow, and waited to see what would develop. The warriors moved, obviously intending to burn their victim again, with him lying helpless on the ground. Drawing the bow, my first arrow flew through the air at the one closest to the injured prisoner and a second quickly followed, aimed at the other warrior. In seconds, one was down with a black arrow through his chest. The second warrior started to turn and the arrow went through his arm into his chest, pinning the arm to his side. Both went down. An instant later, my third arrow was in the air aimed at the thief on his knees, who looked up in surprise at the commotion and died with an arrow in the throat.

The last two warriors dropped the woman's arms and ran away across the clearing. Shouldering the long gun and taking time to aim carefully, I shot at the one on the left. The report of the gun echoed loudly across the clearing. When the cloud of black power smoke drifted aside on the breeze he was lying motionless on the ground. The last man almost reached the trees on the far side of the clearing where he died with two arrows in his chest. Rene and Andre were there.

Glancing back at the campsite, the injured man was on his feet with a tomahawk in his hand, ready to help, although the fight was all over. In the blink of an eye, five men were dead. It reminded me of how narrow a path we walk between life and death. It is never more than a heartbeat away; a very sobering thought.

Staying still while several minutes went by, listening for any sound of movement, my heart slowed after the rapid action. The woman hurried to the aid of the injured man who was likely her husband. Her clothing and appearance indicated she was from the Mandan Tribe who mostly lived farther upstream on the Missouri.

She looked at the shoulder, speaking to the man, who nodded

his head. With both hands she gripped the arrow, snapping off the feathered end. From the front, she braced one hand on his shoulder and pulled the broken arrow shaft out. He didn't move or show any sign of pain.

After carefully reloading the long gun and taking up my other weapons, I stepped into the clearing. The Mandan saw me immediately. There I stood, a man over six feet tall with broad shoulders and rusty red hair, clean shaven since the rest stop yesterday. I was wearing a wool trade shirt, deerskin pants and the knee high moccasins of the woodland Cree that I favored. Behind my leather belt was a pistol, tomahawk and a large hunting knife.

What they couldn't see was the throwing knife hanging down my back from a thin horsehair thread around my neck. It fitted me to fight a war, not for making social calls like people back in Glasgow. Out here, a man got along the best way he could.

Oh, they knew me; there weren't many my size around and red hair was a rare thing on the plains. My black arrows were different and something much talked about. With the talking went the news that Black Arrow was a fair trader who could be trusted. That talk was good for the business we were building. Everyone marked their arrows so there was no confusion as to who shot an animal. Only I went a step further; staining mine black to make them easier to find in the snow during winter. Over the years it became a thing people talked about.

Walking to the fire, I sat down, cross-legged, opposite the man. Using my Cree, along with what Sioux words I knew, we talked, using much gesturing and sign language to help. The woman continued to work on his shoulder. She went into the trees and came back with dry moss which she used to plug the arrow holes. It would stop the bleeding and keep the wounds clean. Next, she put a leather pad over the shoulder, tying it in place with leather thongs. All this time he showed no sign of pain from the wounds or the burns on his sides and chest.

He pointed at his chest. "Red Eagle." He paused and added, "Mandan trader."

Pointing at my chest I told him, "James Richardson."

Red Eagle pointed at the black arrows. "Sioux say Black Arrow."

My head nodded in agreement. My Sioux was not as good as my Cree; I knew only a few words from one year of exposure to the Sioux while trading. My understanding from his words was that they traveled to visit among the Yankton Sioux and were returning to the Mandan villages on the great bend of the Missouri. The family had stopped here at a known campsite where there was a spring of water, plenty of firewood and good shelter from the wind. It was a place often used by travelers.

Red Eagle pointed disdainfully at the five bodies. "Arikara." Four of the attackers were young braves. Only the leader who had been looking through their possessions was older.

Going among them to retrieve my arrows, I gathered up their weapons. Back at the fire, I arranged the captured weapons in a row beside Red Eagle. He watched silently to see what would happen. There were two trade knives and three tomahawks made of iron, the rest were flint, along with quivers of arrows, bows and a few lesser items.

When Red Eagle began to divide the items into two piles, I held up one hand and shook my head no. "Red Eagle keep."

We argued and finally I selected two flint knives and a stone tomahawk which were made by expert hands—each of them a fine example of the craftsmanship of the local people. They would be worth keeping for my collection of odd items; a habit of mine which greatly amused Rene.

Rene came from the trees to stand apart from us, observing the camp, remaining ever alert. He sensed something was amiss, so I kept a wary eye on him. Red Eagle recognized it, too. He spoke to the woman who went to the far side of the clearing, near their two horses, where she called out. A few minutes later a lad of twelve or thirteen years, accompanied by a younger girl, came cautiously from the trees. Red Eagle's wife talked to them, before bringing them to the fire, where the wee girl looked at me wide-eyed. My smile was an attempt to put her at ease.

The boy kept his hand near a flint knife in his belt, looking stern and brave, as he sat beside his father. There was curiosity in his eyes as he watched me; a huge, rough looking man by his standards. If he was frightened, it didn't show.

Rene walked away into the trees and returned to the clearing a few minutes later, leading five horses. We all walked over to have a look. Andre wisely remained concealed. These were typical small Indian ponies which we could use. There would be need for more packhorses if our winter trapping was successful.

The Mandan's two horses were tied at the edge of the trees and they could probably use more. Walking around inspecting the animals, Rene pointed at a triangular brand on one and nodded his head at Red Eagle. In the end, we selected three unmarked animals.

The boy walked away, leading the other two to tie them to trees near their other horses.

Rene studied the Arikara for a moment before suggesting, "Come up river, we send down river." It was a good four hundred paces to the Missouri. We dragged the bodies to the bank and tossed them in. We would never know if they arrived back with their people.

Crossing the river was much easier than expected. All my worrying about the crossing turned out to be for nothing. There was one stretch where the horses swam for about thirty paces; the rest was just wading along a well-used buffalo crossing on the Missouri, where over the years thousands of feet packed the bottom. Much of the crossing seemed to be on a rock ledge of some sort. How the animals selected that spot was another mystery for me to wonder about.

Small packs on the new horses eased the load on the others for the crossing. We needed to make three more pack saddles as soon as travel and time allowed.

Following the buffalo trail up the south side of the river valley, we stopped to rest the horses, taking the opportunity to straighten any packs shifted on the crossing. In doing so, we disturbed an owl. He was a little fellow with long legs, a chest covered in fluffy, grayish white feathers and a round head that seemed too large for his body. He wasn't happy with us intruding into his territory. With his head cocked to one side he squawked at us, sounding much like the warning a rattlesnake would give. The sound would be scary if we didn't know he was there. Rene pointed at the hole beside the bird. "Small owl live underground in burrow." Not wanting to bother the owl unduly we moved the horses away.

Now our course was straight west across very dry country. When we found water, even in midafternoon, we camped, not knowing how far it was to the next source of supply. All these places I was carefully mapping for our return trip. Most of the stream beds were dry and the tall grass was turning brown.

Several times, we stopped to examine strange conical shaped hills that dotted the grasslands. They looked like some giant of a man had filled his derby hat with soil which he turned upside down to make hills. Often they were in rows. I took time to sketch a picture of them in the logbook. It was some freak of nature providing another thing for me to wonder about as we rode.

The tall grass brushed the bellies of the horses while our feet parted it as we passed by. The odor, rising into the air, reminded me of walking through a door into a long closed room smelling of dust. Wind blowing through the grass made a whirring, rustling sound. Wind driven waves for miles around looked much like the ocean rolling away to the far horizon as my ship was crossing from Glasgow to Montreal, a settlement on the St. Lawrence River in this new world called America. My mind wandered back to the old home in Scotland, recalling my boyhood growing up on a small rocky farm and walking two miles to school in the nearest village.

One afternoon in the spring of 1789, the year I was nine, after school closed for the day, it was time to start the two mile walk home. On the edge of the village, a man was unloading a cart near a small cottage, a place that had sat vacant for years. Being a curious lad, I stopped to watch. The man limped with his left leg and there was much to carry so I offered to help. After looking at me carefully, the man accepted.

Mac McGregor was long away at the wars, rising through the ranks of bowmen to become a junior officer in the English Army. Many a Scot and, yes, Irishmen too, went to the armies of England and various other kings, where they fought loyally and well. Many rose to positions of high command in Spain, France and elsewhere. At home, if the Scots cooperated as well with their brethren, Scotland would not be dominated by England. When Mac's leg was wounded by a musket ball, he was sent home to this; a cottage long owned by his family, with a stone wall around it and a garden space behind. The weeds were tall and the thatch needed repairing. Mac explained that there was only time now.

It became my routine each afternoon to stop at the cottage after school. There was much for Mac to teach me about fighting, living, and the troubles women could be to a man and me a mere lad. One day I showed him my sling which got rabbits, pheasants, grouse and an occasional goose for the pot. He was impressed so when the hunting was good he got a share.

Being the youngest of three sons, there would be nothing of the farm for me. Even at that young age, I understood and told him about it. "Aw noo, James, ye be young yet, thar be time tae consider."

Considering was something Mac rated highly. He taught me to think about everything carefully. It was a good lesson and my schoolwork began to improve, which pleased the teacher.

On days with no school, his was the place I wanted to be, slipping away whenever the chores allowed. We talked about fighting; the strategies to be used in attack and defense. Mac stressed that attack was the best way. Always attack to keep your enemy off balance. There is ever a way. The same applied with a lone opponent. Mac pointed the stem of his pipe at me as he often did when making an important point. "Noo, wee James, ne'er go seekin' fer trouble, but whin it comes tae ye, dinnae be waitin', attack. Whin it cannae be avoided, fight tae win wi everything ye hae at hand. Often the first blow, if weel placed, wins the battle."

We wrestled and he taught me how to punch, going through the target. "Whin ye punch tae the nose, dinnae aim fer the nose, aim fer the back o' the heid. Thus wull ye hit wi' much greater force. T'is the same wi' the hert; punch like yer target is at his back, nae the front."

In the forest, we cut walking sticks. These weren't like the canes old people used. They were six feet long with a thickness of a good two inches. My education in stick fighting began, learning how to block, thrust, jab and where it was best to attack an opponent. You don't swing a stick, you thrust with it. The best points to hit are the throat, face, stomach, knee and, of course, the groin. The one place Mac said it was okay to swing was to give the side of a knee a stout blow, which often fit in with blocking a thrust. People paid little attention to you using a walking stick, or leaning on it, and you were always armed.

Without telling me, Mac went to the local blacksmith to have a throwing knife made. We sharpened and honed it together. It was double-sided with a narrow blade and a sharp point for penetration. When I asked why, Mac reached behind his neck to come out with a beautifully crafted knife, explaining that he took it off a dead Spaniard. When I handed the knife back, Mac threw it into the door of the cottage where it stuck. "Ye practice wi' this one frae th' smithy, an' dinnae be hittin' rocks. Mibbie someday ye wull get a better one like mine. Larn tae be fleet an' accurate, it kin save yer life." So I worked hard every day with stick and knife.

At eleven, I was growing, soon reaching Mac's height. He showed me how to craft a long bow like the English used, with arrows longer than my arm. Mac explained that a good bowman could hit a target easily at one hundred paces or beyond. A bow was much more accurate than the muskets of the day. Besides, it didn't make the noise and smoke of a musket. It was two years before my arms were strong enough to draw the bow the full length of an arrow. By then, my accuracy was near as good as Mac's.

We spent many a good day together talking and practicing. Mac seemed pleased with my interest in learning what he passed on. He told me of the many places he visited and lived with the English army, always coming back to the new land of America. His unit was sent there in 1776 after the colonists rebelled against the Crown. He saw very little action in America and much admired the locals, telling me of many a Scot among them. Mac liked the independent way of the settlers. His unit was stationed near a place called Boston, never getting further than the farmlands around the town.

Soon it would be time to leave the farm to find my way in the world. A subject we often discussed. There weren't many options open; only the Army, the Royal Navy that was always short of men, or being a merchant sailor. Staying in Scotland meant a poor existence on some big estate, which did not appeal to me. Mac much admired my skill with weapons and taught me what he knew about sword fighting. Freely admitting his knowledge was very little and that from spending much time around soldiers and picking up a store of knowledge from his observations.

I was appreciative of anything he could pass on to prepare me for a future full of unknowns. Mac looked on me as the son he never had. He didn't like the idea of me joining the military which was a dog's life, especially in the Royal Navy. Every time he returned to talking about America, my question was always the same, "How am I gaun tae git tae America wi' nae dosh tae pay me wey an' what would I do whin thare?"

"We need tae consider, James. Thare is aye a wey if ye consider carefully."

My fourteenth birthday was in June and my father died just a few days later, having been poorly for a time, rarely leaving his bed. I sat with him regularly, reading what he wanted from the large family bible with all the family births, marriages, and deaths. The last entry was for my mother two years before. Now Father was to be added. He kept me in school far longer than the others. That is what he gave me—the ability to read and figure numbers and maybe a better way with the thinking. It was a sad day and for me it was decision-making time. My middle brother was gone to the navy. The farm would pass to the eldest as was the custom of the land. In the night, after Father was buried, I walked away carrying all that was mine plus his curved stem pipe, which I helped myself to. A small thing, a remembrance of him.

At Mac's, I sat on the ground inside the gate waiting for him to rise. When he did we talked while he cooked the oatmeal. "Twa day ago a passerby stopped here tae rest. He said the Bay Company is in Glescae lookin' fer stout lads tae wirk in the fur trade. Ye should sign up. It wull git ye tae America, efter that it wull b' up tae ye."

Mac came along on the twelve mile walk into Glasgow where I had never been before, it being so far away. It was the next morning before we located the Bay men on the docks, near a sailing ship. We walked up to three men having a discussion at the foot of a gangplank to ask, "Be ye the mon hirin' fer the fur trade?"

Barely bothering to look at me, one man pointed. "Gae thru yon door. Thare be a mon sportin' a tap bonnet."

Mac held the door for me and we found the top hat sitting at a table. He watched us come. "Huv ye business wi' the Bay then?"

I stood to my full height to look big and strong. "Ah heard, sir, the Bay be hirin' men fer the fur trade."

He looked me up and down. "Aye lad, that we be." He took a paper from a pile and handed it across the table. "Ye sign this wee contract n' ye wull be af tae America whin yon ship sails."

The agent was impressed by me carefully reading every word in the contract. "Ye huv bin tae schuil, lad. Dae ye ken numbers then?" He was pleased when I showed him and told me, "I kin offer ye the position o' company clerk."

"Thank ye, sir, I accept the position." We watched as he wrote a note on the Bay's copy of the contract. It was July first, 1794 and I was employed for five years as a company clerk at thirty-nine pounds each year, plus all board and keep. Because of the reading and figuring, he hired me at a level above an apprentice clerk where the pay was fifteen pounds annually.

Before leaving to return home, Mac shook my hand, wished me well and slapped me on the back. He pulled the scabbard with the Spanish knife over his head and handed it to me. “Ye tak’ this, lad, tae mind me by. Keep it ever painty. Best o’ luck tae ye, James Angus Richardson.” Mac walked away without looking back and I still remembered everything he taught me.

The ship wouldn’t be sailing for three weeks, or more, so they put me to the task of keeping a record of the supplies being amassed in the warehouse. They were a rough, jostling, noisy lot of men working the ships and docks. Listening to the stories they told of faraway places with strange sounding names, my ears knew not what to believe. There was much news of what Scots were doing, wars being fought and trade in spices, tea, and commodities of all types. Each ship that tied up to the docks brought news from afar. The storytelling was fascinating and mostly hard to believe. Each night, I went to my cot with a head full of new things overheard during the day.

When loading of the ship started, it was my duty as clerk to check each item as it was carried aboard. Sacks, bales, barrels and crates all needed to be carefully identified and recorded. With the record book on a small table at the foot of the gangplank, the workers would stop with the load they were carrying, while I read the labeling and entered the facts in the book. The captain and first mate supervised all aspects of the loading, shouting orders and yelling at any man who deviated from the routine.

All went well the first hours and it seemed everyone was settled in the way the captain wanted, until a man with a bale on his shoulder walked past with me while I was still recording information from the previous load. I called to him, "Ye didnae stop. Nae record is made of whit ye huv thar."

He stopped several paces up the plank and turned to look with a leer on his face. "Ye'r too slow. A mon cannae haud 'is horses oan the likes o' ye."

The first mate glowered from the ship. "Git ye back doon tae the lad."

He came down the plank, smirking. When I stood to look for the label he turned suddenly, hitting me with the bale, knocking me off balance, and I stumbled off the dock into the water.

Not being much of a swimmer, it took time to make my way to a rope hanging down and climb hand over hand up to the dock. Standing there on the dock soaking wet and dripping, I shook my head to rid my ears of water. Everything came to a halt. Men were standing about watching to see what would happen. Mac warned me that many men would test me and to never back down. His words were, "Tak' a beatin' if ye huv tae, bit dinnae submit tae bullyin'."

Putting a grin on my face, my feet walked toward him. "Ye'r nae a nice mon."

He looked startled and put the bale down. It seemed he expected me to submit. His fists came up as my left jab headed for his nose. He took it on the cheek and elbowed me in the ribs, throwing me off balance. Mac's training gave me more skill than he possessed, but he was stronger. There was little meat on my six foot plus frame. A man in the crowd yelled, "Give it tae him guid, Red." Getting my feet under me again I went back at him. My left jab was blocked again, only this time my right fist landed on his ribs. He swung a right that bruised my cheek as I only partially blocked the blow.

Back and forth we went until he bulled ahead and knocked me to the dock with a head butt in the chest.

By the time my feet were under me again, the first mate was there. “Enough noo, lads. Back tae wirk afore yer jobs are lost.”

The sun and breeze dried me and the records were made. In bed that night with a sore cheek and chest, my thoughts were about the fight and what could have been done better.

Next day at the noon break he came down the plank with empty arms and my foot tripped him. He hit the dock on his face. Slowly, he got up and shook himself. We went at it again and this time it was a fair match. The third day he came at me first thing in the morn and he took a beating. He went to his work with a black eye and blood running from his nose. By day’s end, his eye was swollen shut. I’d say I beat him only I was some sore my own self, having gained more knowledge of the world.

After that the men accepted me and finally the ship was loaded.

The crossing of the Atlantic was smooth if slower than normal due to a lack of wind. Many hours were spent watching the sea or working around with the sailors, learning how they handled the ship. They taught me to tie the many different knots that were used onboard, telling me many things about life on the sea. Even the officers seemed taken by my interest. They showed me how the compass was used to navigate along with sightings from the sun and stars. It wasn’t enough learning to be good at navigating, but the knowledge might be useful.

The ship was sailing for Montreal up the Saint Lawrence River instead of to York Factory on the west side of Hudson Bay. It was too late in the season to brave the bay. From Montreal, thirty-six foot long freight canoes, six feet wide, carried us up the river into a vast lake and in late September we landed on the north shore at the new settlement of Fort York in what was referred to as Upper Canada. Fort York was two years old and not much to see. The only buildings that looked like they would stand for long were the Bay post and the Governor's residence. The rest were a huddled mess of low, log shacks, the cracks between logs sealed with mud, and other even less desirable hovels.

The wait was on for the freight canoes expected any time now from the vast, unnamed territory in the west, bringing furs to be processed for shipment to London. Governor Simcoe was scheming to make his Fort York the center of the fur trade in place of Montreal. Again, my work was clerking and so it was to be for the winter.

My first free day was devoted to searching for suitable material for a walking stick and I returned with a strong oak limb that with some trimming would do admirably. It didn't take long to shape it to suit my needs. Now when leaving the fort to walk the muddy lanes it was with my stick and the throwing knife that was my secret. The sling was of little use unless travelling outside the settled area, so it was stored away in a wooden box under my bed. Counting the five of us from Glasgow with six who came from London, there were eleven lads, with me being one of the youngest in age, although not in height, and starting to add pounds. I held my own in the rough and tumble life of the post.

There was a great love in me for the freedom of life on the

frontier. My work was done diligently, expecting the head men would be watching and wanting to get a high rating. The other lads seemed content just doing what would get them by. In fairness to them, most, with little schooling, were hired as menial laborers.

Just as winter was setting in, causing the humid air off the lake water to feel even colder, the Chief Factor sent two of the English boys with me to make a delivery to Governor Simcoe's residence. As we made our way back to the Bay Post, daylight was fading. Passing a tavern built of logs, two dirty, disheveled drunks accosted us, demanding money. We stopped in a line abreast to stare at their long, dirty, greasy hair and beards and rough clothing consisting of dirty leather pants and an assortment of fur pelts.

It was one of the English boys, named Cecil, who replied in a nervous voice, "We have no money, there be not a coin between us." I just watched.

"Be damned with ye and no coins. Take off yer clothes. That will bring us a cup of grog each." Cecil backed up a step making no reply to the threat, so they moved to grab at us.

When they stopped talking and made their move, the stick left its resting place on the toe of my boot. A swift thrust took the first man straight in the mouth, removing most of his remaining teeth. Before the second man could stop himself, the other end of the stick took him full in the throat. Both went down quickly, laid out in the snow, with no fight left in them. My two companions were frightened out of their wits, staring with looks of horror on their faces and not yet comprehending what was happening. They were showing how vulnerable they were. They were city lads straight out of London.

People standing around who witnessed the skirmish were

beginning to talk to each other; soon the questions would start. Urging my two companions into moving, we left at a brisk walk and returned to the post.

Next morning, the Factor called the three of us to his office. With us lined up, he demanded to know what happened. The lads babbled on, making little sense, still scared at what might have happened to them. They finally revealed that it was I, James Richardson, who injured the men. No doubt they were afraid of what the authorities would do.

The Factor's cold eyes turned to me. "Thae demanded money we didnae huv an' said thae wid tak' oor claes tae sell."

The Factor glared. "Did you tell them to leave you be and go away?"

"Nae, sur. Thar be a time fer talkin' an' a time fer fightin'. Thae wur grabbing fer Cecil here, so I acted."

"I see." He watched me for several moments, which seemed like forever. "The man with the crushed throat died right there in the snow."

"I'm sorry tae learn that, sur, bit he brocht it upon himself."

"The other man lost most of his teeth. No one knows what other damage he received. At last report he is still alive."

"I'm pleased tae hear that, sur."

The Factor's expression seemed less severe now. I began to feel more confident. "How old are you, Richardson?"

"I wis fourteen at mah birthday in Juin."

He shook his head in surprise. "A sorry incident. It appears they deserved what they got. My suggestion is you not leave the post for a few days to let this quiet down."

"Thank ye, sur, I wull bide inside the walls." That was the end of it, except my treatment was different from that day on. Even the older hands knew there was fight in me. They were more careful around me while the lads were in awe and maybe a little scared.

That first winter passed slowly. I worked hard, was diligent about the bookkeeping and minded my own business. In April, when the big canoes loaded for the western territory, I was quick to help with the loading and rode in the second canoe when it headed out for Fort Garry. At Fort Erie, on the banks of the river, everything was carried overland around the great falls of the Niagara. From there, the canoes paddled up river into Lake Erie. The route followed the north shore west and again up river into the huge lake named for the Huron Indians which took us north and west until after many days we approached Sault Ste. Marie and joined many canoes coming from Montreal by the Ottawa River. From there, it was across another lake to the Grand Portage, named for the nine miles everything was carried, including six hundred pound canoes.

It was a long, hard trip even for a passenger who was not expected to help. As ever, I wanted to learn about everything I could—wilderness cooking, different ways to make a camp and how to handle a canoe, which was an art unto itself. Gradually, the French speaking voyageurs accepted me as they came to understand my interest was real. They showed me how to do what they did and why. Slowly, a few of their French words came to me. Explaining was difficult for them because it was just natural behavior which they did without thinking. Later I was to learn it was the same with the Indians. It just didn't occur to them that anyone wouldn't know what they had known from childhood.

My second year in the employ of the Hudson Bay Company started during that trip west. The three following would be spent at Fort Garry, although there was no way of knowing at that time what was ahead for me.

The horses stopped. Looking up, the plain in front of us was black with buffalo. Thousands upon thousands of them slowly moving southeast; there seemed no end to them. The wind was towards us, bringing the heat, smell, dust and noise of the herd. The sounds of the animals carried to us clearly; big bulls rumbling deep in their chests, mixed with the bleats of calves and the sound of all those hooves.

Making camp and waiting while they passed was our only choice. We moved into a depression atop a long ridge, where a bit of brush was growing, and unloaded the horses. The hollow was maybe a hundred paces long by thirty wide, deep enough that we would be hidden from the view of anyone on the plains.

The horses were our most precious possession. It was unlikely the buffalo would climb the ridge to interfere with them when the easiest going was on the plain below. Even so, we put hobbles on the horses' front legs before picketing them on grass.

It would be a dry camp for both us and the animals, so what water there was we used sparingly to make tea while our buffalo steaks cooked. There was no good wood for a fire so we used buffalo chips, which were everywhere. They made a hot, almost smokeless, fire.

It was three days before the herd thinned out, allowing us to continue our journey west, winding our way through the last of the stragglers. The big grey wolves were at work pulling down old and crippled animals to feast on fresh meat. Coyotes, foxes and vultures were all there, getting a share of what was left, and there was plenty for all.

The hot, dry, dusty days continued with only a wide, waving sea of grass around us, sweeping away to the sky on all sides. Watching the wind move the tall grass always brought the ocean to mind. As the grass moved the colors seemed to change from green to a silvery grey. More and more of it was turning brown as fall came near. It was good grass growing land that supported the herds of buffalo, antelope, elk, and deer. The top soil was thin; it was no place for a plow.

Birds that nested on the ground were everywhere. Eagles and hawks soared overhead, floating on the rising hot air of midday. Occasionally they would drop like a stone to strike at some unsuspecting prairie dog or ground squirrel in a never-ending search for food.

Impatiently, we waited for the journey to end. It would take time to settle in, become familiar with the area and to get organized before winter arrived. At last the day came when we rode up a long slope and there on the horizon were mountains. Looking small in the far distance, appearing black from where we sat, but mountains at last. It took several more days. Each day the mountains grew larger, looking purple in the morning light and shading to black as the day wore on.

We arrived on the northeastern corner of the mountains, following a small stream the last few miles. First we set up a temporary camp to use while we scouted the area for a good winter location. It would need grass for the horses, shelter from winter storms, plentiful wood for our fires and good water.

With Rene, I worked at setting up camp while Andre rode out to scout the immediate area. We hadn't seen another human since leaving the Mandan family on the Missouri. Even so, it didn't mean there weren't people around. We would be cautious as we slowly became familiar with what was to be our home until the next spring.

With the camp established, I removed my clothes and waded into the stream. It was enjoyable, getting clean again after days of dust and sweat. Ducking my head under the water, I washed my hair until it was clean. It felt good. Swinging my hand, I sprayed water toward Rene who was sitting on a rock with his musket across his legs.

Rene grinned. "No drink water after you wash."

I laughed at him, feeling like a boy again, rolling around and enjoying the cool water. Finally, I waded out to get my two shirts and went back to sit on a rock in the stream to scrub them until they were clean. With the shirts spread out on a willow bush, I sat in the sun to dry off. To the east was the long stretch of prairie grass we had just crossed; to the west, the tree covered flank of the mountains.

This was a place to like. My mind turned to considering how to find the best trapping. First, we needed to establish a good winter camp. After that, Rene and Andre could go south along the range to explore the country. I would handle the smaller area to the north of us. By describing to each other what we saw, we would quickly become familiar with a large area.

Andre came walking in, leading his horse with a large mule deer across his saddle. He brought us a welcome change of diet after eating buffalo for many days. Sitting around the fire, we ate our venison and drank tea while Andre told us what he had seen. “Much buffalo sign. Many deer, elk. Small streams, good grass. Me go five miles maybe.”

“Did yea see any sign o’ beaver in the streams?”

“Streams small, no beaver. See much grouse, rabbits, birds.” Andre pointed over his shoulder at the mountains behind him. “We go there, trap beaver.”

After eating, I baited a hook, hung it on a line from the end of my walking stick and sat beside a big cottonwood tree to see if the trout could be tempted from the deep water in front of me. The fish must have never seen a hook before because in an hour there were seven good-sized trout on the grass beside me.

Just before dark, with the fish cleaned, a little salt sprinkled inside along with some mint leaves from the stream bank, we wrapped them in clay and buried all seven beneath our fire pit. Covered with a thin layer of clay and with the coals from the fire raked over them for heat, we left them to cook overnight. It was a feast we ate for breakfast.

Chapter 3

Riding out to scout for beaver and search for a winter campsite, we left Andre to guard the equipment and supplies. Following the same stream that brought us to the mountains took us in a general southwesterly direction. At first the trees were aspen, with willows near the water. Working higher there were scattered spruce with patches of raspberry and bearberry bushes mixed in. Soon we were passing beaver dams with backed up ponds of water. Around the beaver ponds there were dense groves of aspen, willow, and bushes loaded with berries. The temptation proved too great to resist. Stopping, I tied my horse to a tree and went to pick and eat big juicy red raspberries. After watching for a minute, Rene joined me. It was like having sugar after a summer of eating meat. We ate until we were full before getting back on the horses.

As the elevation increased, the canyon gradually narrowed with spruce trees beginning to dominate as they squeezed out the others. Besides beaver, there were abundant muskrat, ducks, songbirds and the ever present crows and magpies. The dark trunks of the spruce trees stood tall, pointing straight at the sky like long arrows. Leaning back in the saddle to look up, it seemed that many of them were at least sixty feet tall. As the trail took us higher, there were huge pine trees, with yellowish colored bark, towering over everything. The pine needles, each longer than two fingers, formed a thick carpet covering the ground, crunching under the horses' hooves as they stepped along.

A prominent rock ridge loomed ahead of us. The stream was much smaller now and appeared to start near the ledge. To our surprise, the stream made a turn to the northwest so we continued along its route, winding our way around huge chunks of rock and dead trees fallen from the cliffs above. The rock in the cliffs stood on end, often pointing straight up with many water-worn cracks widened by the action of wind, rain and snow melt.

After several hours of climbing, we found ourselves on a high plateau overlooking a long valley that ran mostly north-south. The valley appeared to narrow to the north. We could see it was widening to the south, spreading out with the green of grassy meadows dotted with small lakes. A series of mountain ridges were visible in the distance.

While the horses rested, we talked. "Appears that glen down thar may be wull sheltered from storms, especially right b'low us. Could be beaver further ta' the south."

Rene waved his arm in the general direction. "Much beaver, go look."

I turned sideways in the saddle to look at him. "If we go in there noo, we will have tae stay overnight."

Rene shrugged his shoulders. "Go look."

It would leave Andre alone in strange country. Each of us was often alone. Kicking the horses in the ribs, we started down, winding our way through the trees. Herds of white-tailed deer with smaller groups of larger mule deer grazed on the grass. We passed elk that were as big as our horses. Our presence didn't seem to concern them and they barely moved out of our way as we passed; a sure sign that they weren't being bothered by hunters.

Rene pointed at a tree trunk where the claw marks of a huge bear were visible almost at eye level to me, sitting on my horse. That big bear was marking his territory with a challenge for young bears that might invade his area.

We gradually descended south over a series of benches, each one lower than the previous. The spruce trees were well spaced with coarse brown grass standing knee high to a man growing among the trees. Long lines of aspen covered the slopes descending from one bench to the next with occasional grassy meadows. Lush growths of grass, willows, and berry bushes covered the low drainage areas along the south-trending, rolling hills. Coming down that side to the valley below was much easier going for the horses than climbing up the other side. At the bottom, we started south toward the main valley and almost immediately located what we wanted. A small box canyon completely surrounded by high rock walls with several acres of grass in the bottom. A small stream flowed from the narrow opening, originating from springs and several rivulets of water coming down the sides of the canyon. With a fence across the opening, the horses would have a secure pasture with good grass and water. In front of the entrance was a suitable place for us to build a winter shelter. It faced south, so the sun would be a help in providing heat.

The valley started to widen as we rode and suddenly opened into a series of extensive meadows. There were side valleys with many streams coming down from the higher country. Most important, there were beaver. We rode along slowly, getting familiar with the terrain.

Finally, we turned back, wanting to spend the night at the site where we would settle. The sling got three fat grouse by the time we rode into the little valley to picket the horses. Rene spitted the cleaned birds over a fire while I wrote in the log, including a map of the day's travels, trying hard to estimate distances, and added a description of the site we were camped on.

In the morning, we rode north and the valley did narrow as we expected before widening out as the prairie came into view. We rounded the corner of the hills to turn southeast, looking for Andre and the camp. It was further away than expected. In mid-afternoon Andre was tending a haunch of venison spitted over the fire as he watched us ride in. The camp was a welcome sight.

In the morning, we loaded the packhorses and backtracked the previous day's route to the valley. First, we built a pole fence across the opening to the box canyon, using the living trees for posts with mostly dead wood for rails; this would keep the horses in. With the packs stowed under an overhang of the cliff for protection from rain, we set to work building a place to live through the coming winter using the earth lodges of the Mandan as a model.

A hollow between two hummocks of earth was deepened by cutting the sides straight down and leveling the bottom for a floor. We would be able to walk straight out onto level ground. After four days of shoveling dirt and chopping tree roots, it was a pleasant change to start trimming timbers to serve as posts and beams for a framework to support the steep, two sided roof we planned.

Construction was hard physical work with me more accustomed to it than the others. Every third day, they went out to explore while I worked on alone. Slowly, the framework took shape. The two ends were closed in with logs standing upright in shallow trenches, the tops shaped to fit the slope of the roof. There was space for a door in each end wall. Young spruce trees provided straight timbers for a roof over the beams. To make it weather-tight we cut strips of sod to cover the roof, putting on a double layer. At a distance the roof blended in with its surroundings, so unless you looked closely, the house appeared to be a mound in the trees.

When the house was finished, the main door faced the midday sun. There was a second small door at the back for use in an emergency.

Being a Scot, I knew something of stone. We built a fireplace and chimney of stone using clay mortar reinforced with chopped reeds. Andre found a place where slabs of flat rock, up to three inches thick, had fallen from the side of a cliff. We used them to add a stone hearth and lined the firebox with upright slabs to protect the rock structure.

Rene lit the first fire and the lodge began to fill with smoke until we set the door ajar. With outside air coming in, the chimney began to draw properly. This problem was solved by rigging a vent with a hide covering to regulate the air needed for the fire.

Our roof was strong enough to walk on with its pole base and double layer of thick sod. The two side walls were the cut banks we dug. It would be snug in the cold weather with good protection from the wind. Our chimney was placed so the smoke from the fire would rise through the branches of a tall spruce to be thinned out and dispersed. It made no sense to advertise our presence when we knew not who might be around. Having been here for most of a month, there was still no indication of other people. We knew that didn't mean there weren't any.

We began splitting logs for planks to build sleeping platforms. After two days, the pile of planks was growing, although there was much smoothing of the wood to be done. On the third morning, when I bent to pick up my axe to start again, Andre held out his hand. "You hunt, we split logs." It was a surprise. "Long time you work, no hunt, need change."

Happily, I put the pistol behind my belt with the tomahawk; got my long bow and rode north to a steep-walled canyon there hadn't been time to explore. It gradually narrowed until finally the way was blocked by dead trees blown down by a big wind storm. Probably several storms over the years did the damage. The valley must funnel the winds from big storms in such a way that the force was increased enough to blow down many of the trees. There was deadwood piled up in tangled messes everywhere.

Picketing the horse in a small clearing, I proceeded on foot, finally walking where it was easiest, in the water of a swift little stream. The bed of the stream was fifteen to twenty feet wide with the water only rarely up to my knees. It ran along the base of a steep rock wall that formed the east side of the canyon as it narrowed to become more of a gorge. The trees on the other side of the stream showed signs of floods so the stream probably overflowed the low west bank during spring runoff or heavy rains. It was quiet except for the sound of birds singing and water gurgling over rocks.

In this tangled mess of deadwood there was no sense in shooting a deer because it would be more work packing it out than I cared to do. The sun was shining, the water was chuckling happily and this was my first day since arriving not filled with work.

Walking was easy on the gravel and small rocks that covered the stream bed. The larger rocks were slippery so each foot needed to be placed carefully. There were larger chunks of broken rock that had fallen from the cliff above, but not so many as to slow progress.

Coming to a fallen tree, it seemed like a good place to sit and rest while giving some thought to our situation. We were making good progress on the house, which was almost ready for winter. There were a few other things that still needed to be done like making snowshoes, additional pack saddles and the like. Putting away a store of meat would have to wait until cold weather so it would keep properly. Making up a supply of dried meat would be useful for when trapping started; that was the best thing we could do right now.

Sitting on that fallen tree, not really seeing the water, my mind sorted out the things that needed to be done. For some time the gleam of something in the gravel of the stream bed had teased my eye without me paying any attention to it. Curiously, I knelt down and reached into the water to pick it up.

Holding it up to the sunlight and turning it every which way, my mind didn't want to believe what my brain was yelling. It was a gold nugget! Gold, here in this little stream! If there was more of it, we would have the answer to our problem of purchasing a larger supply of trade goods to start a trading post.

Careful examination of the nugget showed the corners were still sharp. It hadn't been in the water long or they would have been rounded off. The nugget was as large as the end of my middle finger. Carefully storing it away in my leather shot pouch, I began considering what to do. My brain told me not to move, just sit there considering. The first thing was to mark the spot so it would be easy to find again, after which there would be time to look for more of the nuggets. Using the tomahawk, I chopped a blaze on a tree beside the stream and added a second on the opposite side, so they would be visible from both directions. After walking fifty paces back towards the horse, I blazed another tree with one vertical mark.

Placing the pistol and bow on a dry place on the grass, the search began. Going downstream from the sitting tree I looked closely for the reflections. In a few minutes there were three small nuggets in my hat. Moving slowly upstream, the reflections were there, usually on the downstream side of a rock or large piece of gravel.

When I found another nugget as large as the first one I decided the gold was plentiful. Not being a miner, with only what knowledge I had learned from listening to others talk, it would be wise to be cautious and consider carefully. *Don't get excited, think, there has to be a way to get at the gold. Go back to the fallen tree and think this through to figure out the best way to proceed.*

As a lad, I overheard a man telling my father of panning for tin in Wales—not something a boy pays much attention to so there were only vague memories of what was said. What was there to use? We owned a large frying pan which was in our gear. It was unused since there was nothing to be fried. The frying pan would be a start, along with my shovel which was stored away now with the house finished. With those tools I would return to try my hand with shovel and pan.

Sitting there, I searched my mind to remember what gold was

worth; it was vague. My best recollection was around seventeen American dollars to the ounce. With no scale to measure ounces, it would be a guessing game as to how much gold was recovered. If the panning could recover a few hundred dollars in gold, it would provide the funds to purchase a supply of goods to set up a trading post. The trapping should be successful with all the beaver in the area, which would put us in an even better position.

My mind turned to the trade goods to be bought. They would have to be the very best available to encourage customers to return again and again. It wasn't about making a fast profit, rather to establish a permanent, growing business.

Many of the trade muskets were poorly made, often exploding and causing serious injuries. The Indians complained about the guns and no one paid any attention. It was the same with many other items. There should be a better way. It seemed to me that providing the best quality goods would create happy customers, building the kind of reputation that would allow us to trade for only the best furs. A happy customer was one that would return. It was the type of treatment I expected when dealing for things we needed.

Returning to the horse, we took a different way back to camp, that old horse and me. This was for safety and also to see more of the land around. Riding with the long bow across the front of the saddle, it was near onto dark when we arrived.

My two companions put down the axes they were using as mauls to drive oak wedges to split the logs. Andre came to walk slowly around the horse, eying me critically. He grunted at Rene. "Him no good for hunt. Plenty deer. Him no meat."

Rene gave me a sober look. "White man never be Indian."

They enjoyed their joke. To tell the truth, I forgot all about getting a deer, having other things to think about. I fired back. "Ye Cree make so much noise a' the deer ran away. To'morra ye stay quiet n' I'll find a big buck."

While Rene stirred up the fire, I used the last bit of daylight to write in the log. Today there were exciting things to record, along with details to be noted for the maps that I planned to draw. Finding the gold presented a whole new set of problems to be chewed on.

We wouldn't move into the house until the weather forced us—all preferring the outdoors where you could see the stars, breathe the good air and hear the night sounds. It was a fair life which we loved, only it wouldn't last with people like me arriving. There was a burning desire in me to better myself, to own good land and someday raise a family. Now there was a problem. Where would a big, rough, common-looking man like me find a wife willing to share her life with my sort? Already with twenty years behind me and little knowledge of women, my understanding of that particular problem was scant. Most likely many women were just as foolish as men, so somewhere there would be one for me.

Coming awake in the middle of the night, my mind was thinking about the gold and how to recover enough to get us established. *Where did the gold come from?*

Looking at that large nugget convinced me that it couldn't have been in the stream for long or the action of water, sand and gravel would have rounded its edges or broken it into smaller pieces. So the place where its journey in the water started couldn't be far away. The source must be upstream from where the nugget lay when my eye caught the reflection of the sun's rays. My knowledge of such things was limited and out here there was no one to ask. It was up to me. Mac would tell me to consider.

Sliding from under the buffalo robe, I stirred up the fire and put the teapot close to heat. When it was hot, I filled my cup and moved into the trees where the fire wouldn't affect my night vision. While watching around for any dangers my mind gave thought to the problem. It was a rare night when we didn't take turns on watch because there was always the chance of an attack. Besides, the night was a good time to be up. There were owls on the hunt, bats after insects, along with all the other creatures that used the cover of darkness to go about their business. Listening to the night your ears soon came to know what sounds belonged. Anything out of the ordinary quickly drew your attention.

Later, Rene came to join me. We sat there in silence as we often did, enjoying being together. He reminded me of Mac, although life provided him a totally different background and set of experiences. They would have liked each other; two men born so far apart, both wise in the ways of life as they experienced it. I was fortunate to have two such good friends to learn from. The credit for any small success achieved in the future would belong more to them than to me.

Putting down the cup, I commented, "The weather is still ta warm to store meat. We could build drying racks ta make a supply of jerky fer winter ta use when we are traveling or out trapping."

Rene thought about that before pointing south. "We go far there to hunt, make jerky. Leave close game for winter when snows come. Build dugout there for bad storms."

Now there was an idea that hadn't occurred to me. "Yea are right, Rene; we wull be trappin' all down this valley, that wull save travellin' time. If we get caught in a storm thar wull be a place ta stay. Thank yea for suggesting that. The bed platforms should be finished today. After that we can go south to hunt. We need furs ta' make winter clothes, sleeping robes and leather for moccasins."

Rene turned his head. "You no go, stay here." He added, "Bear come or wolverine, maybe strange Indian. Wolverine bad in camp." Rene's experience in the wilderness far exceeded my own. As so many times before, his knowledge and insights, many of them intuitive, were a source of amazement to me. Every day he taught me new things without trying or even knowing it. Well, his suggestion would allow me the freedom to try for more of the gold. That would be good for both our futures.

"The trappin' wull be good this winter; many furs. In the spring, we wull go ta' St. Louis an' buy yea a new long gun an' other things."

He nodded. "Long gun like you good for Rene, shoot far."

We watched the sky grow light. The sun wouldn't come over the mountains for some time yet. There was a chill in the air which was a warning. Rene added small sticks to the remaining coals and when they blazed up, a few larger chunks. We set meat to broil.

They rode away, taking packhorses, axes, shovels, and a string of beaver traps. The beaver would have their winter coats and it was time to start trapping. They planned to be gone for several days. After five days I would go to visit them.

The bed platforms were finished. Taking a shovel and the frying pan, it was off to the gold stream again using a different route where possible as Rene had taught me. That way you didn't leave a well-defined trail and, most importantly, avoided an ambush which was a tactic favored by the natives.

Starting downstream from the sitting tree, I filled the frying pan with sand and sloshed water around in it. The idea was to let the heavier gold settle to the bottom of the pan. Throwing the pieces of gravel away and sloshing more water around, most of the sand went over the side, with help from my finger. Trying to be very careful, I worked on the little remaining sand. Nothing! Nothing at all.

Moving slowly forward, trying again and again, it took a long time until finally there was one small nugget. There were probably gold flakes that were lost due to my clumsy attempts at panning. I wasn't very good at this. I consoled myself with the thought that time and practice would improve my panning.

Working steadily, by midday the bottom of the deerskin bag, prepared the night before, was covered. It seemed like my panning technique was improving. A grouse taken just after first light had been buried under a small fire to cook, so I went into the trees and sat down to eat, with a stream full of clear, cold water to drink. That water was so cold it made my teeth ache.

Sitting there, my eyes were looking at the rock wall that rose up on the other side of the stream. *The gold must be originating from someplace on that wall. How to locate the source?* No idea came to me.

Well before dark I was back in camp. Lifting the bag to weigh it in my hand, it seemed heavy. *There must be two ounces at least,* I thought. Sitting there, my eyes finally focused on the ball mold, which cast seventeen balls to the pound. There were sixteen ounces in a pound, so each lead ball weighed just under an ounce. There was the answer. Just rig some kind of balance scale and use lead balls as counter weights. Doing that, a good estimate of the amount of gold would be possible.

It was exciting and I worked into the night rigging an oak rod with a leather pan hanging from each end on sinews. Using the big hunting knife, I carefully cut a notch in the center of the rod to act as a pivot point so the rig would balance on a sharp-edged stone. With some adjustment, it appeared to be sitting level. A crude affair to be certain. Still, all I wanted was an estimate.

With a lead ball on one side, balanced with gold, it was surprising how little it took to make an ounce. It was late in the night before everything was put away. There was almost five balls worth of gold in the bag.

Five ounces of gold would be worth nigh onto eighty-five American dollars. It was unbelievable and the excitement was too much to allow for sleep. Most of the gold came from a sand-filled hole just downstream of a rock. Maybe that was the secret. The hole was only inches deep and took several pans to clean out. A few more like that would be all that we'd need to set up as traders.

Sitting there in the dark, it occurred to me that there was no need to pour the gold into the pan; a whole bag could be weighted at once. If an empty bag was counter balanced with sand before filling it with gold for weighing, the danger of spillage would be eliminated.

Six ounces would be roughly one hundred dollars, which was enough in one bag. I set about sewing more deerskin bags of about the same size. Gold is always a problem. When it came time to sell, it would be wise not to show too much all at once. Gold drew attention in a hurry, usually from the worst type of people. It's called greed. After considering carefully, my decision was to use a seven ball weight in each bag which figured close to six and a half ounces.

Just after sunup, my horse was picketed on a fresh plot of grass in a well hidden clearing, surrounded by trees. In my pack was cooked venison for lunch. All day I worked shoveling and bending over, all the while standing in cold water. It was slimmer pickings with no rich hole like the day before. This was hard work. It would be worth it if I could find a few hundred dollars in gold. It would be a huge step forward for us. Besides, everything we did was hard work. Building our dugout cabin for the winter or trapping fur was no easier than this.

Next morning, on the second pan, I found a hole under my sitting tree. It was larger and deeper than the first one. When the hole was cleaned out, there were two more bags of gold to add to the cache. Some of the gold was in the form of good-sized nuggets. My panning technique was improving with practice which made the work go faster. More of the fine gold was being saved as well, which improved the recovery.

The fourth day was spent in camp working around. It wasn't wise to follow the same routine every day. While there was no sign of other people, it didn't mean there weren't any. The cache now held three bags, of seven ball weight each, with most of a fourth, so there was close to four hundred dollars hidden away. It was more than hoped for and enough for a start. While I wasn't greedy, there was no sense in stopping now; extra dollars would make it easier for us. We might never return to this place, so it was best to keep working when opportunity offered.

At first light my feet were in the water and it was the best day yet. Working across the stream from the big hole, there was one after the other. All of them were lying just below the lip of a rock ledge where the water dropped a few inches and the holes were rich. By dark, the stock of gold was doubled, both large and small nuggets, with a lot of finer flakes to fill the spaces in the bags. Gold is heavy as I was learning. Now there were nine bags which figured to be worth a thousand dollars. Over three pounds of gold stored in the cache.

My cache was in a crack in the rock wall behind the house, plugged with a flat rock. It was some seven feet above the ground, chosen because it was well hidden and prowling animals wouldn't be able to get at the smell of the leather. It wasn't large, but would hold several more bags.

On the fifth day, with two packhorses in tow, my horse took off south. Happy, he was, to be on the trail again—stepping out with his head up and ears working as he looked around every corner and surveyed the land beyond each rise we topped out on.

It was past midday before smoke rising from the drying fires became visible. My approach was cautious, until everything came into view. With a long gun in the crook of his arm, Rene watched me ride up and dismount. The place they chose was a good ten or twelve miles from our base. They were started on a dugout located in a small clearing in the trees. There was a shank of venison cooking over the fire and Rene watched me shave off slices, chew and look at the campsite. The drying racks were full of thin strips of venison and buffalo meat drying in the sun, with smoke from the fires to keep the flies away. Rene pointed to a bundle sitting on a row of logs. It was the first batch of dried meat and must weigh close to a hundred pounds by the size of the lot, although meat was lighter after being dried.

I stuck a hand in my shot pouch and took out a deerskin bag, with maybe an ounce of gold in it and tossed the bag to Rene. "Take a look at that."

Rene caught the bag and untied the sinew that held it closed. He looked inside before pouring gold into his hand. The gold dust that came out first didn't look like much and Rene didn't react until he saw a nugget. He stared at it for a moment and his eyes grew large, before looking at me. "Where you get gold?"

Pleased with his reaction, I laughed at him. "Found it lying around."

Rene grinned. "Gold no just lay around."

"Yea ar' right, Rene. I found it in that narrow ravine four or five miles north of the dugout. Have been going thar each day ta dig up sand n' gravel. Found enough ta give us a good start on supplies for a trading post, even if the trapping this fall is no so great."

Rene poured the gold back into the bag and carefully tied the sinew. I added, "That stream water be cold an' after a while a mon's feet go numb. Must have close tae one thousand American, in bags like this un."

Rene went around the fire and sat on a log across from me. "Cold water bad for feet."

"Yea be right, Rene. I dinnae plan tae dig much more."

Rene nodded. "Is good. Much beaver, we trap, sell furs. Gold can stay."

That was typical of Rene. I thought he might get excited over the gold. He rarely got excited. "If the weather warms a mite, I may try for more."

Rene pointed at me. "No mine. We trap beaver. Go St. Louis."

For four days I worked on the dugout shelter they had started digging in the side of a bluff and helped with the butchering and slicing. The meat supply grew. We worked on the hides, scraping off the fat and preparing them. We needed several buffalo hides with the hair on for blankets, along with deerskins for making clothing.

Andre came in each day with beaver pelts from the traps. We all scraped, cleaned and tied pelts to round drying rings to cure.

From the ridge above our camp came the deep, resonate sound of bull elk bugling to attract females, along with the clash of horns as the males fought each other for the cows. The sounds reminded us that it was the breeding season. At breakfast, Andre told us he wanted to go hunting for elk meat, so we both decided to take the day off and go along.

No use even looking at a bull elk; they'd be worn down and thin by now from the rutting season. A big fat cow ready for the coming winter would provide several days' supply of meat. Some of those cows were as big as our horses and would weigh as much as 500 or even 600 pounds or more.

Andre took a trail leading farther down the valley so we could climb the ridge to be facing into the northwest wind at the top. Elk were known to have a keen sense of smell. The ridge was really an almost flat-topped bench, one of a series leading to the higher country. Much of the top was covered by widely spaced spruce trees with course brown grass covering the ground. It was easy riding except for the hollows where dense patches of spruce trees and juniper bushes grew. Mostly that seemed confined to where more moisture was available.

This was Andre's hunt, so we trailed behind, not wanting to interfere. He walked his horse along through plenty of elk signs where the animals grazed, leaving their droppings behind. Andre disappeared around another thick grove of trees. When we walked our horses nearer we could see him stopped just inside a small clearing where an elk calf, born the previous spring, was picking at the grass. The calf raised its head, gave a startled bleating sound, which was immediately followed by a whistling bellow and a crashing of trees and brush.

We arrived just in time to see a cow elk charge into the clearing from the side with her ears laid back and hooves churning the ground. She was moving at least as fast as our horses could, running full speed at Andre. He got his gun up and fired; the horse gave a frightened leap and took off running just as the cow went through their recently occupied space. The cow spun around to continue the chase.

Rene's gun fired ahead of mine, the combined noise loud in the small space of the clearing. The cow elk kept going like nothing happened until suddenly she collapsed on the far side of the clearing. The calf was gone.

We reloaded our guns, retrieved Andre's from where it lay on the ground, and went looking for him. He was sitting on the ground under the tree branch that had swept him from the saddle as his horse ran full speed under it. He was winded; otherwise he seemed in good shape except for a sore chest where the branch hit him. Nothing was broken. While Rene checked him over, it fell to me to look for Andre's horse.

Rene and I walked back to camp, leading our horses loaded with elk meat, while Andre rode along behind.

Rene was never one to talk much. Around the campfire that night he started telling us stories of similar happenings when a mother protected her young. All mothers, human or otherwise, were protective of their young. Rene told us, "Many time Cree hunter killed by momma moose, sometime momma elk. When Rene small boy, hunter die at Assiniboine River portage. He shoot calf with bow, momma moose kick him. Moose big, can run in trees much fast. Momma bear very bad. When have cubs will fight, not run. Black bear bad, grizzly momma much bad. Smart hunter not bother momma with baby."

Stories like this were common. The larger animals could be downright dangerous. Moose and elk were known to trample or kick men to death and mother bears were extremely dangerous. It was never wise to get between any mother and her offspring. Andre was fortunate he hadn't been on foot or he could easily have been killed by that irate elk. Listening to Rene, it came to me that he was upset by how close his sister's son came to being seriously hurt.

In the morning, with the horses loaded, I started the trip back, while Rene and Andre stayed to dry more meat and tend traps. This was a new area to us so we had no idea how harsh winter would be. We were preparing for the worst by putting aside a good supply of dried meat. If the cold was bad and the snow deep, it would be hard to find game during the winter. Having starved enough while doing the Bay's hunting, we never would again if we could prevent it by preparing.

My horse stepped right out, forcing the smaller pack animals to trot to keep up. After a mile, I slowed him to ease things because the packs were heavy. With all day to get home, there was no need to hurry.

Putting the horses back in the pasture, I moved the meat packs into the storage room that was partitioned off at the back of the house. It was intended to be a cold room for hanging meat and would serve just as well for storing jerky.

With a fire going and meat cooking, there was time for writing in the log. As every day, I made note of the weather, temperature and things observed such as the weight of jerky put up. On the way back, the sling got a fat goose which was spitted over the fire for roasting. It was browning nicely with frequent turns from me. The grease sizzled and sputtered as it dropped into the flames and tomorrow there'd be roasted, smoked, goose to eat.

It was a bountiful, vast land where there was the freedom to move as you pleased. With hard work, it provided most of what a man needed. I was thankful to Mac for telling me of it; convincing me to try my hand on this new continent called America. Often, it came to me to wonder how he was making it back in that little village in the old country. He had seen his share of the world, experiencing its pleasures and perils. Hopefully he was having an easy time of it now. There was no desire in me to return. If chance offered I would send Mac a note. Sitting up late, I regularly turned the spitted goose because with the night prowlers around, it couldn't be left alone. When it finished cooking and the fire was banked, I brought my bedding close to settle down for the night.

For three days the weather warmed, allowing me to work in the stream and fill four more bags and part of one other. It was enough, besides the water was far colder and there were other things needing to be done. The cache now held the equivalent of fifteen hundred American dollars, a small fortune on the frontier. The weight of it would be a burden to move.

Using slim branches from spruce trees, I fashioned more of the round hoops needed to dry beaver pelts from the winter trapping. When that was done, it was time to make arrows to replace the ones lost or broken. Each shaft was trimmed, straightened and dyed black using charcoal from the fire mixed with blood from game. Each got black feathers for fletching with iron trade points for heads. The feathers were set at a slight angle to cause the arrow to spin during flight, which helped it hold a true course. If you could do that with the ball from a long gun the range might be improved to match the long bow.

It was time to saddle up and head back to see how Rene and

Andre were making out. When I got there the meat supply was growing and our trapping was going better than we had any right to expect. As the days cooled down, most nights there was a frost of several degrees and often first thing in the morning it was foggy until the sun's rays warmed the air enough to chase the fog away. The previous evening, a light shower of rain fell just after dark and in the morning everything was covered in white frost. The grass crunched underfoot and the trees were gloriously decorated in pure white coats of thick hoarfrost.

Chewing on a slice of hot elk meat, I wandered around looking at everything, getting my moccasins wet in the damp grass. The sun was peeking over the mountains to the east and soon all of it would melt and disappear. Coming to a stop on the sunny side of a large poplar tree, now bare of leaves, my eye caught the shine of something on a small twig. Looking closer, I discovered a dragonfly. It was absolutely beautiful. A long, narrow, black body over an inch long with a large head topped by two bulging round eyes. It was the beautiful glistening wings that caught my attention. All four wings seemed overly large and out of proportion to the slim body. My hand started to reach out to touch the dragonfly and I quickly pulled it back, afraid the fly would shatter if touched. What a wonderful broach it would be for a lady to wear on her dress. Maybe the bug was frozen solid and dead. What if the sun's increasing heat thawed it? Would it fly once again? How wonderful.

Breakfast forgotten, I hurried to the get the logbook to record this. My haste drew Rene's attention, so he came to see what was going on. He watched me with his amused half-smile as I carefully studied the dragonfly and recorded my observations, adding a drawing with estimated dimensions.

"Why you draw dragonfly?" Rene asked.

My answer caused his smile to broaden. "Look, Rene, at how beautiful it is an' the wings look like they ar' made from glass."

Rene moved closer and looked to see what I was seeing. "Is just dragonfly."

"Yes, Rene, but look at the small sparkling dots in the wings. Are those natural or from the frost?"

"Rene not know. Is good to look at. Women like." As always, Rene got right to the point with no wasted words as I bent closer and commented.

"Do yea think it is dead or just in some kind of stupor frum the frost? Maybe it will fly again when the air warms."

Rene shrugged. "No fly. New dragonfly when winter over."

While I continued trying to put on paper what I was seeing, Rene returned to the fire and his breakfast. The sun was warming and I sat in its rays and watched to see if the bug would come back to life. When I left to join my companions in the trapping it was still there on the twig. Later in the day it was gone, probably having provided lunch for some bird.

With the racks full of meat, we decided to stop. It was a good thing we did, for in the middle of the night I awoke to something wet hitting my cheek. It was snowing, big fluffy flakes of snow drifting slowly to the ground; the kind that could pile up quickly in a short time. It snowed for a couple of hours, quitting just at dawn. It would take one more day to finish the meat that was drying. We stirred up the fires, adding wood to provide heat for drying because with the overcast sky the sun wouldn't be much help.

Andre took me along to check the traps. We removed the beaver, retrieving the traps so they wouldn't get frozen in. They would go home with us to be reset when the storm was over.

The next morning it was snowing heavily. We packed up, loaded the horses in the snow, and started for home. The cave like shelter, fronted with a log wall, was stocked with firewood and jerky in case we needed to overnight during a winter storm.

Big, fluffy snowflakes kept settling steadily, piling up on the trees and to at least eight inches deep on the ground. Our trip was almost over when Andre, who was out in front, pulled up looking at a trail of smoke rising from the site of our house. Even from several hundred paces away the smoke was clearly discernible. A fire was burning in the fire pit. We looked to our long guns, removing the barrel plugs and Rene took the packhorses in tow. Spread out some fifty paces apart we rode slowly forward, wary as any wild animal. Three horses were in sight, tied under the trees, with two figures sitting beside the fire. We stopped just at musket range and I helloed the camp which brought both men to their feet. They hadn't heard our approach in the deep snow.

One man walked out holding a bow, raising his right hand, palm towards us. I sat there trying to assess the situation, taking care to look for any others that might be hidden. Finally, starting my horse forward, I waved at the others to stay back. When my horse stopped, it was turned so the long gun in front of me was pointing at the stranger. Suddenly I knew who it was. It was Red Eagle, the Mandan from back on the Missouri and the boy, Elkfoot, was with him. He held up his hand and I greeted him.

"Ho, Red Eagle. Welcome to our camp."

"Black Arrow hard find. Red Eagle look much."

Rene and Andre rode forward and greeted Red Eagle. They helped unload the horses. We got our packs stored and put the horses in the pasture. Rene started a fire in the fireplace so we could move into the house. No sense staying out in the snow which was quickly piling up. We talked while our meat cooked. Red Eagle explained. "Red Eagle and Elkfoot look for Black Arrow. Him say go Paha Sapa Mountains. Much hard find."

Red Eagle knew we were heading for the Paha Sapa Mountains. The Teton Sioux gave these mountains that name because they looked black when viewed from a distance. Red Eagle opened his packs to show us the dried beans and shelled corn they had brought. Red Eagle pointed. "Is for Black Arrow. Him much help on Missouri."

It would be a welcome addition to our diet. Mandan women were great gardeners, or more properly farmers, with corn, beans, and squash as their main crops. In the Mandan culture, the woman owned the land which passed from mother to daughter. As a consequence, the Mandan enjoyed a very stable lifestyle. Mandan men were great traders with tribes from all directions around them. Especially in demand was the flint from the quarries the Mandan controlled along the Knife River. It was the best flint available and was in great demand all over the plains. Consequently, the Mandan were well provided with items from great distances away. Things like seashells for decorations and soapstone for pipes, all of which were important to their lifestyle. They weren't a nomadic people like most of the plains tribes, although the men made long trips to trade with neighbors. Red Eagle looked at me explaining, "We find camp on eastern slope. Go south, look for Black Arrow. At Cheyenne River Red Eagle stop, think to go home. Red Eagle know this valley. Come to see. Find big teepee, know it white man place."

It was still snowing when I went out to look around before sleeping. During the night the wind blew hard, piling up the snow into deep drifts. It was cold in the morning. Our house was proving to be snug, well protected from the wind and easy to heat. We settled down to make frames for snowshoes. The two Mandans watched with interest. Rene explained how they were used when the snow got deep. The Cree use rawhide from moose to string the webbing on snowshoes. Here there were no moose. We would use elk or buffalo hide with the hair removed, when we were able to go hunting again.

At midday we all went out to check on the horses. They seemed content in their sheltered pasture. As we stood there, my horse came to get his ears scratched as he nibbled on the handful of grass I brought for him. I fussed over him, rubbing his ears and patting his neck. There were no tracks other than ours to disturb the snow.

An iron kettle of beans soaked overnight and now they were soft, so we cut up meat, added corn, salt and some herbs Red Eagle had brought with him, before setting it in the coals to cook. Soon the house was filled with the smell of the stew as it quietly bubbled. We went back to trimming frames for our snowshoes and getting them ready for bending.

Before dark, I took the thermometer outside to check the temperature. It was twelve degrees, feeling much colder with the strong wind blowing. Back inside, I took out the logbook to write, starting with the date, November 27, 1800. While I was writing notes about the day, adding a few words about the snowstorm, Rene was explaining to our visitors.

"Black Arrow make marks. Marks tell much. Can tell what Rene do long time back. Many white men try make marks, only Black Arrow do it well. Is strong magic."

It wasn't true of course. Maybe Rene half believed what he was saying. His storytelling would do no harm while adding to my reputation among the natives.

For several days the wind blew and it continued to snow, so we were confined to camp. We all worked on snowshoes while the talk turned to trapping. The two Mandans listened as we planned where to start with our traps when the storm ended. Red Eagle suggested, "No have white man traps for beaver. Can set Indian traps for fox, beaver, weasels. In spring you take furs, get gun like Black Arrow."

We looked in surprise and I asked, "You want to stay here for the winter to trap?"

Red Eagle nodded his head. "Get gun like Black Arrow." His finger pointed at his son and at his chest.

All the words needed weren't there. I tried anyway. "In the spring, Back Arrow will go to St. Louis to sell furs. It is a long hard trip with many dangers. Much can go wrong; floods, Indians or bad white men. We may lose everything."

Red Eagle turned to Rene, who explained in a mixture of Cree and Sioux. Finally Red Eagle nodded and looked back at me. "Black Arrow brave, much strong medicine, take furs."

It worried me and I used Cree to talk. "Rene does he understand that we may lose his furs or something could happen to us causing us to never get back? Many things can go wrong on such a long trip."

Again the exchange between Rene and Red Eagle went on for some time and was much too fast for me to follow. Rene turned my way and told me, "Red Eagle say take furs, strong medicine protect Black Arrow. Bring long gun him and Elkfoot. Him not worry. Much more furs." So it was agreed. It would be good having the extra help for the winter with the added safety in numbers. Besides, Red Eagle was acquainted with much of the area.

During the night a small herd of buffalo rumbled past, coming off the plains, hopefully planning to spend the winter in our valley. That was great. It would be like having a herd of cattle on pasture or a ready-made meat shop close at hand.

In the morning, the storm was over. It was beautiful with the sun reflecting off the many shapes the wind sculpted from the snow. In some places the ground was blown bare, while in others there were deep drifts that curved in weird, contorted shapes; some with sharp tops, others with overhangs. Everywhere the sun reached, the snow was sparkling brightly.

The glare was hard on the eyes. Recalling the sun-blockers the northern people wore to avoid snow blindness, I decided to make a shield for my eyes. Theirs were made of wood. A piece of leather would be faster. I set to work making a shield with thin slits to look through and a thong to tie around my head.

We caught the horses, took the pack animals with us and headed north out of the mountains to hunt buffalo. The best of all hides for winter clothing were those from four year old buffalo cows, taken in winter when the hair was long and thick. We didn't need to go far on the plains to find animals. The big bulls were too heavy, some of them weighing 1500 pounds or more. It was a tough job to skin them properly. The cows were much easier to handle so we concentrated on the four year olds. Besides, it was commonly accepted that a fat cow was the best eating on the plains.

In a few days there was a good supply of meat hanging in our cold room, along with the dried jerky. There were new hides to prepare for sleeping robes, boots, clothing and the rawhide necessary for webbing to complete the snowshoes.

My eye shield impressed the others, so they each made a set. There would be many days during the winter when the bright sun was reflecting off the snow and the shields would make visibility easier. Everyone agreed that on a bright day you could actually see far better.

For several days we prepared the furs for winter use, scraping and tanning the hides. When the work was caught up it was time to check the ice on the ponds and streams for thickness, to see if it was strong enough to walk on.

Every day I wrote in the log and each time the Mandans watched with what was close to awe.

Chapter 4

As often happens after the first severe storm of winter, the sky cleared, the sun shone and it warmed up. Snow on the southern exposures melted, causing the streams to begin running again. We hurried to set out all the traps while the ideal conditions lasted.

Our favorite set was to locate a place where the beaver were leaving the water to cut wood or just to sun themselves. A trap was placed on the stream bottom just below the water surface. A sturdy tree branch was driven into the bank at a diagonal so it leaned over the trap and beaver castoreum was smeared on it. Beaver are territorial animals and will fight to keep intruders from another clan from moving in. Each beaver has its own scent so the smell of castoreum from a strange animal attracted the local beaver to defend their pond. When a beaver came to investigate what smelled like an invasion the trap was there waiting.

The immediate reaction of a trapped beaver is to dive for deep water. The ring on the trap chain was put over a strong stake driven into the bottom of the pond. Stakes were trimmed to leave short barbs pointing down where each branch was taken off. The ring slid down past the barbs and couldn't come back up again which held the beaver underwater to drown.

Everyone carried a scent bottle which was constantly replenished with fresh castoreum from the beaver being caught. Most of our traps were a distance from camp, so the beaver were skinned near where they were caught and just the pelts were brought back. After making a round of the traps each morning, the afternoons were devoted to scraping the inside of the pelts to free them of fatty flesh. After scraping, each pelt was tied with leather thongs to round wooden hoops to dry.

Beaver were plentiful and the pelts accumulated quickly, so it fell to me to build a press to compact the bundles; Andre volunteered to help. We planned to put sixty pelts in each pack which would weigh upwards of a hundred pounds. This, of course, depended on the size of the beaver caught. Many of the older animals were huge, often measuring over four feet from nose to tip of tail. Such a large number of beaver indicated that no one else trapped in the area.

We selected a large tree with a sturdy limb at waist height to serve as the anchor and hinge point for a long, heavy lever. A notch chopped in the underside of the limb beside the tree trunk was shaped to fit the lever which was tied in place with heavy leather straps to allow it to pivot up and down.

We hauled in slabs of flat rock for a base to build the packs on and drove thick stakes into the ground on two sides, three in a row, to prevent the pile of hides from tipping over as they were compressed. With a little adjusting, it was ready for use.

We folded each dried pelt in half with the fur on the inside and stacked them in the press until there were sixty. Removing the forked prop that supported the lever, we both pulled down on it to compact the first stack of pelts. It didn't work as well as expected. The pelts wanted to curl up around the lever. After some thought, we put two narrow flat rocks on the top of the pile of furs for the lever to push on and solved the problem. Strong ropes, put across the base before piling the pelts, were pulled up to tie the bale together.

The last step was to wrap each bale in deer hide and tie it with ropes to keep the bale together. After that, the bale was ready to be stored until spring. Making tight, compact bales required two men, so every few days we stayed in camp to keep up with the work.

Red Eagle told us that small groups of Cheyenne often spent the winter in valleys along the mountains, south of our location. As winter settled in, he and I decided to go looking for them in the hope of trading for furs. The other three would stay to trap. The sky was clear, still there was always the chance of a winter storm, so we took time to select what to take with us, including a supply of jerky for emergency rations, snowshoes and extra clothes in case we were forced to walk. Trading would have to be done carefully with our small stock of trade goods. After two days of discussing our route so Rene would know where to look for us, we loaded the packhorses and started south.

Our route was south through the series of valleys we were living and trapping in before crossing the mountain ridges to the west. After that it would be south along the west side of the mountains; checking valleys for signs of Cheyenne. Unless we were lucky or just stumbled on them it could be days before a camp was located. There was always a chance that none of them had come to winter in the area this winter.

After the first day it was new country to both of us, although over the years Red Eagle heard many descriptions of the area. Several times we ran into dead ends which forced us to retrace our route, looking for another way to go. We were climbing and working our way between two high peaks when we came on a narrow animal trail which wound through the tall trees. Following the trail was faster and there was less chance of finding our way blocked. Over time, animals usually worked out the easiest way to move around, eventually creating a trail that was used year after year. At every opportunity we looked back at the country we were crossing, selecting landmarks that would guide us on our trip back. We were leaving blaze marks for us and Rene.

Moving at a walk to save the horses, we stopped after every steep climb to let them rest. The horses expelled long streams of fog from their lungs, causing the sides of their nostrils to flap on each breath. Clouds of moisture-laden air from their lungs froze in the cold air as the horses snorted and breathed heavily. Our progress wasn't fast. There was no hurry and we were crossing country that was worth seeing. The second night we camped in heavy timber on what seemed to be a high plateau with no view beyond a few feet. Red Eagle, with some knowledge of this route from descriptions he had heard, was expecting to find a pass the next day. After that, our route would be south again.

There was snow on the ground and the trees were heavily laden. The large size of the trees prevented the wind from creating snow drifts to slow us down. With the thick stand of tall trees, the ground was well sheltered from the wind. The trail wandered through the trees until at midday we crossed a narrow pass, arriving at a north flowing stream. Red Eagle turned upstream.

For several miles the horses walked beside the stream and often splashed through water. A great many beaver dams and lodges in the stream slowed our progress as it took time to find a way around the ponds. The trail started climbing again. From the occasional clearing I could see another high, rocky ridge ahead sitting across our path. It looked like we would have to climb right to the top unless there was a pass that wasn't visible from where we were.

Setting up camp early, we settled in for the night. Red Eagle pointed at the ridge and explained. "Is small pass, no deep. Next day go through pass. Trail go down mountain. Cheyenne be south."

"How far south will the Cheyenne be camped?"

Red Eagle shrugged. "Not know. Maybe no Cheyenne. Go look. Cheyenne camp, we find."

"Are we looking for a large camp with many Cheyenne or several smaller camps?"

"Red Eagle think small camp. No grass, food for big camp. Many small camp."

He was right about the pass. The next day we climbed and scrambled a winding way right to the top of the ridge, went through a shallow pass and shortly after started down to lower ground.

On the south side of the ridge the snow was melting and in the shaded places it was icy. The horses stepped along on dainty feet, fearful of slipping. In many places, the trail was steep as it made its way through trees and around rocks. We both dismounted to walk, leading the horses. Late in the day, we set up camp beside a trickle of water in a grassy, sheltered canyon on the lower flank of the mountain.

For four more days we worked our way along the mountains,

checking each valley which might hold a village. Finally, we found one in a canyon with a stream flowing along the bottom. A heavy growth of trees covered the slopes. It was well sheltered from winter storms with the advantage that on a clear day the sun's rays could reach the bottom of the canyon.

It was smoke from cooking fires that attracted our attention. When we came around the last bend the village was straight ahead, sitting on a flat bench above the stream.

Sitting there on our horses, we gave them time to notice us, which didn't take long. There was a flurry of activity as people gathered to look and we started our horses forward. Red Eagle had often traded with the Cheyenne in the past, learning much of their language. He told me my Cree would help.

Three men walked out to meet us. Our horses stopped some ten paces away and Red Eagle greeted them. Only a few of the words were familiar to me. "We come to trade with our Cheyenne friends." He pointed. "This man is Black Arrow who the white men call Jar. He is much known among the Cree, Sioux and Mandan who know him to be a friend." He slapped his chest. "Red Eagle of the Mandan. Many times trade with Cheyenne when they lived near us."

They looked us and the packhorses over before speaking. "Red Eagle of the Mandan and his friend Black Arrow are welcome. I am Running Fox, leader of this band of Cheyenne."

They were dressed in leather leggings, with long buckskin shirts that hung below the waist and the low moccasins common to prairie tribes. The village behind them was a partial circle of teepees facing the stream. Their horses were in a corral made by stringing leather ropes from tree to tree.

The whole camp came out to see the strangers. The women wore long deerskin dresses that hung below the knee and moccasins with leggings sewn onto them for the winter weather. Some of the older women draped buffalo robes over their shoulders as the day cooled down.

These were a nomadic people who followed the buffalo. Everything they owned was light and portable to make moving easy. The main decoration on their clothing seemed to be quillwork on the shoulders and sleeves. It appeared to be well done with many creative designs. Both men and women wore long fringes along the sleeves of their clothing. There were short fringes along the bottom of some dresses.

Running Fox took us to a teepee. “You sleep here.”

We unloaded our packs and moved in. An older woman with long white hair came with a bark scoop of glowing coals to start a fire in the central pit while we tethered our horses on a patch of grass. Women were cooking around several fires in the central common area when I sat down in front of the teepee to write a description of the day.

In the grey of predawn, we took our bows and went hunting with the intention of contributing to the food supply and not be a burden to the Cheyenne. Walking north, we followed a narrow animal trail through the trees along the side of the canyon with the stream below us.

Suddenly Red Eagle stopped, pointing at the tracks of a bear in the snow. The tracks were of a big animal and came from the trees on the uphill side of us. He was out there ahead of us on the trail. It was late in the season for a bear to be out; he should be sleeping in a winter den. Maybe he hadn't put on enough fat before the snows came and awakened to look for food. Following along the tracks, we came to a pile of fresh bear droppings right in the middle of the path, not yet frozen, so he was only minutes ahead of us. The last thing we needed was a hungry bear nosing around.

A quarter of a mile further on, the tracks left the trail, turning down the slope towards the stream. We knew he was down there although he was hidden from view. I hoped he was gone on his way and that was the last of him.

I asked, "Do you think he heard us following him?" Red Eagle just shrugged.

It must have been close to a mile further when we spotted seven deer feeding in a grassy meadow. The wind was blowing toward us, so they hadn't caught our scent. Taking time to carefully work our way through the trees to the edge of the clearing, we each selected an animal and prepared our bows.

When we shot, both arrows flew straight and two animals lay in a clearing suddenly empty of the rest of the herd. It took both of us to drag the buck to a large tree where we hung him from a thick branch before going back for the doe. In just a few minutes we field dressed both animals by cutting down from the rib cage, spreading the hind legs and cleaning out the guts and organs. This was important to prevent the meat from being tainted, although not as urgent as in warmer weather. They were ready to be hauled back to camp before the meat froze.

The temperature always dropped just before sunrise and while it would probably melt later in the day, it was cold right then. Red

Eagle went back to camp to bring two packhorses, leaving me to guard our meat. A large rock a few paces away looked inviting, so I walked over. It was peaceful sitting there watching the early morning turn into day. Soon, two ravens with large heads and oversized beaks came to investigate. They moved from tree to tree, each move bringing them closer to the deer; squawking in their harsh voices. All black, with their feathers fluffed up for winter, they were disheveled and rough in appearance.

Soon, they were joined by a healthy looking gray coyote coming across the clearing and cautiously approaching, staying well clear of my rock. It was obvious they knew I was there and were avoiding me.

Their behavior was interesting to watch as they moved closer to the deer until they were picking away at the entrails lying on the ground. The ravens hopped around, getting their share while the coyote ignored them. They seemed to know they were less desirable food and the coyote wouldn't bother them.

Old coyote was wary, causing me to wonder if he would be there if he knew that at twenty paces the bow could easily reach him. He did know he could outrun me. If I moved he would quickly disappear into the bush.

Even while eating they were constantly alert. Watching them lulled me into forgetting the bear. Suddenly, the coyote's head came up and the ravens flew to branches, squawking and scolding. Turning my eyes to where the coyote was looking, the sound of the bear was clear even before he came into sight. A huge black bear lumbered into the clearing. One of the largest I ever saw, coming up from the stream, muttering and snuffling as he came. His dinner was in sight.

The coyote slunk away, looking back over his shoulder as he went and stopped at a safe distance to sit and watch. He could wait, there would be enough left for him when the bear was done.

Yelling would do no good; this was a hungry bear intent on filling his stomach. I didn't intend to give up our meat without a fight and stood up to notch an arrow. The bear spotted me immediately and reared up on his hind legs to look. He was maybe forty paces away, facing right at me, waving his front paws as he sniffed the air. He moved just as the arrow left the bow, causing it to enter below his right shoulder instead of the chest. Accepting the challenge, he charged toward me, growling loudly.

One arrow wasn't going to stop a large bear, unless it was a lucky hit, so I was notching a second. He was coming fast on the far side of the deer. It was hard to wait for him to come from behind the tree where our deer were hanging before shooting again. The distance between us was cut in half when the second arrow went into his left side. He stopped to swat at the arrow with his right paw and tried to bite it. There was no way to know if he was seriously hurt or just annoyed. He looked back at me and charged again. He was too close to get in another shot, so I scrambled to climb a large tree growing near the rock.

Grabbing a branch, I chinned myself and started climbing. Unfortunately, keeping a grip on the bow slowed me down. Quickly glancing down, the bear was right below me, so I lunged desperately to get higher. The bear stood up, swinging his left paw as he reached for me. Before my foot was out of the way, the claws raked my lower leg. It was a big aspen which would probably support him, although it would be rare for a bear that big to climb and I hoped this one wouldn't. Scrambling to a branch twenty feet off the ground, panting from the exertion of climbing so fast, the pain from the claw marks hit me. Sitting on the branch looking at my foot, it was plain to see the leather of the pant leg was torn with no sign of the low camp moccasin I had been wearing. There were deep slashes in my lower leg and claw marks on the side of my foot. The wounds were bleeding, letting the blood drip on the tree and the ground below. Thinking the bleeding would be a good thing for now to clean the wound, my attention turned to checking the bow. It seemed to be unharmed after all the rough treatment.

Now, with the excitement over, the pain really hit me. It was intense and my head felt dizzy. Putting one arm around the tree, I squeezed it tight, afraid of passing out and falling to the ground. The only thing I could think about was the rope we used to hang the deer; wishing I could use it to tie myself to the tree.

The bear was snuffling and growling as he circled the tree, looking for a way to get at me. After a few minutes of resting, I decided to get an arrow ready. This fight wasn't over. With no one to help, it was up to me to defend myself. Maybe my head was starting to work better, even though it still felt woozy. It is not easy to use a long bow from up in a tree, even though big aspens have a habit of shedding branches, which left spaces. I got the bow into position and waited, straining to focus my eyes and concentrate on what was happening.

He was bleeding from both arrows and they were also annoying him. He bit off the feathered end of the arrow in his shoulder before trying to get at the one in his side. It was out of reach. Just when he seemed to have forgotten about me, he stood up to look, growling and turning his head to check me out. He gripped the tree trunk with both front paws, trying to push it over and I thanked the Lord for giving me a big sturdy tree to climb. With both paws reaching toward me and his long black claws gripping the tree, he tipped his head to one side to stare at me. He growled angrily with wide, gaping jaws that looked large enough to swallow me whole. From the ten feet that separated us I could clearly see a red tongue bedded between two lines of white teeth. The lower jaw was narrower than the upper and shaped to fit between two long pointed fangs which flanked a row of sharp teeth across the front of a wide, strong upper jaw. His broad, black, leathery-looking nose was pointed right at me with a gleaming eye on each side looking up to where I sat.

Keeping an arrow notched, I waited for a chance. Finally, he tipped his head back and growled loudly. I shot and the arrow went into the center of his chest, entering at the base of the throat, leaving most of the feathers showing. With three feet of arrow in his chest entering from the top, another in his side and one below his right shoulder, he slowly slumped to the ground.

Hurting as I was, I felt only admiration for that bear, a magnificent animal in the prime of life and a fighter to the end. Here I was, an intruder into his territory, sitting in a tree above him, feeling sympathy for him. It was a hard life we lived, both of us, in a land where it was survival of the fittest and once again fortune was on my side. An old Gallic expression came to me out of nowhere, *'Better yea are ta be lucky than good.'*

Lucky I was in so many ways. Realizing there was no hurry to move, I just sat right there, hung on to the tree and waited on my friend the bear to expire before venturing down. My leg was hurting, with a biting pain, and those gashes needed to be cleaned. Still, there was no energy in me for moving.

The bear hadn't stirred for a long time and there was no sound, so I found a slow, painful way down from the tree and stood looking at him. The claw marks he made on the tree looked to be eight feet above the ground. Standing, his reach was taller than mine. He was in the prime of life and would weigh several hundred pounds. The heavy black fur was long and glossy and would be valuable during the cold weather of the long winter ahead.

Leaving him, I limped slowly down the slope to the stream and found a spot with water flowing close to the bank where my lower leg and foot could soak. The water was really cold. I gritted my teeth and vowed to keep soaking for as long as possible. Drinking the water chilled my teeth, making them ache. There was the need to replace lost blood though, so I kept drinking. Later, pulling some twigs and dry grass together, I got a fire started, adding wood to build a good-sized blaze so my leg could dry and warm up; wishing the whole time we had eaten before leaving camp.

Laying there beside the fire feeling sorry for my stomach, I waited until Red Eagle arrived with the horses, bringing two Cheyenne with him.

They walked around the bear, checking the arrows and could read the story without me telling them. Red Eagle picked up my moccasin, came to the fire and looked at the leg. There was nothing to be done short of camp so he observed, "Him big bear."

I grinned. "He was big and hungry and a brave fighter."

Red Eagle nodded his head at that. "Bear always brave. No get meat."

"No, but he almost got me."

"Huh, you no good eat. Bear want deer."

I grinned again and laid still while he went to help skin out the bear. There were two packhorses for the deer meat. The horses were skittish from the smell of blood so it took extra time to load them. Now there was the bear meat wrapped in its own hide to take back, too. The two Cheyenne walked, with me riding and Red Eagle leading the packhorses.

Back at camp my only wish was to rest. Loosing blood is always a tiring thing and the ride back made my head feel dizzy again. I crawled into my robes and settled down, with two deep gashes on my leg and four scratches on the side of my foot. The bleeding was mostly stopped, so maybe the cold water had helped; it sure didn't stop the pain.

Lying there, the whole scuffle with the bear went through my mind, causing me to wonder what I could have done better. The only thing that came to mind was after the first arrow I should have climbed the tree and not hung around for another shot at him. He very nearly got me. In the future I would be more cautious.

Red Eagle came with a chunk of meat, freshly cooked for me. He put the pot in the edge of the fire to make tea. He was acquiring our taste for tea which the northern people said was the best drink for cold weather. Red Eagle unrolled a square of deerskin to show me the bear claws. "Him big bear, make good necklace. Give Black Arrow bear's strength and courage."

Two days I rested and studied the inside of that teepee. It was an ingenious design that most Europeans would consider beyond the capabilities of a people they thought of as savages. Long grayish white lodgepoles supported a covering made from many well-tanned buffalo hides, neatly sewn and shaped to fit the conical arrangement of the stacked poles. Most intriguing was the arrangement of two triangular flaps at the top that were adjusted with long poles to control the air flow through the smoke hole. Near the top, the hide covering was blackened from rising smoke off the centrally positioned fire pit. The teepee provided a warm refuge from the cold wind and snow outside. It could be dismantled in a matter of minutes and packed to move to a new location. A light, easily transported shelter perfectly suited to a people who followed the buffalo herds.

Restless after two days, I went out to look at the camp and see what was going on. It was good to be up, slowly hobbling around, carefully stepping on my bad foot. The three hides were stretched out with women scraping and tanning them. I stood looking at the bearskin. It was big. Only a fool like me would tackle him. Anyone with a lick of sense would have run or climbed a tree and sat quiet.

Rummaging in our gear for some deerskin, I sat down near a fire to patch my pant leg. My sewing wasn't fancy, just good enough that most things would stay together, so I got with it and started fixing the leg.

Running Fox came to watch me work and from time to time he added sticks to the fire. We talked and many of his words were the same as Cree, although he often put a different sound to them. By going slowly, we managed to communicate, with much gesturing and sign language thrown in.

"Long time before Running Fox born, Cheyenne live far to morning sun beside Great River."

I asked, "Beside the Mississippi River?"

"Ah yes, Mississippi. Running Fox forget river name. Cheyenne no have horse. Cheyenne grow corn, gather in forest, hunt."

"When mother have Running Fox, Cheyenne live on Yellowstone. Have horses. Cheyenne chase buffalo. Now Cheyenne have many horses." Running Fox gestured with both hands. "Cheyenne live north of Paha Sapa Mountains to many days travel south." He pointed west. "Cheyenne live from Paha Sapa many days travel to Mountains of Rock. Some Cheyenne come Paha Sapa for winter. More Cheyenne go Mountains of Rock for winter. Running Fox come here when buffalo scarce and cold winds blow."

Curious about the Mountains of Rock, I considered how to inquire. "Mountains of Rock big like Paha Sapa?"

Running Fox shook his head. "Mountains of Rock much big. Paha Sapa small. Mountains of Rock white with snow in summer when sun hot."

It didn't seem possible. These Paha Sapas were bigger than any mountains I had ever seen in Scotland or in all my travels to get here and he was saying that these were only hills by comparison. Could it be true or was this just a story his people liked to tell around the fire? In my limited experience with Indians they never lied, so maybe I was missing what Running Fox meant.

Red Eagle came back from a hunting trip with the Cheyenne to join us at the fire.

I asked cautiously, "Running Fox has been to these mountains of rock?"

"Much times." Running Fox shrugged and waved an arm. "No buffalo, not stay."

So he was telling me that they went to the mountains of rock and didn't stay because there were no buffalo there. There were many things I wanted to know. Asking questions would cause him to stop talking.

"Someday Black Arrow will ride his horse to these mountains of rock."

"Much sleeps."

I held up ten fingers. Running Fox shook his head and showed me twenty fingers. That could mean anything from 400 to maybe 600 miles. He was talking about time, not distance. It all depended on how hard you pushed your horse. Twenty sleeps would be fewer than it took to come from Peters River.

Returning to my sewing, the last few stitches went in and I pulled on the patch to test it. It held, so that was done. I wanted to ask questions and learn more about these big mountains and what was there. Indians usually went silent when questioned, so I decided not to ask and would wait to ask Rene if he knew of these mountains of rock.

Our stay lasted longer than intended and Rene would be wondering about us, so we did our trading and packed up. The Cheyenne got good steel knives, arrow points, hide scrapers, tomahawk heads that only needed handles fitted, awls, needles, iron kettles, and tin cups. We were going away with beaver and fox furs.

They got items they needed and if we got the furs to St. Louis there would be a good profit for us. To the women who prepared the hides for us I gave a sack of colored glass beads along with a one pound spool of heavy thread.

We travelled back north along the west side of the Paha Sapa Mountains. The first night out it snowed and higher up on the mountains the snow would be much deeper. We wouldn't attempt to return by the trail we used to come south, it would be impassable, so our route would be up the west side of the mountains to enter our valley from the north.

The west wind blew cold with me riding wrapped in the bearskin. Red Eagle put a buffalo robe over his clothes. My leg and foot were still hurting and the bearskin was a big help. It completely covered me and hung below my feet. There were few animal tracks in the snow because of the miserable weather, so the game wasn't moving around. They were smart enough to settle in good shelter to wait for better weather while we were anxious to get home and see how the others were faring.

It took six days of starting early to round into our valley. When we approached the house, smoke was rising from the chimney. It was a welcome sight. The boys came to help unload. Andre took the horses to pasture and me, I limped to the door and went in. No place had ever looked so good.

Chapter 5

It was a long winter with periods of bitterly cold and windy weather. Still, in total, it was good to us. Now, in the middle of March, the snow was melting. Already there were bare patches of ground showing through the snow with water running on the hillsides. We cooked outside now, providing a welcome change after being confined all winter in a small space. Soon we would begin sleeping out in the open.

The beaver cooperated; our pile of fur bales was large and would be a heavy load for the packhorses. There was also a good supply of silver fox, mink, and ermine, some of which belonged to Red Eagle and Elkfoot.

Over the winter we had picked up enough of the Mandan language to make communication easier. Surprisingly, Elkfoot learned English; if what he learned could be called that, coming from a Scot and two French/Cree Métis. As a consequence, the five of us made out well, not that any of my companions were great talkers. Many days there was hardly a word exchanged as each man worked at doing what was necessary.

My logbook was almost full of sketches of things I saw, along with descriptions of the trapping, animals, plants, and what I learned from the others. Like Rene twisting the long chin hairs from buffalo into lengths of twine from which he made rope by braiding four twines together. He produced a good supply of strong rope to tie the packs with. There were always things needing to be done, keeping everyone from being idle. We were all busy making warm winter moccasins, leggings, repairing or making new clothes and fixing equipment. Feeding the fire required a constant replenishing of the wood supply from the many dead trees in the forest around us.

While laid up waiting for the gashes in my leg to mend, I had used the time to make an oil lamp from a buffalo horn fixed to a slab of rock with sinew. Using twisted moss for a wick and buffalo fat rendered in a kettle to provide oil, it added to the light from the fireplace during the long dark evenings. Surprising what a man could contrive when he put his mind to it. The men were curious about the lamp and, having no wish to take credit for something undeserved, I described a stone lamp a trader acquired from the far northern people of the Arctic which they fueled with fat from seals.

So we got through the winter and food was rarely a problem. There was still a small supply of jerky that would be useful to us in crossing the plains to St. Louis.

As the sun rose higher in the sky each day, the snow melted faster, filling the streams until they were running full. Water came down slopes in places that had been dry since our arrival. It was too muddy to move very far from camp, so we sat watching spring arrive.

The geese returned on their long flight north, providing us a change of diet as we waited for the grass to turn green. When it did there would be travelling food for the horses and our trip to St. Louis could begin. There was much discussion of this. In the end, Andre decided he would go north with the Mandan and continue on to Fort Garry to visit his family. Rene would ride with me on the trek to St. Louis. Andre intended to trade for Bay Company blankets to make us new coats and leggings because ours were in a sorry state after the long winter. We set aside furs Andre could trade for blankets, along with extra for him to get the things his family needed.

Each day, we sat in the warm sun watching changes taking place. Grass started to turn green on southern facing slopes; trees were beginning to bud and soon would leaf out. Songbirds began arriving to start building nests, providing music for our ears. It was pleasant hearing them chirping and singing again.

Across the valley from the rock where I favored sitting in the sun was a long grove of aspen trees with here and there a black fir tree showing plainly through the leafless aspens. The aspens stood bare and black looking, with twisted branches reaching for the sky like naked arms. As spring progressed and each day passed, the yellowish green haze around the trees thickened and became greener. With time, the green got brighter as the leaves grew and the skeletons of trees began to disappear. It would be nice to stay to watch the full effect of spring weather. It was time to go.

This must be how my father felt each spring as he watched the miracle of his crops emerging from the ground. He planted seeds, always wondering if they would grow; an annual miracle that kept occurring.

We loaded the horses and there wasn't room for everything. Rene and I discussed what to leave behind. Elkfoot surprised us by bringing his horse with an empty pack saddle cinched up and ready.

He handed me the lead rope. "You take horse, I ride double." He nodded at Red Eagle's horse. He was serious.

"Thank you, Elkfoot; your horse will make a big difference."

He grinned, pointing at my Charleville. "No thank, bring two long guns and powder."

With the extra horse loaded there were still things to be left behind. Ten packhorses loaded with furs would follow us to St. Louis. We rode away, leaving the latch string out on the door, with wood ready in the fireplace. The gold was in a pair of large saddlebags on my horse. Our traps and tools were safely cached, away from the house, in case someone came snooping around.

When the plains opened out in front of us, the other three would go north to the Missouri while we turned east for the Mississippi. At the parting I told Red Eagle, "If all goes well, we will be back on Peters River by summer; you come for your guns."

Turning the corner of the black hills, Rene pointed us south along the eastern slope, staying to higher ground to avoid the mud. The first night out we slept at the spot where we first camped when we arrived in the mountains the fall before. Next morning, our trip south really got underway.

We knew not how far it was to St. Louis. It must to close to 1000 miles. This time of year we would be forced to make detours around lakes or to find crossing places on streams, so it might be further.

With no knowledge of the country ahead and only a general idea of where to go, there was only one thing we knew for sure. The Missouri River was east of us and if we missed it the Mississippi was to the south. It was the Missouri we wanted to find because St. Louis was reported to be just below where the two rivers joined.

Our plan was to go south far enough to avoid the large area of arid badlands that lay east of the Paha Sapas. The badlands were visible in the distance from the high ground where we rode. Red Eagle had told us we would find a good-sized river to the south and, after crossing it, we could turn east.

Working our way around mud and water to find the easiest way for the horses, it was three days before we came up to the Cheyenne River. It was running full with water from the spring snowmelt. Without the packhorses we might have crossed. After watching the water for a while, we decided to go downstream, looking for a ford. If there wasn't one in a few miles, we would have to stay put until the water level dropped.

Several miles downstream the land leveled out and the river widened, causing the water speed to slow. Later in the day, we were lucky to find a ford where several hundred buffalo were coming across from the far side. The river was making a gradual turn to the north with the deepest part of the channel near the south bank. The buffalo were wading in and swimming for a short distance before walking toward the north bank. The horses would have to swim and the packs would get wet, but it looked safe enough to try. Rene suggested we wait until morning to cross so we would have a full day ahead to dry the packs.

My horse was the largest, so I went across to check the fast moving water near the south bank. The horse was able to walk the whole way with the water coming well up his sides. If it was just a little deeper he would have been swimming. I could feel the force of the water which pushed us slowly sideways until we scrambled up the south bank. My horse shook himself to shed the excess water and got his neck patted to show approval.

Riding close to a tree I put my guns, the bow and saddlebags where they would be safe and out of my way for the crossing. On second thought I stuck my hat in a crotch of the tree before going back to help get the pack animals across the river.

The horses were trail broke and accustomed to following along without lead ropes so Rene took off, leading one animal. The other ponies followed, strung out in a loosely spaced column. The smaller ponies started swimming as they stepped into the deeper water near the far side. I came at the rear of the column to herd any horse that tried to turn back. The crossing was going smoothly with the first horses climbing the south bank when a small pony, second from last in line, stumbled as she entered the deep water. It was one of the ponies we took after the fight with the Arikara back on the Missouri.

As the pony went under the water, I turned my horse, slapped him on the rump and he took off, spraying water on both sides, soaking me with the cold water. My horse charged into the deep water just as the pony surfaced and gamely started swimming, being carried downstream by the river current. We followed, slowly catching up until we got ahead and into a position to force her toward the shore. Her eyes were large, her ears laid back and she snorted with fear as the current forced her downstream. I was some scared myself at the prospect of getting tossed into the river. Luckily, the pony was carrying a light load. My horse forced her closer to the bank until her feet touched bottom and she leaped ahead in a series of crow hops and scrambled up the bank to dry land.

Her eyes were large with fright and her nostrils extended as she panted for breath. She was skittish, prancing around, snorting and still frightened. Both horses needed a rest to recover and I was soaked and cold. When the horses calmed down, I dismounted to fuss over the pony, patting her neck, while looking her over for injuries. The pack saddle was shifted to one side, so I got it back into position and retightened the cinch.

The fast water had carried us upwards of a quarter mile. To warm up, I walked back leading the horses. We made our way to where Rene was waiting with the other animals. It was a scare, we could have lost both horses and I wasn't a very good swimmer.

Rene stood near his horse, watching as I approached. "You okay, Jar?"

I grinned. "Got a wee scare and I'm soaked ta' the hide, but I'll be fine."

"Rene will check all the cinches."

"Yeah, do that, Rene. I'm going ta find dry moccasins and fetch ma guns."

I was still wet when we started moving again. The sun was well up in the sky and would take care of that.

Two more days we trailed south before turning southeast into the morning sun, hoping to be in St. Louis in forty days. Every stream bed and hollow was full of water. The grass was really greening up, so there was ample fresh food for the horses. Travelling stayed slow for many days until gradually we began getting into drier, sandy, hill country where our pace picked up.

We hoped to hit the Missouri well below where it made its turn to the south, thus avoiding many of the peoples who lived along the river. Especially, we had no desire to run into the Arikara whose reputation was for being disagreeable.

Every day we kept moving, putting more miles behind us, lucky that the weather cooperated. When we ran out of fresh meat there was jerky which was hard dried. After cutting off a piece you waited for it to soften in your mouth before chewing, taking a fair time to finish. It was nourishing and in a pinch you could shave it into a cup to make a hot drink.

Ours was a small caravan inching along somewhere out on the wide grasslands and each day seemed like the one before. Changes came slowly in this vast, open country with the faraway horizons. It seemed to me we were nothing more than tiny specs sailing on an ocean of grass. The wind often blew and most mornings there was still a cold bite until the sun was well up in the sky to warm us. Slowly, the days plodded by.

Riding along, lost in thought, Rene drew my attention to a storm looming on the western horizon. The black clouds were scudding toward us quickly with an angry look to them. We needed to find shelter immediately. A hasty search finally located a grove of stunted aspen trees growing in a shallow hollow in the prairie. We hurried to unload the horses before picketing them and adding hobbles on their front legs. Rene rigged a shelter on a small rise in the trees using two buffalo hides over poles to make a tent. It wasn't much. Hopefully it would keep most of the rain off and protect us if there was hail in those ominous clouds.

The wind arrived first, bringing coolness with it. Lightning flashed and rumbled as the storm approached with grayish white, rolling clouds at its leading edge. The day darkened as the clouds swept over us. We watched the rain coming like a sheet towards us. With a last look at the horses and the country around, we crawled into the tent just before the rain hit.

Sitting under our shelter, the noise from the rain and hailstones drumming on the hides made talking impossible. Ice stones the size of robin eggs bounced off the hides above us and occasionally one came under the side, blown by the force of the wind. The ice was hard, often with jagged edges. We were lucky to have found a corner out of the storm. I could only hope the horses wouldn't be injured. There was nothing for us to do but chew jerky and wait. My saddlebags were with me so I dug out the log to record the day's events. There was only the storm to write about.

Looking at the few empty pages left, I decided to be sparing of my words until we arrived in St. Louis where there would be a new notebook available. This was the second book filled with my notes since leaving the Bay. There seemed to be a tendency for me to write more words and the sketches and maps filled even more space. I wasn't much on talking, but enjoyed noting down what I saw and experienced. Maybe it would be wise to get two books.

Growling and fussing, the storm finally went on by. The sun came back out before dark. It was late in the day, the ground was wet and there was no sense in leaving until morning. After checking the horses we looked for ways to improve the camp and got a fire going. Sitting there eating broiled meat as the sun fell over the horizon was a peaceful time after the fury of the storm. It was a great, wide country that made you feel small. Still, I loved every day. There had been no sign of people since leaving the mountains, which was just as well as the horses were carrying a sight of furs that would be a temptation to many. We were prepared to fight to protect our property if circumstance dictated and would be happy if it could be avoided.

The river, when it came into sight, was flowing southward. Sitting on our horses looking at it, I asked, "Ye think this is the Missouri?"

Rene shrugged. "Is big river. Goes south. Rene think is Missouri."

"Seems likely, don't it? Never heard tell of another big river going south. Must be the Missouri. This is what we be'n seeking all these long days coming across the grasslands. We may as well see where it goes."

We followed, keeping well away, hoping to avoid people as long as possible. Occasionally there was smoke rising to the east of us. We kept on our way, leaving as little sign of our passing as possible, looking for secluded places to camp and keeping our fires small. The grass was growing tall now and the days were warm.

Fording a wide, slow moving river that seemed likely to be the Platte, we kept on south. Six days later, the Missouri took a turn to the east and we were riding with the river north of us, figuring it would join the Mississippi soon. Ten days it took as the Missouri twisted and turned until unexpectedly we reached a point where there was a fort ahead on the south bank. The sight stopped us where we were, staring in astonishment.

A fort built of stone with a Spanish flag flying from the top, flapping lazily in the breeze. Across the river on the north bank was a collection of wood huts with gardens and a few cows grazing. Wanting nothing to do with soldiers, we turned away from the river to ride a wide circle around the area before returning to the river to continue east. Now there was a cart trail, just two wheel ruts in the grass. We followed along, expecting it would take us to St. Louis.

When we saw the town it was a surprise. All our information put St. Louis on the Mississippi. Here it was on what we believed was the Missouri. Something was wrong. Did we miss the joining of the rivers? It didn't seem possible after following the Missouri for many days and crossing numerous streams with no sign of another large river.

On the river flat below us and short of the town, a boat was being built. Two men sat on it idling away their time. Leaving Rene with the pack train, I turned my horse down the slope and rode up to the building site. Both men walked out to greet me. "*Bonjour m'sieur.*"

"Good afternoon ta yea also, sir. Can yea tell me where we ar' and what place this is?"

"*Oui, mon ami.*" He pointed at the river and switched to English. "This is the Missouri River and the town is San Carlos. The Englishers call it St. Charles."

"Where is St. Louis?" My puzzlement must have been obvious.

The man smiled and pointed. "Ah, m'sieur, St. Louis, it is that way, three days by wagon when it is dry. Much easier to go by boat."

Smiling back I commented, "I don't have a boat, just these faithful horses that have brought us far."

He glanced toward where Rene sat with the pack train. "You

come from the mountains with furs?"

"Yes, from the mountains far ta the west."

He looked at me speculatively. "This fine boat you could have for little."

Now, I wasn't a trader for nothing and I saw the look on his face, so I considered. My horse stamped his feet, shifting his weight and swatted flies with his tail. There was something curious here. "Yea'r boat is fer sale?"

"Not my boat, m'sieur. I was to be Captain when it was finished. The owner was buried nine days ago and here it sits."

There were oak logs stacked on rough timbers to dry alongside a stack of sawn lumber. Nearby there was an overhead rack where two men could saw boards from the logs, with saw dust and woodchips lying around. It was well into the afternoon and we wouldn't get much further today, so what were a few hours spent finding out what was on this man's mind? "Tell me about the boat."

"She is built for the river, pointed at both ends, using dried and seasoned oak for a long life on the water. She is fifty-two feet long with a beam of nine feet and space to store sixteen tons of freight, maybe more. There will be a cabin for cooking and sleeping five men, away from the weather."

He pointed. "See the mast we have prepared that will carry a big sail to push her up the river. Three men will handle her, but five would be better, for the poling. The bottom is flat and curved for shallow water; maybe two feet of water will float her."

He was proud of his boat, which was as it should be. Dismounting, I tied my horse and went to walk around the boat, having a look.

The workmanship was excellent. She was well crafted, obviously built by the experienced hands of men who knew what they were doing. Sitting down on a log and removing my battered hat, I ran the fingers of one hand through my hair. "Dinnae know much about boats. Horses now, I know ma way around horses."

He was sitting on a stump facing me. "All my life has been on the river, first with my father and after, working for others. I know the river and this is a fine boat. You buy it and I will sail for you. Maybe be partners."

Now there was an idea. "What happened ta the owner?"

"His axe, she slipped and cut leg very bad. He bleeds. In two days he is dead."

"Who owns the boat now?"

"Boat belongs to his widow, Madame Chadron. She will sell for cash money. You sell furs and buy boat, we haul freight on rivers."

"How much cash money?"

He held up his hands and smiled. "You talk to Madame."

I looked down at my clothes, all rough deerskin with fringes; dirty and worn from all the travel, mud, and rain. At least I was shaved. "I'm no dressed ta call on a lady."

"You not worry. Madame Chadron has seen much. She will talk."

For several minutes I considered what he said before sticking out my hand. "Ma name's James Richardson."

He grinned and shook the hand. "I am Jean Cabott and this is Joseph who married my sister. He is master carpenter who builds this boat." We shook hands. The horses came down the bank and

Rene met the men. Cabott went to arrange an appointment while we set up camp in the trees near the building site.

You couldn't just call on a lady unannounced. Especially one in mourning for her recently departed husband. We were eating when Jean returned. She agreed to see us at sunset.

It was a stone house of some size, two stories high with I knew not how many rooms. A house like I had never entered before. The maid who answered the door led us along a short hallway to a room set up as a business office. Heavy wooden beams supported the ceiling and the walls were of white plaster. There was a desk and chairs, shelves full of books on one wall, pictures hanging and a small leather-covered sofa to one side. The room was lit by oil lamps on the walls, there was a large pendulum clock standing in a corner and I was surprised.

Cabott's talk of her experience led me to expect a middle-aged woman. Madame Chadron was young, probably no more than mid-twenties. Her dark hair was covered by a scarf and she was dressed all in black; a pleasant looking woman, but decidedly plain. Her brown eyes were appraising me—not boldly, just in a way that gave me the feeling she was accustomed to dealing with men.

Cabott did the introduction. "Madame Chadron, I bring Mr. James Richardson, just arrived from the western mountains."

She stood from her seat behind the desk, resting one hand on its top. "Welcome to San Carlos, Mr. Richardson. May I introduce Father O'let and my eldest son Pierre?" The elderly priest nodded at me without rising. The boy, who appeared to be about seven or eight, came to shake hands.

"Madame, I must apologize fer ma appearance. It ha' been a long journey from the mountains." I didn't think to remove my weapons which she was eyeing. They were as much a part of me as my hands and feet.

"Of no consequence, Mr. Richardson. Would you care for a glass of wine or perhaps sherry?"

"No thank ye, Madame ."

"Would you join us in a cup of coffee?"

"Thank yea, Madame. Tha' would be delightful. It ha' been many months since I last tasted coffee."

"If you please, Marie," she instructed. The maid, who waited by the door, gently closed it as she left. "Please be seated, Mr. Richardson." Her face gave away nothing. "I understand you are interested in purchasing my late husband's keel boat."

"Frankly, Madame, I know little of keel boats an' only stopped tae ask directions tae St. Louis. Mr. Cabott suggested thar may be business moving merchandise on the river. Ma business is in the fur trade and there is a need ta move trade goods ta the western lands."

"Where are you from, Mr. Richardson?" She surprised me with the change of subject. "I do believe you have a Scottish accent."

"I grew up nigh Glasgow in Scotland, Madame."

"Pray tell, how did you get all the way from Glasgow to San Carlos?"

So, I related the travels of a lad from Scotland as briefly as possible. Afterwards, she commented, "The Bay Company, lords of the great white north."

Her comment caused me to smile. "I only wished ta come ta America. The Bay provided a way fer me ta accomplish that."

"I see and now you are an independent trader interested in having a keel boat to move your goods?"

"Yes, Madame, if th' price is within the means of a wee businessman."

Her brown eyes seemed to sharpen. "Mr. Cabott tells me you have many horses loaded with furs. Where do you intend to sell them?"

"St. Louis, Madame, ta whichever buyer will pay the highest price. The only name I have is Mr. Auguste Chouteau. Thar wull be others."

"Indeed there are, Mr. Richardson. Let me assure you that Mr. Chouteau comes highly recommended. When you locate his place of business you will find a holding pen for your horses behind his establishment and alongside the warehouse."

The coffee arrived. Just the aroma brought back many memories. At the first sip my tongue knew what it had been missing. I'm afraid I drank that cup much faster than polite society would expect and was on my second when the others were barely begun. It was embarrassing. "It is the little things like coffee that yea miss most in the mountains."

"Of course, Mr. Richardson. Marie, please fill Mr. Richardson's cup for him."

"Thank yea, Madame, yea are very kind."

She opened a drawer in the desk and removed an account book. After finding the page she wanted she spent several minutes reviewing the numbers. Finally, she looked up. "My husband invested a total of three hundred and twenty-seven dollars and seventeen cents in the boat, not counting his time to cut the oak trees and season the wood. Mr. Cabott informs me the boat can be completed in twenty days, at a further cost of seventy dollars." She studied me for a moment. "Not to delay you, sir, please allow me to consider this matter overnight. Could we meet again in the morning?"

"Certainly, Madame Chadron. What time would be convenient fer ye?"

"It is my wish to inspect the boat in the morning. Mr. Cabott, will you be so kind as to bring the carriage by at sunup to take me to the river?"

Cabott got to his feet, so I stood also. "The carriage will be out front at sunup, Madame."

Madame looked back at me. "Thank you for coming by, Mr. Richardson. We will discuss this matter further in the morning. Now it is time for me to see my children to bed."

Rene was nervous. He explained about a rough-looking man who lingered near just before dark looking at our stacks of bales and the horses. We sat up most of the night with our long guns, taking turns napping. It was just as well, I wouldn't have slept long anyway with so much to consider. In the hour before dawn fully arrived, I stirred the fire and added wood so we could cook meat for our first meal of the day.

Not long after the sun rose, the carriage came from town bringing Madame Chadron, accompanied by her maid. We walked out to meet them. She wasted no time. “Bonjour, Mr. Richardson; come, let us have a look at the boat Mr. Cabott has been constructing.”

Madame was thorough as she looked carefully at all parts of the boat, inspecting the wood, the workmanship and commenting on little details. Madame Chadron was wearing a long black dress that didn’t seem to be a hindrance. She asked questions of Cabott, particularly about what was left to be completed on the boat, the costs and the time required. She even asked for the dimensions of the boat, details of how the cargo would be stowed and what tonnage it could accommodate.

It occurred to me that this might all be for the purpose of impressing me. Being a trader I was familiar with the presentation of the merits of one’s merchandise as part of selling.

Satisfied, she sat erect on the upturned end of a large log. “Are you still interested in owning this keel boat, Mr. Richardson?”

“Yes, Madame, if we can agree on a price.”

Her brown eyes looked steadily at me for several moments. “I have a proposal to put forth, Mr. Richardson. When completed, the boat will have cost three hundred and ninety-seven American dollars and some pennies, let us say four hundred American. You pay me two hundred and eighty American and I will own thirty percent. Mr. Cabott will operate the boat for us as captain and receive ten percent of any profits made, after expenses are paid. I will be responsible for the bookkeeping, act as agent and we will share the remaining profits by our ownership.”

If that woman had hit me with a broom, the surprise couldn’t have been more startling. The previous evening it had been obvious that Madame was acquainted with business matters. That she was this astute never entered my head. The silence lasted while I considered and she sat watching me.

"Ye are a surprising lady, Madame. Such an arrangement may prove ta be profitable fer both of us. I agree."

"Thank you, Mr. Richardson." She smiled for the first time since we met. "There is more to my proposal. On the river there are many risks and the boat may be lost. I wish for us to complete this boat and build another of the same size suited to upriver trade. After the two boats are completed, I believe we should begin construction of a third boat of a larger size for the downriver trade to Orleans. Our ownership to be the same."

It was stunning. How could a lady like her come up with such ideas? "Where wull we find the freight ta keep three boats busy?"

"That will be my responsibility, Mr. Richardson. Of course, I will expect your assistance in the upriver trade. Between this area and Orleans there is a large volume of farm produce, grain, apples, livestock and such that goes south on the river. On the return trip all of our supplies and goods come from there. With sound boats, dependable crews and by providing excellent service, we will capture our share of that trade."

It was a lot to digest. I considered carefully for several minutes and Madame waited patiently. "I accept your proposal, Madame. I can'na pay ye until the furs ar' sold."

Her face took on a quizzical expression. "Sell your furs to Mr. Chouteau and put the money in his care. When we have a signed contract you can give me a letter to draw on your account." That her mind was active I now knew, but she had a way of going in different directions. She did it again. "Tell me about your western lands, Mr.

Richardson."

So I told her about the rivers, lakes and wide prairies where the tall grass moved in the wind looking much like an ocean. I described the great herds of buffalo, mountains and valleys, how the sky looked, the forests of giant trees that grew in the mountains, the Indians, the cold and snow of winter and the freedom to move around as one chose. Probably I got carried away, talking too long, and finally stopped.

She looked at me in amazement before commenting. "You are a poet, Mr. Richardson. I wish there was an opportunity for me to visit your western lands to see what you describe. Being a mother with four children to rear, I shall never have the pleasure of doing that."

"It is na place fer a lady, Madame. The living is rough with few of the comforts of life."

"Do not underestimate us, sir. Women will be where their men go. In the years to come many will go west. Not so long ago this was considered 'no place' for a lady, now we are here."

"Of course, Madame, ye are correct."

Once again she changed direction and looked at Rene. "Is this gentleman a member of your family?" Nothing seemed to escape her attention.

Rene was standing a few paces away with his long gun, listening to the conversation. I explained. "Sometimes he is like a father ta me, sometimes a brother, an' always a friend. May I introduce my friend Mr. Rene Beauchamp?"

Rene bowed slightly and without moving she told him, "I am pleased to meet you, M'sieur Beauchamp. You must take good care of my new business partner."

Rene smiled. "He strong man, take care of self."

"Yes, I believe he can." She studied Rene thoughtfully for a moment, before returning her eyes to me. "Well, I have delayed you long enough, Mr. Richardson. I have a letter for Mr. Chouteau. Would you be so kind as to deliver it for me?"

"Certainly, Madame, as soon as we arrive in St. Louis."

The sun was already three hours high when we loaded the horses and started for St. Louis. Keeping a close watch on our back trail, by midday it was clear we were being followed. They would last no time at all in Indian country, poor fools that they were. Turning off the cart path, we led them a winding way until there was a stopping place to our liking.

It was a narrow clearing with trees on three sides, backed up against a steep slope with a spring of water coming from the side of the hill. A heavy undergrowth of thorny brush made approaching through the trees impossible. If they attacked, it would be from the opening in front.

We stacked the packs in two separate piles in a way to provide each of us shelter from attack. With the horses picketed behind the camp at the base of the slope, we roasted our meat on a fire that was larger than needed. If they wanted us, let it be tonight, because we didn't want to play this game again tomorrow.

Just after dark, with the fire burning, we made a show of rolling out our beds in preparation for sleep. When the fire was down to coals we moved to the shelter of the packs, leaving the buffalo robes stuffed with grass and branches and our hats placed on rocks to look like we were sleeping.

The big dipper turned slowly in the sky, showing it was after midnight when we heard them coming, although they were too far away to be visible in the pale light from a half moon. There were four of them. For town folks, they probably believed they were moving quietly. We heard them long before they came into sight.

There was a mutter of muted voices and suddenly they came with a rush; one swinging an axe, a second with a big club, the last two stabbing with knives. No mercy was intended for innocent sleepers. They made the rules.

My throwing knife went to bed in the throat of the big ruffian with the axe, who stood slightly apart from the others. After that, I followed in with the hunting knife. A second man went down with Rene's tomahawk buried in his chest as I ran the big blade through the ribs of a third. Not to be outdone by me, Rene felled the last one.

It was all over, with four men dead, unless there were others we didn't know about. Fading back into the darkness near the packs, Rene whispered, "You stay, Rene look." He was gone like a silent shadow in the night. More than an hour later, Rene came through the opening to the clearing leading four horses. I went to the fire and dropped a handful of dry grass on the coals and added wood as it flared into life.

They were a sorry looking lot; dirty, unshaven and ragged. Most likely considered tough where they came from. They should have known better, coming at us like that. They might as well have been four lapdogs attacking a big prairie wolf.

Together, we dragged them to the edge of the clearing before settling ourselves against the packs for the rest of the night, neither of us feeling like sleeping. As soon as the sky turned grey we loaded the horses and prepared to leave, not bothering to eat. Their horses would be useful to us except they might be known to the locals and we wanted no trouble with the Spanish authorities. The horses were turned loose before we rode away.

Not wanting to point our direction to anyone who happened on the scene, our tracks went west. There wasn't much we could do to hide our trail unless the weather brought up a rainstorm.

Chapter 6

St. Louis was the largest town I had seen since passing through Montreal almost seven years before. What a sight we were; two men in ragged, soiled buckskins riding into town, each leading a string of horses piled high with packs. We walked our horses along a dirt wagon road into a street with scattered houses on both sides. The business district was ahead, built along the Mississippi and the closer we came, the more houses there were with people going about their daily chores. We carried our long guns in our hands. After safeguarding our furs for many long days while crossing a thousand miles of wilderness we weren't going to let down our guard now. The guns sent a clear message to anyone who cared to take heed.

Rene's eyes were busy, trying to watch everywhere. He had never seen a town until San Carlos and he stayed on the fringes there. Now we were riding right into the very heart of St Louis and Rene was uneasy. He looked ready to bolt for open country. There was nothing to indicate how many people were living in St. Louis; it must be in the hundreds. People along the street stopped what they were doing to stare at us. Most likely many trappers came here over the years, but it was early in the season and we might be the first to arrive this year.

We kept moving until Chouteau's name showed up on a building. Seeing the name, I looked for a way to the back. Just as Madame

Chadron said, there was a pen for horses built from wooden slabs, standing on end, nailed to planks. I rode up close to look over the fence; the pen was empty. Herding the horses inside, I hurried to pull the gate closed. Behind the fence, with no one staring at us, Rene seemed to relax. I suggested, "Yea stay with the horses while I go an' hunt fer Chouteau." Rene nodded his head before settling on his haunches against the fence with his long gun across his knees.

After so long away from crowds, coming into a town felt strange. Rene wasn't the only one who was nervous. With the saddlebags over my left shoulder and the long gun in my hand, I walked back to the street to stand on the plank walk, making a survey of everything within sight.

The town was laid out with two long streets running parallel to the river and a few cross streets. Most buildings were built from wood with the boards nailed vertically on the walls. Some of the business buildings were two stories high with what looked like living quarters on the second floor. On several buildings there were stairs coming down the outside of the walls. The streets were dirt. Only in a few places were there plank walks.

Chouteau's establishment had such a walk with the roof extending out to shade the chairs and benches placed against the front wall. Three old men sat in wooden chairs against the wall smoking pipes and watching me. This was the biggest mercantile I'd ever seen and I stood there like a scared lad, telling myself to get on with it.

Pretending to be interested in the street allowed me to hesitate while building up my courage before finally walking to the open door and stepping inside. The walls were hung with pots, pans, pails, shovels, axes and tools of every kind. Tables were stacked high with bolts of cloth, sewing supplies, ready-made clothes, and dishes. Barrels and sacks of flour, salt and other produce crowded the floor space. The air was full of the good smells of oiled leather, spices, tobacco, and fresh ground coffee. Bonneted mothers, with little children in tow, talked and looked at the goods offered for sale. Across the room from the door was a long counter with several customers being served by male clerks.

Finding a way through the narrow aisles and around piles of merchandise, I marched up to the counter and told the first clerk that looked at me. "I'm here ta talk with Mr. Auguste Chouteau."

The clerk was tall and thin, with grey hair and his face looked doubtful. From first glance he was not at all impressed by my appearance. "Mr. Chouteau is a very busy man."

Placing the long gun in the crook of my left arm, my right hand retrieved Madame's letter from the saddlebag and held it out for him to see. When he saw that his face changed. He knew the name and the handwriting and reached for the letter. He didn't get it. "Madame Chadron told me ta deliver this letter ta Mr. Chouteau, which is what I'm going ta do."

"Please wait while Mr. Chouteau is informed." He was back quickly and asked me to follow him around the end of the counter to Chouteau's office. Standing there, filling the doorway, I took time to have a good look at him. He was a solidly built man of forty some years—not nearly as tall as me, with thinning hair, dressed in a white shirt of some kind with ruffles around the neck. The white shirt sleeves showed below the arms of a black suit coat of a design unfamiliar to me.

"Mr. Chouteau, I'm just arrived from the western mountains

with furs ta sell. Ma name is James Richardson."

Chouteau stood up with his hand out. "Please come in, Mr. Richardson, and take a seat. My clerk tells me you have a letter from Madame Chadron."

When I passed the envelope to him he glanced at it before laying it on the desk and resuming his seat. "You are acquainted with Madame Chadron?" He sounded doubtful.

I understood his doubt. "No sir, I'm not. We were passing by San Carlos an' the lady asked me ta deliver a letter ta yea."

Chouteau sat looking at me for several seconds. "There is something here I do not understand. Perhaps I should read Madame's letter before we continue." It was one page, which he read quickly and a hint of a smile crossed his face. Finished, he dropped the letter into a desk drawer. "You said you brought furs to sell."

"Aye, I did, sir. They are out there in your pen on our horses."

"Please come with me, Mr. Richardson, and we shall have a look." He took me through the back of the store to the warehouse. When he saw all the horses he called several men to assist. They helped us unload the packs and move them inside. First, I opened the smaller packs with fox, mink and ermine furs. While I knelt on one knee to watch Chouteau inspect those, Rene untied beaver packs.

With help from his men, Chouteau checked all the packs while Rene and I stood by watching. Finished, he walked toward us, looking thoughtful. "These are prime pelts, much better prepared than many we receive. There is great demand for fox and mink in the eastern market, also in Europe. It is the style in those places for society ladies to wear mink coats. These silver fox are not that common so will bring a good price."

Stepping away from the piles of furs he asked, "What do you wish to do, Mr. Richardson?"

"If we agree on a value, yea open an account in maw name. We will draw on it for trade goods ta take back west when we go. I will require forty American dollars ta purchase other things we be need'n."

Chouteau sent a clerk to get the forty American while a count of the furs was made. With the tally finished, we followed him back to his office where the value was figured. Beaver were going for eight American each, which came to 480 for each pack. Fox normally sold for the same as beaver. Chouteau said the market was strong and offered ten per fox, four for mink and one for ermine. The Mandan furs brought seventy-five American. In total it came to 4395 American dollars, a tidy amount. I stuck out my hand and we shook to seal the deal.

The same grey haired clerk took us to pick out pants and shirts to fit us and we each got a pair of low moccasins. With the clothes under our arms, he led us up the street to a shop with bathtubs and a barber chair.

The barber and his assistant carried in pails of warm water from a stove behind the building to fill the tubs. They laid out towels and lye soap that the owner proudly told us they made themselves on that same stove. Soaking in that warm water felt so good I stayed in the tub until the water was cold. It was the first soap I'd seen in a long, long time and with it I washed my hair and scrubbed my body clean. Rene was in the partner to my tub, a first time experience for him, so he followed my actions. Climbing out of the water, I tossed him a towel to dry off with. We dressed in our new pants and shirts, sticking our bare feet into clean moccasins.

Rene watched me sit in the chair and the barber start snipping at me. Rene looked doubtful and I figured he would refuse, but he took his turn. Afterwards, we came out on the street feeling like fancy city men; all bathed, trimmed, shaved and smelling something awful from the tonic water. Our pants were of dark grey wool with legs like stovepipes, which we chose over the tapered ones with tight ankles. The cotton shirts were made to pull over your head and hung below the waist. Mine was dark blue and Rene was decked out in bright red. There was a two inch wide leather belt around my shirt while Rene wore a wide woven sash with blue, white and green colors.

We watched people on the street going about their business. The women all wore long dresses reaching to the ground, many with bonnets on their heads and shawls around their shoulders. A number of women wore aprons over their dresses. What stood out most on the men were the wide brimmed leather hats. They were designed for the hot sun and we decided we each wanted one of those.

Wandering slowly up the street, we looked for the boot shop the clerk had told us was there. When we found it, the owner measured our feet and took the order for new leather boots that would reach halfway to our knees with room to wear socks inside. Before leaving we took time to look at the Spanish saddles with big horns for tying a rope. They figured to be more comfortable than the wood and rawhide saddles we made ourselves, so we ordered two of those.

Back at Chouteau's pen, we led out the horses and went looking for the farm outside of town that kept animals for travelers passing through. After our gear was stowed in a shed, the farmer directed us to a boarding house run by a French lady whose husband worked on the river. There were other boarding houses in the town; this was the one he recommended. Mrs. Ruechard turned out to be a plump, middle-aged lady with a room for us and two meals a day for one dollar a week. I handed her a dollar. The way she said her name, it sounded like Roecard.

Rene settled on his bed and watched me as I opened a new notebook and used the dimming daylight to detail the two days since the old book was filled. From long habit we were up in the gray light before sunup and waited until we heard sounds coming from the kitchen before opening our door. The smell of coffee was in the air and we were the first ones there. Later, we were joined by a man with a large stomach bulging his suit pants, who represented several businesses in Orleans wishful of selling goods to people in St Louis.

He talked a great deal and tried to pry into our affairs, asking many pointed questions. All he learned from me was that we were trappers from the far western mountains, along with some general comments on the country out there. Rene didn't speak a word, so the man most likely assumed he didn't understand the language.

Having arranged an appointment with Chouteau, we were sitting in the chairs outside his establishment when he arrived to unlock the doors. "You are an early riser, Mr. Richardson, please come in."

Carrying the saddlebags, I followed him. He glanced at my weapons, making no comment. Seated in his office, I asked, "Could yea give me advice on a business matter?"

Chouteau looked at me in surprise. “Of course, if it is a matter I have knowledge of.”

When I mentioned Madame Chadron he looked at me sharply and listened intently as I related the freight enterprise we were planning. “I know little of the river or the business proposed. Do yea think it is a sound undertaking?”

Chouteau looked straight at me as he answered, using his hands for emphasis. “Madame Chadron is knowledgeable in these affairs and there is much freight to be hauled. You couldn’t find a better partner to start such a business.” He paused. “You told me you didn’t know Madame.”

“I don’t. When I became interested in the keel boat her husband ha’ been building we met ta discuss a price. She surprised me by proposing a partnership an’ that we should build more boats.”

Chouteau’s hands came up. He used them a lot when talking. “There are many risks on the rivers. All too often boats are lost. She is right wanting to build more boats so one loss does not end your business.”

“Madame proposed she wull act as agent ta arrange contracts fer moving freight. How can such a lady do those things?”

Chouteau laughed and waved a hand. “She has many contacts, is experienced in these matters and has people in her employ to assist her. Do not concern yourself in this regard. You told me that the money in your account would be used to buy trade goods. Building these boats will be costly, probably eight hundred American dollars to build and equip two boats. How will you pay for this?” He seemed doubtful and rubbed his chin thoughtfully.

From behind my belt I took a half-filled deerskin sack and placed it on the desk. The look on his face showed he knew what it was without touching it; the way his face changed told me that. “Ye weigh this gold an’ tell me what it is worth?”

“Of a certainty, Mr. Richardson. Where did you get it?” Chouteau’s voice showed a hint of excitement. “You must be very careful showing gold. First, the Spanish Authorities would take a great interest, demanding to know where it came from. Also, there are those along the river who would stick a knife in you for less than this.”

“It was washed frae a mountain stream, far frae ‘ere.”

Chouteau studied me for a moment before glancing at the saddlebags on the floor. He knew. The gold weighed out to three and one half ounces. At twenty per ounce he calculated a value of seventy American dollars. Chouteau was honest; he told me that in Orleans I would get more. He would have risks in storing it and getting it to Orleans, so he needed to buy at a discount.

There was a big iron strongbox in the corner of his office which I looked at thoughtfully for a moment. “Would ye be interested ‘n purchasing more gold?”

Chouteau smiled. “So, Mr. Richardson, you are not a rash man. Is that what you have in those saddlebags?

The bags made a solid thump on his desk. I started removing the sacks and there were thirteen of them. Chouteau sighed. “There is not enough cash on hand to purchase this amount of gold.”

“Just credit ma’ account fer now. When we leave St. Louis I will want one thousand American ‘n gold an’ silver coins.”

Chouteau locked the office door and brought the balance scale to his desk. I watched as he weighed the gold, noting the amounts on a sheet of paper and numbering the sacks as each one was finished. The total came to eighty-seven and one quarter ounces. He calculated the value before looking up. "This is a small fortune; the value comes to 1745 American. Really, Mr. Richardson, you should go to Orleans where you might get as much as another hundred American dollars."

"We plan ta go west ta the mountains fer another season, no ta Orleans. Just credit ma account 'n give me a receipt fer this 'n the furs."

"As you wish, Mr. Richardson." He shrugged, but there was excitement in his eyes. "Is there more gold in your stream?"

"Probably thar is. This is enough fer me, I'm no'a miner. There are many other places 'n the mountains that I hav' no had time ta see."

"You do realize that when this gold gets to Orleans it will raise many questions." Chouteau was serious. "People will come looking. I fear for your safety."

"By that time I wull be well on maw way back ta the mountains."

He wrote out the receipt for 6140 American dollars, less the forty I had drawn and handed it across the desk. The gold was sold; all except the first nugget. That I was keeping.

Chouteau sat back in his chair to study me thoughtfully. "You are now a wealthy young man. This money should not be left sitting idle. What are your plans?"

"We wull set up a trading post ta supply the Indians with whit they need. When the white men start coming in numbers, which they wull, I wull be there waiting fer them with goods, horses, an' cattle ta sell."

"You are wise. Get title to any lands you settle on. If it is Indian lands, pay them for it. Draw up a contract and make sure other whites witness it for you. Is there any chance you would be interested in investing in property in St. Louis?"

It was a surprise. "Such an idea never occurred ta me. Do yea have a suggestion?"

Chouteau smiled. "Let me think about it for a few days."

Rene was waiting beside racks full of the usual trade guns. The tall thin clerk came to help us and I asked, "Do yea have any Charleville long guns?

"How many are you interested in, Mr. Richardson?"

"Four, along with ball molds, springs an' spare flints."

"Excuse me for a moment while I check with Mr. Chouteau."

While we waited Rene picked out five hunting knives with ten inch blades. He checked to see if they were made from good steel and would make sparks on a flint. When the clerk returned we were checking the fire steels. There were three different styles and I wondered, "Which o' these is th' best?"

"The U shaped one with the hole for a thong sells three for five American because they are harder steel and make better sparks. The others are one American each." We added six of the best steels to our pile.

“We want five o’ yer very best axes fer chopping wood. The same in tomahawks.” The clerk disappeared into a back room. When he returned with them, another man brought four long guns.

The guns appeared to be the same as my own. To be sure, we inspected them carefully and checked the bores for size. Rene hefted one, weighing it in his hands and sighted out a window. He looked at me and smiled. I told the clerk, “We wull take this one ta test fire tomorrow. If the accuracy be true we wull buy the four Charlevilles.” Rene put a new knife behind his sash, kept the long gun and we left.

Returning to town the next afternoon after having ridden around the area all day testing the gun, we each carried a deer behind our saddles. We stopped at the boarding house to leave the meat with our landlady. Rene was happy with the Charleville and set about casting a supply of balls using a four ball mold while I returned the horses to the pasture.

With the walking stick in hand, I hiked the short distance back, passing scattered houses. In some blocks there was only one house. They all were enclosed by rough wooden fences with many having barns behind them. Sitting cross-legged in Mrs. Ruechard’s yard, we talked while Rene worked with the melting ladle and mold until we were called for dinner.

Madame Chadron watched the horses leave the river flat, counting the packs of furs, as they climbed the slope. She sat thinking for several minutes before turning to Cabott. “Hire more men to help finish the boat and get as many more as you need to cut trees for the new boats we will build.”

"Oui, Madame, it will be done today."

"Make a large sign that can be seen from the river and the cart trail. Paint our name on both sides of it."

"What name, Madame?"

"RICHARDSON CHADRON BOAT COMPANY, in large letters. I want everyone who passes to see it so talk will spread far along the rivers."

"Please, Madame, you write letters for me?" On a board Madame printed the words so the painter could copy them.

"Tall letters, Mr. Cabott, so they can be seen from far away. In two days I will come to see the progress."

Before the departing carriage was out of sight, Cabott gave Joseph orders to find three men to assist in making a sign and finishing the boat. Cabott knew the men he wanted to cut trees and float them to the site. He would select the trees himself and supervise the work. When Madame returned she would be pleased.

Cabott led the way upstream to mark the trees he wanted, leaving men to fell the oaks; a time consuming, tiring task. He kept on searching for a tree that would make a tall, strong mast. This would be the hardest part of all and he considered going back for a horse. Instead, he kept going until he was sure there was nothing close to St. Carlos. Tomorrow he would take one man and horses so they could go farther to scout for masts. He wanted tall straight trees. Jean smiled to himself, thinking, 'Several to keep ahead of Madame and all her planning. In any case, it would be wise to have spares.' Masts often hit overhanging trees along the rivers which snapped them off.

Across the dirt street from the barbershop was a tavern, owned by a Spanish man. The barber told us it was an acceptable place to eat at midday. The owner's wife prepared the food, so we made a habit of going there. You took whatever was prepared or went without. She favored stews which were made from an assortment of vegetables, with beans, and what meat was available that day; beef, pork, or fish from the river. It made a hearty meal. We each got a large bowl of stew, with a thick slice of bread and a mug of beer for five cents apiece.

The first time we ate there I gave the hard working lady a two bit piece and each time we returned, she favored us with cleaner bowls, even wiping off the table for us.

A rough place with floors and walls built of planks and a few round tables with four chairs each. The owner presided over his tavern from behind a stand-up bar. He kept an assortment of bottles on shelves along the back wall and a tub of water behind the bar where he dunked mugs before giving them a swipe with a well-used towel. The floor was always in need of a good sweeping.

Most of the clientele spoke French or Spanish. Among them were a few Americans from across the Mississippi. Listening to the talk it was a mixture of French, Spanish and English with a few Indian and slang words added. These men used words in their own way and didn't waste any more than was necessary to get their meaning across. The grammar would have driven my old teacher wild if he had heard it. He had a word for speaking several languages, what was it? I mused about that for a moment before the word came back to me. 'A polyglot person,' that was what it was.

Most were men who worked on the boats. A loud, roistering, ever-changing group, living for the day with little thought toward the future. They drank, laughed, and argued. As the day wore on often drunken brawls occurred; mostly using fists. On occasion a man was seriously injured with a knife. The Spanish men favored knives.

At the next table two men were haggling and arguing about a boat one was trying to sell. He referred to it as a pirogue and was praising the ease of handling it. Rene listened to them and when the men moved away I asked, "Rene, what kind of a boat is a pirogue?"

Rene took a sip from his beer mug and wiped his mouth on a shirt sleeve. "Is wood canoe. Pirogue made from tree by chopping out wood with axe. Pirogue heavy. Not good for portage like canoe."

A pirogue was a dugout made from a large tree truck, shaped much like a canoe. Of course you could only make those marvellously light and maneuverable canoes in places where there were birch trees.

Tabletops in the tavern were stained from spilt food and drink. The interior was dimly lit with light from four small windows, one on each side wall and two in the front on either side of the door. Late in the day lamps were provided. The men liked a French card game called Euchre that was played by four people in two teams using half a deck, just the cards numbered nine and higher, with the ace being the most valuable. An old blanket tossed over a tabletop provided a playing surface when they wanted to have a game. Much laughter, shouting, and banging of fists on tabletops occurred each time one team bested the other.

We preferred a table located in a corner between a front and side window where the light was better. It was a temptation to wash the windows to improve the lighting. No one else seemed concerned, so I minded my own business.

Leaving the tavern, we walked along the street to the river and looked at a pirogue. Immediately, I could see what Rene meant. It was near twenty feet long and in the middle more than three feet wide, with thick sides. Mighty heavy to carry! It would haul a large load on the water. With her size it would take two or three men to handle her.

Town life wasn't for us; we were too accustomed to the freedom and quiet of wide open country, Rene even more than me. We got our riding horses, and loaded an extra with a pack, to take off. Mrs. Ruechard asked if we would be coming back, so I paid her two dollars in advance to hold our room. She packed slices off a pork roast along with bread for us to eat on the way.

Getting away from people and noise gave us a chance to think. We made a list of trade goods we wanted to take to the mountains. The subject of long guns kept coming up and we spent many hours discussing what we wanted. Chouteau only had one Charleville left at a cost almost double trade guns. We wanted something better than the usual trade guns the Indians got; guns that were more reliable, more accurate, that would bring our customers back to trade again. Included on the list were kegs of powder, one pound ingots of lead, and molds for casting balls. It was a long list and we might have to trim it or buy more horses.

Eight days after leaving San Carlos we returned. Riding up to the edge of the river valley we were surprised by the changes. Men were working everywhere with a second boat started. A sign made from wide planks fixed to the top of two tall poles and painted white with large red letters, surprised us. Rene pointed. "What that?"

It took me a second to find the words. "It is a sign naming a boat company. It says Richardson Chadron Boat Company." My head was shaking in wonder while trying to understand. "Now who would ha' thought o' doing that?"

Rene grinned. "Me think Madame idea."

Of course, that was the answer. That lady was going to be a trial. How would I ever keep pace with her? Nudging our horses in the ribs, we rode down the trail. Cabott came to meet us, seeming pleased to see us. "What ar' all these men do'in, Jean?"

"Madame say, finish boat fast. She say, start new boat now. We cut trees for planks. Still need to find tall tree for mast."

When my horse was tied, he walked me around, showing off the progress being made. The keel boat was finished, except for a few details, in far shorter a time than the twenty days estimated.

A second overhead rack for sawing boards was set up beside the first one and men were busy sawing planks and timbers. There were stacks of newly cut trees laid out to dry with more being pulled from the river as we watched. Jean leaned against the side of the keel boat. He pointed out details of the cabin being finished and the walkway along each side of the boat with wood strips nailed crosswise to provide footing. After discussing the details I asked Jean, "Are yea going ta have a swivel gun fer defense?"

Cabott pointed. "See post in the bow. It is for a swivel gun."

"Should yea have one in the stern also?"

Cabott was surprised and doubtful. "You think we need two?"

"Yea wull be hauling freight fer many customers an' river rats may try ta steal from us. Two guns would be better wit' a musket fer each man."

Cabott pondered that suggestion before replying, "Swivel guns will have to come from Orleans."

"Yea speak ta Madame, she can order guns."

Cabott seemed to agree. "I talk to Madame." Jean knew who his boss was and I was just a partner who wouldn't be around very often.

He pointed. "You have horses. You look for mast trees?"

"We will ride out tomorrow ta look fer a mast."

"Madame coming to inspect work tomorrow. You stay to talk."

We set up camp in the trees and settled down to watch the activity. Rene was honing his new knife with a piece of fine sandstone, working to get a razor-sharp edge and a good point on it. Using the last of the daylight, I wrote in the log. It was a warm eighty-two degrees, which was about normal for spring. No rain since our arrival and that would probably change. The country around looked like an area that got rain.

For breakfast we ate pork meat and bread by the fire. As the sun appeared above the horizon, men started arriving for work. Propping a small metal mirror in the notch of a tree and stropping the razor on my belt, I proceeded to shave, which always made me feel better. After two or three days' growth, whiskers always felt itchy. Only when the weather was cold was it worth tolerating a beard.

Rene stayed by the fire with his Charleville beside him, working on his knife, while I walked over to talk to Jean. "We wull ride out ta look fer mast trees today. Where do yea think we should start?"

"We went along the river maybe five miles." Jean pointed west. "You go farther or look away from the river. The new boat will be fifty-two feet, mast the same."

"Show me th' mast yea have fer this boat." So we looked. I paced its length before coming back to check the thickness of the bottom end with my hand. The bottom was squared for mounting on the boat with holes bored for the iron pins that would hold it in place.

Cabott suggested, "You find four so we have spares. Many masts break on the river." Jean glanced past me. "The carriage comes."

An older man drove and Madame Chadron brought her son along. After Jean handed her down to the ground, she turned to me. "How nice to see you again, Mr. Richardson. What do you think of our boat construction?"

"Very impressive, Madame." She was pleased by my comment and smiled.

"Come, Mr. Richardson, let us sit to talk of the details and Mr. Cabott can tell us of his progress."

She sat on her favorite stump with us facing her as she questioned Jean on everything done in the past two days. I was learning of her regular trips to the river and how involved she was. There was no detail too small to escape her attention and her memory for facts was amazing. Obviously, she knew far more of boats and commerce than I did. The best course for me was to remain silent, listening carefully to every word. There was much to be learned just by listening and observing.

Rene came with his Charleville in the crook of his arm to watch what was going on. Out on the prairie and mountains one should never be without his gun. Rene was never far from his, a habit I was becoming sloppy about from being in St. Louis.

The sun was more than two hours high by the time Madame was satisfied and started discussing the hauling of freight. There was work lined up for the first boat which would be ready in three days. Rene interrupted, "Jar, soldiers come."

We all looked. There were five of them coming from the west following a Spanish officer. Reaching the trail to the beach they halted. The officer swung his horse and rode toward us. He looked at the sign. When his horse stopped his eyes fell on Madame, who hadn't moved. He removed his hat and bowed from the saddle. "Good morning, Madame Chadron."

"Good morning, Capitan Vargas. May I introduce my business partner, Mr. James Richardson? We are building boats."

His eyes were black, as was his hair and mustache. He looked at me carefully, nodding, before his eyes moved to Rene.

"What brings you to our town, Capitan?" she inquired. "Surely we have caused you no trouble."

"No trouble, Madame. Two days ago the bodies of four men were found some eight miles south of here. We are investigating.

Has there been any word of fighting?"

"Not that I have heard, Capitan. Mr. Cabott, are you aware of anything?"

"No, Madame, there has been no talk."

"These men were known along the river. Ten days ago they were seen near the fort, traveling this way. Possibly they turned off before getting here."

"Could it have been Indians, Capitan?"

"We do not know, Madame. There has been no problem with the Indians for a long time. These men were all stabbed. Their clothes and two knives were not taken. I think it was other white men who did this."

Again she turned to Jean. "Mr. Cabott, have you heard of any problems along the river, rivalries perhaps?"

"There are often brawls resulting in men being hurt. There has been no news recently."

"Thank you for your assistance, Madame. If there is any news perhaps you could send a message."

"Certainly, Capitan, we are pleased to help when we can."

Again, he doffed his hat before turning his horse. We watched him go, riding erect in the saddle as all military men did. It must have been hot in that tight-fitting uniform. I was happy to see him on his way and relieved that he didn't question me. What would my reply have been if he had asked? I was never one to lie. Those men deserved what they got and we wanted no trouble with the authorities. Dressed in town clothes instead of our buckskins may have saved us from being questioned. Mac told me all those years before that appearance was important. His words were, 'When ye ar' around people always be clean n' neat, wearing the best clothes ye can afford. Ye will be judged by how ye look, no by what ye ar.'

We watched Vargas and his column of men start way. Madame commented, for my benefit no doubt, "Capitan Vargas is commandant of Fort San Carlos located on the river just west of here."

"Is that the stone fort we passed coming along the Missouri?"

"Yes it is, Mr. Richardson. A small fort was established by the Government of France many years ago. The stone fort was built by the Spanish Government in 1779 by order of Governor Bernardo de Galvez, governor at that time of the Louisiana Territory."

"Was the fort needed ta keep the peace?"

"No, Mr. Richardson. The Spanish Governor planned to send explorers to map the Louisiana Territory and the fort's purpose was to control traffic on the Missouri. It was believed one of the rivers flowing into the Missouri would provide a route to California and link the two Spanish territories together. Several attempts were made to find that route. The governor even offered a prize of money to any man who discovered the way."

"Ar' the Spanish still searching fer away ta California?"

"Not any longer, Mr. Richardson. Spain was forced by Napoleon to cede the Louisiana Territory to France. Still, the Spanish Governor, the Marquia de Casa Calvo, remains in New Orleans. Since 1799, Upper Louisiana has been governed by Lieutenant Governor Monsieur Charles Dehault Delassus, a Frenchman by birth, who long served the King of Spain and was appointed by Spain."

She paused to push hair back from her eyes. "Now there are

rumors Napoleon will transfer the Louisiana Territory to the United States." Madame Chadron stood and told us, "Well, gentlemen, it is time for me to go to the mercantile, there is work to be done."

Jean and I walked to the carriage with her and watched as it departed.

Jean had searched along the river, so we rode inland for half a mile to start looking through the groves of trees for tall, straight timber that would be suitable for masts. That night we camped beside a small stream flowing north to the Missouri. In the morning, the search resumed. If the trees were tall enough, there were bends or if they were straight, the height wasn't right.

Late on the second day, looking for a camping spot for the night, we came on a thick grove of tall, straight trees growing in a hollow where there was water. Many of the trees appeared suitable for masts. If it were true, Jean would have a good source for many masts. The trees were maybe ten miles upriver and two miles south, a fair distance to drag them before they could be floated down river to the building site. It was tempting to cut several. We didn't because in the end it would be better if Jean selected the trees he wanted. In the morning we rode back to tell him what we had found.

The boat was in the water to check for leaks. Jean explained, "There are only small leaks. They will stop as the wood swells." Her mast was up with rope lines running to the bow, sides and stern to brace it. Men worked at rigging the sail. "Tomorrow we will try her." Jean smiled happily.

We rode back to the trees, taking ropes, with Jean and one man each taking an axe. Jean carefully selected six trees which they felled. While they did the cutting, we started dragging trees to the river with ropes rigged to a harness around our horses' necks. If we had those Spanish saddles we could have tied tow ropes to the saddle horns. The saddles we made ourselves weren't built for such heavy work.

A small boat sent up the river to meet us would guide the raft of trees downstream. The problem of masts was solved and we had contributed. It felt good to be involved.

Madame Chadron came with two copies of a partnership agreement written in black ink on heavy parchment, which we signed. She also brought a letter to Chouteau, authorizing her to draw on my account, after presenting details of the expenditures.

After meeting with her, we saddled our horses and started for St. Louis. This time we followed the river to have a look and see more of the area. From all our riding we had a good picture of the ground between San Carlos and St. Louis. It was always wise to know the lay of the land.

That night it rained, really rained, like nothing we ever experienced. With only our shirts and a blanket each we were soaked in minutes. It was a miserable night, sitting under the trees with the water pouring down and no hope of a fire. Toward morning the rain eased somewhat, but it didn't stop and wind was still strong. Rene suggested, "We ride."

I grinned rather weakly. "Might as wull, we cannae get any wetter than we are now."

Chapter 7

The rain was so heavy we couldn't see beyond our horses' heads. Driven by a fierce wind, the rain was almost parallel to the ground, beating on our shoulders, keeping us soaked and cold. The clouds raced past, thick, heavy and low in the sky, just above our heads. Riding to St. Louis was a slow, miserable trip with the horses slopping through the mud until just at first light, after a dark day and night of riding the farm came into sight. Turning the horses out to pasture, we hurried, carrying our saddles, to shelter in the storage shed. We were out of the storm with respite from the cold wet wind. The sound of rain drumming on the walls was like the beating of drums. Large drops of water fell from several places on the roof. After watching the leaky roof for a few minutes we rearranged our gear to dry places on the dirt floor. Our bows were hanging on one wall of the shed and seemed safe. Both of us were cold and hungry, although it wasn't the first time we had missed eating, often for longer than this. It wasn't going to get any warmer sitting here and there would be a warm kitchen and food at Mrs. Ruechard's, so we headed into the storm again.

Pulling open the kitchen door, we stepped inside and Mrs. Ruechard took one look. "Don't you men move. Stand still while I bring towels."

We stood inside the kitchen door dripping water on the floor, looking at a man sitting comfortably at the table. Grinning at us, he offered, "Looks like you were dragged up the river by a big catfish."

"Dinnae need a catfish, we did this all by ourselves."

Mrs. Ruechard came bustling in with two towels. "You men get out of those wet clothes and dry off. Henrie, you come with me to fetch blankets to make them decent."

After we were wrapped in the blankets Henrie called his wife back into the room. She mopped up the floor before going to the stove to make breakfast. Sitting at the table drinking hot coffee helped to warm our insides until she brought plates of bacon and eggs to the table. We each ate two full plates before sitting back. "Thank ye, Mrs. Ruechard, we haven't eaten fer two days."

"You paid for it. Been gone for a week, leaving me with no one to cook for until Henrie came sneaking in just ahead of the rain." She stood by the stove with her hands on her hips, a disgusted look on her face. "Don't you men know how to build a shelter from bad weather?"

Grinning at her I tried to explain. "Thar was no the time for it; the rain came on sudden in the middle of the night."

Mrs. Ruechard glared at us. "A person would think trappers from the mountains should have better sense."

My grin got wider as my head nodded in agreement. "Yes, we should. The weather ha' been warm since we got here an' it fooled us."

"You have dry clothes to change into?"

"No, we don'na. After we warm up we wull put these back on

an' go buy another set at Chouteau's."

Mrs. Ruechard gave me another disgusted look. "Men are such fools." She shook her head in annoyance. "Henrie, you go down to Chouteau's and get clothes for these men. Tell him Mr. Richardson will pay when the rain stops."

Henrie shrugged and looked at me before going to a peg on the wall where he took down a heavy canvas coat with a hood and pulled it over his head. It hung below his knees. I suggested, "If ye talk ta a tall, thin clerk with grey hair he should remember what we got before. Get us two of those coats like ye're wearing."

We sat there drinking coffee in the warm kitchen. Soon we were warm too. Our landlady put loaves of bread in the oven to bake. There is something about the smell of bread baking that just makes a place a home. It might not mean much to Rene, if anything; to me it brought back memories of growing up on the farm back in Scotland. My parents were gone and maybe the middle brother; who knows what might have happened to him after nine long years in the Royal Navy. My oldest brother was almost a blur; it was Mac I remembered with fondness. He was a good friend to a wee lad, taught me many things and told me much about the world. My hope was for him to be warm and snug and eating well.

The kitchen door opened and Henrie came in, dripping from the rain. He carried a bundle wrapped in a canvas coat just like the one he wore. "You men take these clothes and get changed. You will feel much better. When you are ready, come back. We can talk while Ma does her work and fixes us a midday meal."

Mrs. Ruechard eyed her husband and shook her head. "Fools, all of you. Men are only good at eating and getting in the way. Now,

Henrie, you went and messed up my floor again. You get the mop to clean up. When the sun comes out I will wash these clothes, then at least you men will have a spare set."

We came back to the kitchen to spend the day working on our guns. The powder was wet and caked. It was a job to remove the lead balls and get the bores back into shape. After carefully wiping everything dry, we rubbed grease on all the steel parts to stop rust. It also lubricated the moving parts. Using the ramrod, I carefully worked a small greased patch of cloth up and down the bore of the Charleville. Next, I started on the pistol. Rene was doing the same. All the time we worked, we visited with Henrie. He wanted to know about the western mountains and I told him what I knew, the best I could.

Later, he told us about St. Louis. Henrie described how Auguste Chouteau came up the river to found the town back in 1774. Chouteau was the most successful merchant in town as well as its leading citizen. Henrie estimated there were four to five hundred people living in town or nearby; he said no one knew for sure.

Henrie packed tobacco in his pipe as he fell to talking about the river, boats and all that went on, the good and the bad. His talking gave me the feeling he loved the life.

Henrie told us about growing up and going on the river with his dad who owned his own keel boat. After his dad died he carried on hauling freight and people, using the boat to fish and hunt for meat. It was a good life until two years before when coming down the Missouri a giant tree trunk stuck in the river bed reared its head to rip out the bottom of his boat. Everything was lost and Henrie swam to shore.

"Since that happened I have taken what work there is on the boats, mainly making runs down to Orleans." Henrie turned his head to look at his wife. "It doesn't pay all that well, so Ma started letting out rooms to help."

"We are getting by fine, Henrie. We have this house with plenty to eat. There is no more we need."

Henrie nodded in agreement. "You are a good woman, Ma; it's just that I'd be happier if I got me another boat."

This was interesting. "How far is it ta Orleans?"

Henrie looked at me and scratched his head. He walked over to the stove to relight his pipe with a burning taper, puffed it into life and came back to the table. "They claim it be seven hundred miles. We river men talk in days. Going down river it takes from six to ten days. It varies depending on the water speed and the weather. If there's no moon you daren't travel at night. When the moon is out the trip is much faster. Coming back under sail takes longer. Twenty days if the wind blows and luck holds. Sometimes twice that much. A round trip is thirty to sixty days."

Squinting with one eye down the barrel of the pistol, I asked, "Are these keel boats yea travel on?"

"Mostly they are, only much larger than the ones working the Missouri. These are eighty feet long with a ten to twelve foot beam. They can carry up to thirty or more tons of freight going down river. The trip back is better if you don't load so heavy. The boats usually have three sails and it takes ten to twelve men to handle them, especially to man the oars." This seemed to agree with what Cabott told me.

"Are the holds open to the sky on these big boats?"

"Oh no." Henrie shook his head. "The whole boat has a long cabin to cover the goods, usually with bunks for sleeping at least eight men. Sometimes men have to sleep on the cargo while the boat is tied up to shore."

"Yea were captain of yer own boat?"

Henrie puffed on his pipe, blowing out a cloud of smoke. "More than ten years."

That puzzled me. "Are there no jobs fer captains?"

"Nary a one. Most boats are owned by the captain who runs it or by his family."

While continuing to grease the pistol I pondered that for some time before asking, "Did yea ever meet Jean Cabott over ta San Carlos?"

Henrie sat up straight in his chair. "Knowed Jean for a long time, our dads worked together on the Missouri. Haven't seen him for some time."

Looking up from the pistol, I suggested. "Cabott's building three keel boats up thar at San Carlos an' just put the first one in the water. Why don' yea go talk ta him?"

"Is he hiring?"

"Said he was." After pausing for a moment, I added, "He may still be looking fer experienced men."

Henrie jumped up to pace around the room, banging his right fist into his left hand as he walked; the pipe lay forgotten on the table. He turned to look at me. "How do you know this?"

"We just came from San Carlos an' spent some time watching them build boats. One fifty-footer is in the water an' they have started on a second one. Cabott said the next one would be eighty feet."

Henrie turned to his wife. "That's it, Ma! Jean is building a boat for the Mississippi trade." He was excited and stopped his pacing by the stove. "Got to go see him, Ma."

"You sit down, Henrie, it is still raining. You won't be leaving until the sun comes out; besides Jean won't be building in this rain."

Henrie took another turn around the room, thinking about it. "Have to borrow a boat for the trip and going upstream may take three or four days, now with the water up."

We looked at each other and Rene nodded. "Henrie, yea take my horse an' Rene will ride along fer company. Yea can get there in two days easy by horse."

Henrie stopped in his tracks. "That be damned kind of you, Mr. Richardson."

Mrs. Ruechard waved a large wooden spoon at him and her voice was firm. "Henrie, don't you be using that talk in this house. You are not on the river."

"Sorry, Ma." He winked at us. We kept our faces straight; it wouldn't do to upset the cook.

It rained all the next day. The dirt streets were a mess with hardly a body moving, even the dogs disappeared. Watching out the window, it seemed to me business must be at a standstill. It was a time for resting. Rene and I sat on our beds going over the list of trade goods to be purchased. We discussed how to pack the horses and how much we could take. Rifles would be a problem. With five in a box they were heavy; each box would weigh close to a hundred pounds. With the right pack saddles a horse should be able to carry two boxes; one on each side. Our problem was that with all the other goods we could only spare two horses for guns. It was less than we wanted. No use taking the guns without powder and lead, which would tie up two more horses.

All this talking was tiring. I dozed off. Later, after waking up, the answer was clear. My head argued over the facts while I slept, having found the logical solution. Seemed like a man's brain never stopped working when there was a problem to solve. Rene was sitting by the window. He listened to me explain. "Seems ta me we aren't going ta get enough trade goods back with us ta stock a trading post fer a season's worth of business, so opening a post will have ta wait a year. The valley we found wull still be thar. We wull order what we want from Chouteau fer delivery next year by keel boat up th' Missouri ta Yankton Landing."

"What we do next winter?" Rene's face reflected puzzlement.

"Go back ta the mountains and trap. There's still plenty of beaver there fer another season. We can go farther south through the mountains seeking fer Cheyenne ta trade with. Another season like the last wull set us up. After that we wull let others do the trapping an' bring furs ta us."

Rene nodded his head in agreement. "Good plan."

I grinned, teasing him. "Yea will be able ta sit in the trading post an' get fat. Maybe find a wife to do your cooking."

"No wife. Me too old for troubles wife make. Talk too much." Rene pointed a finger at me. "You young, you get wife. Maybe one in St. Louis."

We laughed together, agreeing. "One day I'll find a wife an' she wull make Rene fat."

Come morning the sun was up. It was a glorious day with a clear sky and the wind down to a gentle breeze. By noon the water was disappearing, the mud was drying in the streets and people were moving around. It felt really hot after three cool days. Late in the day when I checked the temperature it was eighty-seven degrees. That was surprising because it felt more like a hundred, most likely due to the damp air.

Staying close to the house, we made plans for the trip to San Carlos. Rene and Henrie would leave in the morning and be gone five or six days, allowing two days to go each way. Rene would take my pistol behind his sash just in case. While they were away it was up to me to deal with Chouteau. When everything was settled we would start north; back to what we regarded as our home country. It was nearing the end of April. With luck we would be there by June, before my twenty-second birthday.

Where had the years gone? As a lad dreaming of coming to America there seemed no way to make it happen. Now seven years were gone by. I had more money than ever seemed possible and a good friend. Back home in their small little world the Scots wouldn't believe it was true even if I was there to tell them. But it wasn't just about money. I wanted land where my animals could graze, crops could grow and someday little Richardsons could run and play, growing into strong men and women for a man to be proud of. It was a dream which might never happen. No matter, a man needed something to aim for in his life and that was what I wanted.

The sun was an hour in the sky when they rode away. With my walking stick for comfort, it was time to see Chouteau. First the cobbler. My boots were ready so I pulled my new stockings up tight, put on the boots and stomped around the shop trying them out. They felt funny, almost awkward, after years of wearing only moccasins. It would take time to adjust to the feel. The cobbler's helper rubbed them with grease to seal the leather and help keep the water out. Rene's boots and saddle were ready. The cobbler promised my saddle would be ready in two days.

Tying the moccasins to my belt, I took the list of trade goods to Chouteau. Everything we wanted was ready except the number of long guns. In his warehouse he had three boxes of Lancaster model 1794 long guns. Three of them were sold so only twelve remained.

I hefted one, trying the feel of it in my hands, while he told me about them. "These are the best rifles produced in America. They are made in Lancaster, Pennsylvania. The octagon shaped barrel is forty-two inches long. The shape of the barrels makes them heavier than rifles with round barrels. These were ordered with a fifty-four caliber bore. Each one comes with a ball mold, a barrel stopper and a cow's knee to keep the powder pan dry. If you like them you can have ten."

"I'll take the ten, but only after trying one of them out."

"You do that, Mr. Richardson. We will hold these two boxes for you."

"How long would it take ta get more?"

Chouteau rubbed his chin as he thought. It was a habit of his.

"These guns were ordered last fall to be shipped down the Ohio first thing this spring. They just got here a few days ago."

The normal trade gun sold to the Indians and trappers for ten beaver, figured at six dollars per pelt. There was the cost and risk to transport the guns out to the trading point so the normal markup was five times. A normal trade musket was twelve dollars cash, these Lancaster's were sixteen. If we bought at sixteen and traded each one for thirteen prime beaver and got the furs to St Louis safely, there would be a nice profit. Chouteau watched me as I considered. "If these guns shoot straight I'll want ta order more fer next year."

"How many would you want?"

"Probably one hundred, shipped up the river next summer by keel boat."

Chouteau waved a hand. "An order of that size can be placed. They may not be able to fill it." He smiled thoughtfully. "We should send the order immediately which will increase the chances of getting all one hundred. In fact, I am going to Orleans in ten days and can send the order from there."

"I'll let yea know tomorrow after trying one of the guns."

"That will be fine. The clerks will start putting this list of items aside for you. If you come in tomorrow perhaps we can talk about properties here at St Louis."

Outside his office door there were two shelves with books for sale. It was my intention to look through them and now I did. Henrie had mentioned that Chouteau owned a library of several hundred books in three languages in his home and spent hours reading. There wasn't much for me to read since leaving Scotland and it was something I always enjoyed doing. Chouteau came to watch as I sorted through the books and finally chose two.

The first was *Poems Chiefly in the Scottish Dialect* by Robert Burns published in 1786 and *Robinson Crusoe*, written by Daniel Defoe, first published in 1719.

Chouteau commented, "Both are fine books. I had trouble understanding the poems because they are written using old Scottish words." He took another book from the shelf and handed it to me. "Take this one also. Reading it will help you to understand the thinking behind the American Revolution. In fact, many people believe this book is what inspired the colonies to rebel."

It was entitled *Common Sense,* written by Thomas Paine and published in 1776. He was a noted thinker. I knew of him without having seen one of his books before. "Thank yea, Mr. Chouteau. There ha' been little ta read in recent years. Please add these books ta my account."

He waved his hand and smiled. "Not many of my customers show an interest in books, which disappoints me. Please accept these as a gift from me. After you have read them perhaps we can discuss their merits."

Walking outside the town I tried the gun. It was accurate at fifty paces, not as good as the Charleville, much better than the usual trade muskets. The Indians and white trappers should be willing to pay extra beaver to get them. On the way back I stopped to order two pack saddles suited to carrying the rifle boxes. It would be too risky to put all the rifles on one horse, so we would divide the load on two horses for safety.

For two days I wandered around St. Louis. Most houses were built from wood, only a few of the newer ones were of stone. Supposedly this was due to the increasing wealth of the merchants and businessmen. Three churches in the town were built of stone with high bell towers topped with crosses. The Spanish had one and the French two.

Along the river there were no docks. The boats just came into shore and tied up with a rope running from each end of the boat to posts set into the ground. There were stacks of barrels, wooden boxes, and sacks piled on log platforms. Many of the piles were covered with canvas tarps. Oxen and horses pulling two-wheeled carts took merchandise away while others brought loads to put on the boats.

There was one large keel boat tied up to posts with long ropes. It was pointed at both ends with rigging for three sails. She was loading for Orleans. I watched the captain supervising his men as they walked up a double plank incline carrying barrels, boxes and sacks onboard. It seemed like that captain was yelling much more than was needed. It was a trait common to many town folks. Guess they didn't need to worry about noise the way we did out on the plains and in the mountains. Making all that noise they would scare the game out of the country and probably attract some Indian who'd lift their hair.

Several flat-bottomed barges, with both ends squared, were tied up to posts. It seemed to me they would be very stable in the water and hard to move against the current. A number of small row boats, dug out pirogues and birchbark canoes along the shore completed the waterfront. On shore, a few crude wooden huts belonging to men who worked on the boats were scattered around.

The second afternoon found me at the farm checking the condition of the horses. It appeared the rest with time on grass and no work to do had been good for them. Their hooves were hard and in good shape. The shaggy coats of winter were gone now with the warm weather. None of the horses had any problems that were apparent.

Moreau, who owned the farm, walked over. He stood with his back to a post, puffing on his pipe, watching me work. He was growing a few acres of corn, a large garden and several milk cows with their calves were in the pasture where the horses grazed. Satisfied, I slapped the last horse on the rump before walking over to talk. “The horses seem ta be ‘n good shape.”

“They been eating corn along with the cows. Corn fattens them up and makes their coats shiny.” Moreau stuck a finger in his pipe bowl to push down the coals, added tobacco and puffed to get it going again. I waited; seemed like there was something on his mind. “You leave soon, huh.”

Now that was a surprise. We had told no one what our plans were. “We ar’ just lying around St. Louis resting up. It’s nice here.”

Moreau puffed on the pipe again, glancing at me from the corner of his eye. “Talk around that you rich. Build boats, buy many guns, friend to Chouteau.” What he said was true. There was no comment to make, so I waited. “Some men watch horses. I hear them talk. They say you have much gold and trade goods. When you go, look for trouble.”

"Thank yea, Mr. Moreau."

He walked away, going about his business while I lingered with the horses. Looking casually around, it didn't take long to spot two men sitting in the shade of a tree. They looked to be resting with nothing important to do. Picking up the walking stick, my new boots followed the path back to town. At the first house, I stopped to admire the flowers growing alongside the fence. Both men were following. Returning to my room I rested on the bed, intending to read the book Chouteau suggested to me. It was no use, my mind was busy considering what to do, so I put the book aside. Rene should be back in a day or two and we'd leave.

Next morning it was back to the barber shop to soak in that same tub and enjoy hot water and soap, taking clean clothes with me. They agreed to launder my other clothes. The barber trimmed my hair before I treated myself to another store-bought shave with tonic water that made my face tingle. One of the men from the day before, with a different companion, followed me from Ruechard's so there was no doubt they were watching. It wasn't always the same men and now I knew the faces of three of them. They looked like hangers-on from along the river. We would be careful; there might be experienced woodsmen among them when they came after us.

Outside of the barber's shop on the street the sun was high in the sky at its midday position. My stomach was empty and the tavern was just across the street, so it was a good time to eat. My favorite table was not being used, so I pulled out a chair and sat down with my back to the wall. The walking stick went against the wall and I took the book of poems from behind my belt.

It was nice being settled down to read in the light coming through the windows. In a few minutes the proprietor's wife brought the day's offering of stew along with a mug of beer. Eating with the book in my left hand, I dug into the old poems, barely aware that the crowd at the bar was growing as new men arrived. Chouteau was right. Burns was using the old language that few but a Scot would understand. When the bowl was empty I pushed it aside, sipped beer and leaned back, engrossed in reading.

It was a loud, rough voice that brought my head up. A large bearded man was standing near the table with his hands on his hips and a look of contempt on his face. This was trouble, although there seemed no reason for it. He was not someone I had encountered before.

Putting the book down, I inquired, "I'm sairy, were yea speaking ta me?"

"Sorry, are yea. What kind'a man be you? Some flophouse dandy, fancied up and smelling like a woman. You stinks the place up. Y'er smell hurts my nose."

A smaller man was standing to the side and somewhat behind the big man. Everyone else seemed to be just onlookers. Quickly taking stock of the situation, my main disadvantage was being hemmed in by the two walls, leaving me little room to maneuver. I needed to be on my feet. "The aroma is aftershave tonic water from the barber shop. I'm sairy it bothers your nose. Not all noses appreciate the subtle fragrances." That seemed to confuse him and while he was digesting the words I stood up.

"There you go be'n sorry again. What kind'a man is yea? Get out of the place before I throws yea out in the dirt."

Now on my feet, I was as ready as the situation allowed. "Sairy, but I like it here. I suggest yea take your friend an' leave afore there is any further trouble."

"Telling me to leave, be yea?" His eyes bulged and what face was visible above the beard went red. He shouted, "Now y'er gonna take a beating afore I throw yous into the street." With that, he pushed the table, trying to pin me in the corner. I sidestepped to the right. The rough wood of the tabletop hit my left hip a glancing blow that hurt. The bowl fell to the floor and shattered. The half full beer mug was still on the table, so I picked it up by the handle.

He was coming, reaching to grab me, so I kicked a fallen chair into his path causing him to stagger. With my left arm I swung the mug, hitting him solidly on the side of the head, spraying beer over his face. The blow sent him sprawling on the floor where he rolled onto his back, stunned and, I hoped, ready to quit.

His smaller companion crouched and pulled a knife from inside the top of his right boot. He started toward me with the cutting edge up for a belly stab. Slowly, I backed to the wall, watching him and the knife as my hand reached out for the walking stick.

He had a nasty, broken-toothed sneer on his face. "A stick will do you's no good. Yea is gonn'a get carved up as a lesson."

With at least three full paces between us it was too far, so I stepped toward him, moving away from the wall and gaining room to use the fighting stick. That stopped his sidling approach. He was trying to figure out what was going to happen. The pace forward put me nearer the fallen man who was trying to sit up so I gave him a solid kick in the chest with my boot, which toppled him over on his side and away from me. The sound of breaking ribs from the kick was loud. The man who fancied himself a knife fighter yelled angrily and started forward, swinging the knife. My stick moved to jab him in the mouth. He crouched lower at the last second and the stick hit him in the forehead, knocking him over backwards, where he lay quiet on the floor.

He was still holding the knife, so my right boot went onto his hand and pressed. Already, a large swelling was starting above his eyes which were open and looking up at me. Slowly, my weight shifted until his fingers snapped. When he screamed from the pain I stepped back and used the stick to skid the knife across the floor to the front wall.

Neither man was showing any sign of getting up off the floor, so I looked around the room. Pointing the stick at a young man, one of a dozen or so standing near the bar, I told him, "Yea go an' fetch the barber from across the street. Tell him ta bring his shaving gear an' a full bottle of tonic water."

When the door closed behind the messenger I turned to the tavern owner. "Set up a mug of beer fer every man here, I'm buying." They all crowded toward the bar and started talking excitedly.

Pointing at the side wall with the stick I told the two bullies, "Yea gentlemen crawl over ta the wall an' sit with your backs ta it." Watching the two of them, I considered what I was planning. 'Was I being too harsh? No. They chose to pick a fight with a peaceful man who was not even aware of their presence. Now they could suffer the consequences. Possibly it'll teach them to leave innocent people alone in the future.'

Standing there waiting for the barber, there was a low murmur of voices in the room as they all waited expectantly. No one approached or offered assistance to the injured bullies. When the door opened, I looked around. The barber came in with all his gear in a woven basket. He came right to my side and looked at the two men. Obviously, the messenger had told him the tale. "These two men need haircuts an' shaves. Start with the big one."

It took most of an hour. The tavern filled with men who heard the story out on the street and came to watch. Somewhere along there, Chouteau, accompanied by two other businessmen, walked in. The crowd made room for them. Chouteau came to stand beside me. He looked up at me and at the barber as he worked. Chouteau didn't comment, just stood there beside me. My damn hip was hurting. Even so, I wasn't going to let on in front of these men. It could wait until I got away from the tavern.

Their hair was cut short and when the shaving was done I instructed the barber, "Now shave their heads right down ta the skin." He glanced at me with a hint of a smile without saying anything. The barber went back to work lathering up their heads before stropping his razor on a belt. When he was done I thanked him and handed him a silver dollar which was more than a day's wages giving shaves.

Picking up the bottle of tonic water I showed it to them. "Yea picked a fight with me because I smelled of tonic water. It is past time yea gentlemen learned ta appreciate the finer things in life." With that, I carefully poured half of the bottle over each head, making sure the tonic water ran down their faces and soaked their shirts.

Walking to the corner, being careful not to limp, I pushed the table aside and picked up the Burns book. Besides me, only Chouteau knew what it was. When I turned around Chouteau asked, "What do you want done with these men?"

My shoulders shrugged. “I’m done with them an’ have no plan.”

Chouteau called out the names of four men in the crowd and instructed them, “Take my boat and put these men ashore on the east bank. We don’t need their kind in St. Louis.”

At the bar, I paid for the beer and the broken bowl before walking out the door and along the street toward the boarding house. I didn’t limp and didn’t look back.

In my room, I undressed and used the hunting knife to dig wood splinters out of my hip. The bone was bruised and would be sore for a few days. So be it, there had been worse injuries in the past.

Two days later, Henrie and Rene arrived back from San Carlos and came through the kitchen door to find me nursing a cup of coffee. Mrs. Ruechard brought two more cups.

Henrie grinned at his wife. “Got me a job as Captain on a boat, Ma. Jean is going to put me on his new keel boat. When the eighty-footer is completed I’m to move over to her. Jean is bringing a load of freight down in a few days. I will go aboard then.”

“That is good news, Henrie. You will be happier now.”

“Yup, I will.” Henrie’s eyes moved to me. “Madame Chadron was asking after you. She sent a message for you to stop by next time you are up that way.” I nodded my head, causing Henrie to grin broadly. “Ma, it seems Mr. Richardson is partners with Madame Chadron in building those boats. Jean works for them. They got them a big sign up naming themselves a boat company.”

Mrs. Ruechard was coming to the table with the coffee pot and stopped beside me. “You never told me you know Madame

Chadron."

"Don' know her really, just met her a few times in meetings ta discuss boats."

"Madame Chadron is a fine lady who knows her way around business. I mind the days when she kept account books for her uncle, Chouteau."

That hit me out of nowhere. "She is related ta Chouteau?"

"Well, not directly. She is Madame Chouteau's niece. She learned business from him; started keeping books and doing the ordering of merchandise when she was a young girl."

Sipping my coffee in silence, I gained time to ponder. There was no hint of a connection between them. When she asked me to deliver a letter to him it just seemed a natural thing to do. It made me curious as all get out about the contents of that letter, remembering the small smile when Chouteau read it. Just went to show, a man shouldn't take anything for granted and it helped explain her knowledge.

When the coffee was done we walked out on the street, where I told Rene about the men following me. "We should pack up n' leave tomorrow."

Rene nodded his head in agreement. "Leave midday, ride all night, maybe lose them in dark."

"If we don' lose them at least it wull slow them down. We best go an' talk ta Chouteau right now."

Chouteau came from his office to greet us. He didn't say anything about the tavern fight. While Rene picked out shirts and pants to fit Andre, I met with Chouteau to discuss our leaving. "We have decided ta leave tomorrow ta start back ta the mountains. We want ta bring the horses at midday an' load our trade goods."

"That will be fine, Mr. Richardson. My men will have everything ready for you."

"I want one thousand American gold dollars ta take along. Yea keep the rest on account fer me."

Chouteau smiled. "The money is ready. It is in my strongbox right here in the office. The coins are in a cloth bag inside a metal box for protection. That should be better for your trip and the money will be safer on a packhorse, being in the box."

We discussed a few other items, including our property purchases before I took my leave for the day.

Chapter 8

There was help from Chouteau's men loading the horses. We rode down the street and out of town in mid-afternoon, each leading five packhorses. The horses would leave a trail and there was nothing to do about that. Twelve horses were going to leave tracks.

Before dark it was clear someone was following. We held to our direction until happening upon a small stream late in the day. Rene led off, riding in the water of the stream as it followed a generally southwest direction. For several miles the horses splashed through the water until darkness arrived. With no moon the night was darker than the inside of a cave. Stopping in the water, the horses drank their fill while we listened into the night for any sound of pursuit. When the horses were ready, Rene rode up the bank and we continued west for a mile or so before swinging around and taking off north, setting our course for San Carlos.

Rene laid a trail that pointed west, hoping they would think we were headed back to the western mountains and keep on in that direction. If they didn't and continued to follow, we would fight if it became necessary, after trying to avoid trouble if possible. It was up to them. If they were determined and kept coming, we would deal with them when the time came.

The horses were heavily loaded, so we held to a walk, stopping often to let them rest. In the grey light of late night just before dawn, we stopped in a sheltered corner to make coffee and heat meat Mrs. Ruechard sent with us. Before full light we were back in the saddle. Rene carefully hid any sign of our fire and took time to wipe out our boot marks. There were still the hoof prints the horses were leaving. If one among them was experienced in the wilderness he'd work out the trail.

In the pre-dawn of the second day we unloaded the packs alongside the keel boat. Sitting on logs, we settled down to wait. Jean was the first on site and I quickly explained, "We need ta ferry these packs an' horses across the river. There ar' men following us."

Jean didn't waste time asking questions. "You start loading the packs on the boat. I will send a man to bring another boat to take the horses across."

The boat they brought was wide, with a flat bottom and square, blunt ends. There was a mast for a single sail and locks placed where men could row with long oars. We loaded four horses, tying two at each end. Four men hoisted the sail to take advantage of a wind blowing from the southeast and the first load started across the Missouri.

Shortly after midday all the packs, along with eight horses, were on the north bank. Madame and I met briefly at Chadron Mercantile, the general store established by her husband. When I was ferried across with the last load of horses there was no sign of our pursuers. We still felt sure they would be coming.

Originally, we had planned to go straight north along the Mississippi, keeping well back from the river to avoid Indian settlements—trying to slip quietly across the country, all the way north, to Peters River. There was little chance we could do that without being seen. Even so, it would have been worth a try. Now, with men following, we decided to go west along the north side of the Missouri to lay a false trail.

This was Osage country, north of the Missouri. They were a tall, fine-looking people and the men were known to be great warriors. Their numbers had decreased in recent years due to war and white man's diseases. The problem was that a pack train like ours would be to the natives what a Spanish ship loaded with treasure was to pirates. All we could do was be careful, talk or trade if we could and fight when necessary. As for those men coming along behind, our intent was to make it as hard for them as possible. They could travel much faster than our pack train and if they kept coming they would catch up in a few days.

After working our way up the side of the river valley, we started off with the Missouri on our south, letting the trail we were leaving point west again. The country north of us lay between two great rivers, the Missouri and the Mississippi. There should be high ground between them where the drainage went west on one side and east on the other. The high ground would be drier, with fewer streams to cross, providing a travel route easier on the horses. After our try to confuse and lose those following, that was the route we would take.

By holding straight to the west, the Missouri would swing away from us to the south. We would meet it again when it came back north. When we met the river again the plan was to follow it northwest until it swung west again. From that point, we would take off north for Peters River. Looking back in the logbook, it would take six or seven days from where we now were until meeting up with the Missouri further west.

Rene was his old self again, happy to be back out in open country, sitting in his new Spanish saddle with his head up, watching everything. The wind moved the wide floppy brim of his black leather hat and bellowed out the back of his bright red cotton shirt. Our new hats were a good addition; the wide brims shaded our faces and necks, making it easier to see in the bright sunlight. Rene hadn't commented on St. Louis. I knew he was uncomfortable with all those people around and being confined by living under a roof. Now he was out and moving, breathing the fresh air and watching the country around. His eyes were constantly scouting for the easiest way for the horses to travel and watching for potential dangers to be avoided.

Holding generally to the west, our trail wound around hills, lakes and such as we varied our route for safety or to find the easiest going for the horses. It was a chore to load and unload the packs so we weren't stopping at midday, just eating jerky in the saddle and keeping on. Each day, we stopped early to spare the horses and allow them to eat and rest. It wasn't always possible to find a good camping place that was both hard to approach and easy to defend.

The fourth day after losing sight of the river, we found an excellent camping place and stopped. It was on a bench above a small stream with a high bluff rising behind it. A spring of good drinking water bubbled out of the ground at the base of the bluff. Rene spotted it as the horses drank their fill from the stream, so we rode up the slope and moved in to set up camp. There were trees for shelter from the wind with a ring of fire blackened rocks used by other travelers.

With the horses staked out below us to feed, Rene scouted around, while I settled down with the logbook. We cooked our meat over a handful of fire made from dry, smokeless wood. At dusk, we took the horses to water again before bringing them in close to camp for the night. In the last light of day, we climbed the bluff to sit on the high ground and survey the country around us as darkness slowly took hold. Just after dark, Rene pointed east. “White man fire.”

At first I couldn’t see it, having looked west into the lingering light from the setting sun. Finally, my eyes adjusted. There it was, maybe three miles away on our back trail. The fire was close to where we had crossed a stream. It seemed likely they chose that spot to stop for the night. Rene handed me his Charleville. “You stay, Rene go see.”

We always removed our boots and switched to low moccasins in camp. Rene disappeared into the darkness without a sound on his moccasin-clad feet. After glancing at the big dipper to check the time, I sat thinking. It would take an hour for Rene to get there and maybe another to work close to the camp. Depending on how long Rene stayed to watch the men, it would be maybe five hours before he returned. If he wasn’t back soon after that I would go looking for him.

In the dark, I worked my way carefully down the side of the bluff, going from tree to tree. The camp was quiet except for the occasional sound of the horses shifting their feet. To improve our camp for defense, I moved a few dead trees and fallen branches. When the moon came out I used its light to charge two more Charlevilles so we would each have two long guns ready. After checking the pistol and putting the bow handy, there was nothing to do but wait.

It was mainly grassland I had to cross between the two camps and I crossed it quickly. Jar was back at camp with the horses and would stay alert in case the fire up ahead was a decoy and the men tried a night attack. Drawing near the distant glow of the fire, I carefully scouted through the trees along the far side of the stream, checking for guards that might be posted away from the camp. After making two complete circles of the camp, working closer through the trees, it was clear that there was no one on guard outside the camp.

Now, just outside the ring of firelight, I was flat on the ground behind a clump of brush. There were seven men in camp. All but one looked like they were off the river. That other man was bothersome. He was in buckskins, sitting with his back to the fire, holding a musket across his legs. The position he chose allowed him to watch the horses.

A brown colored jug of liquor was being passed around. The men were starting to get drunk and loud, talking about what they would do with all the trade goods after they got them away from us.

Two men besides buckskin carried muskets. The rest seemed to have only knives and clubs. One man stood up and threw wood on the fire. It flared, burning brightly, so I slowly moved back into deeper darkness where there was better cover. The moon was up now, but it was dark under the trees. The men in the camp wouldn't be able to see in the dark anyway, sitting around a fire like they were. I watched as the buckskin-clad man stood up and walked to the fire. He picked up the jug by the finger hole and the sucking sound of the bung being pulled out carried to me clearly. Buckskin took a long pull from the jug while supporting it in the crook of his right arm, banged the bung back in, put the jug down and returned to his former position. Good, that would dull his senses.

Lying there in the dark, I wondered if there was a way to run off the horses. 'If Jar was here we might be able to find a way. It is too risky for a lone man to try.'

Suddenly, buckskin stood up and walked to the horses. After checking the ropes that tied them to the picket line, he disappeared into the trees. I wondered if he heard me move or sensed my thoughts. It was unlikely. All the same, many frontiersmen were like wild animals and often sensed when danger was near.

Slowly, edging back to get further away, I found a spot sheltered by bushes with two large trees at my back. There had been no noise from my movements. I crouched low near the trees to better see the guard if he approached. With a knife in my hand I was ready if buckskin came looking. The men around the fire were just visible from this distance. After a time, the guard returned to camp and took another drink from the jug. He said something to the others, the words being indistinct from my position.

With that large fire they wouldn't last long if there were unfriendly Indians in the area. Time to go! I turned my head and looked into the darkness until my eyes fully adjusted and night vision returned. Silently circling the camp, I started away, hurrying back to tell Jar what we were up against.

In the darkness of the camp, Rene explained about the seven men, nine horses and their weapons. He described the man in buckskins and the way he acted around camp. Rene finished by suggesting, "They catch us early tomorrow. Stay here. Be ready."

"Maybe they wull miss us an' go on by."

"No miss. Follow many days. Come early tomorrow."

"Of course yea ar' right, Rene. Okay, we wull stay put. When they come we wull be ready. Yea get some sleep while I keep watch."

Seven men were a lot for just two of us to handle. We did have some assets on our side. They would have very little cover coming up the grassy slope from the stream while there were trees around us and our packs were arranged for defense. We could expect the man in buckskins Rene described to be the most dangerous. When the fight started he had to go first and after that the other two who were carrying muskets. If we got those three, the odds would shift in our favor. I hoped they finished off that jug of liquor and maybe there was another at hand.

In the first grey light of morning, we changed our minds, deciding to move into the trees on the edge of camp. I found a small hollow with deadwood and trees around it. My hat was propped up on the packs where it would be visible when they neared the top of the slope. Hopefully, their eyes would be on the camp as they came, not expecting anyone to be in the trees. It took a few minutes to shift branches to improve my cover and also get them out of the way for fighting. Rene did the same on the other side of the camp. If they came straight up the slope we would have them boxed.

The bow was ready with five arrows laid out, along with two charged long guns. I was ready. There was nothing to do now but wait. Rene disappeared in his cover some thirty feet away, so I hunkered down, chewing on a piece of jerky.

It was peaceful sitting there with the sun starting to come up behind us. It was hard to believe there was danger anywhere near. My few years on the frontier had taught me otherwise. Our camp would be in shadows from the bluff until the sun was high, after which the sun would be shining in the eyes of anyone coming up the slope.

Birds sang, occasionally a horse stamped its feet, while flies buzzed around. Magpies were always out first thing in the morning, bobbing their long tails as they sat on a tree branch or hopped around on the ground. They always came with the whole family, rarely alone, being very quick to spot any discarded food around a campsite. Magpies were good looking birds with glossy white and black feathers. Sometimes the black feathers took on a bluish/green sheen in the sunlight. They were one of nature's ways of keeping the country clean. Their feathers often provided fletching for my arrows.

The sound of horses coming along the little valley reached us before anything was visible. They came into sight and rode up to the stream where we had watered our horses. Their eyes followed the tracks up the slope. They couldn't see our camp; still, it was obvious where we had gone. They tied their horses to trees before starting toward us on foot. The fools just walked up the slope, hardly even spreading out.

It seemed to me they must feel formidable, being all together like that, gathering false strength from each other. Thankfully, it wasn't Indians coming; they would never be so foolish.

As they drew near the top of the slope the packs became visible. A large man with a black beard called out, "Hello the camp." When he got no answer he tried again. "We are goanna take your goods. You can leave now and have no trouble."

Three of them I recognized from being followed in St. Louis. It was the buckskin-clad man I was keeping an eye on. It was surprising to me that he stayed with them out in the open like that. Buckskin was at my end of the group, standing slightly apart. I notched a black arrow for him and waited on developments. He would be the most experienced of the lot and was likely to be the quickest to act.

Black Beard yelled again. "There be but two of you and we are coming in. Leave now while you can." There was a slight French sound to his voice; still, he seemed more like an American from across the Mississippi. The silence went on for seconds before he yelled once again, "Go get them." They charged the camp, running up the last of the slope. One man saw my hat, lifted his musket and shot at the packs. When he fired, my first arrow was on its way, hitting Buckskin in the chest. One of their muskets was empty and Buckskin dropped his. My next arrow took out the man still holding a loaded musket just as he started lifting it to fire. Rene put an arrow into Black Beard.

The four remaining men stopped where they were at the top of the slope, staring around at their dead comrades. With no noise from the arrows, they seemed to hesitate for a moment, not sure what was happening, before they scattered. Rene downed another with an arrow as I shot a fifty-four caliber lead ball into the man who shot at my hat. I lifted the second Charleville, but it wasn't needed as Rene fired from his cover. I could have shot the last man, but for what purpose? We had won.

When it was over, there were six men dead on the slope. The one remaining man didn't think about a horse, he just ran like a cat with its tail on fire, back the way they came. He faced a long walk.

We stayed hidden in the sudden silence following the action. Smoke from the black powder slowly drifted away, taking the sharp, biting smell with it. Nothing moved as my heart slowed from the rapid action. We were lucky. Their lack of wilderness experience was a big help and the whiskey they drank likely dulled their senses, giving them false courage. Whiskey was bad, ruining lives and families. In the life Rene and I were living, you needed all your senses about you. You wouldn't last long if you failed to be alert.

That I enjoyed fighting I knew and possibly I was too good at it, although there was little satisfaction in taking a life. They gave us no choice after following all the way from St. Louis. Their intentions were clear, so we did what needed doing.

Back in Glasgow they would be critical of my actions, saying I should have talked. Outside the cities, the Scots weren't so peaceable themselves. Here, talk was of little value. There was no constable or court to settle an argument. This was no settled community with laws and authorities to protect your rights. Here, every man stood on his own feet acting as constable, judge and, yes, executioner.

Rene saddled his horse and went to follow the escapee to make sure the man kept going. With a rope tied to my saddle horn, I dragged the bodies away one at a time, leaving them in a hollow down the valley where they wouldn't be a bother to us.

We were in the best campsite since ferrying across the Missouri, so decided to stay another night to rest the horses. They were breaking into the traveling well; still the rest would do them good. Here there was plenty of water and good grass to fill their bellies.

Our attackers left us with three more muskets, seven knives, several pounds of powder and lead, blankets, cups, cooking gear, and assorted other items, plus nine more horses. There was a half-empty gallon jug of whiskey. I poured the whiskey on the ground and spent some time washing the inside of the jug clean. A good jug with a finger hole for picking it up would be useful for carrying drinking water.

Rene watched me washing the jug before suggesting, "Find one jug, maybe one at camp. You look, Rene stay with horses."

The ride was pleasant in the morning air before the full heat of day arrived. They chose a poor site for a camp, one which we would never use. The camp was messy and sitting by a tree was an empty jug. Now we'd each have one. When time allowed, I would wrap the jugs in a tight covering of sacking which was an old trick. Keeping the sacking wet, the evaporation cooled the water. Back on the farm, each time you took a drink you would deliberately spill a little water on the sacking to wet it.

In the group of horses there was one that was larger and looked strong, along with two others that would be worth keeping. Now we each had an extra riding horse. There were twenty-one horses on the meadow beside the stream filling their stomachs on the long grass. It was a large number of horses to travel with. We could turn loose the six we didn't want, except that went against my grain. I was a trader and it seemed to me we should get something for them. In the end, we decided to take all the horses along.

Resting in the shade, we caught up on missed sleep, roasted meat and checked our gear. In the evening, we cut tobacco to load our pipes and watched the sun go to sleep in the west. A man could get lazy lying around like this.

Three days later, there was the Missouri right in front of us, flowing down from the north. We followed along, going upstream, until late in the day when the bend to the west showed up. This is where we would leave the Missouri behind. From where we sat on our horses, we could see the river stretching away to the west. Turning north, we looked for a spot to spend the night.

Day after day we rode beside shallow streams that were flowing southeast. It was easy going, much better than we had a right to expect; no doubt it wouldn't last. This was good country with long grass growing and tall trees in the hollows. The scattered buffalo were moving slowly north, eating as they went. These weren't the big herds. Those were already long gone. These were stragglers. There were hundreds of them with late spring calves trailing their mothers and, of course, the wolves were there for the banquet.

Buffalo never stopped moving for long. If they did the grass would be gone in no time. They were forced to be nomadic to survive, seeming to move maybe five miles each day, as did those creatures that followed them.

During the night, there was a strong shower of rain and the morning was cloudy. Underway for only a few miles, we came upon a fresh trail in the wet grass crossing in front of us. Rene walked out to look and followed along a short distance toward the stream on our left. He returned to remount, explaining, "Woman, with little one. Wander, look for food."

He pointed. "We go look."

As always, the long gun was in my hand. There was no other way to carry it except on a packhorse where it would be of no use to me. I followed after Rene until we topped out where the little stream valley was visible below us. There were four people.

An old man with two women and a boy child. They knew we were coming and were standing up to watch for us. As far as I could see, they had nothing but the clothes they were wearing. By the look of them they were Osage. The old man had been huge when he was young, taller than my six plus feet, with his head shaved except along the top. Long decorations hung from his ears. The two women were almost as tall and rather stately looking. Good looking women wearing deerskin dresses.

Looking around there was little to see. No cover in the area and no sign of any other people being nearby. Dismounting, I walked toward them with Rene watching over the scene. Using a mixture of English, Sioux, French and sign language they told me the story.

Three days before, Indians from the west had attacked their group. Everyone was killed or taken prisoner except these four who managed to slip away. They were attempting to make their way back home. Between them there was not so much as a knife and I surmised they hadn't eaten anything in several days. The old man was sick, most likely from exposure and lack of food; still, he was standing up straight and with dignity.

Gathering together a few sticks with some dry grass, I struck steel to flint to start a fire before returning to the horses. The eldest of the women took over tending the fire. The gear taken from our attackers was packed on two of the new horses. Finding a coffee pot and three tin cups I brought them to the fire. The younger woman filled the pot with water from the stream and set it in the side of the fire to heat.

Walking back to my horse to get the bow, I watched Rene from the corner of my eye. The butt end of the Charleville was resting on his saddle horn and he was amused by my actions. On his own he would do much the same.

A buffalo cow was grazing on the far side of the stream some fifty or sixty paces away. With the bow, I put an arrow just behind her shoulder. At that range it went all the way in. Wading across the shallow water of the stream to butcher the animal, the women splashed through the water behind me. I took out my hunting knife and the younger of the two held out her hand. She was far better and faster at butchering a buffalo than I was.

They positioned the animal on its side and cut along the back bone starting from the head all the way to the tail, then across the top of the neck and down along the belly. The hide on the inside of each leg was cut to join the belly incision. While one woman finished the cutting, the other started pulling the hide loose. In minutes, they peeled the hide off the upper side and stretched it out behind the buffalo. A few quick, sure cuts produced several steaks which they took to the fire.

When the meat was spitted to cook, she cleaned my knife and handed it back. While the Osage waited for the meat I thought about the travelling ahead of them, especially the old man. Going to the horses, I brought three of them to a lone cottonwood tree near the fire and tied them. Rummaging in one of our packs, I got out a knife taken from the river men and laid it by the fire. The old man began thanking me.

The older woman held up my black arrow, broken in two places, to show him. His eyes grew large, telling me the story of Black Arrow had spread along the river. He told me as best he could, "You come Osage."

Pointing north, I held up both fists, flashed my fingers three times and using Sioux tried to explain, "We go north thirty suns." Using a stick, I drew in the dirt an outline of the Mississippi as I was told it looked and added the Missouri. At the north end I drew in Peters River.

Using the stick as a pointer, I tried to explain, "Here Missouri, this Mississippi." He nodded understanding.

"Here is Peters River." I stuck the stick in the ground west on Peters and pointed at my chest. "Me go there."

He nodded his head again; then stuck a stick in the ground by the Mississippi, before pointing at his chest, then the stick. "Osage."

I nodded my head in agreement. The point he indicated was east and a little north of where we were. He pointed at me and then at the stick. "Osage."

Signing thanks, I pointed north. He nodded, understanding.

Looking around the bare camp made me feel selfish, so I went to the horses to get three blankets to give to them. The blankets were dirty. Picking up a handful of dirt to show him and pointing at the blankets, then at the stream, I rubbed my hands together in a scrubbing motion. He nodded at the women.

Standing up to leave, the little boy caught my eye. He was standing erect behind the seated man, who was probably his grandfather. He was looking at me. I went back to the horses to get another metal cup so the little fellow would have one of his own. That seemed to make him happy, which made me feel better than anything else. Besides, growing up being mostly left out by my older brothers, I knew how it felt.

With the packs retied, I swung into the saddle. They were eating meat when we rode away. At the top of the slope, we stopped to wave at them and they returned the gesture. A mile or so of riding went by in silence before Rene glanced at me. “Jar poor trader. Give much, get little.” Rene held out his empty hands.

Shrugging my shoulders I replied, “They needed help.”

“Strong woman, make good wife. You trade.”

I laughed at him. “Yea stop trying ta get me married. I’ll find my own woman when I’m ready.”

Rene grinned. “Jar slow finder, bad trader.”

Chapter 9

Rene kept our horse's noses pointed north. The days were warm with green grass growing on the gently rolling hills and it was easy travelling. Of the many varieties of trees, most were unknown to me. Only a few could I identify such as willow, ash, aspen and several different oaks. There were huge birch trees with their peeling, papery bark which looked to be eighty feet tall. On the lower ground, more moisture allowed smaller bushes to grow under the big trees. One that interested me had white flowers with a sweet smell like the perfume that a lady might wear.

Many different types of flowers, some growing around water, others out on the grasslands, added bright colors to the landscape. A tall reddish-purple flower stood waist-high near water where it could have its roots in damp soil. Its long head was made up of tiny purple buds which flowered from the top down, creating a shaggy appearance caused by a white hair sticking out of each small flower. At a distance, the combination made the top of the head look pink. During stops to rest the horses, I tried to sketch pictures of the plants and describe them. What I really wanted to know was what they were. The local Indians probably used many of these plants for tools, food or medicine. It would take years to learn all these things and we were just passing through the area. Our route was along a divide between streams flowing east to the Mississippi and those flowing to the Missouri on our west. Two great rivers, each with a drainage area, and we were travelling the higher ground between them.

Both of us were paying careful attention to our back trail, constantly checking for anyone following. With this many horses, there was no way to hide our trail although we tried, using the buffalo herds whenever chance offered and with frequent changes in our direction of travel. On our left, fewer streams drained the area so we often veered to the northwest for several miles before coming back to our main route. Always alert to ambush, we rarely took the easiest or most obvious way. Constant maneuvering took time, which slowed progress. It was tiring on a man, always being alert.

Resting the horses at the top of a rise provided a good view of a large lake on the northern horizon which appeared to be several miles long. A faint hint of smoke indicated people were living near it. We veered off to the northeast, aiming to bypass the lake by several miles. Crossing the grasslands, the course of a good-sized stream ahead of us was indicated by a long line of trees growing along it. When we came up to the bank the water was wide and deep, flowing from the direction of the lake toward the Mississippi. After a short ride upstream, we found an animal ford and easily crossed to the far side. In the tail end of the day, we hurried to set up camp in a thick grove of trees on the north bank.

The land we had been crossing for many days was ideal for farming and raising cattle. The rich soil supported many types of plants. It was sparsely occupied by scattered groups of natives who grew corn, squash and beans on their small plots, using this vast area for hunting. It was an open land stretching for hundreds of miles, lying unused except for the numberless buffalo and other grazing animals. No other Europeans were within days of me, the last being those we had fought way off to the south. Behind me there was San Carlos and far to the north, Fort Garry. We were somewhere in the middle, a long way from anywhere.

Back in San Carlos, Madame Chadron would have the first boat hauling freight with construction of the second progressing. By summer, both would be working and late in the year the big boat would be ready. There were risks on the rivers and sooner or later an accident would befall us. It amused me to ponder how little control a man truly has over his fate. If we hadn't stopped at San Carlos to ask directions, the conversation with Jean Cabott wouldn't have occurred. In which case, none of these things would be.

Also there was Auguste Chouteau, the founder of St. Louis in 1774. Most of my fortune was on deposit with him except for the gold dollars packed in the saddlebags. There was a big order for rifles and trade goods to be delivered next year to Yankton Landing, north up the Missouri. On deposit was sufficient money to pay for the goods. Even so, transporting the goods all the way north was risky.

Well, our start two years before was with very little. If it didn't work out this time, we would try again. Rene and I were now partners with Chouteau in several blocks of farmland outside of St. Louis, with one having a house and barn on it. We also agreed to purchase similar parcels on the American side of the Mississippi in Indiana Territory.

Chouteau explained to me there were rumors that Spain would be forced to transfer the Louisiana Territory to France which would cause unknown changes. It was worrisome because the Americans were arriving in ever greater numbers. Chouteau was expecting that France was too far away to maintain its claim to the area or French officials might simply lose interest.

He was planning ahead for when the United States took over. Having a non-French partner with a name like Richardson might help in maintaining property rights. Chouteau even went so far as to write the partnership agreement so that a reader would see me as the lead partner and Chouteau as an investor and the local manager. My name was prominent in the agreement and it was stated that Rene Beauchamp owned one fourth of my interest. The agreement was registered with the Spanish Authorities. Chouteau was wise, with experience in both business and local politics. In this situation the greater risks were in the politics between countries. Who could predict what America would be inclined to do if they took over? They might not recognize Spanish or French agreements.

My progress this past year was faster than I ever imagined or dreamed. After all the scrimping and saving to put together a stake, everything really got underway with a trading trip out west to the Mandan villages on the Missouri where we heard of furs in the Paha Sapa Mountains; then I stumbled on the gold. The good supply of trade goods on the horses would improve the next season of trapping and trading with an opportunity to look for more gold.

Best of all was having a friend who was dependable. Rene was more of a brother than the two back in Scotland ever were. All those people back there on their small, rocky farms or crowded up in cities were unaware of all this great wide land with water, wood and the soil to grow crops. Here was a climate far more favorable than the damp, rainy, cold place where they lived. As discussed with Chouteau, white settlers would come. When they did, we would be ready to provide the things they needed.

Thinking about cold, rainy places was a jinx. It started to spit rain, so we hastened to improve the shelter built between two large trees, working in the light from our cooking fire. It was a sheltered little glade with trees large and small growing around. There was grass enough for the horses with a spot for us. If it was going to rain this was a good place to be. We all, man and horse, could use the rest after days of constant travel.

It didn't really rain, just kept spitting, occasionally getting heavier, so we sat there for two days. Regularly, one of us was watching or scouting around. We boiled beans to start a stew with corn, venison, wild onions and mushrooms for flavor. By the second day, we were eating well. The third afternoon the sun came out, so I decided to put a fish hook in the stream using a big worm for bait. It was a lazy day, just idling away time sitting there in the shade waiting; with no luck. Rene came through the trees to stand beside me and point downstream. "Indians come, have families." I looked to my guns, just in case, and stayed right there with the long gun beside me.

They came along the far side of the stream in a group that appeared to be two families coming up from the Mississippi. Whether they were coming home or going away for some reason there was no way to know. They saw me sitting there and stopped to stare. Raising my right hand with the palm toward them, I tried to determine which tribe they belonged to. Their dress was different, so these people belonged to a tribe not encountered before. They seemed surprised to see me.

Two men started wading across the steam. Rene stepped from the trees a few paces away from me and they stopped in mid-stream. They now knew there was more than just me, not knowing how many men might be behind me. Finally, they came on, glancing curiously at my fishing pole. The rest of the group settled in the shade to start a cooking fire, so it looked like they would be around for some time.

They knew a few French and Sioux words so with signs we managed to communicate. I asked if they wanted to trade. The upshot was an invitation to their village which was one sun's walk upstream. They had corn, beans, and furs to trade, so we agreed to meet at their village the next day. We watched them eat before resuming their trek homeward.

Back in camp, we sorted the goods to take to their village, setting out the muskets, ball, and powder we had captured as well as three knives, blankets, tin cups, along with the odds and ends still left. We added steel arrowheads, double-ended awls, needles, beads and fire steels. Rene cleaned the muskets for use if the Indians demanded a demonstration.

At first light, we loaded the horses, putting the selected trade goods on the three poorest horses, which were also for trade. We rode out, keeping well away from the river until we saw smoke from the village. Rene took the horses into a small sheltered ravine in the midst of a dense growth of trees to wait for my return.

It was unlikely there would be trouble. All people depended

on trade to obtain things they needed from outside their local area, especially items they couldn't make themselves. Traders were always welcome. Still, there was no sense in advertising the load of trade goods. There are always those with no regard for traditions or proper conduct.

Midday was near when my horses followed a well-worn path along the river to a small village located on both banks of the stream. There were maybe twenty families living in permanent domed dwellings covered with large strips of tree bark. Spring crops were growing, with women in the fields pulling weeds.

They saw me coming and several men gathered in the center of the village to wait. I pulled the horses to a stop and sat there looking around until the headman stepped forward and started speaking. Indians loved speeches and I wasn't getting any of it. People gathered around as he went on for some time, no doubt telling me and those within hearing the great deeds of his people.

When he finished, I sat up straight, slapped my chest, and announced, "Jar." I repeated the process twice more. Showing twenty fingers after pointing at the sun, I held my arm out to the north. He nodded his head as though understanding. I launched into a speech reciting my history since leaving Glasgow, knowing they understood none of it, just going on to match his time.

Stepping down from the horse, I presented the chief with a fine steel tomahawk as a gift. It pleased him and hopefully made a good impression which would bode well for trading. Spreading out a robe with a musket, knives, kettles, needles and other items in a row, I sat cross-legged to trade. They could see still more trade goods on the horses.

The headman or chief, I knew not which, spoke to his people before sitting down across from me. Quickly, a woman appeared with a white deerskin hunting shirt decorated with quills, which she handed to me. A return gift and she motioned for me to put it on. Setting aside the wide brimmed hat, I pulled the shirt over my head. When I looked up they were all staring. It was my hair. Wearing a hat with my head out of the sun, my hair had returned to its deep rusty, red color which seemed to amaze them. Probably they had never seen red hair before. Very soon the whole village was gathered around.

Men brought furs; beaver, fox, otter, along with deer and buffalo hides accompanied by leather pouches of corn and beans. We haggled; bartering, the way trading is done the world over. In the end, all my goods were exchanged for a large stack of furs, corn and beans. These were a settled people, feeling no need for horses, which was okay; there were all the furs to take away.

With the sun three hours from setting, I packed up, preparing to leave. They invited me to stay. I pointed north, flashing those twenty fingers. At the end, I took a metal comb from my saddlebag to give to a little black-haired girl who was brave enough to come close and examine my red hair during the trading. The chief's wife got a fire steel.

Ready to go, I paused and, using the point of my knife, drew a map in the dust showing the rivers and made a mark to show where the trading post would be and signed trade. I pointed to the chief and at the spot on Peters River and signed trade again. Maybe they would come. If they didn't nothing was lost.

While the light lasted we got moving, riding north all night. It was into the morning before we stopped to rest. The following evening, we came to a large river flowing southeast like most of the others. It wouldn't be easy to cross, so we camped.

For three days the river led us to the northwest until we came to a crossing place that showed signs of much use. Animals crossed here and we found horse tracks in the mud that were only a day or two old. The horses came from the west, crossed and went off to the east. We hoped they would keep going until we were well away. These were probably hunters out for whatever they could find. If they were returning home we were safe. Rene believed they were from farther west, probably out to raid villages along the Mississippi. If they returned soon they would see our tracks and most likely follow us. Crossing the river, we turned north for the higher ground visible far ahead. Now, we looked for even more secure, easy to defend campsites.

Short of dark, we took to a depression to go west for several miles, away from our line of travel. Switching to a shallow valley that pointed north, we found a place for the night. With luck it would be dark before anyone following got to the point where our trail turned off.

Next morning, we waited as it grew light until we were satisfied that no one was around. While I loaded packs, Rene scouted the area. When he came back we started, riding spread out, each leading a string of horses. For two days we changed direction often, switching around as much as the terrain would allow between two rivers flowing parallel to each other on their way to the Mississippi.

Well into the third day, we stopped at a small stream to water the horses. The stream flowed down from a range of hills which looked like they might provide shelter. Riding single file in the water, the horses climbed a gentle slope into the hills. The stream passed through a narrow cut which was maybe a hundred feet above the main valley. Luck was with us. There were a few acres of grass in a small canyon in the side of a hill with a trickle of spring water flowing down the center. The entrance was narrow, the sides steep and it was well suited to us for defense.

With the packs stacked and the horses turned loose on the grass, I took my weapons with me to find a place in the trees, just inside the entrance. With some work we improved it for defense. Afterwards, Rene went to watch our back trail for anyone who was following.

Sitting there, slowly chewing on jerky, I wished it would rain to wipe out our tracks. The sky was clear, so that wasn't going to happen. It never seemed to rain when you needed it. Looking around at our position, the biggest problem was the shortness of the entrance. It was only about ten paces from the stream bed we rode up and if a group of men charged they would be on us fast.

I went out and pulled a few dead trees across the entrance. It wouldn't stop anyone, but it might slow them down. With the water and food on hand, we could sit here for several days if need be. The day dragged on. Waiting is tough when you are more suited to action. Besides, Rene's long absence was starting to be worrisome. He came in just at dusk. "Far down trail, they come. Find us in morning."

"How many are there?"

"Four, maybe five. We eat now, make tea, ready for morning."

Leaving him there on guard, I went around the corner from the entrance to get a fire going. When the fire was burning nicely with a bed of hot coals I hung meat to broil and put a pot full of water in the side of the fire. Rene stayed on guard just in case. When it was ready, I took Rene his meat with a tin mug of tea, returned for mine and came back to sit with him as it grew dark. It was peaceful sitting there enjoying our food together. As the light dimmed before full night, a big owl went past on silent wings, flying out through the entrance. If you weren't watching, you'd never know he passed by. Those long, wide wings made no sound.

Done eating, I put another pot of tea on the coals to boil before the fire died. We both settled down to wait in our chosen spots, each with a buffalo robe to keep the night's coolness away. It was useless to hope they would go on by; they weren't following our trail by accident.

In the grey of the early morning light, I went through the entrance and worked my way through the trees to a point where yesterday's trail was visible, settling down there to watch. The place where our trail met the stream was down the gentle slope in front of me. As the sun came up the dew on the grass glistened and sparkled in its rays. A finch landed on a willow branch to look me over. It had a gold-colored body with black wings. White markings on the wings looked like tiny waves on the ocean. The top of his head was black, giving him the look of wearing a brimless hat. After looking at each other for a few seconds, he went about his business, most likely searching for food for his family. They needed to eat, just like me.

The ponies came at a fast trot and stopped at the stream. One Indian rode his horse ahead, splashing through the water to look for tracks. When he returned they looked both ways on the stream. One of them pointed uphill. He couldn't see me, but it felt like he was pointing straight at me. There was an argument about something.

There were five small, lithe men, their dusty brown bodies bare, except for loincloths. One was wearing leather leggings. Young, but that didn't mean they weren't dangerous and they all carried bows. If they got our horses along with all the trade goods they would be big men among their people.

After tying their horses to trees, they started up the gentle slope. I faded back through the trees to our little canyon to tell Rene there were five of them and they were coming.

Sitting down, I switched to boots from the moccasins worn around camp. For the fight that was coming, boots were better in case my foot stepped on a stone or root and noise wouldn't matter once things started. The long gun would be of little use this close up, so it went against a tree. Holding the long bow with three arrows lined up in a row for quick access, there was only waiting to do.

A gentle breeze was blowing, the birds were singing and it didn't take long for them to come into sight. Standing where our trail turned into this side canyon, they looked at the dead wood. Obviously, it didn't belong where it was and they weren't fooled. One Indian pointed at our horses in the small valley before they started forward.

Rene may have moved on purpose for suddenly one of the Indians shot an arrow in his direction and died with Rene's arrow in his chest. The rest charged, yelling loudly. Maybe they thought there was only one man because they charged toward Rene, leaping over logs. My first arrow didn't get the man intended because another man jumping over a log got in front of him and the arrow took that one high in the leg. After that there was no more time for the bow.

With a tomahawk in my left hand and the big hunting knife in my right, I leaped into the fray with the two men in the lead. The remaining one fell when my arrow took his companion and the injured man fell on him. He would be up and coming very quickly.

Surprised by my charge, they hesitated for just a moment, which allowed me to get close. Rene came from the other side. My man swung his tomahawk, which I blocked with mine, catching his hand on the shaft. He dropped his tomahawk and it cut the back of my shoulder as it fell. Shifting to the right, my right fist hit him hard on the nose, just the way Mac taught me and it stunned him. My tomahawk came down to cut along the side of his chest as he fell back. That fist I hit him with was holding a big knife and I should have stabbed, not punched.

Swinging to hit him turned me more to the right, which saved my life. The Indian who had fallen over the one I shot charged at my back to stab me. With my turn to the right, his knife went past me, cutting my side. Completing my turn, the man's whole right side was open; with his arm extended, he was looking back over his shoulder. This time I stabbed with the ten inch blade and it went all the way in and cut backwards as his momentum carried him past. Pulling the knife back, I turned to help Rene. He didn't need me; his man was down.

Rene was unharmed while I was bleeding from at least two cuts. Once again we had survived. Three Indians were dead and two injured, one of those was out cold from my punch. We stood there looking around, amazed at our good luck.

Once my breathing was back to normal I walked over to retrieve my arrow. The Indian was lying on his back, partially under a dead tree, still holding his knife. He watched me approach, probably expecting to die. His black eyes were wary and he looked to be younger than me. After bleeding for several minutes, most of his ambition had drained away.

Watching him carefully, I moved the dead tree away, gripped his right arm and removed the knife. Rolling him on his side, I snapped the arrow before pulling the shaft out. He didn't yell. With the arrow gone the wound started bleeding harder, so I plugged the holes with moss and used a strip cut from my shirttail to hold the moss in place. I sure hated to cut into that cotton shirt, but a man did what he needed to. Gathering up his weapons, I left him lying there. Rene stood watching the other Indian who was awake now. His nose was broken, probably his head was hurting and he looked scared. The cut down his side was barely bleeding, so it wasn't serious. They watched us warily as we went about picking up the fallen weapons.

Rene heated water to clean my cuts. The shoulder cut was not serious. The gash in my side was hurting and bleeding a fair bit. When it was clean, Rene found moss to cover it, using a wide strip from the bottom of my shirt to hold everything in place. At this rate there wouldn't be much of that shirt left and there was only one other.

Rene went to get their horses while our meat cooked. Sitting there on a log with the long gun across my knees, I had both Indians in sight. When Rene returned we ate meat and drank tea, taking our time. These men had interrupted our breakfast so they could wait on us.

Keeping the three best Indian ponies, we turned those two

renegades loose on the other two. Rene followed them to make sure they went south. If they had made enemies in their travels, hopefully they would be able to avoid them on the way home.

Rene loaded up the horses with me only managing to help tie ropes and we took off out of that place. All the horses were carrying loads except the three new ponies because we didn't have pack saddles for them. My collection of Indian bows, flint knives and other assorted items had grown again. These were tied to the Indian saddles as we rode away. There were nineteen horses following us now.

Chapter 10

Wearing my cut-off shirt now hanging outside my belt, we kept going, staying between two rivers which were flowing down from the northwest. As we went, the horses were slowly climbing a long gentle increase in altitude as the land rose higher before us. It wasn't all that noticeable as we traveled because it was gradual. When you checked the back trail the change was easily seen.

Three days after the fight both rivers took a slight turn, which allowed us to travel north again. Dark clouds scudding low overhead on a strong wind gave warning of a storm coming. Turning the horses into the river valley on the west, it wasn't far until we found a good place to camp, with water nearby, a stand of tall trees to block the wind, material to build a shelter and tall grass for the horses. We took the time to build a good shelter with a slanting roof to shed rain. When the sides were closed in, we hauled logs to build a reflector for our fire and gathered wood to stack in the shelter where it would stay dry. Rene came in with two old bird nests to use as tinder.

Wherever the buffalo went the grass was eaten down by their wide front teeth and the ground trampled and churned, looking like someone had used a hoe to chop at it. After the herd passed by the grass and other plants grew quickly, taller and thicker than places where the herds didn't go. Buffalo left well-worn trails that were followed year after year, usually finding the easiest route across the land. The meadow beside us was yellow with flowers standing almost knee-high above the ground. When you looked closely you noticed they weren't yellow flowers, those were the leaves. The blossoms were tiny dark brown flowers clustered together in a round knob above the yellow leaves. Rene came to sit beside me, reached out to pick one of the plants and explained the brown flowers could be boiled to make a refreshing tea.

Just at dusk, Rene was sitting at the edge of the trees when a big buck crossed the meadow heading to water. The Charleville dropped him with a shot behind the shoulder. Hanging the buck from a branch, Rene quickly skinned out the deer. We took the meat wrapped in the hide back to camp and soon there was meat cooking over the fire, although it would be after dark before we ate. While grease dripped from the meat and sputtered in the fire, Rene worked on the deerskin, scraping it clean and I sat with the Burns book to read another poem.

In the night a gentle rain fell for a long time, gradually becoming heavier while the wind truly started to blow. We were warm, dry and comfortable in our robes, lying there listening. This was the first rain in many days and now our trail would be wiped out. Until we moved from here there would be no sign that we were in the country.

It rained all through the day, so we stayed put, only going out to check on the horses. Rene took them to water even though they were getting enough moisture off the grass they were eating. Our most important asset was the horses, so we were careful to care for them. The rain jackets made from heavy canvas sailcloth were effective only for a short time after which the rain soaked through. Each time they were used, we hung them up to dry for the next time.

The Mississippi was east of us and as we travelled further north it would swing back towards the west. We expected to meet it before getting to where Peters River flowed in from the west. Once we reached Peters River it would be familiar ground, country where we traveled the past two summers. Both of us were looking forward to getting there. Day after day of traveling, always being on the outlook for trouble, was tiring. Not that we weren't getting enough sleep, it's just that it wore on a man's nerves and after a while you got jumpy.

My side was still sore. Even so, the wound seemed to be healing with no problems. With the bandage off, I picked at the bits of moss still stuck in the wound. Filling one of the captured cooking pots with water and hanging it over the fire to heat, I rummaged through our gear for a piece of rabbit hide with the fur on. Dipped in hot water, I used the soft rabbit fur to slowly dab at the scab covered wound to soften it until the moss could be pulled out. Using my metal shaving mirror allowed me to slowly work around to the back. It was a slow process, but I worked at it until done. Several of the spots were seeping blood so I just sat quietly to let the air dry them.

Rene went back to working on the deer hide to pass the time. He was shaping it up to tan for future use. The cooking fell to me. Beans had soaked since we arrived so the first thing was to change the water and hang the kettle over the fire to start boiling. With meat spitted over the fire and coffee water on to heat, I put my back against a tree to watch Rene; just being lazy. The water boiled and I mashed coffee beans and dropped them into the pot and set it on a rock near the heat. Rene liked his coffee strong and his meat barely singed. With all this sitting around we were eating three times a day, which meant more meat would be needed soon.

During the night the rain eased, but didn't stop. When morning came the clouds were higher with the wind down to a tolerable breeze. From time to time the sun would peek through holes in the clouds. Birds started coming out, singing and chirping to each other. When we walked our boots made squishing sounds as we stepped on the soft, wet ground. No sense trying to travel in the mud, much better to wait until the sun dried the ground. In any case, it would be hard work for the horses with their loads if we left before the ground dried up.

Beans were cooking, with corn and some wild onions added to the pot. Rene came in with his hat full of fresh mushrooms. We cut several of them into pieces along with chunks of venison for the pot, adding shaved buffalo jerky for flavor. Come night we'd eat well with plenty left over for the next day.

We woke to a clear sky with the sun just coming up. In the afternoon I went to the stream to soak and splash around and washed my shirt and pants. It took a lot of scrubbing to get the blood stains out. That shirt was inches shorter than when it came out of the store. With the clothes spread out on a black willow bush to dry, I sat on the grass, letting the sun dry my wet skin.

After idly digging at the ground with my knife I picked up a handful of soil. It was rich loam that looked like it would grow anything that was planted. This wasn't a thin layer of top soil that a plow would ruin. It was deep. If we weren't so far from anywhere I'd start looking for a good place to locate a farm. It was just a passing thought. There needs to be a market if you're going to grow crops to sell.

A redheaded woodpecker went to work on a tree on the opposite side of the stream. The sound of his beak hitting the tree was as loud as a hammer pounding nails. Every few seconds he would stop to look around. His redhead was like mine only his was brighter, almost a pinkish red and came down below his neck. His chest and stomach were snow white. From where I sat it looked like his back and wings were a dark grayish black. He worked steadily and I sat there watching, wondering how his little brain could take the pounding. How he avoided getting terrible headaches.

Thinking back to St. Louis, for some reason I recalled overhearing a group of men talking about a lead mine on the Mississippi River run by a French Canadian named Julien Dubuque. Five years before, the Spanish Governor of Louisiana issued him an exclusive grant to mine lead along the west side of the river.

There we were packing lead on our horses all the way from St. Louis when it might be available much closer. If we could locate his mine and he was still operating, there would be a big advantage for us. Lead was very heavy to move and the distance would be far shorter than packing it from St. Louis. Two of the horses were carrying lead and those packs needed to be loaded every day.

It was an exciting idea. After hurriedly dressing, I went looking for Rene who was out scouting around the area. I paced around camp, impatiently waiting for him to return. When he rode in there was deer meat behind his saddle, which he hung in a tree while I told him my idea. "We ar' packin' four hundred pounds o' lead on the horses while there's a lead mine over on the Mississippi where we could be getting it."

"Where on Mississippi?" Rene frowned. "Mississippi long river."

"Ah dinnae know where. They said it was on the upper Mississippi."

"It past Peters?"

"Probably not, more likely south o' Peters."

Rene looked at me as he thought about the problem. "We go east, find river, find mine." He liked to tease so he added, "You hurry get home, now many days more."

That put a grin on my face. "It wull be worth it if we can get lead from the mine, besides yea will get ta see more country."

"See much country, not need more country."

"Yea're getting old, Rene. Soon yea wull just want ta sit around an' eat."

"No sit." Rene smiled slyly. "Madame say, Rene protect Jar."

In the morning, we started out, turning east to look for a lead mine that we hoped was still in existence. Every time we came to a good-sized stream we were forced to follow it southeast until there was a place to cross, so in general our course was to the south of east. It was five days before we rode up to the edge of a bluff with the Mississippi below us.

It wasn't nearly as wide as down at St. Louis, but it was still a big river. There were tree-covered islands in sight from where we sat, mostly near the far side. We made camp beside a small stream, in heavy forest. Next day we started north, following the river. That night we camped above a bend where the river took a turn to the northwest. We were finding plenty of signs that people were in the area, but so far we hadn't come across anyone.

Midway through the second day, we spotted smoke from fires over near the river. It was slow going as we made our way through the rough breaks toward the smoke until finally we sighted an Indian village. It was built on high ground above a small stream and back from the river a fair distance. Now we were following a man-made trail and as the horses splashed through the stream people came out to see us and the string of horses we were leading.

We came to a halt at the edge of the village where a man walked out to meet us. From his actions and appearance it was obvious he was a man of authority; giving me the feeling he must be the chief. He was bare-chested except for a bear claw necklace hanging around his neck. He wore moccasins on his feet and deerskin leggings, decorated with quillwork, along with a knee-length breechcloth held in place by a woven sash that hung almost to the ground. Long fur tassels dangled from bands around his upper arms. Along the top of his head was a porcupine quill roach that reminded me of drawings of Roman army officers seen one time in a school book.

A number of people followed him from the village. They stayed back several paces, giving all of us room. The chief stopped to stand looking from one to the other of us and at our pack train. I held up my right hand, palm forward. He did likewise, asking in broken French, "You come trade?"

"Maybe trade. We look for Dubuque."

His face didn't change. "Dubuque come soon, you stay."

Pointing at my chest, I told him, "Jar."

He nodded, pointed at me. "Jar," and tapped his chest. "Peosta." When I repeated his name he nodded again.

Indicating a group of large aspen trees, maybe 200 paces outside the village, I inquired. "Can we camp there?"

"You camp, Dubuque come."

Our campsite was upstream from the village, which was best. We unloaded the horses, stacked our packs for the night and tethered the horses on a patch of grass, not wanting them to wander into the woods. There were cultivated fields where women were weeding crops of corn and beans, with pumpkins growing between the corn plants. We also saw rows of squash and tobacco plants. With all the game available in the area, these people had built a good life for themselves.

I sat with my back against a tree where there was a good view of the village. The lodges looked to be thirty paces long, built with domed roofs covered with bark. Smoke rose from several roof holes along the top. Fish were hung on racks to dry in the sun. Most likely they did the same with deer and buffalo meat. A woman was tending the smoky fires that kept the flies away.

There was activity everywhere. A number of women were gathered in the shade weaving baskets, tanning hides, and making clothes. I could see men busy shaping various items that weren't discernible from this distance. No doubt there was gossip and news to be exchanged. Now the arrival of strangers would give them something else to discuss.

A group of men arrived with four deer slung from poles that

they supported on their shoulders and a little later other men came in with fish. From the number of lodges, there must be several hundred people living in the village. It would take a lot of food to feed them all.

Our packs contained tobacco bought in St. Louis for trading with the Indians and white trappers out west along the Missouri. If these people would trade tobacco, corn and beans and Dubuque could supply our lead needs from his mine it would save the long haul from St. Louis. Of course, the other trade goods would still have to be brought in. It would be less weight to move all that way. Trade would depend on what these people needed or wanted, especially the women.

Peosta came from the village accompanied by a grey-haired man wearing deerskin pants, a cotton shirt and leather boots up to his knees. He was none too clean, but then mining would tend to do that to a man. Getting up to await their arrival, Rene came to stand beside me. I looked like what I was, a redheaded European. When Dubuque saw Rene he grinned, speaking to him in French. "I'm Julien Dubuque, you are French?"

Rene tapped his chest. "Rene Beauchamp, father French, mother Cree."

Dubuque laughed heartily. "Good people those Cree. So you are Métis."

"Me just me." Rene shrugged and turned toward me. "This friend, James Richardson. Call him Jar. Sioux name him Black Arrow."

"Ah, Black Arrow, we have heard of him." He turned to Peosta to talk in a language we didn't understand. They both looked at me. "You are welcome, Black Arrow. What do I call you?"

"Jar will work fine; it is the name Rene uses." I gestured at a big oak tree where our camp was. "Come and sit in the shade."

When we were sitting cross-legged in a circle Dubuque asked, "What brings you to Saukenuk? That is the name of Peosta's village and the area around it."

"We heard that you are mining lead so came to see if you will supply us with what we need for our fur trading out west on the Missouri."

"Why not sell to you? My lead goes to St. Louis and New Orleans, so what you buy, I not need to ship. Give you good deal for American cash. In Orleans I get one American for four pounds. Give you five pounds for one American, cash."

In St. Louis the price was one dollar a pound. "Can you make lead in one pound blocks?"

"Will do. Our lead is poured in eighty pound ingots for shipping. We make one pound for our own use." He fell silent for a few minutes before suggesting, "You stay to see how we dig lead from the ground and see my smelter. It is the only one on the Mississippi."

"It wull be a pleasure to see how yea make lead."

Dubuque laughed at that. "I don't make lead, I find it."

Curious, I asked, "Have yea lived here long, Julien?"

"Came down the Mississippi over twenty years ago. Stopped here to look around and became friends with Peosta. Married one of his sisters. The people here were making decorations from a soft metal they found in caves along the river. It was easy to pound and shape. A few years back I came to realize it was lead. I took a canoe down to Orleans and made a deal with Governor Francisco Luis de Carondelet to mine lead. Have been operating the mine for five years now."

He wasn't a young man. His hair was graying and he was energetic, full of enthusiasm and seemed proud of his mining operation. Anything I learned about mining could prove to be useful. Besides, this would give me an opportunity to observe the way Sauk Indians did things. When we settled down permanently at the valley, gardening would be an important part of our lives. The Sauk knew what worked best for the crops they grew.

Dubuque came for me when we were eating our morning meal. He accepted a tin cup of coffee. We had taken to having coffee in the morning with tea at night. Walking stick in hand, I followed him through the village which proved to be larger than it first appeared. From there, we took a winding path through a thick forest which made it hard to judge distance. There were steep places where the stick was handy. The pistol and hunting knife were behind my belt. Close up, the stick would be the most useful. From experience, I knew few people had any knowledge of stick fighting.

At last we came to a large open area on a bluff above the river where all the trees were gone and only the stumps remained. There were a few crude huts for shelter with a group of men sitting around a fire. Dubuque immediately began yelling instructions in a mixture of French and English which started the men moving.

One group walked off toward the river while five men gathered around a wooden winch built over a square hole in the ground. Motioning me to follow, Dubuque explained that the four foot square hole went down thirty-five feet. At that depth, the diggings were along a crevice where the lead was found. Attached to the round winch was a long handle on each end that two men held onto while a third man climbed onto a wooden platform. When they turned the winch, he disappeared into the hole. In this manner, three men were sent into the ground.

The ocean crossing had given me some knowledge of pulleys. Dubuque's winch was rigged with two lines which cut the travel time in half and made the work of turning it harder. It also reduced the weight that could be moved. Peering over the edge of the hole, as far down as was visible the sides were supported with wood slabs, each made by splitting a log in half. Dubuque explained it was necessary for about nine feet to stop the sides from falling in. Far below, the light from candles made a dim glow in the deep blackness. You could hear the clink, clink of tools chipping at the rock.

A few minutes later, a voice called and the winch began turning until it brought to the surface a cut off wooden barrel filled with chunks of rock. These were dumped into a roughly fashioned wheelbarrow and the empty barrel was lowered back down the shaft. One man wheeled the barrow to an open-sided shed where he began sorting the rock.

Observing the way the men moved, I developed a feeling that if Dubuque wasn't there the work would be going a lot slower. These men weren't very enthusiastic about their jobs and were moving no faster than was required to keep Dubuque from yelling at them.

After midday, he led me down a winding path to the bottom of the cliff where the mighty Mississippi flowed past only a few feet away. You could sense the power in the surging water as it rushed along on its way south. There was a cave in the cliff side, which we entered to find three men working with picks and shovels. To me it was a cave they were enlarging, but Dubuque referred to it as a crevice. He explained that on occasion they found nearly pure lead, although it was normally mixed with other materials.

Being underground wasn't a comfortable feeling. I felt like the walls were closing in, giving me a cramped feeling. It was a big relief when Dubuque finished his explanation of the operation and I could escape without being rude. Back in the sunlight, I looked up at the cliff face. It seemed to be made from two layers of different rock, one a reddish brown with the other a grey color. The whole cliff was about thirty feet high. Dubuque had his mine to supervise, so I took my leave. "Thank you for showing me your operation. It is time for me to be getting back." My French was much improved from the time spent in St. Louis and San Carlos.

"Tomorrow we will be moving the ore from below the cliff here up to the shed. The next day we will smelt it to recover the lead. You come back to see us refine the lead."

"Thank you, I would like ta do that."

On the way back, I came across a group of the large birds that Dubuque referred to as turkeys. They were new to me. Dubuque had talked about how good they were to eat so with the sling from around my waist I killed one. Picking it up by the legs and letting it dangle with is head dragging on the ground, I toted it back the way we came, crossing the village to our camp.

Rene was busy cutting out a pair of moccasins. I cleaned the turkey while relating to him the details of the mining operation. When the bird was spitted over the fire to cook, it was so large that it wouldn't finish cooking until the next day.

While we were talking, Rene pointed. Chief Peosta was coming with two women, bringing us a cooked fish on a wooden platter along with a type of bread they made from ground corn. It was the first food we hadn't cooked for ourselves since leaving St. Louis.

Peosta stayed to share the fish with us. When I asked, he agreed to take us out to the fields to see how they planted and grew their crops.

On smelting day Dubuque came by our camp at sunup to take me with him to see the process, leaving Rene with the packs. Alongside the sorting shed were several flat-topped rocks that had been there on my first visit. He put men to work smashing the ore into small pieces using square-shaped blacksmith hammers.

While the ore was being broken, other men started a fire in a rock-lined pit with a low rock wall above ground. As soon as the fire was well established a barrow-load of charcoal was wheeled out and part of the load was added to the fire. That explained all the tree stumps; Dubuque was cutting down the trees to make charcoal. Next, a flat iron plate with a round hole in the center was placed over the fire pit. A man came with a bellows and started pumping air through a hole in the stone wall. Very quickly, the fire became so intense I could feel the heat from several paces away.

Dubuque showed me the melting ladle, a round iron pot with a pouring lip on one side. Round handles stuck out on the other three sides. "This ladle will hold over a hundred pounds of lead so we can fill one mold and get started on a second one with each melt."

The ladle didn't completely fill the hole as it rested on its handles. Hot flames came up around it. In just a few minutes he gave the order to start filling it with ore. As the lead melted, it settled to the bottom of the ladle and a shallow iron spoon was used to skim off the bits of rock, sand and grit that floated to the top. As soon as all the debris was removed more ore was added. This process continued until the ladle was full of lead.

Four molds sat side by side on the ground. Three men lifted the ladle and positioned it over the first mold. The men on the side handles held it steady while the third used his handle to tilt the ladle. Lead poured into the mold, which they filled before moving to the next one. It wasn't much different from what we did when we cast balls for our long guns, except for the use of charcoal. As we watched I asked about that. "Why do ya go to all the trouble of making charcoal when a plain wood fire will melt lead?"

Dubuque laughed heartily. "Because, you see, I need a hotter fire to get the impurities out of the lead. When first I started mining we used wood fires and everyone complained about the grit. They said I was cheating them. Now my lead is better than what comes from Spain."

We stayed on for five days, went hunting with Chief Peosta and traded for beaver, muskrat, mink, otter, and wolverine. We traded carefully, making sure to be fair. The Sauk were shrewd, intelligent people. Their furs were well prepared and we were interested in repeat business. The wolverine furs were a problem because I knew not if there was a market for such fur. Reluctantly, we accepted them. Peosta looked on when I drew a map in the dirt to show him where the trading post would be on Peters River. He nodded, saying he had been in the area. Dubuque told us about his Spanish Mining Grant that covered 300 square miles on the west side of the Mississippi. He winked at me when he related that each year the Governor received a share of the profits.

Our last night there the Sauk invited us to a feast where Chief Peosta gave a long speech with Dubuque interpreting for us. Peosta related the history of his people, who came from far to the east on a big river where they lived for a long, long time before being pushed out by white men arriving. After many years they found this place, on the River of Rock, where they built their village. The people increased in numbers, spreading out to establish other villages. Now the Sauk and Fox people lived in a large area to the west and south of Saukenuk.

The Osage were on the south and the Sioux on the north. In good times they traded with each other and in times of disagreement went to war. The great river protected them on the east. His speech was long and the people listened carefully, although it was a story they must have heard many times.

Long into the night they talked, danced, sang and ate a wide variety of food. Venison, buffalo, elk meat, several types of fish and from their stores corn, beans, pumpkin seeds, nuts and other things gathered from the forests around. They were a healthy, industrious people living a well ordered life together in a land that provided almost everything they needed, except for the iron and brass tools they wanted to make life easier. These things had to come from trade with the white man.

By being fair in my trade with them, hopefully in the future we could supply much of what they wanted in return for furs, corn, beans and tobacco.

Late into the night we talked. Dubuque told us about growing up in Montreal until he was seventeen before coming west with his father to work in the fur trade. Dubuque became sentimental as he remembered his youth and the family he left behind. "Always intended to go back, now forty years have passed. I wouldn't know anyone and Montreal will be changed. I wouldn't fit in and my French is not so good anymore. They would all look at me from the eye corners and laugh behind my back." Dubuque seemed to enjoy talking French with us and recovering his skill with the words.

Eventually, he returned to the present to complain about the boatmen who were unreliable. "The keel boat is many days late bringing my supplies from St. Louis. It should have come a month, no more, ago." Julien slapped his hand on one leg in frustration. "I need to take my lead to St. Louis and Orleans two times between winters."

Listening to him, I heard only opportunity. "Do you send two loads of lead south each year?"

"Yes, I do. All winter we mine lead. It must be sold in the spring to get money to buy supplies and pay my men." Julien waved his hands. "Before winter comes the lead must be sold to buy all the things necessary to mine over winter." He jumped to his feet and paced around the fire. "Now everything is late. I should be in Orleans by now. No, I should be coming back by now. These lazy boatmen cause me much trouble. What is there to do?" Julien shrugged and came back to sit by the fire. He sat quietly, obviously worried and feeling helpless.

Waving my curved stem pipe I inquired, "Do you know Auguste Chouteau in St. Louis?"

Julien's head came up and he smiled. "Met old Chouteau twenty years ago when he was just a *jeune homme.* Why do you ask?"

"Chouteau has a niece in San Carlos, Madame Chadron, who manages the Chadron Mercantile."

"That so! Last time in San Carlos I talked to Chadron. How come his wife is doing his job for him?"

"Chadron died last spring. Madame Chadron runs the mercantile and has keel boats to haul freight on the Missouri and Mississippi for anyone who needs to have goods moved."

Dubuque eyed me with a doubtful look on his face. "Do they do a good job and on time?"

"We have hired them to bring our trade goods up the Missouri." While he was thinking, I added, "You can contact Madame Chadron through Chouteau or just stop in San Carlos and talk to her."

"By damn, Julien will do that. If the boats come on time, Julien will keep using Chadron's boats."

"Rene and I have furs on hand. Could you take them to Chouteau when you go down river with your ingots of lead?"

"Why not? Lead is heavy, still it takes little room. Julien will take your furs to Chouteau."

"Thank you, Julien, it will lighten the load on our horses. Could you take a letter to Chouteau for me?"

"Damn rights, you write letter, Julien will take it."

First light found me sitting at the fire writing on letter paper brought from St. Louis; for the first time using black India ink and a pen with a metal nib. There were ink blobs along with the writing for which I apologized to Madame, promising to improve. The ink was intended for the maps I planned to draw on a supply of heavy paper purchased for the purpose. When the letters were done I wrapped them in oil cloth to keep them dry and sewed both into a deerskin pouch for further protection. If Dubuque got to St. Louis the letters should arrive in good condition. On the outside I printed Chouteau's name in black ink.

At our parting Dubuque told us, "Word off the river is of fighting to the north. Indians from across the Mississippi are trying to push the Sioux off their lands. You ride careful."

Chapter 11

Riding west to clear the river breaks and be out on the grasslands, we used up the last of the day. With Dubuque taking the furs to St. Louis, the horses were carrying lighter loads, allowing us to travel faster. Now we were anxious to get back. It was very tempting to cut across to the northwest to save time. The problem was this was still new country to us. It was better to go north until we found something familiar. This was the safest route, staying with the river until we recognized landmarks. After a hurried breakfast, Rene led off, setting a faster pace, both of us now wanting to end the traveling. Around midday, the horses waded across a good-sized stream that was flowing east to the Mississippi, stopping in the middle to drink their fill.

Next day, we came up to strange-looking mounds of dirt with the Mississippi below us on the east. There was forest as far as the eye could see on the other side of the river and the islands in the river were covered with trees. Turning in the saddle to look west, it was tall grass all the way to the far horizon with trees growing only in the drainage areas along streams and lakes. Riding through the scattered trees, we stopped to look curiously at the mounds. They made no sense, all being different shapes and sizes.

"These ar' too irregular ta be natural like the conical hills we saw last fall oot West."

Rene shrugged his shoulders, leaning both hands on the saddle horn. “Old people make, long time ago.”

Frowning, I looked at him. “Yea thinks these piles were made by people who lived here?

“Old people live here long time ago.” Rene shrugged again. “Now forgotten.”

“It took a lot of work an’ time ta move all this dirt. Why would they do that?”

“Not know why. Maybe great spirit tell old people to make.”

“Yea may be right, Rene.” I looked at him thoughtfully. “Do yea think they wur’ buryin’ their people in these piles?” Rene just shrugged again, not being prepared to comment, which was his way. He rarely spoke of anything he wasn’t sure about.

Two hours later, I was still thinking about the mounds when we came upon more of the same style of dirt piles. Only now many of the mounds were out on the grassland where it was easier to see the shapes. Ground hitching my horse, I swung down from the saddle and climbed the side of one small mound to better see the others scattered around. Right beside me was a peculiar looking mound. After puzzling over it for some time it came to me. The mound was shaped like a dog with its back to me.

In surprise I yelled, “Rene, come here an’ see this. It’s shaped like a dog.”

Rene climbed the mound to stand beside me. He looked for a long time. “Not dog, is bear.”

After he told me it was clear. The shape of the body and head was a bear. Looking at other mounds, Rene pointed. “Bird.” Later, he pointed to a long curving shape to announce, “Snake.”

Walking around them, it wasn’t easy to recognize the shapes for what they were. Why would they go to all the trouble to do this? “Rene, do yea think the old people who built these mounds worshiped birds an’ animals?”

“Rene not know. Animals, trees, rocks have spirit.”

“Yes, yea are right. Could they have built these shapes ta honor the things they needed in their daily lives?”

Rene grinned. “You too much think, just is. Not matter why.”

Laughing, I agreed. “Yea ar’ right, my friend. All the same, I sure would like ta know why yer old people built these.”

“Not matter. Not my people.”

What Rene said caused me to think that this was just one more sign that people had been living on this land for a long, long time. I wondered what other secrets were waiting to be discovered. If I knew more about this type of thing, maybe I’d be able to make sense of the signs the Old People left behind. Well, at least with the log it could be recorded in a small way.

Shaking my head, I told Rene. “Guess we should be going an’ make a few more miles afore dark.” Rene walked to his horse and swung into the saddle to sit waiting for me.

Continuing to travel north, two days later the river took a decided turn to the northwest. Keeping well out on the grasslands where the going was easiest, we became even more cautious. We were getting close to Sioux country. If they were being invaded we didn’t want to be surprised by any enemies from across the river. Three days later, back in familiar country, Rene turned west, leaving the Mississippi behind; Peters River was ahead. The route we chose would go around the south end of the elbow where the river made a turn to the northeast, allowing us to avoid fording Peters twice.

We camped for the night in a small glade with our backs to a steep bluff, well sheltered and hidden from view. I climbed to the top of the bluff from where the country all around was visible. While watching for any sign of other travelers, the sun slowly set. The horses were on the grass below the bluff where I could see them while Rene was scouting through the trees. As darkness claimed the land we both returned to camp for the night, satisfied that no one was around.

Sitting in camp after eating, with our pipes lit, Rene told me, "Six days, you home."

"Ay, it wull be good ta get back." I blew smoke and puffed to keep the pipe going. "Since winter ended we hae made some miles mah friend." Rene nodded in agreement. "Do yea think Andre wull be at the valley when we arrive?"

Rene shrugged. "Andre come soon. Maybe him there now."

"We wull need ta set up a guid camp with shelter from storms. After that, we can start cutting trees ta build a trading post."

"Andre know. Him cut trees."

That hadn't occurred to me. "Yea ar' right, Rene, if Andre is back he wull make a start afore we arrive."

Rene observed. "Need make two buildings. One for sleep, one for trade. Better if fire come."

Of course Rene was right. Fires were always a danger in the

winter when you tried to keep the inside of a cabin warm. With two separate buildings there would be another place to take shelter if one burned down. I pointed at him with the pipe. "Yea ar' smart, ma friend. We wull do just that."

Rene nodded in agreement. "Rene see many cabin burn. Is bad when big storm come." The campfire was down to just a bed of coals. We found our beds and settled in for the night.

Progress was slowed by our caution. Constant changes in direction to avoid any place suited to ambush used a lot of time. Rene was out in front, always taking the least likely routes; not the easiest or fastest for travel. By mid-afternoon we were looking for a place to spend the night. Our route was pointed at a gap in a line of low hills and bluffs ahead of us. Nearing the entrance to the gap, Rene suddenly veered left to start south along the slope. Riding half-turned in the saddle, I kept an eye on the gap as we moved away. Nothing showed. I had learned long since to trust Rene's instincts. There might be no danger waiting there for us, but it was the obvious route for a traveler to take, so he was avoiding it.

No good campsite showed, so we kept going until Rene stopped to wait for me to catch up. He pointed at a shallow dip in the ridgeline. With my head tipped up to scan the ridge and before any comment could be made, three Sioux warriors rode from the trees to sit their horses, watching us. They were from the local Santee branch of the great Sioux Nation, people we had traded with for two years. These would be members of the Akicita Society which trained warriors to protect the rest of the community. They each wore a single eagle feather at the back of their heads and were armed with bows, tomahawks, and spears.

Holding up my right arm, palm toward them, we waited. Finally, one warrior responded and they rode down the slope toward us. From exposure to sun and wind I was as brown as Rene so one hand removed my leather hat while the other rubbed my head; it let them see the red hair. Replacing the floppy hat, I sat with the Charleville across the saddle, waiting.

They stopped some three horse lengths away to look us over. The oldest of the three looked at the bow behind my saddle before turning his eyes to Rene. I spoke to them in Sioux. "Greetings to my Santee friends."

He looked steadily at me for a moment. "You Black Arrow?" I nodded and waited. "Where you come?"

My left arm pointed south. "Many suns along the great river. Trade furs."

He digested that before replying. "Black Arrow come Santee camp, talk chief." Turning their horses, they started up the slope to the shallow pass with us following. The horses climbed the slope through the trees into the pass where three more Sioux warriors stood beside horses. Obviously, the Santee were on guard and concerned about anyone who might enter their lands. One warrior nodded as we rode by and continued through the pass. It was almost dark when we arrived at a large encampment set up between two small lakes.

There were five chiefs from different villages, come together for a council. Two we knew from trading along Peters River. They greeted us and sent for food. The other three chiefs were from villages located north of Peters along the Mississippi.

They didn't make long speeches as was the custom. Instead, they explained quickly that the Chippewa from far to the northeast had attacked a Sioux village located up the Mississippi where the Crow Wing River flowed in. Many people were killed and lodges burned. The Chippewa took women, children, food and many items away. Chippewa warriors were now moving slowly south toward the next two villages. This gathering of Sioux was a war council to discuss the best way to deal with the invaders. Chief Crow Foot, whom we knew from trading explained, "There are many Chippewa. They have muskets from the French with much powder. Sioux have only bows and spears."

After considering all they said, I asked, "Do the Chippewa have horses?"

"No horses."

"That is good because they must move on foot." I was searching for positive factors to encourage them. "Your horses give you great speed to outmaneuver them."

"That good where no trees, not good by river."

I nodded in agreement. "What you say is true. In times of war one must use whatever strengths he has to the best advantage. With horses, Sioux warriors can move quickly to attack in many places. You can surprise them many times and give them no rest."

"Black Arrow speaks wisely, but Chippewa muskets scare horses. Sioux must get close for arrows to reach enemy."

A few moments considering brought me to a decision. Holding up my Charleville to show them I explained. "This long gun will shoot further than the muskets the Chippewa have." We waited while the two local chiefs explained about my shooting, getting nods of agreement from the other chiefs. "We have ten guns like this." I held up ten fingers. "They will shoot much further than the Chippewa muskets."

"Black Arrow will trade guns?"

"My friends the Santee are at war. Santee take the long guns to use for fighting your enemies. Next winter you trap beaver to trade."

"Does Black Arrow have powder?"

My hands showed twenty fingers. "Powder to shoot twenty times. Tomorrow we will melt lead to make musket balls. Chiefs pick ten warriors to use the guns. We will clean the guns and show your warriors how to load and shoot them."

The silence lasted as they thought about my offer. A ring of warriors standing outside the circle listened and watched. Glancing at Rene, his impassive face showed nothing. Finally, one chief asked, "One gun, how much beaver?"

So I explained. "These guns are much better than the muskets the Chippewa have. They will shoot farther and are more accurate. Better guns take more beaver for Black Arrow to trade in St. Louis. One gun, powder and shot for twenty prime beaver. Santee bring beaver next summer." We sat quietly beside the fire until, after much discussion among the chiefs, it was agreed.

Wrapped in robes, we settled down for the night with our backs leaning against our packs. Stars came out and I watched them, wondering how many there were, just as I had done as a lad back in Scotland. There was no way of knowing how many although there were plenty. As the big dipper made its circle I woke from time to time to look at it. When the eastern sky began to lighten, the camp came to life.

Rene helped me carry the two boxes of guns to the center of camp. The chiefs gathered around as we opened the boxes, using hunting knifes to pry up the lids. Each long gun came with a barrel plug, a ramrod for loading and cleaning, along with spare flints, springs and screws. The cow knees were in place, covering the powder pans. While the chiefs inspected the guns we brought a keg of powder, ten one-pound blocks of lead and a ladle for melting the lead. Rene went back for ball molds.

Rene positioned a ladle over a fire and added a pound of lead. The warriors learned how to cast balls, each of the ten men taking a turn at doing it. When the guns were distributed I used the Charleville to demonstrate how to clean the grease off and make sure the mechanism was working smoothly. With the ramrods we cleaned the inside of the barrels. They were adept students and soon the rifles were ready for use.

Rene picked up a deerskin and with charcoal from one of the fires, drew a circle as big as his head in the center of it. We hung it between two trees and stepped off fifty paces, where Rene drew a line in the dirt using a stick.

Now for the hardest part. Beckoning them to follow, we went back to the deer hide with the whole camp gathered around watching. Using an arrow to demonstrate, I explained. "When you shoot an arrow you aim above the target." Placing my hand a foot above the circle, I repeated. "You aim here so the arrow hits in the circle."

Stepping back a few paces I pretended to shoot a bow. With the arrow in hand I showed how it arced up and then came down to hit the target. The crowd was howling with laughter. This was something everyone knew and they were enjoying the show. We laughed along with them.

Taking a lead ball from my pouch, I held it up for them to see. "It is the same with a gun." This time I put my finger just above the circle. "With the gun you aim here and the ball hits in the circle." The warriors nodded their heads, understanding the explanation.

A group of young boys crowded around, interested in the demonstration and I got them to stand in a line. It was a quiet morning with no breeze. Getting them to blow like the wind, I demonstrated how the wind would affect a ball, just like an arrow. Now even the warriors laughed along with the crowd.

Going back to the line they learned how to aim a long gun. I loaded the Charleville, going slowly and taking time to explain each step. Shouldering the gun, I shot at the target. We went to look at the hole which was very near the center of the circle. Rene marked a cross over it with charcoal. As each of them took a turn, we inspected the holes and crossed them off. No one hit the circle. They all hit the deer hide, which was as good as many white men could do at fifty paces.

Each warrior loaded his gun and shot at the target twice more while everyone watched. We cleaned the guns again so they could see the bits of unburned black powder from inside the barrels. I explained the importance of keeping the guns clean. A few more days like this would improve my communication skills in the Sioux language.

The war council resumed with much discussion among the

chiefs and elders. They were all members of the Naca Society which governed the villages, making vital decisions such as going to war with neighbors. In this case, it would be a decision involving five villages.

We sat in the shade of a tree to listen to their debate. The chief of the Crow Wing Village, which suffered the attack, gave a long speech lamenting the loss of life and property, urging the others to join him in going to war. Watching the people, I was impressed. They were mostly tall with fine features, although the older people tended to be wrinkled and weathered from much exposure to the elements. From experience, I knew the men were brave, great hunters and excellent horsemen.

The younger men were bare-chested while the older men wore deerskin shirts. The women's deerskin dresses were decorated with quills with each dress having a different design. They all wore their black hair in two braids.

In true Indian fashion, every member of the Naca was given the opportunity to speak. The orations went on as the sun worked its way toward the west. Just at dusk two scouts rode in on tired ponies to report the Chippewa had moved south to the little falls of the Mississippi. They would be at the Mnisota River in three days which would put two more villages at risk. Mnisota was the Santee name for Peters River. In the Sioux language the name meant 'water reflecting the sky.'

They believed in open discussion, but when necessity required decisions were made rapidly. The women, children and old people would remain in camp with a handful of Akicita to provide security. A warrior came to bring us to the council where the two chiefs we knew from trading were standing up, waiting.

"Council asks will Black Arrow and his friend Rene join our warriors to fight the Chippewa?"

It was a serious question; one to be considered carefully. I looked as grave as they had all day. The Chief continued. "Black Arrow has brought good long guns to the Santee. He has shown our warriors how to shoot. Black Arrow is a friend to the Santee and we would be honored if he joins our warriors. He can shoot far which will bring much fear to the Chippewa. Black Arrow has strong medicine in signs he makes and always he speaks truth. Santee need strong medicine to make war."

There was the logbook again and my habit of making notes, which they had seen me do many times. It was a small thing to white men that was impressive to the natives who didn't understand what it was. Of course, Rene's storytelling encouraged their beliefs.

I considered gravely before speaking to Rene in English, keeping my voice low. He answered, "Is great honor they give you. Believe your strong medicine will help. Must do."

"What about our trade goods?"

"They won't be touched while we are fighting with the Santee." Rene's arm swung in a circle to point at all the people around us. I nodded at him in agreement. Honestly, if they hadn't invited me I would have volunteered. There was something in me that liked a good fight. Maybe it was in all Scots. The clans certainly had a long history of fighting with the English and when there were no English, with each other.

Turning back to the Chiefs, I spoke solemnly. "The Akicita of the Santee Sioux are great warriors. The Chippewa will tremble in fear when they see them coming. It is a great honor for us to be invited to join our friends, the Santee, to fight their enemies. We will fight with the Akicita and thank the Naca for honoring us this way."

Warriors quickly prepared to leave. We saddled our horses, leaving everything behind except our weapons. Pulling a leather hunting shirt over my head to cover the cotton shirt, which was wearing thin from use, I prepared to leave. Rene did the same.

The three warriors who had guided us to the camp waited for us. In minutes the horses were carrying everyone into the night to join those who were tracking the progress of the enemy.

All night and into the day we rode, passing two villages where more warriors joined. At a ford I didn't know existed, we crossed Peters River, continuing on the north side to the joining with the Mississippi. There, at midday, meat was cooked and we ate and rested. The horses especially needed rest after sixteen hours of travel.

The Sioux were planning to set up an ambush where the Sauk River meets the Mississippi. With the horses, we would be able to get there well before the Chippewa could as they came down the west side of the Mississippi on foot. After only a few hours of rest the caravan of warriors was on the move again. Next morning, just after first light, we halted well away from the Sauk River crossing.

We listened as the leaders discussed setting up the ambush. The Chippewa would be wary of an ambush at the ford on the Sauk so no one would be there to alert them. Sioux warriors would be waiting for them at a gully about an hour's walk south of the ford when the enemy would be relaxing and letting down their guard. Two groups of warriors, including those from Crow Wing Village, would cross the Sauk further upstream and be ready to attack from the rear after the fight at the ambush started. They would get any stragglers or those fleeing from the ambush.

Our group would be on the west side of the ambush with four long guns. One of the War Chiefs asked, "How is best to use guns?"

My answer was, "Place the warriors with guns fifty paces back from the trail and use them to shoot the Chippewa warriors carrying muskets. After that Sioux warriors with bows and spears can move more safely." Motioning with the Charleville I added, "It takes time to reload a long gun. Two men shoot while two wait until guns half-loaded before they shoot. Always have rifles ready that way."

He nodded and spoke to the others too fast for me to follow. From his gestures, he was explaining my suggestion.

The Sioux were masters at arranging an ambush to catch an enemy at a disadvantage. We watched as the war chief positioned his warriors. He sent scouts to watch the ford from a distance and bring word the enemy was approaching. He stationed three young warriors on the trail where the Chippewa would see them as they approached the north side of the gully. The young warriors got instructions to flee south down the trail as soon as they were seen by the Chippewa.

Everyone settled into hiding to await the arrival of the enemy. It was uncommonly quiet in the forest, with only a few small birds flying from tree to tree. Even they seemed subdued. With so many warriors present in the area the wildlife was in hiding. If the Chippewa were sensitive to this unusual condition it would be a warning to them.

A Sioux warrior came silently through the trees to report the enemy was approaching the ford with an advance party of scouts crossing first. As expected, the Chippewa were wary of a trap. An attempt to attack them at the Sauk River would have been detected. Now there was time for them to relax if they behaved as expected.

The Sioux on the Mississippi side of the ambush would attack first in order to drive the enemy away from the river and west toward us. Behind our position, additional Sioux warriors were waiting on their horses for any enemy that got past us.

Whilc waiting, I recalled Mac talking about battles—how a few of the best archers were always designated to watch for enemy officers and aim arrows at them. His words were clear in my head. *'Many a time, Jamie, if yea eliminate the officers the battle is won. Without leaders the others soon lose heart an' their discipline falls apart.'* It might not be the same with the Chippewa. If this thought had come earlier, I could have asked how the chiefs would be dressed. Rene was beside me so I whispered to him. "If we can identify the Chippewa leaders we should try ta shoot them first."

He thought about that. "You want to shoot war chiefs?"

"If we get the chiefs, the warrior's wull have no leaders ta direct the battle."

Rene nodded thoughtfully. "You smart for white man."

"Learned everything from Métis. How will we know who the leaders ar'?"

"Just look." He shrugged as he often did when there was no answer.

It seemed to take forever. From our position, trees hid the

approach to the gully so the enemy wouldn't be visible to us until they were close. The three young Sioux being used as bait to lure the Chippewa into acting rashly were on the trail where we could see them standing casually, carrying on a discussion as if they had no concerns. One was standing where he could see the gully, another was leaning on a tree looking relaxed and obviously not expecting trouble.

They were playing a vitally important role in the ambush which was intended to cause the enemy to rush forward hurriedly in an attempt to capture them and prevent news of the Chippewa presence being reported. If it worked the Chippewa in their haste would forget about their flanks for a short time. It was a serious responsibility. The calmness of the young Sioux in the face of the risks they were taking was admirable, even if it was only on the outside. The Sioux loved any type of game, war being their favorite one. War was a way for the young men to display their courage and skill to win great honor in the tribe.

Suddenly, the Sioux warrior facing the gulley straightened and pointed down the trail saying something which caused the other two to turn and look. They stood there staring for an instant, just out of arrow range of the enemy. Hurriedly, the Sioux lifted their bows and shot arrows towards the Chippewa, which appeared to fall short into the gully. Turning, they started away, looking back over their shoulders.

Chippewa warriors came running across the gully in pursuit, yelling as they came. We heard the yelling before the warriors came into view. In size they were similar to the Sioux. While the Sioux wore their black hair in long braids, the Chippewa hair was piled high on their heads with pieces of vegetation woven in. The effect was to make them appear much taller. Their mostly naked bodies were marked with lines and designs that appeared to be war paint. There were a lot of warriors. We were outnumbered so our surprise better work. Five Chippewa warriors came out of the gully, running fast and raced past us in pursuit of the Sioux bait. Our war chief patiently waited, allowing them to pass by until the main group of Chippewa warriors came surging out of the gully.

Edging the Charleville forward to rest on a branch, I picked my first target. He was older than most of the others with the look of a leader, so my eyes followed him. He was armed with a long-handled tomahawk, not a musket. I was going to get him first before the warriors with muskets.

You couldn't load a long gun lying down, so we were behind big trees to have shelter after the first shot. Suddenly, the Sioux on the far side of the ambush opened the battle by firing their guns and raining a shower of arrows on the Chippewa, hitting several of them. The Sioux charged toward the enemy with spears, tomahawks and knives, going for close-in hand to hand fighting. Yelling was a normal part of Indian fighting and both sides were making the forest ring with their war cries.

My long gun followed the man who appeared to be a leader. As expected, there was some confusion and the Chippewa stood still for an instant as the Sioux charged. When he stopped moving, I shot and watched him go down. Now there was no time to watch what was going on. While I reloaded, Rene shot. We would be lucky if each of us got two shots away before it became hand to hand fighting.

The Chippewa with muskets were easy to spot because of the

smoke from the black powder. Their first shots were towards the Sioux on the other side, so the smoke didn't hide them from our view. My second shot hit a warrior while he was reloading. He dropped his musket and staggered back toward the gully.

Moving fast to reload, I glanced up to see a big Chippewa warrior coming straight at me with a spear. There was no time to finish reloading. I dropped the long gun and grabbed the pistol from behind my belt, pointed it and fired without lifting it above my waist. As he disappeared from sight in the black smoke, I dropped the pistol and dodged left in case it was a miss and he was still coming. Grabbing my fighting stick, a two-inch thick seven-foot long oak rod, I leapt into the battle. The Chippewa warrior was down, shot in the chest.

Now there was fighting, yelling and the clash of weapons everywhere. The noise was deafening. War cries mingled with screams from the wounded and dying. Rene grabbed a fallen spear as we waded in. It was too close for arrows; this was all knives, spears and clubs. At close quarters, the fighting stick was more versatile, allowing me to react faster. It was more effective than knives and spears.

A Chippewa warrior ran at Rene, swinging a tomahawk. Thrusting hard, the stick crushed the side of his neck and dropped him. Another warrior came at me holding a knife with the cutting edge up. Knocking the knife arm aside with the stick, I kicked the warrior in the groin with my right boot and followed with a hard thrust into his throat. After that, I kept moving as Mac taught me. The fighting became a blur of thrust, parry and kick. I never did get my knife or tomahawk out. It was hot and sweaty with the noise deafening from the yelling and the cries of the injured. The visibility was good after the long guns went silent. Rene and several Sioux were fighting alongside me.

As suddenly as it began, it was over. The Chippewa warriors were scattering with the Sioux in pursuit. Carefully checking around for any enemy warriors who might remain, all I saw were the wounded and dead. I looked for Rene and saw him leaning against a tree with blood all over his hunting shirt. Seeing him like that scared me more than anything ever had before in my life. Rene was injured and it looked bad. Nothing else mattered as I ran to get to him. As gently as possible, I helped him to a sitting position with the tree trunk to support his back. Rene explained, "Spear cut side."

With his help we got the hunting shirt off. Then the red cotton shirt he was so proud of. There was an ugly gash across his right side just below the ribs. It was gaping open and bleeding badly. "We have to close this wound. Hold yea'r shirt over it while I run fer my sewing kit."

Sprinting as fast as the forest would allow, I got to my horse, grabbed the saddlebags and raced back. Still panting, I suggested, "It wull be better if yea lie on your side." I eased him down to the ground on his left side.

Threading a needle with heavy thread, I pulled the sides of the gash together and Rene held it closed with his left hand. Sewing the wound was slow work, trying to be careful and gentle, as I pulled the thread through Rene's flesh to close the gash. He lay on his side with his jaws tightly clenched, making no sound, just watching me work. My mother wouldn't have thought much of the rough stitches. Even so, they were good enough to hold the two sides of the wound together. When the sewing was finished my forehead was wet with sweat. I looked up as I wiped my brow and several Sioux warriors were watching intently. I instructed Rene, “Yea keep the wound covered with yea’r shirt while I gather moss.”

Rene was getting weak from the loss of blood and the shock from the injury was setting in. He managed a weak grin. Finding dry moss this time of year took a while. Finally, the wound was covered and held in place with Rene’s sash. “Yea rest easy now while I fetch the water jug. Yea wull need ta drink plenty of water ta replace all this blood that leaked out.”

Returning with the horses and the jug of water, Rene needed help taking a drink. Clearing a space on the forest floor, I gathered material to start a fire. With the fire burning, I shaved jerky into Rene’s tin cup, added water and set it close to the fire to heat. A little hot broth would help to restore his energy. Who knows, maybe it would also cheer him up. Rene kept drinking from the jug of water, which would help. While the broth heated, I retrieved our long guns and other gear. Rene watched me clean the guns and reload them. Sitting down beside him, I offered the tin cup of broth. Rene took small sips from time to time and we talked quietly until he dozed off.

Sioux warriors gathered the fallen weapons and herded the captured Chippewa together in the gully where they could be held. It was difficult to ignore the screams from the wounded Chippewa when the Sioux began getting their revenge.

Many Sioux went off in pursuit of fleeing enemy and might be gone for several days. After the noise of battle, the silence was deafening.

Setting about making a camp right where we were kept me busy while Rene slept. I cleared forest debris in a circle around the cooking fire to stop it from spreading and placed rocks in a circle to make a guard to keep the fire contained. With young fir boughs, I put together a thick bed and added a covering of grass to make it softer. When Rene's buffalo robe was spread over it and he was moved, he went back to sleep. Rene would be warm and rest easier now.

The cup was empty, so I refilled it and set it near the fire to heat. Sitting there near Rene, I cut a bite of jerky and slowly chewed. Later, wandering around, I picked up a few items, spears, knives and tomahawks and found a musket the enemy left behind and stood it against a tree.

I went to look at the man my first shot killed. The lead ball had entered the left side of his chest and didn't come out. He was laying beside the trail, a sturdy looking man of about Rene's age, towards whom there was no animosity in me. Under other circumstances we could have been friends. Such were the ways of war. It could easily have been Rene lying there. What appeared to be war paint turned out to be patterns tattooed on his skin in various interesting designs. They probably told a story or had some special meaning to the Chippewa. To me they were just a curiosity.

When Rene woke up, he asked for the bark of a willow tree to ease his pain from the injury. Taking the cooking pot with me, I cut long strips of inner bark off young, pliable willows and shredded them into the pot. When the pot was nearly full I returned to our camp. Rene was awake, so I gave him some of the bark to chew on. It might not help but it would give him something to do while the rest of the bark boiled to make a drink. When the water was boiling, I used a small stick to stir the pot and keep the bark mixed to get the most value out of it. When it seemed to be ready, the stick served to remove strands of the bark until most of it was gone. Using my hunting knife to serve as a dam just inside the lip of the pot, I strained out the remaining bark and filled Rene's cup, setting it aside to cool.

The next time Rene woke up the broth was ready and he drank it before going back to sleep. I added more bark to the pot and boiled it again to have another batch ready.

For three days we lazed around until Rene got back on his feet. He was weak, needing more time to heal and build back his strength. Our camp was too close to the battleground where the stench from decaying bodies was bad, so Rene agreed we should move to a small spring of water located west of our present site. It was near the edge of the trees and well sheltered. Rene insisted on helping. I didn't object. He wasn't used to sitting idle and while he couldn't do much, just being useful would be good for him. We would be there for several days, so we built a shelter in case of rain with a reflector for our fire. We did many things to make the camp comfortable; things a man wouldn't normally bother with.

With Rene and the gear settled, it was time to go hunting. It was great to be back on a horse moving around the country again. It was most of five miles to a small stream. Riding at a walk upwind through the scattered trees, it wasn't long until a large buck feeding with his does showed ahead. Leaving the horses securely tied to trees, I managed to work my way close and dropped the buck with an arrow. A man feels proud riding into camp with fresh meat for eating. Rene watched me unload the meat from his horse and hang it from a tree branch. Now there was plenty to eat and a deer hide to be scraped and tanned.

The Sioux held a council which lasted for two days. Afterwards, the old Chief of the Crow Wing Village came to sit at our fire. He just sat there saying nothing for a long time. We waited, knowing he'd talk when he was ready. After the long silence, he looked carefully at Rene before turning his old eyes on me. Those eyes felt to me like they were looking into my very soul. A number of warriors came to listen and stood around the campsite watching.

Finally, the chief started. "Black Arrow is great warrior, fight bravely, good friend to Santee. Always talk truth. Give Santee wise advice. Sioux have won a great victory over the Chippewa. Black Arrow helped. Council asks. What Black Arrow do with Chippewa prisoners?"

I took a long time to consider. He watched me as my mind searched for the right answer. It couldn't be a short answer in such serious circumstances. When he arrived I was writing in the log. Picking it up, I opened the pages and read out loud the description of the fight that was partially finished, mumbling the words. If any of them knew English words, the exaggerated Scottish accent would prevent them from understanding. My finger held the pages open when I looked up. Everyone was staring at the book which they considered to be great magic.

The old chief sat, watching me. After looking back at him for several minutes, I started. "Crow Wing Village suffered a great loss from the Chippewa attack. Many lodges were burnt, much property stolen and many friends killed. This brings much sorrow to the Sioux. Santee went to war and have won a great victory, with many Chippewa killed. There will be much wailing in Chippewa lodges.

Santee have captured many muskets, knives and tomahawks. The Chippewa have paid a great price for their treachery. After this they will not attack the Santee for many seasons and long will they tell their young of the bravery of Sioux warriors. Now they know the Sioux have long guns that shoot far. The Chippewa will be afraid."

When I glanced at Rene, he nodded his head slightly. "To be a great chief of the Santee you must be wise in all things. A great chief makes decisions that are good for all his people. Old men wish to sit by the fire in peace while young warriors look for war to prove their bravery. A great chief must decide what is best for all his people. The Santee will rebuild their lodges better than they were before. Warriors will hunt for deer and buffalo to replace all that was lost. Soon, the Santee will be better and stronger than before. A great chief must also think of the Santee women and children who were taken from their lodges and are missing their families."

Stopping for a moment to look around at the faces watching, I decided to let the silence last before continuing. "Black Arrow says this to the Chief and these brave warriors listening." My arm swung to point at the braves gathered around. "Pick two Chippewa warriors from those captured and send them home with a message for their chiefs. Tell these warriors to say. 'Bring the women and children of Crow Wing Village back to the great river. The Santee will trade your Chippewa warriors in exchange. If you do not do this all the captured warriors will die.'"

His eyes never left me while I talked. He looked at the book, eyeing it for a long time. Slowly, he got to his feet, his old knees creaking from the effort. "Black Arrow is wise as always. I will tell his words to the council."

Five more days we stayed there before Rene was ready to ride. His side was sore and was just starting to heal. It wouldn't stand up to much abuse. We were both tired of sitting idle, so I brought in the horses, saddled them and began packing our gear.

The chiefs came to see us off and Crow Foot asked, "Where you go?"

Pointing west, I told them, "There is a valley south of the Mnisota River that is half one day's walk long. There are high hills around it with many trees. A small stream that comes from the top of the valley flows out the south end. Many springs of water come down from the hills. We go there to build a trading post."

"One summer from now our trade goods will come up the Missouri River by keel boat. Sioux bring their furs. We will make good trade, sit by the fire and talk of old times."

One chief nodded his head. "We know this valley. The Sioux will come. Where Black Arrow when snows are deep?"

"We will go back to the black hills of the Paha Sapa Mountains to trap and trade for another winter."

Chapter 12

It was a time to move slowly and with caution. The fall weather was warm, until with no warning a storm blew in from the south west, catching me a day's travel from our trading post. It started with blowing rain. After several hours the temperature dropped and the rain turned into snow, which quickly covered the ground, sheathing the trees in a thick white blanket. Shortly after leaving camp in the early light, the wind shifted, coming out of the west, blowing harder and drifting the snow. If this turned into a real old prairie blizzard I was in trouble.

This was the same route we followed two years earlier after the big fight with the Chippewa. That was in June with warm sunny days as we crossed the grasslands at a leisurely pace because of Rene's wound. It had been the breeding season for buffalo and we watched the bulls with their large flat heads, wide-spaced eyes and short, curved horns as they head-butted for mates. It was an amazing spectacle involving two bulls charging at each other at full speed, roaring from deep in their chests and when their heads met, the loud thudding noise of the collision could be heard from up to mile away. We watched and heard it many times.

Arriving at our valley, we immediately set to work building a trading post. Now, two years later, it was a fast growing, profitable, fur business with a trading house, storehouse, bunkhouse and a cabin shared by Rene, Andre and myself. Each season more trappers, Indian, Métis, and whites came to trade their furs.

Lifting my head from watching past the big roan horse's ears, the snow blew under the wide hat brim, stinging my face. It felt like being hit by a dust storm. Visibility was less than twenty feet. Reality hit me. I was already in trouble even if the storm only lasted the day. I needed shelter from the wind soon and this was wide open country. My best hope was to find a creek bed with trees to break the wind and fuel for a fire.

The surface of the wet ground was frozen and now, with the snow, there was no way to see the icy patches beneath. As good a horse as that roan was, his feet had slipped several times already. Holding to a steady walk, I considered the situation. In the saddlebags there was a little coffee along with enough dried meat to carry me for two days if used sparingly. Behind the saddle was a thick bedroll, covered by a canvas ground sheet. The Cottonwood River bottom was off to the right. Along there the side of the river valley was steep and not something to be tackled under these conditions. The only choice was to keep going until we found the next stream drainage where there would be shelter.

That conclusion had just entered my head when the roan stopped walking, shook his head and snorted softly. Right in front of us was a trail in the snow cutting diagonally across our path toward the northwest. It was a wide trail with too much snow disturbance to be a deer, so it was probably an elk or moose. Dismounting and keeping the reins in my hand, I knelt in the snow to look closer. There were no hoof prints to see as drifting snow was already filling in the trail and the snow was knee deep. The animal that trampled the snow was only minutes ahead of us and fresh meat right now was vital if this storm lasted for several days.

Standing beside the roan, I dug the bowstring out of my pocket, strung the long bow and took two black arrows from the leather quiver. Remounting and reining the horse into the trail, we started off. The roan knew immediately we were on the hunt, which he enjoyed, always being ready to go. He possessed a good nose for a trail and stepped right out, following along this one. With the poor visibility, there was no way to accurately estimate distance. A sense of time gave me the feeling we had probably gone half a mile and the river valley couldn't be much farther. Judging by the trail, we were gaining.

Hunching my shoulders in the leather hunting shirt, it occurred to me to get out a blanket for protection from the wind, which was getting colder. A blanket would be a hindrance to using the bow though, so there was nothing left except to tough it out and hope we caught up soon. Suddenly, I realized, the trail was holding almost a straight line which was unusual for wild game. Wherever the animal was going, he was heading straight for it.

Following the trail brought us to the edge of a cut bank that dropped off steeply for ten or fifteen feet toward a creek bed. It was one of many creeks that fed the Cottonwood River. At the bottom was a pony standing on three legs with an Indian girl beside it. A woman was lying in the snow. Either they hadn't seen the steep bank or had tried to ride down it and the horse slipped. The snow was all scattered and torn up where the horse fell and skidded to the bottom. From my vantage point it looked like the woman was hurt. Certainly, she wasn't moving. The roan pranced around, snorted and the girl heard him. She looked up at me and her hand reached for her belt knife. Looking up like that it was obvious she was young.

I held up my hand for moment to reassure her before dismounting and leading the roan to a lone tree growing close to the bank, where I tied him securely before starting along the bank, looking for a way down. Remembering the woman lying there, I hurried back to the horse for my blanket roll. With it under one arm and the bow in hand, I kicked a way through the snow. A short distance along the ravine a shallow wash showed in the storm, providing an easy path down the bank to the bottom. Returning along the bottom, I passed below my horse and came face to face with the girl. She stood there, knife in hand, ready to defend the woman. With the knife out in front of her, cutting edge up and knees slightly bent, she was ready to fight. She was young, slim and most of a foot shorter than me. The knife was for real and I didn't doubt she knew how to use it. Here, the trees growing along the stream provided partial shelter from the wind and snow. Speaking in Sioux I asked, "Do you need help?"

She watched me with wary eyes, looking at my clothes, the bow and the blanket roll. With her looking on, I placed them against a tree and removed my hat so she could see my red hair, which the Sioux found fascinating. I was hoping she had heard stories from members of her tribe. Her eyes went from the hair to the arrows. I pointed at my chest. "Black Arrow." Pointing at the woman I asked, "Is your mother hurt? Can I help?"

The girl watched me a moment longer and to her credit she didn't waste time on long explanations. "Mother hit head on rock, no wake up."

"Show me where the rock hit her." She went to kneel beside

her mother still holding the knife and put her other hand on the left side of the woman's head. Feeling beneath the long black hair, my fingers located a lump the size of a chicken egg. Leaning close to look carefully, there was no sign of bleeding so the skin wasn't broken. Hopefully, it was just a bad bruise and the woman would regain consciousness before long. Right now, the cold was her greatest danger so we needed to get her to shelter and start a fire for heat. In the meantime, I brought the bedroll and spread it on the snow beside her. With me picking up the woman's shoulders and the girl lifting her legs, we moved her onto the blankets and covered her from head to foot. Another problem was apparent. The bone in the woman's right leg was broken below the knee. That would have to wait for now.

A short distance up the creek, there was a thick growth of willows and young poplar trees. Pushing a way into the trees, I used my hatchet to clear a round space by chopping the slim aspen off at ground level and setting them aside. Next, I pulled down an aspen from one side and tied it to one from the opposite side using a leather thong from the long fringe on my shirt. After repeating the process several times a domed framework took shape over the cleared space. My young helper knew what to do. With her knife, she started trimming the slim aspen cut to clear the space and quickly weaving them into the sides of the frame. With branches, we covered the dome until the snow began to pile up and cover it like a blanket.

Gathering dry sticks, slabs of bark and dead grass from under fallen trees, I laid a fire and struck a spark with steel and flint. Leaving the girl to tend the fire, I brought fir branches from lower down the water course to make a bed for the injured woman.

Something had to be done about the broken leg before she could be moved all the way to the shelter. Searching through the trees, I cut four sturdy willow branches, brought them back and sized them to match the length of the woman's leg from knee to ankle. While I was shaving and smoothing to flatten one side on each of the sticks, the girl watched everything carefully and was quick to perceive my intent. When the splints were ready, she gripped her mother's knee firmly while I pulled on the ankle to put the bone back in place. Together, we tied the splints in place to immobilize the break.

With the woman in my arms, her daughter moved the bedroll into the shelter. She hurried back to help move her mother, as carefully as we could, to avoid bumping the leg. With them settled in the shelter, I took time to improve the thatching on the lower part of the dome to stop the wind from coming through. After narrowing the opening into the shelter, I hung fir boughs across it for a door. It allowed air for the fire to get through while stopping the wind. Using a stick, I poked a vent through the snow on top of the dome to let the smoke that was beginning to fill the shelter escape. When I went back for the roan, the trail we made getting there was gone, filled in and wiped out by the storm.

We were settled in now and safe from the storm. It was getting late in the day and there was only one thing left to do. Adding a few small sticks to the fire, I looked at the girl. "Your pony has a broken leg. We need meat to last out the storm."

She didn't flinch from the suggestion. Her dark brown eyes switched from watching her mother to look at me. She nodded her head in agreement. "Me help."

Together, we walked to the pony where she used her knife to slit its throat. In minutes, the horse was skinned and there was meat to last us for several days. The girl impressed me. Young she was, but brave, didn't waver from what needed to be done and proved to be capable. Her long black hair was braided in two pigtails, a pert little nose and brown eyes set in a narrow face seemed to match her slim build. Only the brown skin and high cheekbones indicated she was native.

Packing tobacco in my pipe and lighting it with a taper from the small fire, I sat and smoked while considering our situation. Before settling in for the night, I went out to check on the roan and fed him an arm full of grass. The roan was pawing through the snow and getting to the grass on his own; even so he deserved a little pampering. Snow was still coming down steadily and our shelter was now thickly covered. It was warm and snug inside.

Waking late in the night, when it was still dark, to maintain our small fire, I leaned back against the saddle the Spanish cobbler in St. Louis had made for me and let my mind wander, occasionally adding a stick to the fire. It was over two years since the big fight with the Chippewa. After that, it took all summer for Rene to fully recover from his wound. We moved to our valley where we built a log trading post at the outlet where the creek flowed through the south end. Andre, Rene's nephew, returned from Fort Garry and was waiting when we arrived. Andre's younger brother and a cousin came south with him and stayed for the summer to help trim the logs and put up walls. Andre's new Charleville long gun was far superior to their trade muskets. After they tried the new gun they asked how they could get guns like that. Around the campfire, I explained there were a hundred Lancaster long guns coming up the Missouri by keel boat in the spring. If they returned at that time they could trade for what they wanted at thirteen prime beaver for each gun. The repercussions that conversation was to have on our trading were totally unexpected.

They spread the word of the new long guns and returned the next year with a caravan of other Métis with packhorses of furs from the northern lands. That group went away with forty of the new guns, powder, lead, rolls of cloth and many other trade items. This past summer two keel boats brought trade goods to Yankton Landing. Again, the Métis returned, this time in larger numbers, accompanied by Cree relatives. Trading was brisk and our business grew rapidly. Rene and Andre were kept busy overseeing the post. Our friendship with Red Eagle of the Mandan gave us entry to those people. Red Eagle came the first summer with his son, Elkfoot, to pick up their long guns as agreed at the parting when we left the Black Hills. They returned this past summer, proposing that we establish a trading post at the joining of the Yellowstone and Missouri rivers to trade with the Mandan, Cheyenne, Teton Sioux and other native peoples living along the Mountains of Rock. Many times, Red Eagle, Rene, Andre and I sat around the fire talking of the details and all that it would entail, until finally it was agreed. When this new winter was over Andre would go west with a team of Métis to establish a trading post.

The keel boat that delivered supplies to us the first summer went back to St. Louis piled high with bales of furs, taking Andre and I along to do the selling and order trade goods for the next year. This past summer two keel boats brought trade goods. In St. Louis, the furs were sold and trade goods bought from Auguste Chouteau, after which I spent time in San Carlos discussing the keel boat business with our partner, Madame Chadron. The business was thriving, both in hauling freight and in custom building boats for other people. Our own fleet was being expanded to five boats.

Sitting up to put sticks on the fire, the light was reflecting from two sets of eyes watching me from the blanket roll. Picking up the coffee pot, I ducked outside to fill it with snow and returned to place it in the side of the fire. While it heated, I went to visit my horse and stood rubbing the roan's neck and talking to him. He had trampled down most of the area he could reach, so I moved him to a fresh spot and promised to bring him grass after eating myself. The snow was well over knee deep, even here in this protected creek bottom, and still falling. The wind was down to a breeze. Returning to the shelter, I crushed coffee beans, added them to the pot and set meat to broil over the fire, pretending not to hear as the woman chided her daughter for letting me do the work of a woman. Soon, the girl hurried past me and ducked through the entrance to do her morning nature call. She returned with her hands wet and cold from washing with snow. While she warmed her hands by the fire, I asked, "How is your mother feeling this morning?"

She looked straight at me for the first time, her eyes large. "Head hurt, leg hurt." The girl paused, still looking at me. She frowned. "Mother say bad me not cook meat."

Nodding my head, I told her, "You cook the meat." She immediately rearranged the spits before pointing at the pot. "What that?"

With a piece of leather, I lifted the lid to let her smell the coffee. She wrinkled her nose as I explained, "It is white man drink. Very good in cold weather, warms the insides and gives you energy." She looked at me doubtfully. I sat back and let her take over the kitchen duties. I couldn't blame her for being concerned about the company of a huge white man who was totally different from everything she was familiar with. She seemed to be gaining confidence that no harm was meant to her. A young girl dealing with a stranger and an injured mother while away from her own people should be concerned. Now which tribe did they belong to? As though she could read my thoughts she said from across the fire, "You Black Arrow, you trade beaver."

Nodding in agreement I asked, "What is your name?"

The girl pointed at her chest. "Willow Flower." After hesitating a moment, she pointed at her mother who was sleeping. "Morning Sun Woman."

Willow Flower was a name that suited her. She was as slender as a willow and pretty as a flower. After considering what she said for a moment, I told her, "Willow Flower is a very nice name."

That got just a hint of a smile from her. "Is good Sioux name." She moved the meat and asked, "How you want meat?"

"Cook it until the red is gone." Willow Flower wrinkled her nose again. "Too much cook, not good." I laughed at her, liking the way she wrinkled her pretty little nose and she smiled back. She ate her meat with dainty fingers, leaning forward to avoid dripping on her deerskin dress. I watched her eat until mine was ready. Pouring coffee into my tin cup, I handed it to her and she held it, sniffing the aroma and inspecting the cup before she took a sip and tried it on her tongue. Willow carefully assessed this new aroma and taste before taking another larger sip and swallowing. She nodded her head and took another drink. When the cup was empty she handed it back and asked, "What is name, white man drink?"

"The drink is named coffee."

"Caw fee." She smiled. "Willow like caw fee." She went to check on Morning Sun Woman and tucked the blankets around her, before returning to the fire where she watched me finish my coffee.

I handed the empty cup to her and she reached for the pot as I asked, "Where is your home?"

Willow's brown eyes looked over the cup at me. "Yanktonai Sioux village on Mnisota River, below falls." That was northwest of here and further away than my trading post. Moving the injured woman would be a problem. The best solution would be to take her to the post and send word to her people. I lapsed into silence, considering the alternatives. It came down to building a sled or a travois. Any kind of a sled I could build here with limited tools would sink in the soft snow and act more like a plow behind the horse. So, a travois it was, which was much simpler to put together and the ends should slide easily through the snow. With Morning Sun Woman on the travois and Willow Flower riding on the horse behind my saddle, we should be able to make the post in one long day. By starting to build a travois today, it would be ready when Morning Sun Woman could be moved. My head came up to find Willow watching me. "What you think?"

The girl seemed to be a mind reader. It amused me, realizing she was very alert and sensitive to my reactions and, yes, my thoughts. "Thinking about how to build a travois to move your mother when the weather improves and she is able to travel. We will go to the trading post. From there, someone will go to tell your people what happened so they can come for you."

She considered my idea. "Willow Flower will help."

It was still snowing. We tramped through the drifts, following the stream, looking for two tall slim poplars. We cut and trimmed them and I shouldered the thickest ends. Willow started out carrying the smallest and lightest ends, one on each of her shoulders. With the hatchet, we flattened and rounded the thickest ends to better skid over the ground. I cut notches for cross pieces, which would be from willow, a strong resilient wood. Regularly, my young helper went to check on her mother. Daylight was fading by the time the framework was ready. All that was left was to complete a bed to support the bedroll and Morning Sun Woman.

I woke with a start to hear the roan snorting and neighing. I quickly pulled the hunting jacket over my head, grabbed the bow and quiver and ducked through the entrance into the predawn light to see what was disturbing the horse. It was still snowing lightly and at first there seemed no reason for the roan to be excited. He was at the end of his rope tether, rearing and stamping his feet. I started toward him, calling out to calm him and a shape in the snow moved. Wolves! Standing still, I soon located six of the big grayish white wolves facing the horse. From the corner of my eye, the movement of a seventh slowly creeping up behind the roan caught my attention. While the six were distracting him, the other wolf was moving in to hamstring the horse. They were cautious, wary of those flailing legs and the damage horses hooves could do; crushing ribs and breaking legs. Time was on their side, eventually they would get him, unless he broke the rope and was free to run. Even then, with the deep snow, they might wear him down in the end. One lone man wasn't much of a threat to a pack of hungry wolves, except for the bow, which they would quickly become aware of. I checked around me to make sure there wasn't a wolf stalking me also. The roan moved around nervously. Smoke started rising from the shelter, so Willow was up and adding wood to the coals. It would be best if she stayed inside for now. Wolves were familiar with smoke and if they got a scent of that it would worry them.

Notching an arrow, I waited for the big wolf behind the horse to stop moving. He did and the arrow flew true, hitting him behind the front leg. There was a startled yelp, he turned his head to bite the arrow and fell over in the snow. Quickly, I got another arrow ready and shot the wolf closest to the horse while they were all looking and wondering what had happened. He yelped and staggered around before falling over in the snow. Two wolves down and five to go. Standing up with arms extended to look big, I walked toward the horse, yelling at the wolves and waving my arms to scare them. They could smell blood and backed away. Suddenly, at some unfathomable signal they all turned and disappeared into the brush. They would regroup and hopefully look for easier prey to pursue.

The roan was still nervous, so I patted his neck, telling him how brave he was. I walked over to look at the wolf behind him and recover my arrow; he followed along, prancing and snorting softly. When I stepped back with the arrow in my hand, he reared up and came down with both front hooves, trampling the dead wolf. He was making sure.

Willow Flower arrived just as I was recovering my second arrow. She watched, before walking around looking at the tracks. Going to a sheltered space near the stream bank, I came back with grass for the horse and Willow was skinning the wolves. Before the raw wolf hides could freeze, we used them to cover the bed frame, wrapping them around the main poles and tying them in place. They would freeze hard to the poles and support pieces, providing a solid base to lay the bedroll on.

In the shelter, Morning Sun Woman was sitting up. We talked quietly while the meat cooked and coffee boiled. Willow watched the pot come to a boil and moved it away from the fire to cool before she poured half a cup and held it out to me. “Give the first cup to your mother, Willow; it will be good for her.” She thanked me with her eyes and took the cup to Morning Sun Woman. Willow held the cup so her mother could smell the aroma and explained how caw fee tasted. Willow Flower watched anxiously as her mother tried the drink, looked at the cup and tried it again. They chatted softly and Morning Sun Woman smacked her lips in approval after each sip. The next half cup came to me and I drank while Willow tended the meat. She took meat to her mother and came back to start eating hers. Soon mine was ready and I handed the cup to Willow before picking up the spit and cutting a slice to chew on.

Before dark, we pulled grass for the horse and fed him. He sniffed the girl’s hands and finally pushed her shoulder with his nose, a sure sign that Willow had his approval. Back in the shelter, I wrote in my logbook about the weather, the wolves, and the injured woman. When I finished Willow was curious. “What that?” she asked.

Opening the book to what was written, I showed it to her. She bent her head to look closely and touched the pencil marks with one finger. I explained. “The Sioux keep their history in the stories they tell. My history is kept in these marks.” She bent to look again. “Look here, Willow. These are white man’s words. Follow my finger and I will tell you the history they speak.” Using a finger to point at each word, I read. "Willow Flower skinned the wolves. We used the hides to finish the travois."

She looked at me with astonishment and shook her head no. She pointed at herself. "Here Willow Flower."

I smiled in agreement. "You are Willow Flower, daughter of Morning Sun Woman."

She pointed at the book. "That not Willow Flower." I nodded agreement, wondering how to explain. After a moment an idea came. With the pencil, I drew a sketch of a buffalo. While I did, she came around the fire to sit beside me. Willow looked at the picture and told me "Buffalo." I nodded, wrote her name and showed her. "This picture says buffalo the way the Sioux do and this says Willow Flower the white man way."

She took the book and murmured to herself as she studied the page carefully, before telling me, "Sioux make good picture of buffalo, Black Arrow make bad picture of Willow Flower." She studied me and slyly asked, "Make white man picture of Morning Sun Woman?"

I turned the page back and showed Willow Flower what was written from the day before. She followed my finger. "Morning Sun Woman fell, hit her head on a rock and broke her leg." Willow gasped in astonishment. "White man picture talk much." She moved to the other side of the fire and was silent for a long time. I missed having her close. Very seriously, she announced, "White man picture strong medicine."

The morning of the fourth day, Morning Sun Woman declared she was ready to travel. We filled our stomachs with meat, drank the last of the coffee and packed up. With the saddle on the roan, we put the travois in place, tied to the saddle horn. I picked up Morning Sun Woman and carried her to the travois while Willow Flower hurried to bring the blankets and arrange them just so. Morning Sun Woman was stocky, her face round, with wrinkles from the weather starting to crease her face. There was a hint of grey in her black hair and she would weigh a good hundred and forty pounds.

With our passenger wrapped up and tied to the travois so she couldn't roll off, we mounted the horse and started for the post. It was a bright sunny day and the sun would be behind us, at least for the first half of the trip. The glare off the snow was strong. We found a way out of the gully and headed west with Willow Flower riding behind me, hanging on with her hands on my waist. Never in all my life was I as acutely aware of a woman as I was of Willow Flower on that ride. Woman! She was a young girl. I could feel her heat on my back and it was disturbing. Every time those thoughts came I shook my head, trying to clear it. Regularly, Willow would turn to check on her mother. When she did, the heat disappeared and I found myself waiting for it to return. It would be a good fifteen miles to the post. After the first five, we stopped to check on Morning Sun Woman.

Willow hurried to ask, "How you feeling?"

Morning Sun Woman nodded her head, looking up at us. "Morning Sun Woman is warm. Go trading post."

Not long after the second stop, smoke from fires at the post became visible on the horizon. Soon after the stop, I saw riders coming toward us. As they got nearer I recognized Rene and one of his Métis helpers. Rene looked carefully to check me, rode around the travois and came back up the other side to stop beside me. His long gun was in his hand. "Jar okay."

Grinning, I reassured him. "Had ta hold up an' wait oot the storm. It is good ta see yea, my friend. Hope I didn't cause yea ta worry."

Rene looked at me a moment longer, glanced at Willow Flower and turned his head away. "Jar gone, good quiet." Rene kicked his horse and we went home.

Chapter 13

Rene rode beside us right to the cabin. All the men came to see what was going on and would be waiting to hear the story. Lifting my right leg over the roan's neck, I dropped to the ground and held up a hand to help Willow down. She half surprised me when she accepted it and came down beside me. We walked to the travois to check on Morning Sun Woman and Willow stayed close beside me. It was because of the strange men, even so; I tried to believe she wanted to be near me. Willow untied the ropes and helped her mother sit up.

Beckoning for Rene to come near, I told him in Sioux, "Rene, this is Morning Sun Woman from the Yanktonai Sioux village located north of here on the Mnisota River. She took a rap on the head from a rock when her horse slipped and she has a broken leg."

Rene nodded his head solemnly. "Greetings, Morning Sun Woman, welcome to our teepee." Morning Sun looked at Rene briefly, nodded and demurely lowered her eyes.

From the corner of my eye, I observed Willow taking all this in with a very serious face. Rene turned and I added, "This very brave lady is Morning Sun Woman's daughter, Willow Flower."

Rene nodded his head and smiled at her. Willow managed a small smile. I think she liked my comment about her bravery. "Greetings,

Willow Flower, welcome to our teepee." Andre came to meet the women.

"Yea open the door, Rene, I wull bring Morning Sun Woman ta the cabin." Rene went ahead and had a chair pulled back from the table for her to sit on when I carried her in. Willow stood beside her mother and her eyes were busy. It was just one big room, some twenty feet long and twelve wide, with a door in each long wall. On the east end was the kitchen with a cast iron stove hauled all the way from St. Louis along with a table and four chairs. Wooden pegs were set in the wall for hanging clothes and utensils and there were a few shelves for storage. At the other end there were four bunk beds, two in each corner. There was a small glass window in each wall.

Turning to Rene, I asked in English, "Is it okay wi' yea if we sleep in the tradin' post an' let Morning Sun Woman an' Willow Flower have the cabin?"

Rene nodded his assent just as Andre came in, bringing the bedding from the travois, neatly rolled. He crossed the room and dropped in on my bunk. Andre came back and asked, "Where you want to put travois?"

"Lean it agin the cabin. It wull be needed in a few days."

"Andre will do and give roan rub-down before putting him in pen. He worked hard today."

"Thanks, Andre." He went out and Rene went with him. I turned to Willow and switched to Sioux. "Will you help me get your beds ready and Morning Sun Woman can lay down when she wants to?"

She followed me to the other end of the room where I picked up the bedroll and leaned it against the wall. Willow pointed at the bunk. "Black Arrow sleep here?"

"Yes, Willow. Rene and I will move to the trading post so you can sleep here tonight."

Willow looked at me with curiosity. "This Black Arrow teepee. Black Arrow sleep in teepee."

How to explain that it wasn't proper, even with her mother here? Looking at Morning Sun who heard every word, there was a hint of approval on her face and I assumed she was going to support me; it was a surprise. "Black Arrow sleeps in snow shelter with Willow Flower." She pointed at the bunk and said firmly. "Black Arrow sleep in teepee." There was a glint in Willow's eyes; she'd won the argument. We fixed the other bottom bunk for Morning Sun and Willow used buffalo robes to make a place for herself on the dirt floor beside her mother.

Willow walked around the cabin, looking at everything, touching nothing and avoiding the hot stove. She stopped to look at the shelf with the books. Rene came in and sat at the table across from Morning Sun Woman. He watched Willow Flower with amusement, knowing full well all the surprises awaiting her in the strange white man things. It was starting to grow dark outside when Willow stopped by Rene. "Where meat? Where Willow make fire?"

Rene grinned at her as he stood up. "Food is ready, Willow, come and look." He took her to the stove and, with a square of leather, lifted the lid on a pot of stew that was simmering quietly. Using a large wooden spoon he had carved from oak, Rene stirred the stew and Willow leaned over to sniff. It was Rene's special meal with chunks of meat, corn, carrots, onions, potatoes, salt and often mushrooms or whatever else was handy on a given day. He always boiled it down until it was thick and would stand still on tin plates. Rene asked her, "You ready to eat, Willow?"

She nodded her head. "Willow eat, Morning Sun eat." Rene went to a shelf and came back with tin plates and spoons. He spooned stew onto a plate and handed it to Willow. "For Morning Sun Woman." Willow took it to her mother. Rene filled another and told her, "This for Jar."

Her head swiveled. "What Jar?" Rene smiled.

"Give to Black Arrow."

After sitting down and putting the plate on the table, I laid the spoon beside it. Morning Sun followed my example. Rene was enjoying Willow's excitement and the surprises he was popping on her as she watched his every move closely. With all our plates ready, Rene brought four tin cups and a jug of cold spring water. He filled the cups and handed them out. Willow looked at the water in her cup before asking, "Where caw fee?"

Smiling, I told her, "Rene likes to drink his coffee after he finishes eating."

Willow nodded. "Is good, Willow make caw fee." Rene started eating with the spoon and they watched to see how it was done. Willow spooned up corn from the stew and chewed it. She fished out an orange piece of carrot and looked at it. Holding the spoon toward Rene she asked, "What this?"

"Taste it, Willow. Name is carrot." She chewed slowly before commenting. "Willow like cawot." It was the same with each new thing she tried. She was curious about the taste of the stew and Rene put salt on a spoon. He wet a finger and dipped it in the salt before licking his finger. Willow did the same and wrinkled her nose at the taste. Rene laughed. "The salt gives the stew flavor. Is same as the sage plains Indians use for flavor in food." He held the spoon toward Morning Sun who tried it and nodded her agreement.

Andre came in and filled a plate before sitting on my bunk to eat. Willow kept glancing that way, obviously trying to decide where he fit in the family. I explained. "Andre is the son of Rene's sister. Rene is Andre's uncle."

She nodded her head and announced. "Rene is uncle to Andre. Rene is Black Arrow father. Where is mother? Why mother not look after teepee?"

The stunned look on Rene's face caused both Andre and I to laugh. Both women looked on in amazement that what seemed so obvious to them, could cause such laughter. Rene looked at me and I told him in English, "Yea better explain, father o' mine."

Rene smiled before turning to Willow, pointing at his chest and explained in Sioux. "Rene is uncle to Andre. Rene not father to Black Arrow, Rene is friend. Rene is not married, there no mother here." Willow mulled that over and looked at me.

"Rene has been my friend for many seasons." Finally she nodded in agreement.

It was unusual for Rene to talk this much. Something about Willow loosened his tongue and he explained, "Black Arrow and Andre very young. Rene show them how hunt, how make teepee, how live like Sioux. They much to learn." Willow glanced at me and her eyes were wide with wonder. "Rene protects them from bad Indians and wild animals so they learn look after selves."

Willow looked back and forth between us, trying to decide what to believe. She glanced at her mother, before suggesting, "Santee say Black Arrow great warrior, have much strong medicine."

Morning Sun Woman added, "It is so. Strong medicine much talked about in council." Mother had spoken and supported Willow; that stopped Rene.

Rene shrugged. "Rene was teasing Black Arrow. Is story Rene make up."

Willow looked at him for several moments before turning to me. "Rene not speak truth. Rene tell story, he make joke?" I nodded in agreement. Willow told me, "Ho, this white man Rene is trickster, like old coyote." It was Rene's turn to laugh and after a moment Willow joined in.

They went to the stove and put coffee on to boil. It was almost dark so I brought the oil lamp and set it on the middle of the table. We didn't use it very often. Finding a sliver of wood, I opened the stove door and held it in the fire until it began burning and used it to light the wick. Once again, Willow was full of questions. We cut tobacco for our pipes and smoked while waiting for the coffee.

In the night, the wind picked up and blew strongly. Willow Flower opened her eyes, listening to the storm, as the wind whistled around the cabin. It was dark except for a faint light from the stove. There was a stirring from Black Arrow's bed and Willow watched as he appeared walking across the room to the stove. He opened the front door and added wood to keep the fire going. Willow marveled at the great size of him standing there wearing no clothes, just like her father in his teepee. When he turned to come back, she closed her eyes tightly so he wouldn't see the reflection and know she was watching. Soon, she heard his soft snoring and snuggled into the robes, content with her thoughts. This white man was very interesting.

As usual, I awoke in the first grey of morning and sat up. The women seemed to be asleep. Pulling on my dark grey wool pants and sticking my feet into a pair of moccasins, I padded across the dirt floor to the stove to add wood, filled the coffee pot with water and put it on to heat. Picking up the pail of spring water Rene had brought in the night before, I set it on the stove to heat. Through the window the storm was just visible. It was snowing again and a strong wind was drifting snow around the trees and buildings. Not a day for travelling. Willow startled me when she suddenly arrived at my elbow to ask, "What you see?"

"It is storming again. Black Arrow was going to send a man to your village today to tell them you are safe and they can come to take you home. Now it will have to wait."

Willow glanced at him, wondering if he wished to be rid of her and the idea made her sad. She had hoped … well maybe Willow was foolish to have such thoughts; there was much she didn't know about this white man and his ways. She moved to the window. Yes, it was snowing and old man wind was blowing at them from the southwest. It was not a good day.

The good smell of coffee was in the air when Rene and Andre arrived. Rene greeted her with a big smile. "Willow Flower, sleep good?"

"Willow sleep good." Rene noticed her voice sounded a little sad and looked closely at her. All through breakfast he wondered what had happened. Her usual liveliness and curiosity was missing. Rene wasn't the only one to notice, Morning Sun Woman was also watching Willow. After breakfast, when Rene prepared to leave, Willow asked, "Where Rene goes?"

"To the trading post and later to see the horses." Rene felt a sudden flash of intuition. "Does Willow Flower want to go with me?

"Willow Flower go with Rene."

Willow went to get a robe to put over her deerskin dress. Rene watched her for a moment before going to a peg in the wall and taking down his coat made from a three point blanket. "Wear this, Willow, it will keep you warm and you won't have to hold it in the wind. It was too bulky for her and hung almost to her feet. Rene got a length of rope and tied it around her waist. Willow rewarded him with a smile. Andre followed when Rene opened the door. All morning Rene showed her the many trade items in the post and her enthusiasm and curiosity were boundless; her questions endless. Rene explained everything to Willow and couldn't remember ever talking so much.

At midday the wind temporarily dropped to a breeze, so Rene suggested, "Let's go and see the horses." He slipped three carrots into his pocket on the way out. Willow led the way along the path through the snow until they arrived at the rail fence. Rene explained how the fence was built and she went from post to post, looking at what held the rails up. Finally, she grabbed a rail and shook it. Willow giggled. "White man fence strong."

"It has to be, Willow, so horses not push it over." She nodded her head in agreement. They leaned on the rails and Rene's horse came to be petted. Rene took out a carrot, broke it and held out one half for the horse. Willow gasped. “You feed horse white man food.”

“It is treat and horses like carrots. Here, you feed her.”

Willow put the carrot on her hand and held it out. The horse’s whiskers tickled her hand as the lips nimbly picked up the carrot. Jar’s roan came to the fence and Willow rubbed his ears. He pushed her shoulder with his nose. She turned her head to ask and Rene was holding out a carrot. Willow laughed happily and took the carrot. She looked at it carefully and the roan pushed her again. “Where you get cawot?”

“They grow in the garden. The orange part grows below the ground and green top grows in air.”

“Ho, you grow like corn.” Willow broke the carrot and held out a piece to the roan who quickly crunched it and looked for more. Willow took a bite out of the other half and chewed thoughtfully. She looked at Rene. “Is good.” The roan pushed her shoulder again; Willow laughed with delight and held out her hand. Willow spied the shelter built in the edge of the trees and her eyes grew large. She turned to Rene. “You have teepee for horses?”

“It is a windbreak and a place where they can get out of the rain and snow.”

She watched him for a moment and Rene wondered what she was thinking. “Rene think horse is people?”

Rene explained, “We want them to be in good shape when we need them to hunt or travel.”

Again Willow watched him and finally she opined, “Rene is wise, treat horses good.”

Rene held out another carrot. Willow asked, "What we eat?" Rene laughed and she fed the roan again. The horses wandered away and they leaned on a rail to watch. Willow inquired, "Black Arrow Santee name. What white man name?"

"Black Arrow white man name is James Angus Richardson." She gave Rene a startled look. "Is hard name for Willow." Rene held up his hand. "Morning Sun Woman," and with each word he extended a finger. "Three names." Rene put up one finger, "James." She came back with Yames. Rene slowly recited the name and Willow practiced until she got the J sound. Happily, she kept repeating to herself, "James, James, James." Her eyes sparkling, she told Rene. "James, good name."

It was mid-afternoon when they came back to the cabin. Morning Sun Woman was lying on her bunk and Jar was working on two long thick sticks. Willow hung up the blanket coat and went to her mother to talk for a moment, before coming to see what Black Arrow was doing. She noted the bark had been removed from the sticks and the wood smoothed. He was busy shaping and rounding one end of a stick. He would shave the end and then pick up another wood piece and try to push it onto the stick. When he put the small piece down, Willow picked it up and studied it. On one side was a neat round hole. She stuck her finger in the hole and looked at it in amazement, it was so smooth and round. Willow couldn't contain herself. "How you make hole?"

Jar looked at her and smiled. "We have a tool to make round holes. Rene, show Willow how we do it." Rene picked up the brace with its spade bit and showed it to Willow. While she looked at it he fetched a chunk of firewood, put it on the dirt floor and demonstrated the drill for her. Willow clapped her hands in glee. It was like magic. She moved a chair and sat beside Jar so she could see everything. He was acutely aware of her presence so close to him. This morning she seemed to be upset with him and he could think of no reason why that should be. After breakfast she left with Rene and was gone most of the day. He felt jealous. Now, she was back and everything seemed normal again.

Finally, Jar fitted the pieces together and stood up with one in each hand. Willow watched him lean down with one stick under each arm and walk with them. He handed them to her. "Try these crutches, Willow." She stood up and followed his example. When she leaned her weight on them he told her, "Pick your right foot up off the floor and walk with one leg." After several tries, Willow was hobbling around on the crutches. "Good, Willow, very good. Now let's see if your mother can walk with them."

Suddenly, Willow realized what he had done. He had spent the day making these sticks so her mother could walk with her broken leg. She felt a rush of happiness. He was a good man who did good things. She would try hard to show him she was a good woman.

Morning Sun Woman was nervous about falling. That didn't cause her to hesitate. After watching Willow, she knew what to do. Willow walked beside her and soon she was getting around the room on her one good leg. What a relief to be up and able to move around. She stopped in front of Black Arrow. For the first time Morning Sun looked him straight in the eye. "Morning Sun Woman say thanks, Black Arrow. Him do much good for Morning Sun Woman."

Jar nodded his head in agreement. "Morning Sun Woman is welcome."

Rene and Jar cleaned up the wood shavings and chips and put them in the stove. Jar moved the table over close to the stove and placed a metal basin on it. He filled the basin with hot water from the pail on the stove. He brought a towel and soap from a shelf and put them on the table. Next, he pulled his cotton shirt over his head. The women watched in amazement. Willow looked at Rene who whispered, "Just watch." Willow wondered if this was more white man magic. Jar stuck his head in the water and rubbed his red hair. He lifted his head, letting the water drip back into the basin. Next, he picked up the soap and dipped it in the water and rubbed his hands together. When his hands turned white he rubbed the white into his hair. He did this twice. The women knew he was washing his hair. What was this white thing he put in his hair?

When Jar picked up the towel to start drying his hair Willow couldn't contain her curiosity any longer. She jumped up from her chair and went to the table to look at this strange thing. She poked it with a finger and put the finger to her nose. It smelled strong. Willow wrinkled her nose, not a bad smell, it smelled fresh. She tasted the stuff on her finger. Ugh, that was terrible. Willow hurried to Morning Sun to let her smell this strange thing.

The women watched as Jar used a small cloth to wash his neck, shoulders, arms and chest and use the towel to dry his body. Willow saw the battle scars from fighting. Done, Jar went to a shelf, got a clean shirt and pulled it over his head. He took the basin and poured the water into a pail beside the door. He looked around and told them, "Ah, it feels good to get cleaned up."

Willow was still on her feet, looking at him. "What white stuff?"

"It is called soap, Willow. Come here and try it on your hands."

He poured warm water into the basin for her and Willow washed her hands. She smelled them while they were still wet, dried them on the towel and sniffed again. She liked that. Willow looked up. "Soap good on hair?"

"Yes, Willow. It makes your hair and your head feel good."

"Can Willow put soap on hair?"

"Of course you can. In the morning, after I heat another pail of water for you. We will put the pail on the stove tonight and it will be warm in the morning."

"Willow wash with cold water."

"Soap doesn't work in cold water, Willow. You wait until morning." Willow nodded her head in agreement. When he used the last of the warm water to wash the towel, Willow hurried to help. She pushed him aside and washed both the towel and his shirt for him. Morning Sun Woman's face didn't change, but inside she was smiling. Willow was learning. A few more days like this and Black Arrow wouldn't want Willow to leave. Willow had said nothing about it; still, Morning Sun understood what her daughter wanted. Morning Sun missed her husband and family. Still, she hoped the storm lasted.

Each day Willow Flower watched everything with an intensity and concentration that amazed the men. She looked at the thermometer when James went out to take the temperature, she watched him make the magic marks in his log, and she was fascinated when he used the straight razor to shave and wrinkled her nose at the tonic water he rubbed on his face. James' shaving mirror was an exciting new world for her. Willow followed Rene as he went about his daily routine, constantly practicing her words. Plate, cup, spoon, table…

and most important James Richardson.

Rene was patient with her and talked far more than was normal. Willow loved washing her hair, using the metal comb James gave her and scrubbing her body with soapy water. Each time she prepared to do that, James would hurriedly leave the cabin which she didn't understand. After the second time it happened she came to the trading post, her hair freshly braided and smelling of soap. After idly looking around for a while she asked Rene, "Why James go away when Willow wash?"

Rene pondered how to answer. He grew up much like Willow, living in a teepee, which was no place for modesty. In a teepee people paid little attention to someone being nude, getting ready for bed or going about their normal lives. Rene leaned his elbows on the trading counter and started. "Rene family live in teepee like Willow family. Many times see people with no clothes. Many times wash in stream and see people with no clothes." Willow nodded her head in agreement. "James not grow up in teepee. He never see woman with no clothes."

Willow gasped. "How that be?"

Rene shrugged. "Rene not know. James not looks at woman without clothes until she his wife."

"Is very strange." Willow mused, "James run away, Willow think coward."

Rene rubbed his nose. "James Richardson not coward. He very strong and brave warrior, fight like silver bear." Rene stopped, searching for the right words. "He very brave with men. He shy with woman."

Willow came to the counter and jumped up to sit on it near where Rene was leaning. "What this shy?"

Rene scratched his head. Damn woman, he wasn't used to talking like this. He sighed, how to explain? "Not know Sioux word for shy. It is like modest or having great respect and being a little scared." Willow was silent for a long time; Rene was thankful and started to relax. He liked this Willow. He had great hopes for her and Jar.

She startled him. "James shy with all womans?"

Rene considered that. "He always very respectful to women. In St. Louis there are two women." Rene heard the sharp intake of breath and the ah. "When James in St. Louis he stays at the teepee of Mrs. Ruechard and she feeds him. James has a business partner in San Carlos named Madame Chadron."

"What business partner?"

"They work together. When Willow and James worked together to build the travois they were partners. James and Madame have a boat company to build keel boats. They own five keel boats to haul goods on the rivers."

"Why Madame not at trading post with James?"

That surprised Rene. "Madame has a trading post to run in San Carlos and four children to raise."

"Huh, James not shy with Madame. He make four babies with her." The force of Willow's outburst startled Rene and he stood up straight to look at her. Her face was grave and her eyes angry. Rene stared at Willow for a moment and started to laugh. Willow glared at him. "Four babies no funny."

Rene reached for her hand. "Willow right; four babies not funny.

James not make babies. Madame has other white man for husband. She lives in a big stone teepee. Two floors." He paused. "Two teepees high." Rene watched as Willow's face relaxed and her eyes softened. "Willow, James has no woman; he waits to find a wife to live with him."

Suddenly, her eyes were smiling and happy again. She watched him for a moment. "Is good, Willow thanks Rene. Willow go see what James do."

Rene watched her jump down from the counter and put on the blanket coat. When she opened the door, the cold wind blew in snow. Rene went to the round potbellied stove to add wood. Deciding to make coffee, he filled the pot and set it on the small flat top of the stove to heat. He sat down on a wooden crate to think. 'Maybe, just maybe.' Rene was sure Willow was interested. Jar saw her as a young girl, not yet grown up. Willow was sixteen summers and most Sioux girls were married before that age. Jar better not wait too long.

The storm blew itself out. The snow stopped and a day later the sky cleared. All around the trading post the country was white and the sun glared off the snow. The men at the post began preparing to go hunting. To get buffalo, deer, elk and moose for winter meat and hides for the many things they were needed for. The two women watched all the activity with interest; their people would be doing much the same.

Early in the morning, James dispatched a rider to take word to the Yanktonai village. Willow knew that tomorrow or the next day her father would arrive to take her home. She had cooked, sewn and looked after the teepee like a woman should. She showed interest in everything James did, asked questions, trying to learn his ways. They laughed together; still he treated her like a sister. Willow didn't want to be a sister. She wanted to be a wife, to live with him and have babies with him. What to do? Dejectedly, she went seeking Rene. Willow found Rene in the trading post talking to one of his helpers. When Rene saw how sad she looked he sent the man on his way and asked, "What troubling Willow?"

"Willow is sad. Willow wait for James to ask me to live in his teepee. He does not see me. He thinks Willow is sister. Willow not wants be sister. Willow wants be wife."

"Come here, Willow, and sit down. Do you want a cup of coffee?"

Her shoulders were slumped; she wasn't the lively, curious woman Rene admired. "Yes, coffee good." Rene filled two cups and came to sit beside her on the wooden crate.

"Tell me about it."

Willow looked at him with sad eyes. "Why does James not see Willow as woman?"

"He does, Willow. Rene has watched his eyes follow you. He knows Willow is a woman, a very beautiful woman, who can do everything a woman should."

"James not show Willow she is woman."

They sat in silence while he pondered that. "Rene is Cree, from far to the north. Cree and Sioux are Indians. Much of what we do is the same, but not everything. James is from far away across the great lake far to the east. His people do many things different than Cree and Sioux. Their customs are different, they think different.

James treats Willow like he would a woman in this Scotland he comes from."

"Huh, Willow not likes this Scotland."

He smiled. "Rene would not like go this Scotland. James not know all Sioux ways. Willow must be patient. When Willow goes to her village, James will be lonely, soon he come see Willow."

Her face brightened. "Rene think he do this?"

Rene grinned. "Yes, he will come and he will come again. He bring Willow gifts and court Willow."

Willow frowned. "What this court?"

"Where James comes from a man goes to talk to a woman he likes, to get to know her better and to know her family. They say sometimes this takes several years."

Willow's eyes grew large in amazement. "Several years, Willow not like this court."

"It is the way James knows. He will court Willow. In time, he will go to your father and Morning Sun Woman and say. 'Can James marry your daughter Willow Flower? I be good husband to her, protect her, keep her in my teepee forever.'

"Ho, Willow like that." She smiled. "What else James do?"

"If your parents say 'yes James can marry Willow Flower' he will look for a white man spirit leader to say prayers and ask the Great Spirit for happy marriage and many children. James will look for a ring to put on Willow's finger."

Willow frowned. "What is ring?"

"Give me your hand, Willow. No, no, the other one." Rene held her hand and explained. "See this finger. James will get a shiny metal hoop that is just the right size to slide on this finger to here. Willow will wear ring on her finger for all her years with James. The ring tells all white men that Willow Flower is married. All white men will call Willow, Mrs. James Richardson or sometimes Mrs. Willow Flower Richardson."

"Ho, Willow like that. How many seasons this court take? Willow is sixteen summers now, soon be old woman."

Rene laughed and dropped her hand. "Rene will be very happy when Willow comes to live here and keep her teepee."

It was mid-afternoon when Andre opened the door and stepped in. "Jar, riders coming."

"Okay, Andre, do the men know?" Andre nodded yes. "I wull be oot in a moment." Willow Flower and Morning Sun Woman watched as Black Arrow put a knife and tomahawk behind his belt and hung the powder and shot bag over his shoulder. He picked up his long gun, checked the powder pan, and went to the wall to add the pistol to his belt. He walked to the door before turning. "You ladies stay in here until we know who is coming." It was an order and Willow acknowledged it. She hoped this would be her man one day and he was doing what warriors did. As soon as the door closed, Willow put the knife in her belt and hurried to a window to watch.

The approaching riders slowed to a walk; the tough, seasoned warrior leading them was Willow's father. He carried a spear in his right hand and five warriors followed him, along with the messenger Jar had sent to carry the news. His hard old eyes gleamed with understanding as he looked at the men deployed around the buildings. He could see four in position to fight and there were probably others. The door to one of the white man teepees opened and a large man with hair like the setting sun stepped out to stand waiting. The man was carrying one of the white man fire sticks that could kill at long range. At the base of the slope leading to the bench where the buildings stood, the warrior turned his horse and rode straight at the big man. He came to a stop, at a comfortable distance, while his men ranged out on each side of him. The messenger rode toward another building and dismounted. The hard, experienced eyes watched everything with appreciation. This was the white warrior the Santee talked about at council. He started to hold up his hand in greeting. Before he could, the door opened again.

Willow Flower walked out, leaving the door open and stood beside the big man. Her black hair shone in the sunlight as he looked to see if she was healthy. Father and daughter looked long at each other with passive faces. His heart leaped with pride. He noted that Willow was standing erect and proudly beside the white warrior. There was movement and Morning Sun Woman came through the door, leaning on sticks. This was his number two wife. He had searched in the storm for her and finally accepted that she was lost. The messenger told that her leg was hurt. She was walking and now he had her back. He acknowledged her with a nod of his head and she smiled at him.

The warrior stuck out his right arm toward the man beside him who took the spear. He lifted his leg over the horse's neck and dropped to the ground. His measured stride took him to his wife. He stopped two paces away and looked her up and down, his eyes staying for a moment on her right leg. He nodded his head as she told him, "Morning Sun Woman is happy you have come." He watched her for a moment before moving sideways to stand in front of Willow, who was more beautiful than he remembered. "Welcome, Father. Willow Flower is happy to see you."

"You are in good health, Daughter?"

"Yes, Father, Mother and I have been well cared for." She surprised him with her next words. "May I introduce you to this man with the hair of fire?" His eyes glinted with amusement and he nodded. "Father, this man is the one the Santee named Black Arrow. He is a brave warrior and a great medicine man. His white man name is James Angus Richardson. He came out of the storm to save us."

Jar was surprised when she used his name. Now how did she know that? Rene, that was how. Willow spent a lot of her time with Rene. He heard Willow say, "Black Arrow, this is my father, Chief Red Thunder *(Wack-haw-en-du-tah)* of the Yanktonai Sioux. He is a brave warrior who has fought many battles." Jar stuck out his right hand. Red Thunder hesitated at this strange act before he took it. Both grips were firm.

"Red Thunder thanks Black Arrow for saving women from storm and sending word to my village."

"Welcome to my teepee, Chief Red Thunder. Will you stay the night before starting home?"

"The horses need rest. We will start at first light in the morning for long ride."

Willow interrupted. "Father, take mother to the teepee so she can sit down. Her leg gets tired standing this long." He started to object at being ordered. She continued, "Come James and meet my uncle."

He stared at Willow's back as she walked with Black Arrow to the horses. Red Thunder turned to look at Morning Sun Woman who smiled. "Your daughter has found man she wants, he not know it."

There was just the two of them, so he smiled. "Willow Flower is sixteen summers, is time."

The sun was just coming up when they were ready to go. Rene came with his blanket coat and held it out to Willow. He was pleased at her surprise. "We have many good talks. Willow Flower made Rene feel young again. Wear coat, keep warm."

"Thank you, Rene." Willow took off her buffalo robe and put on the coat. Rene produced the rope and tied it around her waist. "We talk much. Rene tell Willow advice. Rene think advice good?"

Rene nodded. "Much better than I thought. Willow Flower take care of self."

"Willow will do what Rene say. Rene come visit village, talk more?" He nodded his head yes and Willow smiled.

Jar listened to the conversation, wondering what this was all about. Willow waved to Jar and turned her horse. Willow was going home with her comb, a tin cup, a bar of soap, needles and thread, and awls to punch holes, all of which James gave her. Rene put a bolt of blue cloth in her blanket roll when he helped pack her bed. Willow was happy; there were many stories to tell around the fire during the long winter ahead.

Chapter 14

Two men rode away, going west, to scout for buffalo. Jar and Andre took packhorses and went along the Cottonwood River to hunt moose and elk. The animals were out feeding after being holed up in shelter for days, waiting out the storm. Although the snow was starting to melt it was still deep and animal tracks were easy to follow. At the end of the day, they came back with a moose and two elk to hang in the meat house.

Rene stayed close to the trading post. With cold weather he expected that trappers would start coming soon with fall furs to trade for items needed during the winter ahead. The post and separate storage house were packed full to the roofs with trade goods brought up the Missouri on two keel boats during the summer. Rene was planning for a busy fall and spring. The trading business was growing quickly, in large part due to the high quality of goods they stocked and also the fact they treated everyone fairly and never took advantage of the Indian, Métis and white trappers. Jar said over and over that treating trappers fairly was important and they were making a huge profit trading the right way.

Jar quit the Hudson Bay Company in 1799 to come south as a free trader. Rene joined him as a partner. Jar put up all the money to buy trade goods and insisted that Rene was to have a one quarter interest in the fledgling business. Since the year 1670, the Bay had claimed all the land west of the great lakes and north of the Missouri River, by grant from the King of England. The Bay would not tolerate free traders in their territory which they governed with an iron fist.

Fort Garry's Factor threatened Jar with retaliation if they traded in the company's territory. Their post was north of the Missouri, in that territory. Even worse in the company's view was the large amount of trade they attracted from Métis along the Assiniboine River. This past year many Cree also bypassed Fort Garry and made the trip south to trade for the better quality guns and supplies available from Richardson. These visitors related the anger of the Fort Garry factor and the threats he made against them. Together, they prepared as well as possible. The buildings were located to provide coverage of each other in case of an attack and each of their men was armed with a 1797 model Lancaster long gun and ample powder and shot. Rene, Andre, and Jar each carried Charleville long guns which were even better than Lancasters. The past summer Jar came back from his annual trip to St. Louis with two swivel guns like those used on keel boats. These were positioned for defense.

The post was manned by the three of them plus five men from the Red River country, which was more than they needed. Next summer, Andre would go west to meet Red Eagle at the Mandan villages and build a trading post where the Yellowstone flowed into the Missouri. Two men would go with Andre. The new post would give them access to a vast area of the west and the peoples who lived there. Jar prepared for this by buying larger, better quality horses. Two years before, he bought a roan stallion and two large mares from a Spanish man at San Carlos and started breeding all the mares in their herd, to get better quality colts. The first of those new colts were with their mothers in Long Valley which stretched away behind the rail fence. All horses carried the Bar R brand on their left shoulder. Rene smiled remembering his last trip to St. Louis in 1801. Jar knelt in the dust of the blacksmith shop drawing diagrams. He wanted an arrow over the R. The blacksmith explained it was too difficult to make and would result in a poor brand because the heat distribution would be uneven. Jar settled for a thick bar over the R and ordered two identical branding irons made.

The brand was burned into the outside of the door at the trading post with a black arrow nailed above it. Everyone who came to the post saw them and went away knowing who the post belonged to.

Rene barred the back door of the post. He firmly closed the front door, snapped the large iron lock in place and put the key in his pocket. He walked to the cabin to begin the evening meal and Jar looked up from the table as he came in. “How was your day, Rene?”

“It good. Now post organized way Rene want. Soon trappers come with furs to trade.”

“Yes, I was thinkin’ about that. When Andre has the post built and operating oot west on the Yellowstone we ar’ going ta need a clerk fer the recording an’ keepin’ of accounts. We need a record of all the trade goods an’ where they go. When trappers ask fer credit that has ta be recorded. It means hiring someone from Fort Garry or St. Louis.”

“St. Louis better. Factor mad with us. Hiring his man push him over edge.”

Jar ran a hand through his red hair. “Yea ar’ right, Rene. It might be better if I wait until the next trip ta St. Louis. Should have thought of this sooner an’ hired a man last summer. I will talk ta Madame Chadron. She may know of someone around San Carlos who is available."

Rene stirred the pot of stew. "We have tea tonight?

"Sure, Rene, it wull be a good change. We drank a lot of coffee durin' the storm."

Rene saw his opportunity to get in a reminder. "Willow like coffee. She always put pot on." He turned away from the stove so he could see Jar without being obvious.

Jar stood up and paced around the room. "Willow is a nice girl an' she learns new things real fast. She is young. Did yea like her, Rene?"

Rene turned back to the stove to hide his smile. He was pleased; Jar was thinking about Willow. "Rene like Willow. She interested in everything. She good worker." Rene paused thoughtfully. "Jar wrong, Willow, not young. Willow, sixteen summers. She take husband soon."

Jar came pacing up to the stove. "Is Willow getting married?"

Rene shrugged. "Rene not know. Many Sioux girls married before sixteen. Willow marry soon."

"But, Rene, she is a sixteen-year-old girl, that's mighty young." Rene could hear the concern in his voice.

"Jar not knows women; Willow not girl; she woman." Rene threw out his best shot. "How old Madame when get married?"

That stopped Jar and he stood still, thinking. "I donnae know. Her eldest son is ten now so she must hae been about sixteen when she got married an' maybe seventeen when he was born." Rene kept his peace and waited. Jar was thinking, which was what Rene wanted him to do. It was five days since Willow left and it wasn't the same cabin without her.

The next afternoon the scouts arrived back to report a small herd of buffalo near the lake on Flandreau Creek. In the morning, Jar, Andre, four men and a string of packhorses left to hunt buffalo. They expected to be gone two or three days. Rene and one man stayed to look after the trading post. It couldn't be left unguarded with trade goods worth thousands of American dollars stored inside.

Jar watched the land as the roan trotted along beside Andre's horse. The snow was melting quickly since the storm ended and was mostly gone now, except in the shade and in gullies where the wind piled it in deep drifts. Melt water made the land soft and they detoured around low places where water was accumulating. Jar expected the creek to be running full with new water and the lake level to have risen. They came to the campsite where the scouts stayed, located in a thick stand of cottonwoods and set up camp. The best time to hunt would be first thing in the morning when the ground was firm from overnight frost. With meat spitted to cook, they discussed the hunt. Andre noticed Jar was unusually quiet; all he contributed to the conversation was 'we want fat, three or four year old cows.' Everybody knew those were the best eating and provided the warmest hides.

The men loved to hunt and Jar left them to it. When they dropped the first cow he stopped with the packhorses and started skinning the animal to recover the hide and the meat. He peeled the hide back and was cutting out meat when he remembered Willow Flower skinning the horse when they needed meat during the blizzard. In his mind, he saw her working quickly and deftly. He missed her talk, all the questions and her happy, surprised, reactions to new things.

Andre came back for a packhorse and found Jar standing with the knife in his hand, unaware of the approaching rider. Andre dismounted and walked over. "You need help, Jar?"

Richardson was startled at the sound of the voice. "Oh! Andre, what did yea say?"

"Wondered if you needed help?"

Richardson shook his head. "No, be finished here in a few minutes. Why did yea come back?"

Andre watched Jar quizzically, thinking. 'Rene is right, Jar is in love and he doesn't know what to do.' "The men got another buff. I come for packhorse."

Richardson nodded. "That is guid! Yea go ahead. When I finish up here I'll come ta pick up your meat an' take the two packhorses back ta camp."

In Chief Red Thunder's village, Willow Flower was settled into the routine of looking after her mother's teepee while Morning Sun Woman's leg healed. At night, sitting around the central fire in the teepee, she described to Red Thunder, her uncle and half-brother from Red Thunder's first wife, the blizzard, the accident and the white man who appeared out of the storm to help them. Willow told them how he put his hands on the big lump on Morning Sun's head, said she would sleep for a while and would recover. In Willow's version, it sounded like magic. Morning Sun Woman and Willow slept in the white man's blankets, while he sat up tending the fire and guarding the entrance. She told them how the big white man with the hair of fire frightened her, until she saw he was gentle and intended them no harm. Her story went on and on in great detail, with some unintended exaggeration, as seen through the eyes of a young woman. Red Thunder saw her eyes shine when she talked about the white man. They discussed at length the magic hands that could heal a lump on Morning Sun's head and fix her broken leg.

Several days later, Red Thunder asked her, "You like this white man?"

"Yes, Father. I waited for him to ask me to live in his teepee. He did not speak and I was sad. One day, I went to the trading post to ask Rene why Black Arrow did not speak to Willow. Rene says that Black Arrow comes from far away at a village named Scotland. He does not know the ways of the Sioux. Rene say that after Willow goes to her village, Black Arrow will be lonely and he will come many times to talk to Willow. He will do this. One day, he will tell Red Thunder that he wants Willow for wife."

Willow waited patiently, her heart beating fast, as Red Thunder thought about all she said. He looked at her and studied her face before asking, "Does Willow Flower wish to be wife to this white man?"

"Yes, Father."

"If the white man asks, Red Thunder will tell him yes. Willow Flower must remember it is not proper for an unmarried woman to be alone with a man not from her family. Can Red Thunder trust Willow Flower when she talks to the white man or walks in the village with him?"

"Willow Flower knows Sioux ways. She will talk with him, she will walk with him, maybe Willow will ride big horse with him, if Red Thunder approves."

"Red Thunder approves. Willow will cause much talk in the village."

"Thank you, Father." Her eyes were smiling. He glanced at Morning Sun Woman and she was happy. This strange white man worried him; still, he knew what he had said was the right thing.

Every night they talked and often others crowded into the teepee to hear the stories, many of which they found hard to believe. Whenever anyone doubted what Willow Flower said, Morning Sun Woman would support her in the firm voice that brooked no argument. The entire village discussed these things and argued about it. When asked about it, the elders related stories from the council meetings, telling of this white man's strong medicine.

The fall buffalo hunt was on and in the village everyone was busy with hunting, butchering, hauling the meat home, tanning hides, and all the other tasks to prepare for winter. The corn harvest was completed and stored away earlier in the fall and soon they would settle in for a long winter of storytelling around the fire. The snow melted away and at midday it was warm and Willow waited.

Fall trading was brisk. The warm afternoons made it easy for trappers to travel to the post with their furs. A few Métis came from the north. Rene told Jar the Cree would not come until spring. Sioux from various tribes came including their cousins the Mandan, Omaha, Iowa and also French from along the Mississippi. On a sunny afternoon, standing outside the trading post, Jar pulled the wide brim of his leather hat down to shade his eyes as he watched a rider with two packhorses approach. The man rode up to the post and tied his horses to the tie rail. His hair was long with a thin, scraggly beard on his chin, wearing dirty, stained buckskins, with gaps in the fringes from long wear. The man never looked directly at Jar, just walked past into the post. A moment later, Jar heard a booming voice. "By damn, if it ain't Rene Beauchamp himself. How are you, old son?"

Richardson leaned against the wall and listened for the answer. Rene's soft voice came through the open door. "Well I'll be, Pig Eye Parrant. Heard you went out west for the Bay and the Blackfoot got you."

"Well now, Rene, I did go and those ornery Blackfoot came close, more than once, to lifting my hair. Blackfoot be something else. Cussed mean they is."

"What you doing down this way?" Rene didn't know if Parrant had any sight in his left eye. That white ring around the pupil gave the eye an evil look. He got the name Pig Eye from that eye.

"Bay want to send Pierre up the Saskatchewan again. Said no to them. Don't care for their ways. Took my pay and come back to the big river. The Mdewakanton Sioux along the white cliffs of the river be telling stories of a great warrior with red hair. Say he helped them defeat the Chippewa a while back. Chief Little Crow, he right sure about it. Little Crow tells Red Hair lives in a wood teepee and trades. Caught me a passel of furs and come to see that red hair. Got my pelts out there on the horses."

Richardson heard Rene suggest, "Let's look at your furs, Pierre," and took up his long gun from where it leaned against the wall and walked around the corner of the post smiling. He'd heard of Pierre Parrant, but never seen the man before. 'Only a few years older than me,' Jar mused, 'he has been around and is still alive so he knows how to handle himself in wild country.' Richardson went back to the cabin to catch up on his bookkeeping.

Pierre Parrant loosened the ropes on the pack saddles and let the packs fall to the ground, before he knelt to untie the bundles. As Rene watched, Andre came through the post from the storehouse and walked up beside him. They watched Pierre together. When the bales were open both knelt beside Pierre to inspect the furs. Pierre looked at Andre with his one good eye. "You that Troyes boy from up on the Assiniboine?"

Andre's expression didn't change. "Grew up there. Name's Andre."

"You some kin to Rene here?" Andre nodded his head in agreement.

Rene asked, "How many beaver you got?"

Pierre wagged one hand and replied, "You count, Rene."

Carefully looking at each pelt as he went, Rene made two piles. "Pierre, I make it eight good pelts and four that you did a poor job on."

"Expect so, Rene." Pierre tugged on his scraggly beard. "You want those four?"

"Sorry, Pierre, you keep them." When they finished inspecting the furs, there were eight beaver and seventy-one muskrat that were acceptable. "What do you want to do, Pierre?"

Pierre rubbed his grizzled chin and allowed. "Could use a new blanket, powder, lead and a mite of tobacie. You got a new pipe? Chewed mine up some."

"Come inside, Pierre, and Andre will tally up what you have

here." Muskrat were valued at four to one American and beaver at six each. While Andre did the tally, Rene got a heavy three point wool blanket off a shelf, brought five pounds of black powder and five one-pound billets of lead. Pierre watched all this and his eye kept going to the long guns. When Andre finished the tally and listed the trade items he asked, "Them good long guns?"

Andre got one down and handed it to him. "These Lancasters are best guns available."

Pierre hefted the gun and commented, "Some heavier than mine."

"They are that." Andre smiled. "Never heard of one blowing up."

Pierre allowed. "Them Mdewakanton Sioux of Chief Little Crow's have a number of these guns. Claim they shoot some good. The extry left over enough to get one of these?"

Andre shook his head. "Sorry, Pierre, five beaver short."

Pierre paced around the small area in front of the counter and came back. "If you was to keep a credit for me, I could fetch five prime beaver."

"You got a deal, Pierre. Bring the beaver and you got a new long gun."

"Pierre will do, Andre." He lifted a hand. "Good seeing you, Rene."

Rene came around the counter. "Getting late, Pierre, you stay the night. We talk, you go for beaver tomorrow."

Pierre blinked. "There extry bunk for Pierre?"

"There's an extra bunk. We will pen your horses and show you where to put your gear. Andre, you take Pierre's goods to bunkhouse?" Andre nodded and started gathering up the items on the counter. Together, Rene and Pierre led the horses over to the rail fence and turned them in. Rene threw out hay for all the horses and showed Pierre where he would sleep before they walked to the cabin. Pierre brought along his new pipe and a twist of tobacco.

Trading was slowing down as time moved deeper into winter. It appeared that all the trappers that intended to come had. Nine days after leaving, Pierre returned with eight beaver, got his long gun and a credit he could draw on. He was restless and Rene waited, figuring there was something on Pierre's mind. After some pacing Pierre leaned on the counter and commented, "You got as solid a setup here as Pierre ever seen. Rene got work Pierre do for bunk to spend winter?"

Rene was surprised and he hesitated for a moment. "We go talk to Jar." When they came through the door, Jar looked up from the book he was reading and Rene told him, "Pierre would like to work for his winter keep."

"Sit down, Pierre." Jar watched him as he thought about his plans. Ever since Willow left he couldn't get her off his mind and he was considering putting a wooden floor in the cabin and cutting timbers for another building. "Pierre, we have a sawin' rack set up out in the valley and I want ta' cut planks for a floor in this cabin. We need to cut timbers fer another building. If yea want ta work at that with the men yea are welcome."

"*Oui,* Pierre will do. Pierre start tomorrow."

"Very good, Pierre. I pay the other men two American dollars an' found each month. Yea will get the same if your work be as good as theirs an' no fighting with the men. Everyone here must get along together an' help each other."

"Is good, Pierre will work, you see. Who is *bourgeouis?*"

"Most days Andre wull organize the work. When he is busy with other things it wull be Rene or me."

"Is good, now Pierre go zee bunkhouse."

Trading was over and Richardson was restless. Rene watched him and figured he knew what was bothering Jar, so he suggested, "Why don't you go see her?"

Jar stopped pacing and looked. "What's that?"

"Rene say, Jar go see Willow."

Jar was surprised. "I admit tha' she is on my mind. It donnae seem right fer me ta call on a young girl like that."

"Jar is fool. Willow Flower soon be seventeen summers. My Marie was fifteen summers when we married. Jar not visit, Willow not wait."

That startled me. I had heard the story, but this was the first time Rene ever mentioned his wife, who died two years after they were married. "Do yea think I should, Rene? She made this cabin come alive when she was here an I cannae stop thinking about her. Dam'it, I cannae even settle down ta read my books fer very long until she is on my mind. Will yea go with me?"

Rene nodded. "In morning, Rene saddle horses. One packhorse

be good?"

"Donnae know, Rene. We wull need bedrolls an' food. Extra robes an' clothes in case it storms. Let me think."

Rene smiled at Jar's back, 'Finally.' He commented, "You take presents for Willow Flower, Morning Sun Woman and Chief Red Thunder."

That stopped Jar. "What should I take fer her?"

Rene shrugged. "Willow like coffee, you take pot and coffee beans. Take scissors, tin plate and spoon. Many things Jar can take."

The young Sioux scout raced his horse into the village, causing the dogs to chase after him, barking. He pulled the horse to a stop near Red Thunder, who was sitting cross-legged on a buffalo robe in front of his teepee, shaping a new spear. "Greetings, Uncle, your brother sends word. The white man the Santee call Black Arrow is coming along the river."

Red Thunder looked up. "He comes alone?"

"No, Uncle. He comes with one white man and a packhorse."

Red Thunder stood up. "Thank you for bringing the news, Spotted Tail. Put your horse away and come to see these white men." As the scout rode away, Red Thunder ducked through the entrance into the teepee and waited for his eyes to adjust to the dim interior. He didn't need to tell them. Morning Sun Woman and Willow Flower were already putting everything in its proper place. Willow Flower pulled her everyday dress over her head and took a clean deerskin dress from her par fleche to wear. Red Thunder remembered the summer Willow was twelve and he had given her the rawhide from a buffalo to make that par fleche. She scraped it clean of flesh and hair and stretched it to dry in the sun. When it was dry she cut and folded it to make a stiff rawhide bag as long as her arm and half as wide with a flap that folded over the top. All winter she painted designs on the sides.

"Morning Sun Woman will make a fire so you can talk to these white men." Red Thunder nodded his head and returned to his seat on the buffalo robe to await the arrival of the visitors. News travelled fast and the village was stirring with activity.

From half a mile away, Jar saw the village located on the south side of a creek that came in from the west to meet the Mnisota River. A location well protected by trees and the west side of the river valley which rose up behind the village to meet the plains. They held the horses to a steady, ground-eating trot. Both carried long guns across their saddles, with Rene leading the packhorse. At the edge of the village, Jar pulled the big roan down to a walk and steadied the horse, as barking dogs danced around its feet. The roan blew air through his nose and sidled sideways nervously at all the noise and confusion.

People were gathering in the center of the village. As they neared the crowd, Jar saw Chief Red Thunder standing beside a fire in front of a large teepee. The crowd left a wide space around their chief. Stories of this white man were retold many times and everyone was anxious to see him and hear his words.

The horses came to a stop six paces from the fire and Red Thunder held up his right hand. The white men did the same. The crowd went quiet; they all wanted to hear the words. A woman kicked a camp dog and it ran away yelping. The chief looked grave as he said, "Red Thunder welcomes Black Arrow and his friend Rene to this village of Yanktonai Sioux people. Come and sit by my fire."

"Black Arrow thanks you for this invitation and is happy to see Chief Red Thunder again." People in the crowd exchanged glances. This white man knew the proper way to behave. Jar dismounted and for the first time the people saw the Spanish saddle and marvelled at its size and elaborate design. Rene took the reins, saying in English. "I'll tie the horses to that cottonwood behind the teepee."

"Thank yea, Rene." What were these white men saying? Everyone noted that Black Arrow kept his long gun, as a warrior should, with a knife and tomahawk behind his belt. They marvelled at his great size. The other white man seemed normal. Jar walked to the fire and held out his hand. What was this? To everyone's amazement, Chief Red Thunder reached across the fire and squeezed the hand.

When Rene returned, the Chief pointed to the robes and they sat down cross-legged. Immediately, Morning Sun Woman came from the teepee with the ceremonial pipe, in its decorated leather covering. Red Thunder carefully removed the long-stemmed pipe and cut tobacco to load the bowl. With a taper from the fire, he lit the pipe and offered it to the four directions before puffing and blowing smoke to the sky. When the tobacco was glowing he held it out to Black Arrow who took it, solemnly puffed and blew the smoke skyward, before passing it to Rene, who did the same. Rene passed the pipe back to the chief who puffed several times before giving the pipe to Morning Sun Woman who took it and disappeared into the teepee. Red Thunder observed Black Arrow's eyes straying toward the teepee. He asked, "Your fall hunt for meat was successful?

Black Arrow nodded. “Very successful, Chief. We have a good supply of meat stored for winter. And your hunt, was it successful?”

While the chief answered, the village elders came, to sit in a circle around the fire and the people crowded in close behind them. “Sioux have great hunt. Many buffalo and elk. Much meat and hides. Red Thunder is happy.” The conversation went on as they worked through the pleasantries and courtesies. Red Thunder heard the flap on the teepee move as it was folded out and knew the women were coming. He watched the white man to see his reaction.

Jar was quick to see Morning Sun Woman step out and hold the flap. Willow Flower ducked through the opening and straightened. Black Arrow came to his feet, staring at her, his face breaking into a big smile. Rene put a hand on his leg, afraid he would leave the circle. Jar stood still as the women came and sat on either side and slightly behind Red Thunder who was pleased with what he saw. This big white man loved his daughter, there was now no doubt. Jar settled back on the robe, still drinking in Willow with his eyes.

Willow’s heart was beating fast. She allowed no emotion to show on her face to indicate she was bursting with happiness. James did love her, just as her friend Rene told her and finally he was here to talk.

It almost didn’t register on him when Red Thunder said, “Does Black Arrow remember Morning Sun Woman?” The Chief was pleased with his little distraction.

“Black Arrow is happy to see Morning Sun Woman again. Has your leg healed well?”

“Yes, Black Arrow, the leg is almost healed. Thank you for using your strong medicine to heal Morning Sun Woman’s leg and the big lump on her head." Her hand went to the side of her head.

"Black Arrow is happy to hear that Morning Sun Woman is in good health."

Red Thunder was enjoying the subtleties. He knew the white man's eyes were only for his daughter. "Red Thunder thanks Black Arrow for saving his daughter from the big storm." No need to introduce them, they were staring at each other. Black Arrow removed his hat as he looked at Willow and the crowd murmured in amazement at the hair of fire. Willow smiled and he was lost.

Long moments went by, Rene jabbed him in the ribs and told him in English, "The chief talks to you." Jar tore his eyes away from Willow and focused on the chief, who was happy. Jar dared not look back at her.

"Morning Sun Woman and Willow Flower have told about the storm and how Black Arrow found them. This village would like to hear Black Arrow tell about the storm."

Jar nodded in assent and started. "Black Arrow was coming from the morning sun (he pointed east), returning to the trading post. It rained and toward night, froze. The rain turned to snow and in the morning it was very icy and my horse's feet slipped many times. Black Arrow was hurrying to get home and the storm got worse. The wind was blowing, the snow was up to my knees and Black Arrow couldn't see past his horse. The horse walked for a long time. We came on a trail in the snow. Black Arrow thought it was a moose or elk, so he got his bow ready and followed the trail. The storm was filling in the trail, so he hurried. The trail led to the edge of a stream bed that fell away steeply. When Black Arrow looked he saw where a pony fell and was standing on three legs." He pointed at Morning

Sun Woman. “A woman was lying in the snow, not moving. A young woman,” Jar pointed at Willow, “was standing looking up at me. I tied my horse, took my bedroll and searched for a way to the bottom. When I came along the stream and got close, Willow Flower was guarding Morning Sun Woman.” Black Arrow paused, looked at Willow and smiled. “Willow Flower was holding her knife out in front of her with the cutting edge up and her face looked like a big silver bear. Black Arrow trembled with fear and his knees shook. He told himself, this Sioux woman is a fierce warrior, Black Arrow better walk carefully.”

Willow laughed at his story, Morning Sun Woman laughed and soon everyone was laughing. Red Thunder’s respect for Black Arrow increased. It took a strong man to make a joke about his own courage.

“Black Arrow talked very nice to Willow Flower before she would let him look at the lump on Morning Sun Woman’s head and all the time she kept her knife pointed at him. Willow Flower and Black Arrow built a shelter from the storm and we stayed there for three days until Morning Sun Woman told us it was time to travel. In one day, we traveled to the trading post and after the storm was over Chief Red Thunder came to take these women home.”

Willow leaned toward her father and whispered a request. He nodded his head and she talked to the circle. “Black Arrow does not tell about healing Morning Sun Woman’s head or how he tended her broken leg so she can walk again. He does not tell about the wolves that attacked his horse and he ran from the shelter to stop them with arrows. Black Arrow does not speak of the travois he built or the walking sticks he made so Morning Sun Woman could walk with a hurt leg. There is much he does not say."

Morning Sun Woman explained to Red Thunder that this strange white man did not think it was proper for him to sleep in the same teepee as Willow Flower. He and Rene were given their own teepee to use during the visit. The first day, Willow rode behind his saddle as she took him to see the cornfields, the creek that flowed from the west and they traveled north to see where the river fell over the rock ledge. They walked around the village holding hands and the older women of the village turned their heads away to hide their smiles. For hours they sat, drank coffee, and talked, telling each other about their lives. Often, they did not know if anyone else was in the teepee. Morning Sun Woman cooked. Rene was happy. Red Thunder waited for the white man to ask for Willow.

On the morning of the third day, Rene packed their gear. Black Arrow told Red Thunder it was time to go. He presented Red Thunder with a Lancaster long gun including everything needed to use it. He gave Morning Sun Woman a large iron cooking pot. Willow got a metal mirror, a pair of scissors, a coffee pot, and a bag of coffee beans.

When Black Arrow went to get the horses, Rene walked to her. "Soon Willow Flower will come to live in the cabin. Rene will be happy." Willow smiled happily.

At the last moment Willow asked, "Will James come to see Willow again?"

Chapter 15

Winter settled in a few days after they returned from the Yanktonai village. James Richardson was happy; he just wanted to figure out how best to arrange to marry Willow Flower. He wanted to provide her with a good house where she could be comfortable, live like a lady, with all the things needed to make it a home. In his mind, he saw Willow living in a house like Madame Chadron in San Carlos.

Each day that wasn't stormy, the men went out to the valley to saw planks and timbers. Everyday Jar went along and while they sawed planks from logs stacked to dry the winter before, he selected and chopped down trees to be cured for future use. Andre worked alongside him. They took turns, one chopping and the other trimming off branches, while Rene towed them to the storage site using a rope tied to the horn of his saddle. Jar enjoyed the physical labor after an autumn of relative inactivity. He swung the heavy double-bitted axe with authority, making the woodchips fly.

The valley was more than five miles long and in most places well over a mile wide. It was surrounded by high hills covered in a thick forest of trees; cottonwood, spruce, and oak. Along the creek there were willows mixed with berry bushes that were heavy with fruit during the summer.

One surprising thing about the valley which caused the men to wonder was the climate. Somehow it was warmer in the valley than outside where the buildings were located. With the high hills covered in tall trees, the wind was much less of a problem, still that didn't seem to be the complete answer. It was a subject of much speculation. After days of listening to the men talking, Pierre announced, "Why you talk? Just is. God make valley this way."

Pierre was the bottom man on the two-man saw crew because with just one good eye he couldn't accurately follow the scribe mark. He was always covered in sawdust, complained very little and worked steadily. He chuckled to himself. This was the easiest winter living in a long time; there was plenty of good food, a warm bunk to sleep in and tobacie for his pipe. Pierre found himself wondering about the summer, after winter ended. Andre was going to the Yellowstone to build a trading post and he would need good men who knew how to work. Pierre pulled even harder on the saw as the idea came to him.

Richardson always carried a book with him and at rest breaks or lunch time he would sit and read. None of the others had any schooling. They watched him, thinking it was a waste of time.

Jar spent days dreaming about what he wanted for Willow. Finally, he realized that to build the house he visualized would require bringing carpenters and stonemasons from St. Louis. He could afford it. Anyone who knew what his assets were would consider him rich. Thousands of American dollars on deposit with Auguste Chouteau in St. Louis, seven parcels of land on both sides of the Mississippi at St. Louis and the boat company in San Carlos. Any money left over from selling his furs in St. Louis was brought home as gold coins. Right here in this valley, in a place only he and Rene knew, were iron boxes full of gold and silver dollars, more than enough to last them for the rest of their lives. During their second trip to the Black Hills, he panned more gold from the little stream and it was stored in the iron boxes, twenty-three leather bags each containing seven ounces of gold. The first sale of gold caused too much of a stir in St. Louis and New Orleans. He didn't want a crowd of gold-crazed men following him everywhere he went.

Jar turned his mind to the house plan. It would take two years or more to get the men here and build a house. He wanted to marry Willow and waiting two or three years was too long. They would have to live in the cabin. With that decided, he turned to considering the problem. He would put a plank floor in the cabin and widen his bunk to make room for her. Rene and Andre would need a place, so as soon as the weather permitted, a cabin would be built for them.

Often, the horses came to nose around the worksite. The snow was piled up out on the flatlands while here it was no more than half as deep. The native grass grew tall, giving the horses no problem pawing through the snow to find food. Only the horses needed for riding were kept in the pen and fed grass cut in the fall. Each time the horses visited, Jar and Rene took time to admire the colts. Two of the colts would be ready to train for riding when winter was over. In two or three years, they would have a vastly superior herd of horses for their own use and after that there would be horses to sell.

Jar wanted to obtain beef cattle to graze in the valley to start building a herd that would provide another source of meat for the trading post. The nearest animals were north on the Assiniboine River. When time permitted, someone would go to purchase animals and herd them south. With a beef herd, together with the garden, they would be almost self-sufficient, if for some reason buffalo became scarce for a season.

Finally, the day came when Jar was ready to tell Rene and Andre what he was planning. The evening meal was over, their pipes were lit and he surprised them. “I’m going ta ask Willow ta marry me.”

They grinned at him. Andre leaned back in his chair with the comment, “Is time.”

Rene came around the table and slapped Jar on the shoulder. “Rene afraid you never ask. We go tomorrow?”

“Now, Rene, don’ yea go an’ rush things. We need ta build a cabin fer you an’ Andre ta live in. I want ta put a plank floor in this place an fix it up fer Willow before we get married.”

Rene’s sudden happiness was dimmed. He growled, “Rene and Andre can sleep in trading house. Willow like cabin as is. You marry now. Jar fool.”

It was a rare outburst from Rene and Jar stared at him. “But Rene, I want ta have things right fer her. Need ta find a preacher ta do the marryin’ an’ get Willow a ring.”

“You want ring, Rene make ring from gold money. Where you find preacher, huh? We go and Jar talk Red Thunder. Bring Willow Flower home.”

Jar held his hands out, asking for understanding. “I cannae do that, Rene. I want her married proper with a signed paper. I won’t have white folks looking down on her because she is Sioux. Willow will be my wife an’ a lady.”

“Willow is lady.” Rene looked belligerent. “Rene not care what white people say. No white peoples here."

"Thar wull be Rene. White people wull be coming up the river. Already there ar' white trappers coming ta the post. Soon white people wull be here."

Andre watched the two men. He rarely saw his uncle so worked up about anything and it was unusual for him to argue like this. Rene went back to his chair and sat down. He looked across the table at Jar and shrugged. "Jar worry much." Rene was silent for a while and Andre went for the pot to refill the coffee cups. Jar waited. "Where we find preacher man?"

Jar sighed. Rene was onside. "There was talk the Presbyterians were sending a man out frum Scotland ta preach ta the Indians an' Métis along the Red River."

Rene asked. "Jar want Rene go find preacher?"

"No, Rene, not in the winter. The trip would be too hard an' dangerous. We wull send one of the men next spring."

Rene tried again. "Rene think Jar talk Red Thunder. Chief say Willow and Jar married."

Jar grinned. "If Willow wants that we wull do it, Rene. I also want a white preacher ta sign a paper saying we are married."

Rene shrugged and looked at Andre. "White man make marry too hard. Indian way better."

Andre agreed. "White man think much, worry much." He looked at Jar and smiled. Jar smiled back. They liked to poke him from time to time and he didn't mind.

Rene insisted they work on the cabin floor first, so they did. They cut and fitted planks and slowly the floor extended its coverage from one end of the cabin to the other. The planks were sawed two inches thick and varied in width from ten to fourteen inches, depending on the size of the log they were cut from. Using hatchets, they carefully trimmed the sides until the cracks between planks were as narrow as they could manage.

After one long day of fitting, Andre slyly suggested, "Jar should leave big cracks. When Willow make Jar clean floor can sweep dirt into cracks."

With sandstone, they worked to smooth the rough places on the boards until Jar was satisfied it was as good as they were going to accomplish. He liked the result and stomped around in his boots testing the floor, finding little give in the thick planks. Rene watched him and suggested, "In spring we get black bear in valley, make rug."

Jar was surprised. "Tha' is a great idea, Rene."

The days were getting longer as spring approached. They cleared a space for the new cabin and started laying slabs of shelf rock for a foundation. With squared logs, the base for the walls was laid. It was slow work, cutting the angles and trimming the ends of the timbers to fit together at the corners. It was something they had all done before and slowly the walls began to rise. They were building an exact copy of the other cabin. Rene was helping to wrestle another timber into place when one of the men said, "Riders coming."

Rene stood up on the wall to look. He saw the blanket coat. "Looks like Willow coming."

Picking up their guns, everyone moved to defensive positions just in case. Jar and Rene walked to the cabin and stood waiting. As the horses started up the slope they could see Willow Flower, Chief Red Thunder, Willow's uncle Running Buffalo, and his son Spotted Tail. The men pulled their horses to a halt. Willow rode right to Jar. Rene held the rawhide hackamore and Jar held up his hand to help her dismount. They were both smiling. "How are you, Willow Flower?"

"Willow Flower in good health. Willow can see James Richardson is healthy."

They forgot everyone else. Rene walked to the men, knowing the courtesies were being neglected. "Welcome, Chief Red Thunder. We are happy you have come for a visit. Welcome Running Buffalo and Spotted Tail. Will you come and sit so we can talk?"

Red Thunder nodded his head toward the cabin. "Black Arrow has eyes only for Willow Flower."

Rene glanced toward the cabin as the two were disappearing inside. "That true, Red Thunder. Always Black Arrow thinks of Willow Flower."

Red Thunder almost smiled. His eyes showed amusement. "Willow Flower not wait for white man to come. She say Willow Flower go talk Black Arrow. Morning Sun Woman say Red Thunder ride with Willow Flower. Must keep teepee happy."

Rene nodded his head in agreement. "Is important, Red Thunder. Come and see what Black Arrow has done to his teepee."

They tied the horses and followed Rene into the cabin. Willow and Black Arrow were on their knees examining the new floor. They quickly stood up. This time, James was aware. "Welcome, Chief

Red Thunder."

The Chief stepped forward and put out his hand. Black Arrow shook it. It was a strange habit. His daughter loved this white man who was a brave warrior, so Red Thunder would accept it. Black Arrow went to greet the other two men.

Willow exclaimed, "See, Father, James made a floor from trees." Willow stamped one moccasin-clad foot. "It is strong." Willow was pleased and that pleased Red Thunder. He jumped up to test the floor with his weight. It didn't move. He agreed. "It is strong, Daughter." It was amazing what these white men could do. They did not always follow proper courtesies and there was no ceremonial pipe to smoke with guests. Red Thunder knew there was much to learn about this strange white man with the hair of fire.

James walked back and Willow pointed at the stove. "Willow Flower make caw fee?" James smiled and nodded. Rene went to light the stove while Willow filled the pot with water. James watched for a moment before turning to the chief. "Will Red Thunder and his party sleep in the cabin?"

Red Thunder wasn't going to show that this teepee made of trees worried him, so he replied, "Weather is good, Red Thunder make camp in trees. Long winter, too much sleep in teepee." Willow listened as she worked around the stove. If she slept in the cabin, James would go to the trading house. The idea made her tingle inside. 'Foolish man.' Willow would sleep in the camp and not disturb him.

They sat around the campfire and roasted meat. Willow put the coffee pot in the side of the fire. She sat beside her man and listened to the men talk about hunting. When spring came, the Sioux would hunt buffalo just like in the fall, before winter arrived. After much talk, the camp fell silent. James looked across the fire at the chief. "Black Arrow would ask Chief Red Thunder for great favor."

Red Thunder's weathered face remained impassive. He saw Willow turn her head to look at the white man. "What is favor?"

"Black Arrow asks for permission to marry Red Thunder's daughter, Willow Flower."

The chief noted the happy look on Willow's face and he remembered her words of what this white man would do to marry her. He remained silent as he thought about it. Willow put her eyes down just the way Morning Sun Woman did when there was serious man talk. This is what Willow wanted, it was what Morning Sun Woman wanted and yes he would be proud to have this white man marry his daughter. He looked at her. "Does Willow Flower wish to marry this white man?"

Her low voice came across the fire. "Yes, Father, Willow Flower would marry James."

He turned his hard, experienced eyes on Black Arrow and the white man looked straight back at him. "Willow Flower say she marry Black Arrow. Red Thunder say yes. When the sun rises in the east, Red Thunder say words to make Willow Flower wife to Black Arrow." He watched Willow Flower start to raise her hand and the startled look on her face. Her head turned to look at the white man, she didn't speak. He waited, amused inside, to see if this white man would do what Willow Flower said.

"Black Arrow thanks Red Thunder for approval to marry Willow Flower. My teepee will be her teepee and I will always protect her. Willow Flower is Sioux. Chief's words good for Willow Flower, good for Black Arrow. Black Arrow is white man. Need white man spirit leader to say white man words, so all Sioux and all white men will know Willow Flower is Black Arrow's wife."

Chief Red Thunder was impressed. The white man was serious. He was doing as Rene told Willow Flower. He watched them for a moment. "Where this white man spirit leader?"

"There are spirit leaders far down the Missouri at St. Louis and north at Red River. When the snow goes, Black Arrow will send a rider to find spirit leader."

"Black Arrow not marry Willow Flower when sun comes up; Red Thunder take Willow Flower back to Morning Sun Woman."

"Black Arrow wishes to walk with Willow Flower, to talk with Willow Flower." The chief nodded his head in approval and watched as they walked away into the night, holding hands. Spotted Tail added sticks to the fire. After a long silence, Chief Red Thunder turned to Rene. "Black Arrow wants Willow Flower to come to his robes. It is in his eyes. Why he not marry Willow Flower now?"

"Chief is right. Black Arrow thinks always of Willow Flower." Rene smiled. "Many times Rene speaks to Black Arrow. He not hears Rene. In mind, he talks to Willow Flower. White man ways strange to chief. Black Arrow thinks only of what good for Willow Flower. He wants Willow Flower get great respect from white peoples."

"When Black Arrow take Willow Flower for wife?"

"Rene thinks in summer. When corn grows high."

"Huh, Red Thunder thinks Black Arrow much foolish." He raised his hands in resignation. "Chief see. Willow Flower agree, chief agree."

In the morning, Willow Flower came to the cabin to make coffee. She sat at the table with them to eat stew. She poured water, washed the tin plates, and put them back on the shelf. Rene requested, "Willow Flower walk with Rene?" She put on her blanket coat and Rene held the door open for her. Jar sat there wondering what this was about.

Rene took her to the trading house and seated her on a crate. He came with a canvas bag full of spade bits and compared them to the third finger on her left hand. He selected one and drilled a hole in a thin slat. Holding it up, Rene asked, "See if finger will go in hole."

Willow tried and it wouldn't go past the knuckle on her third finger. She knew what Rene was doing. He found another bit and was drilling a second hole in the slat when Red Thunder pushed the door open. Seeing the two of them come out of the teepee and go to this place, he came to see for himself what was happening. Rene finished the hole and gave the slat to Willow. Her finger slipped easily into the hole. Rene held her hand and slid the slat back and forth on her finger. "Does feel good, Willow? Not hurt finger?"

She smiled at him. "Willow finger not hurt."

Rene went behind the counter and came back with a gold coin. He handed it to her. "With this, Rene will make Willow wife ring."

"Willow thanks Rene." Rene was pleased with the happy look on her face. "Does Rene have cawot? Willow go talk big horse."

Rene nodded. Red Thunder said, "Time to ride, Willow Flower."

"Yes, Father. Willow wishes to talk to big horse. Will Red Thunder come?" Willow led them out the back door and up the path to the horse pen. Red Thunder followed her and Rene came behind with carrots in his hand. Willow leaned on the rail fence with a man on each side of her. The big roan came and looked at them from a safe distance. Willow spoke to him. "Come, big horse." He came and pushed her with his nose. Willow laughed and scratched his ears. He pushed her again and she gave him a carrot. "Big horse look after James. Not slip on ice, not fall down." She got another nudge and he got a carrot. "You run fast when James say." Willow fed him the last carrot and turned away. The men followed her back to the cabin. The horses were standing ready to go. Willow held Jar's hand and looked up. "James come talk Willow Flower?"

"James will come."

She nodded and squeezed his hand. "Is good." Willow went to the horse and mounted. She looked at him for a long moment, waved, and turned the horse toward home.

The days grew longer, the sun got warmer and the cabin walls slowly rose with openings for doors and windows left to stare like vacant eyes. One moon of time passed, the snow was gone except in the shade, birds returned and they framed the roof structure in preparation for the planks that would cover it. The evening meal was over. Rene made tea and filled three cups. He suggested, "Long time since Willow leave. Jar go talk."

"Been thinking on it. I miss her. When she goes th' spirit of this cabin goes with her." Andre glanced at Rene and saw the trace of a grin. "By damn, I'm going ta do that. I will leave at sunup." Jar went for his guns and came back to clean them.

"When Rene expect Jar back?"

Still working on the guns, Jar replied, “Four, five days.”

Richardson stayed for three days. He and Willow walked, they talked about the future, much of which Willow didn’t understand. She liked his enthusiasm and she would learn. They found a rock above the village where they could see the river valley and the village below them. Sitting in the warm spring sun, he surprised her, by putting his arm around her shoulders to pull her close. She found she liked that. In the evenings, he sat by the fire and talked to Red Thunder about war, hunting, different trails each had travelled and Red Thunder asked about the Black Hills of the Teton Sioux. Willow listened, proud of her man who soon she would marry and stitched the hunting shirt she was making for him.

Jar decided to take a different route home and instead of coming along the western side of the hills he came around the east. There was a plan forming in his mind, to see if the Sioux would trade the valley and the hills surrounding it, in return for trade goods, giving him title to the land just as Chouteau had suggested. Now that he was to be married it was important to him. This was dangerous country and accidents happened in many ways. If something happened to him, Willow and Rene would have a place.

He would have to prepare a map with a diagram and a description of the land, with carefully set out boundaries. For this purpose, he was using the return trip to look for landmarks, to define what would be the eastern boundary. At one point, he stopped to look up at the sky. Jar was sure he heard thunder rumbling in the distance, even though the sky was clear except for a few scraggly white clouds floating on the wind. Continuing along, intent on his plan, it was midafternoon by the time he rounded the southeast corner of the hills and rode toward the stream and home. Stopping in the stream to let the roan drink its fill, something about the trading post struck him as odd.

Jar sat there, not moving, while he sorted out his surroundings. There was no activity; the men weren't working on the cabin roof, which he could clearly see. There was no sound, nobody was in view. He turned his head. There were no horses in the pen. There should be two; of course, Rene and Andre could have gone off somewhere. Where were the men? He sensed trouble. Something was wrong.

Nudging the horse with a heel, Jar rode across the water into a shallow hollow and tied the roan to a sturdy tree, where it was hidden from view. He checked the powder pan on the long gun, made sure his other weapons were in place and started working his way slowly up the slope toward the horse pen. From there, he would have a good view down the gentle slope to the buildings. At the edge of the trees, he got down and crawled along the path with the long gun across his arms. He was getting muddy. More importantly, he was hidden from anyone looking out from the buildings. Making the corner of the rail fence, he continued on, coming slowly to his knees behind the third fence post. Jar watched the buildings. There was no smoke, no sign of activity. He waited, knowing that often the first person to move was the first person to die. Rene had taught him the value of patience. Glancing around, he noticed the section of rails used for a gate lying on the ground. They never did that. When one of them opened the gate, they just lowered one end of each rail and let the horses step over. Someone else did this.

Jar wished for the long bow. He hadn't taken it because he was thinking of visiting Willow, with no intention of hunting. Now, he regretted his mistake. Dam'it, he was living too comfortably and getting lax. This was a warning and he better remember it. The sun was slowly moving toward the western horizon while he waited. Finally, he detected movement through the back window of the bunkhouse. Jar watched until the door edged open and one of the men ducked out, holding a long gun, and ran to the back door of the trading house. A long gun followed him. Well, at least two of the men were alive.

Still, he waited. If it was some kind of trap, he might be the only one who could act. Jar was tempted to move closer and was considering the best way to do it when Andre opened the back door of the trading house and called to whoever was in the bunkhouse to come over. Jar stood up, Andre spotted him immediately and started up the slope past the two men hurrying out of the bunkhouse.

Jar decided to remain where he was, letting Andre come to him while he kept an eye on all the buildings. Andre came up the path with his long gun in trail position for easy carrying. There was blood on the side of his face and one shoulder was bleeding. He looked at Jar. "Andre glad you back."

Jar demanded, "What happened, Andre?"

"Just after midday nine men come with packhorses. We think they are bringing furs to trade. Rene was in the trading house. Andre send two men to help Rene. We work on roof. Old Pig Eye stuck his head up to look and told me, 'Those are Bay men.' We scrambled to get down to long guns. Before we can, they start shooting. Both our men at trading house were killed and Rene took a ball through leg. He got inside and slammed the door shut. Andre send two men to bunkhouse to cover the rest of us. When we tried to move, they shot around corners of trading house.

"Balls was flying. Dem trade muskets they have don' shoot so straight. Andre got ball into one and they rode off some, to regroup. Rene loaded a swivel gun. When they charge back, old Rene he let them come close and fired off gun. It make big roar like thunder. Many balls in gun. Two men and one horse go down. Maybe more hurt. They ride off, we hole up. Andre think they come back. Long time now, maybe they go."

"How's Rene?"

"He bleeds some. Andre tie up leg. Rene say Andre watch, be ready fight."

"Yea did good, Andre. Let's go an' see how Rene is. Anyone else hurt?"

"Don' think so. Just Andre on shoulder."

"We wull have a look at that shoulder an' get yea fixed up."

On the walk down the slope Jar was thinking. 'That swivel gun did some damage. They lost two men and at least one more is wounded from Andre's shot. Most likely, they have started back north to Fort Garry.' Andre led the way in by the back door, past stacks of trade goods, to the front. Pig Eye stood in the front door, watching for the attackers. Rene was lying on the dirt floor with his long gun beside him. His pant leg was all red. Jar stopped beside the counter and looked at Rene carefully. "Seems like every time thar is a fight yea get hurt."

Rene grinned. "You got cut a time or two."

"Aye, I did and yea fixed me up. Did th' ball pass on through?

"Andre says it did."

"Good, I will go ta the cabin an' get some things ta fix yea up. Sorry I wasn't here ta help out." Rene nodded and relaxed. As Jar went past Pig Eye, he slapped the man on the shoulder, "Good job, Pierre, thanks."

Glancing around, Jar could see two dead men and one horse lying on the grass not more than fifteen paces away. He thought, 'Andre must have moved our two men to the storehouse.' He went to the cabin and took from a shelf white cotton bandages, a pair of scissors and the pint bottle of whiskey kept to sterilize wounds. With those in his hand, he walked back. Pig Eye and three men were standing outside. Jar stopped beside them. He sent two men to get the roan from the creek, told the third to get a rope to drag the bodies away. Pig Eye was posted as lookout. Inside, Jar squatted beside Rene and asked, "Dunna suppose yea want me cutting up those pants so I will pull them off. First, need ta get rid of Andre's bandage." Rene untied the sash around his waist and Jar eased his pants off. The ball went through the inside of Rene's right leg a hand's width above the knee. There was a neat round hole in the front and back which started oozing blood. Jar looked at them and commented, "Doesna look too bad. Now, Rene, I'm going ta pour whiskey on these cloth pads an' put one on each side. It wull sting some and kill any infection that might want ta start up. Yea okay with that?" Rene nodded. "Andre yea come here an' hold these pads in place while I put a bandage on." Rene gritted his teeth, not making a sound, as Jar wrapped the bandage around his leg. When it was done, Jar asked, "Yea want your pants back on?"

Rene grinned. "Don't want to go bare-assed."

Both men laughed at him and pulled his pants on. With one on each side, they lifted Rene up, so he could stand on his good leg while leaning against the counter. Andre put Rene's long gun on the counter close at hand.

"Now it's your turn, Andre. Get that shirt off so I can look at yer shoulder." There was a nick on his right ear which was where most of the blood came from. There was an angry looking mark across the top of Andre's left shoulder that wasn't much more than a deep scratch. Jar poured whiskey on a cloth and sterilized the cut. Andre winced. Jar smiled and told him, "Probably best ta leave your shirt off fer a time. That way the air wull get ta this shoulder. It wull be okay in a day or two."

With Rene's arm over his shoulders, Jar walked him to the cabin and settled him in his bunk.

They dug two graves up on the rise, overlooking the buildings, to bury their men. Nothing was said about the dead raiders. The sun was down by the time the graves were filled in.

While Andre cooked, Jar lit the lamp and started cleaning his guns. He got his saddlebags and began packing supplies. He set the long bow and the quiver of arrows by the door. Rene watched the preparations. "You go after Bay Men?"

Jar looked up from the knife he was honing, his eyes hard. "They are going ta pay fer what they did. If even one of them makes it ta Garry, I wull have failed."

Rene propped himself up in the bunk. "Andre go with you."

"No, Rene, yea may need him here. Soon trappers will be coming ta trade furs."

“Rene be okay. You take Andre, two better than one.” Jar thought about it and nodded agreement. He and Andre would leave at first light. They were all in their bunks when Rene asked in the darkness, “How is Willow Flower?”

Chapter 16

With enough light to follow a trail, we started, each with a spare horse to ride and a packhorse to carry supplies, in case a late winter storm blew in. We carried our Charleville long guns, with bows for backup. Andre figured there were seven men left, one or two of which might be wounded. He had shot one of them while the horses were prancing around and couldn't be sure how solid the hit was.

The trail was plain to see and easy to follow at a steady ground-eating trot. After a mile, Andre commented, "They not go far last night. Need eat, fix wounds."

Jar considered that. "Yea think they will get as far as the Parle before stopping?"

"Is too far. They not think we come." Jar was still thinking about it when they found the horse. Both dismounted to have a look. There were three ball wounds in the shoulder and the horse had slowly bled to death. This horse must have been ridden by one of the men killed when the swivel gun blasted at them. The horse only made five miles before faltering. Two hours later, they found the campsite in a grove of trees, beside a small lake. The first thing they saw was a dead man who had been left behind. Andre walked around, looking at the places where men slept. He held up six fingers. Jar nodded in agreement. Jar knelt to sift the ashes of the campfire with his hand.

There were still warm coals. He looked at Andre. “Two, three hours ahead of us.”

Back on the horses, Jar asked, “Which way do yea think they wull go? My guess is they intend ta stay west of the Mnisota an’ follow the Sioux north.”

Andre waved his left hand. “Is best way.”

Jar nodded. “Close ta four hundred miles ta Garry. We got time.”

They approached the Parle River with caution, expecting the raiders might be camped for the night. There was no camp. Jar mused. “An hour’s travel from here is the west branch of the Parle. They wull stop there for the night.” He turned the roan. “Let’s find a hidden corner an’ eat before it gets dark. Won’t hurt to let them settle down an’ stop worrying.”

Eating meat while the coffee boiled, Andre suggested, “Run off horses, leave them afoot.”

Jar wiped his greasy fingers on the grass. “By tomorrow night they should be close ta the lakes at Big Stone. If conditions ar’ right we can try ta move in an’ sneak the horses away.” They drank coffee and let the fire burn down. Jar took the first watch, thinking about Willow Flower; it kept his mind off those two men they had buried.

Lazing around the breakfast fire, they waited, there was no hurry. They were only an hour behind and could move much faster with their better quality horses. This was slightly rolling, open country and they didn’t want to be seen if the raiders checked their back trail from some stopping place on high ground. Riding west of the trail, they followed along. By midafternoon, the gap was closing. Andre spotted the riders going over a rise maybe two miles ahead. Staying where they were, Andre suggested, "Them camp at lake."

"What I figure." Jar rubbed the red stubble on his chin. "It is wide open country around those lakes. My recall is of a small stream with a heavy growth of trees a couple of miles west of the lakes. If we wait fer dusk an' stay west of this trail it should take us ta that stream. Good place ta keep out of sight an' we wull be able ta look right at their camp."

They located a hidden dale inside a bend of the stream with enough grass to picket the horses on. A low ridge on the east of the stream separated them from the lake. Moving through the trees and wading across the shallow stream, they crawled to the top of the ridge and looked out through a clump of low bush. The camp turned out to be farther than expected because the men had gone farther along the lake before stopping.

Bellied down in the grass to watch the activity, Andre looked for the best way to approach the camp. Smoke started rising from a fire. Two men mounted horses and rode out of camp, coming west toward them, carrying long guns. Had they been spotted? The men rode along what looked like a shallow drainage that would bring them to the stream a short distance north of the ridge. Andre whispered, "Hunt for meat, look for deer."

Worming back down the slope into the trees for better cover, they waited and watched the men ride past and disappear west along the drainage. One of the men was puffing on a pipe while riding Rene's horse. Jar climbed the ridge again to watch the camp and make sure the other men were staying put. Returning, he whispered to Andre, "We wull let them get ahead an' follow. There should be good places ta set up an ambush along that dip they ar' following. If they come back this way we can cut down the numbers against us."

Having switched to moccasins before leaving camp they were able to move silently, staying on the grass beside the horse trail. From a short distance ahead came the sound of a gunshot. Jar judged that the sound was loud enough to carry as far as the men back in camp at the lake. They found a short straight stretch along the trail and discussed the ambush. Jar moved into the trees right where they were, while Andre went ahead about twenty paces and disappeared into the trees on the other side.

Waiting is never easy. It was growing dim as the sun set before Jar heard the sound of horses coming. He watched as the two men came around a bend and started toward him. When they got to where he wanted them to be, he stepped into the trail and stood there holding his long bow, an arrow notched and a spare arrow gripped in his left hand. It was only a moment until the riders saw him and stopped their horses. In the dim light, they could see a big man in a buckskin hunting shirt, with a black, wide brimmed, leather hat on his head, standing silently in the trail. The man with the pipe spoke. "Who are you?"

Jar's voice grated. "That mare yea are sitting on is wearing mah brand."

The man seemed to sag. "Now see here, we were just following orders." Jar just watched them silently. They looked at each other; Jar could see their lips moving as they whispered. Suddenly, both started to raise their muskets, probably thinking, 'it's just one man armed with only a bow.' Jar pulled the bow and put a black arrow into the pipe smoker's chest. The pipe fell to the ground, the gun followed and the man slowly slumped and fell from the saddle.

Andre's arrow hit the other man a moment later and he toppled to the ground; neither got off a shot. Jar stood silently, watching for any sign of movement. After a moment, Andre's man slowly straightened one leg and sighed before going limp.

Jar walked forward to look at the men. Neither was familiar to him. Andre said the same after looking at them. They gathered the guns, knives and tomahawks, mounted the horses, and rode away, following the drainage west for half a mile before turning off and working their way back to camp. It was a cold camp, with no fire. Chewing on jerky, they discussed strategy. Two men disappearing like this would throw a fright into the four remaining men. In the dark, it was unlikely that anyone would venture out to look for the men. Tomorrow, the raiders would be frightened and most likely short of food. Logically, they would assume the two men were killed by Indians and this would add to their fears and fear would work on them. It was amazing what a man's mind could do to him if he allowed it to get out of control and run wild.

In the morning, from the same perch on the ridge, we watched the men hurriedly break camp and leave. They were moving fast and if they kept that pace the horses would tire. It was likely the men would get to the far west bend on the Mnisota where a small river flowed in from the west. Back in camp, we roasted fresh venison, ate a morning meal and packed up. Andre fussed over Rene's mare, patting her neck, and decided to ride her.

With the string of horses following, Andre led the way to the abandoned campsite to look for anything that would give information about these men. It was clear from the camp that the raiders possessed no great experience at wilderness living. The camp showed little knowledge of things that could make a camp more comfortable. One man was heavy with large feet. Andre decided another was just a boy. The place where this one slept was short, the footprints small. Andre glanced at Jar who became more silent with each passing day, his face mostly expressionless and a hard look in his eyes. Jar said none of them would make it to Garry. Andre wondered, 'what about this boy?' Andre knew Jar felt responsible for the two men killed and was worried about Rene—feeling that if he had been there he could have prevented Rene getting hurt.

Andre recalled Rene's descriptions of fights Jar and he were in on the trip to St. Louis and the journey back north to Sioux territory. Rene went into detail about the big battle they fought with the Santee against the Chippewa. This was so Andre could learn and benefit from the descriptions. Rene said that Jar always fought only to win, like a wounded grizzly that was cornered. In battle, he was merciless. Afterwards, Jar became caring. Again, Andre wondered, 'what about this boy?'

The raiders were pushing their horses too hard, rushing to get away, letting their fear override good judgment. This would wear down the horses and the men also. From the campsite, Andre knew that food was in short supply. There were no spits for roasting meat which was why two men had gone hunting.

Only fools behaved this way. They were rushing toward the safety of Fort Garry when they should have looked for an easily defended campsite, hunted for meat and rested the horses. Andre wondered if the raiders knew he and Jar were following or were just running from imagined fears. Curious! The raiders were sent to murder innocent competitors; probably with orders to burn the trading post and all the buildings. These men weren't brave warriors; they were cowards who had no place being out here in Indian country.

Late in the day, it was a surprise to find the raiders didn't stop at the bend of the river. They kept going and soon it would be dark. There would be no moon tonight with the overcast sky. The fools would stumble around in the dark. Jar turned west and they rode along the small river, crossed to the north side at a wide horseshoe-shaped bend and camped in the trees.

Shortly after picking up the trail in the morning, they found where the raiders stopped for the night, after wandering around in the dark. No fire. The grass was cropped were the horses were tethered. Watching the trail as the day wore on, it was obvious the horses were tired and starting to plod. Jar tried to think ahead. Somewhere, the men would have to stop and it would probably be near the Wild Rice which flowed in from the west and turned north, paralleling the Sioux. Most likely, the men would camp close to the Sioux as it seemed obvious they were not familiar with the terrain. Tomorrow they would continue north toward the Red. A plan began to take shape in his head.

Jar and Andre watched the four remaining raiders set up camp on the west bank of the Sioux. Andre led the way west to the Little Rice, where they found a sheltered place. With the horses picketed on good grass, they roasted venison and Jar told Andre his plan. After dark, they rode back to the Sioux and found a spot in one of the many twists of the river to light a campfire where it would be visible from the raider's camp. Jar cleared the ground, so the fire couldn't spread, while Andre gathered wood. When the tinder caught, Andre added small sticks until there was a good sized blaze.

With wood piled on the fire caught and flared up, throwing out a bright light. Walking the horses to a vantage point closer to the raiders, they watched for a reaction. It wasn't long in coming. The big man stood up and went into the darkness and quickly hurried back to point at the fire a mile or so south of them. Andre laughed softly as the raiders rushed to put out their campfire and darkness descended on the camp. There were two options open to the men. They could sit in the dark camp until morning or saddle their horses and ride off into the night. Either way, they would get little sleep. If the decision was to leave, it would be soon. What figured to be an hour later, there was still no sound of horses. On the ride back to camp, Andre commented, "Dumb white men, Indian not light big fire on high ground."

When the sun came up, the four raiders were gone. This was wide open grassland, or prairie, as the white man named it. As a consequence, they stayed well back so the raiders wouldn't see them following. 'Well, it wasn't all that open,' Jar thought, 'there were rolls in the land, water courses, and occasional shallow ravines. Still, all in all, you could see for miles.' Sitting in the saddles, they looked at the campsite before riding away, following the horse tracks. Once they were sure the raiders were headed north, they turned west and crossed the Wild Rice. It was unlikely the men would go east across the Sioux. If they came west, Jar or Andre would find the trail. By being out here west of the Wild Rice they could move faster with less chance of being seen by the raiders.

Shortly after midday, Andre pointed. "Riders over east, horses walk." Sure enough, there they were. Jar thought about it. "Andre at that pace I doubt they wull make th' Sheyenne afore dark." Andre nodded agreement. "I have been thinking on it. We have ruined two nights sleep fer them. If nothing disturbs them tonight, they may sleep sounder than they should."

Andre grinned. "We take horses?"

Jar smiled; the first smile in days. "Been thinking that. The sky is overcast an' if this wind holds it wull hide any noise we make sneaking in on them. If we put them afoot they are in trouble. Must still be two hundred miles to Garry?"

Andre agreed. "Dem not travelers like Jar. Long way walk. Need make moccasins."

Jar nodded. "We wull just trail along an' see where they stop. If it looks good we can try tonight."

Grey clouds scudded down from the northwest on a brisk wind and it felt like rain. There was a little light through the clouds that helped with visibility, even on such a dark night. Two dim figures sifted through the trees along the Sioux, slowly working toward the six horses, tied to a picket line strung between a pair of cottonwoods. The wind in the trees made a constant rustling sound. They had started watching shortly after dark and now it was well past midnight. Jar was suspicious. The raiders were camped on a spit of land where the Sioux swung around in almost a complete circle. There was water on three sides of the camp. What made Jar worry was the raider's position at the closed end of the spit, with the horses staked out between them and the opening. It seemed like they were using the horses as bait.

Andre argued the men were afraid of being attacked and put the horses between them and the open country to the west for safety—not realizing the horses could more easily be stolen. Now, after letting hours go by so the men relaxed, they were moving in.

They came with only knives and tomahawks. Jar brought his pistol because if they were discovered, using it would cause confusion and buy them a few extra seconds to escape.

The raiders' horses were tied to a picket line facing away from camp, so they wouldn't have to be turned, just led away. Ever so slowly, they crawled across the ground, their buckskins blending in with the late winter grass which was still brown with only a hint of new grass showing. Andre aimed for the near end of the picket line and Jar for the far end. Jar crawled to the base of a big cottonwood and lay still, listening, scanning the ground toward the camp. The horse closest to him stamped his feet and sidled sideways.

Satisfied, Jar came to his feet and grabbed the picket line with his left hand as he reached for his knife. The line went slack as Andre cut the other end. One slash with the big knife and Jar's end of the picket rope was free. Jar turned and took a step, feeling the resistance of the horses to moving. Andre must have done the same and the horses started forward. One slow step at a time, they led the horses away. The clop, clop of hooves seemed loud enough to wake an army.

After leading the horses well clear of the opening, they turned south. When they felt there was a good half mile behind them, Jar spoke softly. "Let's rig this rope so we can ride an' lead th' other four."

Sitting bareback on the horses, they rode south for two miles before turning west to ford the Sheyenne. Riding along the west side of the stream, they got back to camp just as it began to spit rain. If the sun showed its face this morning, it would be in an hour or so. With the additional horses added to the herd, there were now thirteen animals and Andre had his gelding back.

Andre picked up his long gun in its buckskin travelling sheath and cradled it in the crook of his left arm before picking up his bow. “Andre go watch, see what men do.”

“Better take some jerky. Don’na go too close an’ yea take care of yourself.”

Morning arrived, bringing a dull, grey light to the day. It stopped spitting and the ground was barely damp. Andre watched the campsite from a half mile west, lying in a shallow depression with last year’s tall brown grass around him. He saw a man sit up and stretch, before walking to the stream bank to relieve himself. As he stood there, he looked around and up at the sky. Turning back, he walked to his bedding and rolled it up. With the roll under one arm, he walked through the scattered trees toward the picket line. Suddenly, he stopped, just standing there and Andre felt sure he was staring in shock. The man dropped his bedroll and ran back to camp, his arms waving. He appeared to be yelling, although Andre couldn’t hear him. The rest of the camp came alive all at once.

Andre watched them rush to the picket line. The big man picked up the rope where Jar had cut it, looked and threw it down in disgust. He stomped around, waving his arms and probably cursing. A slim man started looking at the ground under the trees. Andre smiled to himself. If the man could read tracks he would see footprints made by moccasins. If he was really good, he would recognize them as Cree-style moccasins. Two men rushed out through the opening, looked at the ground and started to follow the trail south. Soon, they realized they didn’t have their muskets and hurried back to camp.

Arguing took a long time as the day continued to brighten.

Finally, they started a fire and put a coffee pot in the side of the flames to boil. Andre cut off a good-sized chunk of jerky and held it in his cheek to soften before beginning to methodically chew. He watched all morning as the men argued. They didn't seem to be able to agree on a course of action. Finally, at about midday, they started moving, carrying bedrolls and muskets, with very little else.

Clearing the opening, they turned north and started the long trek to Fort Garry. Four dejected looking men, walking in a line. Andre wondered how far they would get before blistered feet started giving them trouble. He watched them until they disappeared into a dip in the land.

After eating their fill of meat and drinking coffee, Rene led the way to the vacant campsite to recover any gear that might be useful. Just before dark, Andre used his bow to bring down a deer. They dressed out the meat and wrapped it in the hide, ready for travelling the next day. The raiders wouldn't get far—with the late start they made, twenty miles at the most. They would need to hunt, which should be easy with all the deer along the river. It was their feet that would be a problem, provided one of them didn't break a leg or sprain an ankle. It was relatively easy to cross the flatland along the Red River.

With eleven horses on lead, Andre picked up the tracks and they trotted along the trail. The raiders didn't make twenty miles. They now had meat. There wasn't much to the campsite, so Jar moved them on. Andre had half-expected Jar to turn back, now that all the horses had been recovered. He was surprised Jar was pressing on. They found the remains of a fire where the raiders had stopped at midday. Jar commented, "I want ta get ahead, let's pull off ta the west an' go around them."

Andre was puzzled. "You go to Garry?"

Jar looked at him. "Have business there. Yea can see your family." Feeling sorry for his gruff manner, he added, "We are over halfway there now, so we may as well go all the way." Jar thought, 'It isn't Andre's fault for what happened, I must remember that.'

The men made an estimated twelve miles during the morning, so they rode about the same distance and came back to the river, located a good campsite and picketed the horses. Jar packed the ropes they had found in the abandoned camp on a horse and commented to Andre, "Let's go meet them."

South they went, four or five miles, until they saw the men plodding toward them. Long guns across their saddles, they kept the horses walking. Jar stopped near a group of large cottonwoods. The men finally saw them and waved as they picked up their pace. When they were within range of his Charleville, Jar held up his hand. "That is close enough."

The men stopped, looking puzzled. The big man waved and called, "Sure glad to see you. You come from Fort Garry? We could use some help. Indians stole our horses and we have walked for two days." He started forward.

Jar held up his hand. "Yea stay there. We don'na know yea. Put the muskets down an' we'll talk."

The leader hesitated, wondering who these unfriendly white men from Fort Garry were. Finally, with a nod of his head, he laid his musket on the grass at his feet. The other two followed his example.

The small man at the back of the line didn't have a musket. Jar pointed with the Charleville. "Move over ta that big cottonwood an' sit down."

Jar dismounted, ground hitched the roan, and walked to within ten paces of the men with the Charleville cradled in his left arm. They were a dirty, discouraged group, obviously tired. The big man wore boots, the others moccasins. There was a hole in the sole of one man's moccasin. Jar asked, "Where ar' yea men coming from?"

The big one answered. "Down to the south. We'uns is in the employ of the Bay, up to Fort Garry."

"If yea are in the employ of th' Bay at Fort Garry please explain what yea ar' doing in Sioux country."

"This be Bay territory." The voice was loud and blustery. "The Factor sent us to get rid of renegades that be trading Missouri furs what belongs to the company."

"What right does th' Factor have ta claim the furs belong ta him?"

That puzzled the man. "The Factor be the law. Always been that way."

"Yea say th' Factor is th' law, so he metes out justice. What would his justice be if an Indian were ta murder one of his men?"

"That uns easy." The big man laughed. "Last fall a Cree knifed a trader for bedding his young daughter. De Factor said it was murder and we'uns hung dat Indian."

"So th' Factor is th' law, judge, an' jury?"

The big man laughed. "Dat so. Factor be next to God."

Jar was silent as he considered his course of action. He looked carefully at the men and suddenly realized one of the men was a mere boy. In his cold fury, he hadn't noticed before. He walked over and asked, "How old are yea, son?"

"Be fourteen this coming summer."

"An employee of the Bay. What is your job on this expedition?"

"To tend the horses, take them to water, see they eats. Rustle firewood."

Jar stepped back. "As yea say, gentlemen, the Factor is the law at Fort Garry. Yea are in my territory an' here I am the law. Yea invaded my territory, stole horses, murdered two of my men, an' injured two others. Yea are under arrest. Andre, please bring ropes an' tie their hands."

Andre started with the big man, tying his hands behind his back and did the same for the next two. He looked inquiringly at Jar. "Leave the boy be, he is no part o' this." Andre felt a huge sense of relief.

"Now, gentlemen, I have arrested yea fer murder an' thievery an' all of us know yea are guilty as charged. Therefore, using th' same justice your Factor employs, I sentence each of yea to hang."

The men were in shock and frightened. The big man became angry and shouted, "You'uns can't do that. We followed the Factor's orders. He decides." He raved on and Jar ignored him as he picked up a rope and began tying a hangman's noose.

With the boy riding on the packhorse, they rode away, leaving three men hanging from a large cottonwood branch.

Chapter 17

North we rode, following the Red River past the Goose and Forest, until we came to the Tongue and Pembina rivers, all running full from the snow melt, adding their waters to the Red. Once across the Pembina, Andre felt he was home. Pointing the horses to the northwest, Andre led the way across country toward Fort la Reine on the Assiniboine River where he was born and grew to manhood. Andre explained that the old fort was the starting point for the *portage la prairie* where trade goods were hauled over the grassland for fifteen miles to the big lake the Cree called *Manitou wapow.* Andre's family found work each summer moving trade goods north to the lake and packs of furs south to the Assiniboine. In recent years, the local Métis began to refer to their scattered collection of cabins as Portage la Prairie.

They kept the boy with them. He was an orphan named Louis Chouart; he spoke French, Cree and ragged English. He had been raised by an uncle until he was twelve and after that the uncle left.

Louis was handy around camp, a good worker who was willing to help with anything that needed doing. Initially, he was frightened of Jar and tried to stay near Andre as much as possible. Jar was still withdrawn and quiet, causing Louis to wonder what troubles he was wrestling with in his head.

A short day's travel from la Portage, they settled into camp. Jar watched Louis gather wood and start a fire. The lad had filled out some since joining them, probably because he was eating more regularly than in the past. Suddenly, it occurred to Jar; Louis was the same age as he was when he signed a contract with the Bay and left Glasgow for America. Not often did he think of those times. He remembered Mac McGregor, the man who did so much to help him, to prepare him for the rough, tough world and encourage him to go to America. Thank God for Mac.

His mind drifted back through the years, remembering the old farm, Mac, coming across the Atlantic in a Bay Company sailing ship and the canoe trip west to Fort Garry. He got lost in memories from those years and didn't hear when Andre told him his meat was ready. Andre stood up and came around the fire. He nudged Jar's leg with the toe of his boot. "Your meat is ready."

Jar's head snapped up. "Thank yea, Andre."

Andre watched Jar stand up. "Don't thank, Andre, Louis cook meat for you. Soon you so spoiled Willow Flower not want Jar."

For the first time in days, Jar grinned and slapped Andre on the shoulder. He picked up the spit that held his meat, cut a slice and chewed. He looked across the fire at Louis and smiled. "Good job of cooking, Louis, thank yea."

Louis replied with a tentative smile, in awe of this big redheaded man who was so strong and sure of himself. Like no one Louis had known before, he washed almost every day, shaved and kept his clothes clean and neat. Louis was scared almost to death when Jar hung the three men for murder, sure he would be abandoned, or worse. Instead, they took him to their camp and fed him all he could eat. Andre handed him a bedroll. Next morning, when they rode away he was sitting in the saddle that belonged to the leader of the raiders. It took him several days to become accustomed to a saddle, the first one he had ridden in. Louis was surprised when Jar spoke to him again. "Now that yea are back an' close ta home, *Louis*, what ar' yea going ta do?"

That was something Louis worried about constantly. *"Louis* don know, *Monsieur."*

Jar fell silent as he chewed another slice of meat. 'Of course; the boy said he was an orphan. There was most likely no home for him to go to.' When they finished eating, Jar suggested to Andre, "A man like Louis should have an outfit. The saddle an' mare he is riding would be about right fer him. One day he can get himself a colt out of that mare. Yea take Louis an' go through the gear we picked up an' get him a good outfit. Everything he needs."

Andre was pleased. The old Jar he knew over the years was back. He glanced at the boy to see the startled look that slowly turned into a happy grin. Andre started with trade muskets. He knew how important a long gun would be to the boy. Together, they checked all the guns, finally selecting the one that seemed best. They cleaned it, loaded up and test-fired the gun. Louis was happy. Andre set out powder, shot, and additional lead, along with a ball mold. Louis got a large knife and a tomahawk. Andre glanced across the camp. Jar was writing in his log, a daily task he rarely neglected. Louis pointed to a fire-steel and Andre handed it and a flint to him.

Louis took his gear and put it with his saddle before walking over to the mare to fuss over her. After riding her for days, she was now his. Andre put the packs back together and tied them, keeping an eye on the happy boy and his mare.

In the morning, they went hunting. Andre wanted to arrive at la Portage with fresh meat for the table. He and Louis each shot a fat buffalo cow; cut out the tongues, shoulder humps and best cuts of meat, wrapped it in the hides and loaded the packs on horses.

When they rode up to the cabin where Andre had lived as a boy his mother was sitting on a bench outside the door, enjoying the spring sun. Andre suddenly realized his mother was no longer young. She had raised three children and worked hard all those years feeding and clothing them. She looked up and stared at him. It was three summers since Andre had come to visit and she worried; maybe he was no longer able to come. Now, here he was. She got slowly to her feet, her knees stiff and hurting. Ignoring the pain, she stood up to greet her son. Andre leaped from his horse and hurried across the hard-packed dirt that fronted the cabin to hug his mother. When he stepped back to look at her, she was laughing and crying at the same time. Using a corner of the ever-present apron, she dried her eyes. "So good see you, my son. I worried. Your Papa says you come this summer."

Andre looked around. "Where Papa?"

"He helps with horses. Papa come soon. Come, sit, tell me how Andre is." She remembered her manners and turned toward the horses. "Greetings, Monsieur Richardson, come, sit with us."

Jar removed his hat. "It is nice ta see yea again, Mrs. Troyes." Her eyes shifted. "Andre, who this other man?"

Andre waved his arm toward Louis. "Mama, this is our friend Louis Chouart. He rides with us." Louis heard the 'our friend' and his happiness swelled. He almost missed her greeting.

"Greetings, Monsieur Chouart, come, sit."

"Bonjour Madame, thank you." As the men dismounted, she asked, "Where Rene? Why you not bring Rene?"

"Rene stayed to look after the trading post, Mama." Andre glanced at Jar. "Rene hurt leg, Mama, he not want ride horse."

Jar and Louis unloaded the meat while Andre sat with his mother on the bench. There were many things to discuss and catch up on after three years. Leading the horses to water and coming back to tether them on grass, the two men went about setting up camp under a large poplar tree. The location provided a good view of the hard-packed area in front of the cabin. A young lad came around the cabin and Jar watched as Andre stood to grab the boy around the shoulders. Mrs. Troyes pointed, said something to the lad and he ran off. Not long after, people started to gather. Word was spreading that Andre was home to visit. Family and friends crowded around to hear and tell stories. It was an occasion for a party and soon the Métis had a fire going under a large kettle hanging from a tripod; the women were busy cooking, while the men talked and children ran everywhere. In the evening, one man produced a fiddle and soon they were dancing and singing the old songs. There were more than fifty people gathered. Jar wondered if they could all be relatives. It didn't matter. The Métis were a close community and everyone was welcome.

Jar lay in his blankets, listening to the shouts and noise. Light from the fire flickered on the tree branches above him. He dropped off to sleep while considering the things he wanted to do while here. In the morning, when he looked, Andre was sleeping in the bed they had rolled out for him. Jar dressed to start his day and Louis joined him.

Over tin plates of stew left over from the night before, Andre and Jar talked about the day. First, Andre and Jar would deliver the remaining possessions of the men who were killed by the raiders to their mothers. There was a small purse from each man containing money saved from the wages Jar paid them. To each purse, Jar added fifty American dollars. Jar wanted to trade for a white mare to take back and Andre said he would ask around. Andre needed to find new men to fill the vacancies created by the fight.

Louis listened to this talk and wondered.

Andre and Jar rode away to complete a task neither wanted to do, leaving Louis to look after the camp. It would be sad informing these mothers their sons were dead. Still, Jar felt it was his responsibility. They were back before midday. Jar rolled his bedding and tied the bundle behind his saddle. Louis watched and listened as Jar told Andre, "Going ta ride over Garry way. While yea are looking fer tha' horse ask about beef cattle. See if yea can find two cows an' a bull. Good stuff that wull help us ta start a herd."

"Andre will see what he can find. When Jar be back?"

"Three, four days, I expect." Jar gathered his gear and turned to the roan.

Louis interjected, "Monsieur Jar take Louis to Garry?"

Jar turned back. "Yea want ta go ta Fort Garry, Louis?"

"Oui, Monsieur Jar. Fort Garry Factor say pay Louis five dollars to look after horses."

Jar was surprised. "Well now, Louis, yea ride along an' we will collect yer five dollars." Jar grinned at Andre. "Expect we better take a packhorse along ta carry meat an' supplies."

"You want me to come, Jar?" Andre was clearly worrying about what Jar was up to.

"Yea stay an' visit with your family. See if yea can find a horse an' those cattle."

Louis came with his horse saddled and brought a packhorse. While they were loading the horse, Louis spoke, "Andre hire men. Louis need work, you hire Louis?"

Andre glanced at Jar, who nodded his head in agreement. Andre smiled at the boy. "You go to Fort Garry. When you come back you can start work."

"Oui, Monsieur Andre, thank you." A very happy Louis climbed into his saddle and, long gun in hand, sat ready to ride. Jar glanced at Louis, swung into his saddle and turned the roan east.

The ride would be close to fifty miles and they set a steady, ground-eating pace which brought them close before dark. They established a camp in a well hidden and protected nook on the north side of the Assiniboine River.

In the first grey light, Jar packed up and got ready to go. Arriving at the scattered log buildings, he stopped his horse and looked around. Nothing much had changed in the years since he left in the summer of 1799. There were a few more sod-covered cabins and the usual teepees. Again, he thought how odd it was that this jumble of shacks was referred to as a fort. The Bay wasn't noted for putting money or effort into providing accommodations for employees and many spent miserable winters trying to survive. There were a few people moving around, starting the day's tasks. He noted smoke rising from the chimney of the Factor's house and a few of the other buildings.

Louis followed as Jar rode toward the Factor's house and stopped sixty or so paces from the door. Jar carried a leather quiver full of black arrows on his back and was holding the bow that always amazed Louis with its length. A man came out of a nearby cabin and walked toward the house. Jar spoke. "Tell th' Factor that two gentlemen ar' here ta talk wi' him."

The man was startled, stared at them and hurried to the door. He knocked before opening the door and going in. Several minutes went by and Jar sat calmly waiting. Finally, through the open door two men came out. The Factor looked even seedier than Jar remembered. The man was always a regular drinker of the rum provided by the company. By the look of him, he drank a few mugs the night before.

The Factor walked out a few paces before stopping. He put a hand above his eyes for shade from the morning sun, which was behind Jar. "Who says he wants to talk to the Factor?"

Jar waved one hand at Louis. "Yea owe Mr. Chouart five dollars. He is har ta collect his money."

The Factor squinted. "Louis, is that you, Louis?"

"It is me, Monsieur Factor. Louis wishes to collect his five dollars."

"Yes, yes of course, Louis. Where are the other men? Tell me how the trip went."

Jar cut in. "First th' five dollars. Then yea wull hear th' news."

More people were gathering out of curiosity to see what was happening and hear any news that would relieve the boredom of the trading post. Who was this big man with the wide black hat? The

Factor turned to his clerk and instructed, "Go to the office and get Louis' five dollars and give it to him. Hurry now, I want to hear the news."

The clerk ran back and handed the five dollars in coins to Louis. The Factor came a few more paces and moved to one side to avoid the sun in his eyes. "Now, Louis, tell me the news." He was focused on Louis without really looking at Jar.

Jar answered. "Louis' business with yea is finished. Now, there is the matter of one hundred American dollars yea owes me."

The Factor blustered. "I owe no one a hundred dollars. Who are you to make such a claim?"

Jar removed his hat to let the red hair show. After a moment, he resettled the hat on his head. "James Angus Richardson at your service, yea cowardly, louse-infested, rum-soaked sot. Yea sent nine men south ta burn mah trading post. They murdered two of mah men an' wounded two others. None of your men are coming back. I gave fifty American dollars ta each dead man's mother. Yea owe me one hundred dollars. I rode four hundred miles ta collect an' ta tell yea that if yea or any man working fer the company ever comes south again I wull wipe yea out."

The Factor was never talked to like this. No one dared to question his orders. He flew into a rage and shook his fist. "No one talks to me like this. Ridiculous; utter rubbish. I won't stand for it!" The Factor turned to leave and took three steps. Jar notched an arrow and the gathered onlookers gasped. He was going to shoot the Factor. Jar pulled the bow and sank a long black arrow into the door of the log cabin where it vibrated for a moment.

The Factor stopped, afraid to move, as he stared at the arrow in his door. He couldn't run fast enough to get inside to his musket before an arrow would find him. He shivered with fear, he wanted to run, he tried to run and found his feet had grown roots. "Now hear this, yea gutter snipe. Your orders resulted in two men being killed who were far better men than yea have ever been. In three days, I will return. Yea have a hundred dollars ready or I will cut out your heart to feed the camp dogs an' stick your head on a pike fer everyone ta stare at."

Jar turned his horse and rode away with an amazed, awestruck Louis following with the packhorse. The crowd watched until the riders disappeared. The post clerk went to the Factor, who hadn't moved; the man had wet himself. The clerk took the Factor's arm and tugged him toward the house. Several men followed. One pulled the arrow from the door. They handed the black arrow around for everyone to see. A Métis commented, "The Sioux be telling stories of a great warrior with magic medicine who shoots black arrows." The story spread with the speed of a grassfire in a strong wind. Andre heard it the next day.

Jar and Louis rode south to the *Riviere Sale* where a few Métis were starting to farm, forded the river and carried on south over the amazingly flat grasslands spotted with small herds of buffalo. Jar speculated on how the land could be as flat as a tabletop. Some twenty miles south of the river, they came to another group of farms. Riding up to a small cabin and crude barn, Jar saw a broad-shouldered young farmer leading a cow in from pasture and recognized immediately that he was Scottish. The man wore a plaid tam. The farmer stopped and waited for them. Jar turned on the old language. "Noo laddie, be ye from th' auld country?"

"Aye, 'at Ah am an' yea noo, yea hav' th' hair tae be Scottish if yea nae be from Irelain."

Jar laughed with delight. "Nam is James Angus Richardson frae nie Glasgow an' it be a pleasure tae meet yea."

"Aye laddie an' Ah be John McDonald frae th' far west coast, forced aff th' land by th' Laird McDonald who cares mair fur sheep than he diz fer th' clan."

"That be a sorry thing they dae." Jar wondered before he asked. "Hoo long hae ye bin here?"

"Th' misses an' Ah cam th' past summer. We built 'at cabin yonder an' dug up a wee garden. It was tay late ta plant seed. Any day noo will be a braw time tae start. Got thas milch coo an' not much else; noo th' misses tells me thur wull be a wee McDonald come fall. We'd invite ye tae table, laddie, except we scarce got enaw fer oorselves an' it nae fittin' fer company."

Jar turned his head to look out at the prairie beyond the small farm. "There ar' buffalo all aroun' ye what make fine eating."

"Aye, laddie, Ah knows. Ah naw got a gun an' wouldna ken hoo tae use it if'n Ah did."

Jar smiled. "Noo thaur we can be ay help tae ye. Have ye room in yon barn to hang meat?"

McDonald looked relieved. "Ah' tak' that kindly ay ye. All we got is whit milk thes coo gives an some greens. Wi' meat we might make it till th' garden grows. Th' misses told me Ah was a fool tae try farmin' in thas great open land wi' th' long blowing wind."

Jar nodded at Louis. "My partner here is as good a hunter as there is on the plains. We will go and fetch yea a buffalo cow; they are the best of eating." McDonald watched them ride away. He tied his cow quickly before hurrying to tell his wife the good news.

A mile or so away, the men found a suitable buffalo cow. Louis dropped the animal. Together, they skinned the buff, took the best cuts of meat, wrapped them in the hide and rode back to the farm.

Louis started a fire in the yard to roast meat. John and Mrs. McDonald sat with them. Jar explained how to scrape and prepare the buffalo hide, telling them it would make a warm robe. Mrs. McDonald kept eyeing one particular piece of meat that was over the fire. Finally, she asked, "Whit is 'at peculiar slice ay meat?

Jar looked at the meat. "That, Mrs. McDonald, is buffalo tongue. Everyone oon th' plains wull teel ye it is th' choicest part ay a buffalo."

She looked doubtful, so Jar decided to change the subject. "What did ye do in th' auld coontry, John?"

"Ah' went ae school till sixteen and thin apprenticed ae a bookkeeper. Faither cam doon ill ae Ah went back ae th' farm ae help out. Julia and Ah were only jist married when the Laird chased us aff th' land. We heard abit thes land an' th' need fer farmers ae we sold whit we could an cam tae make a new life. After we got haur we foond th' Bay Company does'nae want farmers here coz they ur scared ut will hurt th' fur trade. We ur tryin'. As Julia says, we may hae ae move oan."

Jar observed. "T'is good land, John, much better than th' rocky farm I grew up on."

"That it is, James, except there's naethin' haur. Only a handful ay settlers an' thaur is nae support fer any of us except whit we can do fer each other. Given a chance, thes land woold grow great crops. Ah woold be happy ae get a garden an' a bit ay oats fer the porridge."

Again, Jar changed the subject. "Be there a preacher among ye?"

"Aye, thur is. Th' Reverend Miles Christie, a Presbyterian, cam oan his own ae care fer us. He is trying ae make it oan a wee farm like oors an' preaches come a Sunday."

"Could yea tell me how tae locate him?"

"Anither group ay settlers ur south ay here about five miles located jist above th' flood line oan the Red River. Ye ride doon thaur an' someone will point ye ae his place."

"Thank ye, John." Jar took the buffalo tongue and cut it into four pieces. He handed the McDonalds each a piece and watched them cautiously try it. After a small bite, they seemed convinced and ate the meat. Jar smiled to himself. They would learn. It was tough on people coming into this land with no preparation. Most of the early ones would fail; he hoped the McDonalds would make it.

They left the McDonalds to hang the meat and rode south. It was late when they found the settlement so they looked for a campsite for the night. Morning would be soon enough to look for the reverend. The first man Jar asked leaned on his shovel and pointed with one hand. "Yea wull be finding Miles spading his garden plot two farms that way."

"Thank yea, sir, we will just ride over that way an' have a word with Christie." The farmer watched them briefly before taking up his shovel again. Jar saw Christie from afar, a tall, lean figure, his wild hair flying in the breeze as he dug away at the ground, turning over the soil in a fury of activity. Christie saw them as they arrived and watched as Jar dismounted, hung his hat on the saddle horn, and stepped away from the roan. The Reverend smiled. "Now, laddie, with hair lik' that ye must be a Scot."

Jar smiled back, lowered the butt of his long gun to the ground and replied, "Aye that I am. Are ye th' Reverend Miles Christie?" Christie was as tall as Jar, only thin and a good thirty pounds lighter.

Christie showed he possessed a streak of humor. "Well noo, laddie, that all depends. Be ye a bill collector, Christie may have left some time ago. Now, if ye ur looking fer a wee bit of preaching, ye have found him."

Jar laughed, he liked this man already. He stuck out his hand. "Nam is James Angus Richardson and it is th' bit of preaching that interests me."

Christie shook the hand and his grip was firm. "Angus, is it? As fine a Scottish name as a mon could want. My grandfather was named th' same an' he was never late when called to plate. Come, let us sit an' talk awhile. Ah would hear more of this preaching yea mentioned." Jar sat on the grass cross-legged like an Indian with the Charleville across his knees. Christie leaned on one elbow, his legs extended. "Noo, Angus, tell me what is on 'ur mind."

"I plan ta be married this summer an' want it done up proper, wi' a prayer an' a signed paper."

"Aye, Angus, that is th' way it should be. In th' two years since arriving Ah have buried two people an' baptized three babies an' nary a wedding. What be th' lassie's name?"

Jar laughed. "She is no lassie, reverend. Just th' most beautiful lady in this great wide land. Slim as a willow tree an' beautiful as a flower. Quick to learn an' as full of questions as any three people. Her name is Willow Flower."

"Flower is no a family name Ah am familiar with. Where is th' lady from?"

Jar looked at him steadily and Christie noticed the eyes go cold. He felt he might have done something to offend. "Willow Flower is from th' Yanktonai Sioux Nation. She is a lady an' I have asked her ta marry me."

"Of course, Angus, Ah meant noo harm with my comment. It is normal for a minister ta acquaint himself with both parties ta a wedding." Christie watched Jar relax and continued. "Will yea an' th' lady come here fer th' wedding?"

Jar was suddenly more formal, less friendly. "No, sir. I own a trading post south of here on th' Mnisota River. I will pay fer your time ta travel there an' perform th' wedding."

Christie stared in amazement. "Ah can do that. Only thing is, how wull Ah find my way, Angus? Ah dinna own a horse an' am no familiar with th' country."

Jar considered. "Mr. Chouart yonder works for me an' will be bringing cattle an' other things south in about ninety days. If yea agree ta come, I will give yea a horse an' saddle to keep an' pay yea for your time."

Christie was amazed. This man could afford to give him a horse and pay him while he and the other settlers struggled just to provide food for the table. With a horse, he could get around to visit all the settlers; it was like a gift from heaven. He closed his eyes and quickly said a prayer of thanks. "Hoo long wull Ah be away from this settlement?"

"With the cattle it wull take thirty days or so ta travel south. If yea stay with us fer thirty days, th' total time wull be around eighty days."

Christie knew he could not pass on such an opportunity. To earn a couple of dollars and receive a horse was beyond his dreams. Maybe this was an opportunity sent from the Lord so while he was there he could do a wee bit of the Lord's work among the natives. He was full of questions and Jar tried to satisfy him. They discussed the details and Jar promised to stop by in a few days on his way south.

Finally, Christie went back to his shovel. He watched as his visitors rode away going north.

Two days after the threat, people started arriving at Garry. French Voyageurs, Orkneyman, Métis and a few Cree coming for the entertainment. Two-wheeled carts with wives and children drove slowly into the settlement. Lives here were full of hard work and struggle, with very little entertainment; that only what they made for themselves. Now, someone was challenging the Factor for doing something they all knew he had done. Everyone knew at least one of the nine men recruited for the raid. The men talked, discussing every detail of what was happening until there was nothing left to say, so they turned to speculating.

Crude shelters sprang up and campfires burned all around the trading post. It was the largest gathering of people ever seen at Garry. The Factor didn't show his face and only the chief clerk was allowed into his house. The sun rose on the third day accompanied by great expectations. The morning the challenge was made the man came from the east so the sun was in the Factor's eyes and they waited for him to reappear the same way.

At first light, Andre rode his horse into the compound. He stopped where there was a clear view to the Factor's house and the trading post. He sat with his Charleville across the Spanish saddle, pointing at the buildings, offering to talk to no one. This gave the crowd more to speculate about. Maybe the lone man wasn't alone.

Andre was barely in place when a Dakota Sioux Indian chief leading a group of warriors rode up to the post and stopped on a slight rise in the land to the south of the buildings. The warriors were armed with bows, spears and a few trade muskets obtained from this very post in exchange for furs. They spread out in a line on each side of their chief to watch the spectacle. The chief clerk sent a trader to see what the Sioux wanted. At first, the chief ignored the trader. Finally, they conversed in a mixture of Sioux and French before the trader walked back. Many in the crowd pressed close to hear his words as the trader reported to the chief clerk. "The Sioux chief says they have come to see Black Arrow, the great warrior and medicine man, who fought with the Santee when they defeated the Chippewa." This news spread rapidly through the crowd, causing a stir.

As the sun rose in the sky, the crowd started to become restless. In his house, the Factor began thinking Richardson wasn't coming. He even considered going out to talk to the crowd. His fear of what happened the first day kept him inside.

Shortly before midday a warrior spoke to his chief and pointed. The Sioux moved their horses to leave a gap in the line beside their chief. Word spread through the crowd that a rider was coming and people craned their necks to be the first to see who it was.

The big roan horse came up the rise and stopped between the two groups of Sioux. People saw a big man in grey pants and a deerskin hunting shirt, wearing a wide-brimmed black leather hat with a long gun across the saddle in front of him. Those close enough heard him speak to the chief in the Sioux language. Warriors looked at each other. This Black Arrow was no fool. He didn't use the same trail in case of an ambush. Truly, he was wise.

Jar sat and waited. From the corner of his eye, he saw Andre across the packed dirt compound and smiled inside. 'Good old Andre, should have told him.'

It took a few minutes. Finally, the door of the house opened and the chief clerk came out carrying a leather bag. He walked up the rise until the long gun moved to point at his chest. He stopped, holding up the bag.

Jar didn't greet the man, he just said, "Count it."

The clerk knelt and emptied the bag on the ground. Jar watched him as he counted out loud and dropped the coins into the bag. The clerk stood up and walked close enough to hand the bag up to Jar; turned and walked away. Jar watched him for a moment before he swung the roan and started away. Andre kicked his horse in the ribs, rode around the Sioux to follow and Louis came in from the other side.

Chapter 18

As they followed the Assiniboine west, Jar gradually relaxed. The bad business with the Factor was over. They didn't push the horses and rode at a leisurely pace. When the trail permitted, they rode three abreast with Louis in the middle position. The horses were at a walk, going up a long slope named High Bluff as Andre related, "Andre trade two long guns, powder we capture for two cows with new calves. Those calves are females. Dey be at la Portage this day. Orkneyman has young bull, no family to cows. He say nine dollar for bull. Andre tell him Jar will come talk."

Jar nodded in agreement. "How far ta his place, Andre?"

Andre removed his hat and scratched. "Andre think ten miles from la Portage."

"An easy ride. We can go tomorrow an' if he wull deal, bring th' bull back. How long before those calves wull be able ta travel?"

"Farmer says three months for calves to get good legs."

Topping out on the bluff, they stopped to let the horses rest. Jar shifted in his saddle, inquiring, "Have yea found men ta hire?"

"Andre tell people need two men and look for good mare. They come, you see."

Jar smiled. "Louis, can yea herd those cows south ta th' Mnisota

River an' bring along Reverend Christie?"

"Oui, Monsieur Jar, Louis will do."

"Good man, Louis. Andre, when yea find those two men they can stay at la Portage an' come south with Louis. You tell them Louis wull be th' man in charge." Jar rubbed the red stubble on his jaw thoughtfully. "I promised to give Christie a horse an' saddle, so remember that, Louis." Andre looked past Louis as he listened to Jar and noticed the way Louis sat up straighter in his saddle. Louis was gaining in confidence every day. He was responding to being treated like a man.

The screech of cart axles reached them before a sturdy ox lumbered into sight coming around a corner in the trail, pulling a wooden cart with tall wooden wheels. These carts were made locally, totally from wood and because the axles were not greased, they made a terrible noise that was irritating to the ears. The screech coming from axles could be heard for long distances. A Métis man walked beside the cart, carrying a prodding pole to control the ox. As the cart came abreast of them, the Métis called to the animal to stop. Leaning against a high wheel that reached above his head, the man fished in a leather sack, brought out a clay pipe and began tamping it with tobacco. In height, he was about five foot nothing with legs curved like barrel staves. His clothing was a mixture of leather and wool with a fur hat on his long white hair. When the pipe was tamped to his satisfaction, he gathered together dry grass and a few small sticks to start a fire. With a burning taper from the fire, he lit the pipe and puffed several times. Sitting down cross-legged by the fire, he added sticks before looking up. His eyes took in all three men before settling on Andre. "By hap you have spare coffee for pot?"

Andre dismounted and went to the packhorse. He came back with a handful of beans. Watching all this, Jar decided this was a man who spent his time alone and wasn't accustomed to conversation. His eyes were sharp, missing nothing, even though he avoided eye contact. Those sharp eyes saw Andre get the beans. He got to his feet nimbly for a man his age and went to the cart, found a blackened pot and filled it with water from a jug.

Back at the fire, he added sticks and set the pot to heat while watching Andre wrap the beans in a square of deerskin and use the side of his tomahawk to mash the beans. When the water boiled, Andre lifted the lid to add the beans. Jar and Louis took the horses aside and tied them to trees where they could crop grass. They came with cups and sat at the fire with long guns across their legs. Andre reached to move the pot away from the coals so it could stop boiling. The old Metis watched the pot closely as it cooled and held out a cup. Andre filled it for him. He tasted it, then tasted it again and smacked his lips. His sharp eyes slanted toward Jar. "You clerk usta be Garry?" Jar nodded in agreement. "You friend Beauchamp. Where Beauchamp?"

"Rene is down south a ways running a fur trading post on th' Mnisota River."

"Ah." The old man nodded his head and returned his attention to his cup to drink coffee. He held out his cup and Andre refilled it. He took a mouthful and swallowed. "Snowed in, no beans long time."

Jar stood up, walked to his horse and removed a cloth bag of coffee beans from his saddlebag. He came back and set it on the ground beside the Métis. The old man looked at the bag, finished his cup, and commented, “Thank ye.”

They gathered their gear, mounted up and started away. Without looking up the old man commented, “Old Joe hello to Beauchamp.”

The horses trotted into the yard at la Portage well short of sundown and Papa Troyes came to visit as they settled into camp again. They were here, so their business with the Factor went well. He would hear the story soon enough. Mama Troyes came with a kettle and filled their tin plates with stew. Andre hurried to bring the bench, so his parents could sit while dinner progressed and darkness came. Papa Troyes told them stories of when Andre was young.

In the morning, they rode across the grasslands to see the bull. He was two years old and as far as they could detect sound of limb and body. The Orkneyman wanted nine dollars. He showed them the big bull that sired the two year old and praised his attributes. Jar went back to the two year old and looked again. He offered six dollars and the Orkneyman shook his head. Jar walked around the young bull again, stood back for a good view and rubbed his clean-shaven chin before asking, “Do yea have a halter ta fit this bull?”

The Orkneyman went into a shed and came back with a heavy rawhide halter, slipped it over the bull’s nose and tied it around his neck. Jar tugged on the halter and it was strong. There was a loop of rawhide to tie a rope to. Again, Jar rubbed his chin and stated, “Yea throw in that halter an’ I will pay eight dollars.”

The Orkneyman nodded. “Sold.”

Louis led the bull home and staked him out on a fresh plot of grass to graze with the cows. Several men were sitting in the yard and Andre found there were three men looking for the two jobs. Over the next two days, men kept coming with mares for sale and

Jar inspected each horse. He rejected all of them as they weren't what he wanted. Andre hired two men and there was nothing else to keep them in la Portage. The unneeded gear recovered from the raiders was all sold or traded. They would leave in the morning.

Louis helped with loading two spare riding horses with packs and Andre went to say goodbye to his mother. At the sound of hooves approaching, Jar looked around and watched a man ride into the clearing, leading a snow white mare. The man came to a stop beside the loaded horses. "Is the man looking for a riding mare around?"

Jar stepped forward. "I am th' man."

The man tossed Jar the lead rope. "You have a look. You like her, we see if a deal is to be made."

Jar walked, hand over hand, up the lead rope until he got to the horse and patted her neck. He looked at her eyes, checked her teeth, lifted each hoof to check the feet and hocks for soundness and walked around the mare, running his hands over her, checking the muscles. Louis held the lead rope while Jar switched his saddle from the roan to the mare. Jar rode her out of the yard and turned her using the halter and lead rope. She handled well and responded quickly. Jar tried different gaits until he was satisfied. Trotting her back to the yard, he removed the saddle. Louis took it and went to saddle the roan. Jar walked around the mare, checking her again. He walked away to see her from a distance.

Satisfied, he came back and asked, "What yea asking fer her?"

"Eighteen dollars."

"Give you twelve."

"She a mighty fine horse. Four years old this spring, trained well. Easy riding. Tell you what. Fifteen dollars, you can have her."

Jar smiled. "Leave th' halter an' lead rope on her an' yea got a deal."

The man nodded agreement. Jar took fifteen dollars from the Factor's cloth sack to pay him. They shook hands and the man rode away.

Leaving the new men to look after the cattle and spare horses, Louis rode with them to call on the Reverend Christie. The first night they found a camping spot on the *Riviere Sale* and next day were passing near the McDonald farm at midday, so Jar decided to ride by to see them. John McDonald came from the cabin to greet them. He looked discouraged. Jar inquired, "Yea are no looking happy, John, is something wrong?"

"Aye, James. Th' buffalo cam' two days ago an' trampled th' yard an' mah garden. Did th' sam to th' neighbors. Julia says if 'at happens when things ur growin' we will hae nothing. She is reit, James. Aw our wark would be fer nothin' an' we will hae little fer th' next winter. Julia says it is time tae move oan."

"Whaur will ye go, John?"

McDonald shrugged. "Ah dinna know, James."

Jar remembered the previous conversation. "When I stopped here a few days back yea said yea were a bookkeeper."

"Aye, James, Ah apprenticed but thaur be wee chance th' Bay Company will hire me. Th' Factor is mair interested in seein' aw of us gone."

"Tell ye what, John. I have a fur trading post located near th' Mnisota River an' I wull hire yea to clerk. Yea bring Julia ta th' post an' go to work."

McDonald's face brightened. "Noo 'at be th' best news Ah hae received in a lang, lang time, laddie. T'is mighty fine of yea tae offer me a job. Whaur be this tradin' post ay yoors?"

"It is all th' way south up the Red River an' a ways off to th' east. It is a fair distance, John, an' yea told me yea don'na have a horse. Louis here will be coming south this summer with cattle we purchased. Louis wull come with horses fer yea an' Julia to ride. Th' Reverend Christie wull be ridin' with yea."

"Bless yea, James. Julia will dance wi happiness when Ah tell her."

"Yea are welcome, John. Louis will stop by from time ta time when he is in th' area an' will keep yea informed. Louis can't come south until th' wee calves have legs enough fer th' journey.

"We wull be on our way now, John. I will be waiting fer your arrival." They rode away, leaving a happy would-be farmer and future bookkeeper watching them go.

They camped in Christie's yard and Jar explained the arrangements to him.

Rising in the grey of early morning, Jar handed Louis ten dollars. "Louis, yea look after th' McDonalds an' Christie. See they have food. Ride over this way an' bring them a buff when they need it. Go ta th' trading post at Fort La Reine an' get them coffee, corn, an' beans. Use th' rest of th' money ta buy provisions fer your trip south. Yea are responsible fer th' animals an' people, so bring them safely to th' trading post. See yea this summer."

Jar slapped the boy on the shoulder and walked to the roan.

Andre came and shook Louis' hand. "See you this summer, Louis."

Louis watched until they were out of sight before mounting his horse and turning back to Portage la Prairie. He was given great responsibility; he was entrusted with cattle, horses, and people. He, Louis Chouart, would guide them all to the trading post safely.

Setting a ground-eating pace, they rode the days away. The white mare came to heat and the roan stallion tended to his job. Eating early morning and late evening, the miles disappeared beneath the horses' hooves. Pleasantly warm spring days with the grass starting to green made for easy travel and Jar sat his saddle, thinking ahead.

The first keel boat would be coming on the spring winds; striving to be tied up at Yankton Landing before the annual runoff from the snow melt in the shining mountains far to the west came sweeping down the Missouri. Using packhorses, the men would move bales of furs to load the keel boat and bring trade goods back across country to the post. Several trips would be required and the captain would be anxious to be away to ride the runoff downriver to St. Louis.

Drawing a map of the lands he wanted to claim for the post and farm needed to be completed with landmarks to define the boundaries. When that was completed, negotiations with the Sioux to trade for the land could begin. Now witnesses would not be a problem with Christie and the McDonalds coming.

It was time to get the garden planted to grow potatoes, carrots, and corn for the coming year. Hopefully, Rene would find time from the trading to get the men started on that task. So much to do! Losing all these days chasing the raiders and spent at Portage la Prairie would put things behind. Jar squirmed in the saddle and Andre watched, wondering why.

Coming down off the grasslands into the valley of the Mnisota the horses got within a mile of the village before two Sioux scouts rode toward them, one from each side, and fell in alongside the horses for the ride toward the teepees.

Willow Flower and Morning Sun Woman were in front of their teepee, scraping buffalo hides in preparation for tanning. Jar dismounted and walked toward them. Willow looked up and came to her feet with a big smile for him. In Sioux, she greeted him. "Welcome James Richardson, have you eaten?"

Jar smiled back, happy to see her. "Yes, Willow, I have eaten." They stood looking at each other. Finally, Willow took his hand. "Come and greet mother."

Jar followed her. "Greetings, Morning Sun Woman, you are healthy?"

She nodded her head, braids bouncing on her shoulders. "Red Thunder hunting, you stay talk?"

"Thank you, Morning Sun. We must get back to the trading post. Tell Red Thunder I will talk to him another day."

Willow asked, "Where you come, James?"

"We have been to Fort Garry. While there, I talked to the chief of the northern Sioux. We are going back to the trading post." He smiled at her. "I found a white man spirit leader who will come in the summer to marry us."

"Ho! Willow like that."

Jar grinned. "Come and see what I have brought." Morning Sun Woman watched them leave, thinking, 'Black Arrow shows much teeth when looks at Willow Flower.'

Willow greeted Andre and Jar took her to look at the mare. He had brushed the horse carefully that morning and her white coat shone in the sunlight. Willow greeted the horse, patted her neck and the mare bobbed her head. Willow ran a hand along the mare's neck and over a shoulder before exclaiming, "She beautiful horse. So big, James. What name?"

"Yes, she is big; makes a good match for the roan. Do you like her?"

Willow turned to look at him, her eyes sparkling. "Yes, Willow like."

Jar grinned. "Good! The horse is for Willow to keep. Willow name horse."

He watched her eyes grow big. "Horse is for Willow!" She came so he could hug her, something she learned to do from him. He liked to put his arms around her. She stepped back. "Can Willow ride?"

Jar laughed happily and handed her the lead rope. Willow took it, grabbed a handful of mane and jumped onto the horse's back. She sat there, proudly looking down at him. "Willow will ride with James."

They rode out of the village and a mile south before Willow stopped the horse. "Willow much work to do. Red Thunder hunts, much hides to prepare. Willow say thanks for horse."

He didn't want to leave. Andre waited patiently as they talked together. Finally, Willow turned her horse and started away. She stopped a short distance away to wave at them before riding back to the village, sitting proudly on her horse. Willow was thinking, 'Wait till Red Thunder see horse. Ho, he much jealous of Willow.' She laughed softly to herself. 'Will ask Red Thunder help find name.'

The swirl of people and horses was visible long before Jar and Andre rode up to the cabin. For a quarter of a mile in front of the trading house there were campfires burning, horses staked out to graze and people talking. There were a few of the short teepees that were common before the Indians got horses and they used dogs to haul their travois when moving.

Jar's first thought was, 'Poor Rene, they must be running him off his feet.'

Together, they unloaded the packs and took the saddles inside. Andre disappeared around the cabin, taking the horses to the pen. Jar hung the long guns on pegs beside the door, picked up his seven-foot long hiking stick and walked to the back of the trading house. He pushed the door open, bumping one of the employees who was bent over untying ropes on a bundle of trade goods. The man looked over his shoulder in surprise. "Oh, Jar, Rene be glad you back. Rene been trading from can see to can't see every day. Is getting some worn down."

Jar chuckled and slapped the man on the shoulder. "Andre an' I are both back an' glad ta be, we wull help out."

Jar found a way through stacks of furs and a diminished supply of trade goods to the trading counter where Rene and Pig Eye were working. Rene glanced his way and grinned before looking back at the trapper he was dealing with. The counter, set back from the door, enclosed a small area with room for three or four people at one time so they didn't have to deal with a big crowd all at once. Right now there was a Métis trapper and his Indian wife handing them furs. Rene was inspecting the furs and sorting them into piles, after which they would be counted and the tally entered in a ledger. That was when the trading would start.

"What can I do ta help, Rene?"

"We finish beaver. You count. Big pile good ones, little pile seconds." Rene continued to inspect muskrat pelts. And so it went until dark when Rene locked up and they went to the cabin.

Things speeded up with Andre helping Rene. Jar worked with the press to compress the stacks of furs before tying them in canvas-wrapped bundles for shipment. Rene's two men shuttled between the store and trading houses, taking trade goods one way and coming back with furs to be baled.

For a rest break Jar took a twist of tobacco, some colored ribbons and walked out to talk to the people camped on the grass. He sat talking to a group of Cree and cut tobacco to fill pipes. Jar moved from group to group visiting, exchanging news, giving men tobacco and ribbons to the few women present.

A Sioux family with their camp off to one side attracted Jar's attention and he walked over, recognizing the warrior as belonging to the Wahpeton Sioux village east on the Mnisota River. The warrior sat beside a cooking fire with his young wife and a little girl with black braids who was about three; old enough to run around the camp. Jar kept smiling at her and slowly the little girl grew brave enough to come closer. Jar held up a red ribbon and watched her eyes light up with excitement as she watched it flapping in the breeze. He pointed at a braid and asked, "Can I put the ribbon in your hair?" She backed up, looking at her mother who urged her on. Slowly, she came close enough for Jar to tie the ribbon around the end of one braid. The little girl ran to her mother, holding out the braid to show her. When she looked at him, Jar held up a yellow ribbon. The girl hurried back and he tied it on the other braid. Before he left he held out a red and yellow ribbon and pointed at the girl's mother. The little girl came and took the ribbons to her mother. When Jar got up to leave four braids were brightly decorated with ribbon.

The next day, Jar stopped to talk to five trappers from up north on the Wild Rice River. They told him of seeing three men hanging from ropes on a cottonwood tree on the west side of the Red. He looked shocked and asked what that was all about. The talker replied that they didn't know. With the Red in flood they did not try to cross. Another shrugged and remarked that the men must have made someone mad.

Slowly, the activity waned and the trappers drifted away. Jar sent Pig Eye to Yankton Landing to watch for the keel boat. They baled the last of the furs. Andre and two men worked in the garden, turning over the soil with shovels. Jar spent time helping every day.

Marking out the land he hoped to trade for was a demanding task. In places he was able to use natural landmarks. Often, there was nothing to use and he drove wooden stakes into the ground. It was his intent to claim the valley and the high hills that surrounded it. His first description described the boundary on the west, north, and east as the bottom edge of the hills where the land flattened out to become grass prairie. On the south he wanted to include the grasslands for half a mile out from where the trading post was located. Using his compass, Jar established an east-west line through the trading post and pounded tall stakes into the ground at each end. From those end points, he walked 880 paces south using the compass to align his path so he was straight south of the stakes and pounded in corner stakes.

With Rene helping, they fashioned markers to be erected at the four corners. Sturdy fir logs squared on two sides for six inches at the top. To those flat sides they nailed short planks, each with one pointed end. The Bar R brand was burned into each pointer. At the corners of the boundary, they dug holes to plant the posts and hauled rocks to erect a stone cairn around them.

Riding the boundary lines, Jar and Rene figured it marked out an area that was approximately two miles wide and seven miles long.

Jar labored long over drawing a map and writing a description of the land block to use in a bill of sale trade agreement with the Yanktonai Sioux. His draft was ready and changes marked for the final copy when Pig Eye rode in to announce the keel boat was tied up at Yankton Landing.

Andre rode into the valley to herd the horses back to the pen. Pack saddles were cinched in place and the horses loaded with bales of furs for the two day trip to the Missouri. By getting a start now at midday they would only have to camp two nights before arriving. Jar was going south with the keel boat, so he packed a spare shirt and pants and took his weapons.

The first camp was on the headwaters of the Sioux Rock River. In the morning, they rode past the pipestone quarries where the Sioux mined rock to make pipe bowls. Late on the second day, they watered the horses at the joining of two small streams and crossed over to camp for the night.

A short distance north of the Missouri, the horses turned south to follow the James River to Yankton Landing. While the horses were unloaded the boat crew started bringing trade goods to shore. Jar went to greet the captain and crew of the Lady Marie; number three in the fleet of Missouri keel boats. Jar stuck his hand out. “Good ta see yea, Captain Bouvier. How was your trip?”

The captain shook the offered hand. “Greetings, Mr. Richardson. This boat just slides through the water with its shallow draft and smooth lines. The barest of breezes will move her. The crew rowed very little on this trip and now the water will carry them home with ease. I fear they will grow fat and lazy.” The crew laughed at their captain’s joke, which pleased Jar. They tried to hire good men, paid them fairly for the work and wanted a good attitude on the boats. Captain Bouvier had started as a member of a boat crew before being promoted to captain the previous year. All the men knew there were similar opportunities for them.

Bouvier inquired, “How was your winter, Mr. Richardson, and the trading?”

Jar pointed at the horses. “As yea can see we bring many bales. It was especially busy this spring with many trappers coming ta trade. Winter was not so bad this time with only a couple of blizzards an’ not as much snow as some winters. There was time ta read.” Pausing to consider the boat it seemed to Jar that it was smaller than the others, or maybe it was just slimmer. “We have brought what I estimated would be a boatload. What do yea think?”

Bouvier ran a practiced eye over the bales that were piled on the shore. “It will be a load. We shall see.”

Trade goods were stacked ashore until the boat was empty before the bales of furs went aboard to be stowed. Andre sent a man to start a cooking fire so tonight they could all eat fresh buffalo together, tell stories and hear the news.

Chapter 19

Floating down the Missouri was easy. The sail was rolled, the mast folded down and secured along the top of the cabin. Captain Bouvier rotated men on a regular basis; one on the steering oar and one sitting in the bow beside the swivel gun watching for sandbars, sawyers, or any other obstruction that might be a danger to free passage along the river. At night the boat was tied up to large trees on the shore. Meals were eaten around small fires and washed down with strong coffee before returning to the boat to sleep. Men took turns during the night, a man always on guard in the cockpit at the stern of the boat. My overestimate of the capacity of the boat resulted in it being cramped for space. Each night my blankets were unrolled on top of the cabin to sleep in the open, watch the stars and listen to the night sounds; the Charleville always handy. Coyotes entertained us at night as they called to each other with sharp yip, yip, barking sounds from both sides of the river.

It was easy traveling, making maybe eight miles an hour at which rate the boat would be in San Carlos in seven or eight days. Late on the second day the boat passed the Platte River, out letting its sandy water and debris into the Missouri. It reminded me of the first year we crossed these far reaching plains, coming from the Black Hills with horses loaded with furs and fording the Platte just upstream from the Missouri. It was a long trip; crossing country neither of us knew, with only a rough idea where St. Louis was located. It turned out well, our furs were sold and we returned north, the horses loaded with trade goods.

Rene didn't complain about St. Louis, even though he was uncomfortable all the time we were there and didn't want to go back. Rene was happy staying at the trading post to look after business. He wanted nothing to do with towns and all those huddled up people. Jar laughed softly to himself. Rene didn't like St. Louis. He sure liked Willow, having expressed disappointment, even anger, when he thought I wasn't moving fast enough to marry her. Mid-summer should put me back at the trading post and when Reverend Christie arrived we would be married.

The boat stopped just south of the Platte, close to a fresh water spring and tied up to the Missouri's east bank for the night.

Seven days after leaving Yankton Landing we came to shore at San Carlos and tied up beside other boats at the Richardson Chadron Boat Company. Sitting on the cabin roof provided a good view. Jean Cabott stood talking to two men on some detail of boat construction. One man pointed, saying something to him. Jean turned to look and came hurrying toward the boat. He stopped at the edge of the water and called, "James, welcome to San Carlos." Adding, "It has been way too long since you were last here." Jean hurried on. "Captain Bouvier, have the men put the plank out so James can come ashore." Jean's English was much improved from when we first met.

Bouvier turned from directing his men. "Of course, Jean, as soon as the boat is properly secured." You had to appreciate Lee Bouvier. He never neglected anything that affected the boat, was always calm and addressed his men politely. Even when we sat together on the cabin roof to talk, Bouvier watched everything. When the ropes from the posts set in the shore were pulled tight and tied, the gangplank was extended and I walked ashore, carrying my gear. We shook hands. “It is good ta see yea again.”

“You too, James. You only come once a year; not nearly enough. Will you stay the night?”

“Yes, I want ta talk with Madame Chadron about merchandise I need. Could yea send word ta her and ask if I can visit th’ mercantile tomorrow morning?

Jean waved a hand toward town. “Madame will have many things to talk to you about. We built a cabin to store tools. Madame told me to build bunks so you have a place to stay when you come. Here, let me help you with your gear and you will see.” On the way to the cabin, Jean stopped a young man who was going past carrying a coil of rope on his shoulder. Jean gave him the message to take to Madame. “This way, James, right over here.” Jean pointed, “Watch your step; we don’t keep things as neat as we should.”

The cabin wasn’t large. At one end there were two bunks, a table and chairs, tin plates and an oil lamp. What really caught my eye were the curtains on the small windows. I was impressed; they made the cabin look like a home. ‘I should have curtains in my cabin back at the valley.’

Jar stowed his gear, rolled his bedding out on a bunk, kept the walking stick and turned towards the door. Jean watched the broad shouldered man, over six feet tall with rusty red hair, dressed in grey woolen pants and a pullover cotton shirt that hung below his waist. A wide leather belt kept the shirt in place. Jar removed the tomahawk from his belt and added it to the other gear on the bed.

The big knife stayed in place behind the belt. Jean remembered the story of what that walking stick could do in a fight like the brawl in the St. Louis tavern when two ruffians attacked Richardson. Jean told himself, 'Everyone will see that big knife and it is the stick they should be wary of.'

Richardson asked, "Do yea have time ta take me around ta see what all these men are working on?"

"Of course, James, come and we shall see." Jean held the door open, thinking. 'He owns two thirds of the boat company, yet does not act like an owner; being important and giving orders.' They stood outside the cabin and Jean explained, "We are finishing one keel boat and two more are started. All for different customers who come with their plans for how they want the boats." Jean shrugged. "They are foolish, thinking only of space for big load, not how the boat will handle. I tell Madame. She say, 'they pay, build what they want.'

Richardson looked across the yard at the boats, trying to see what the difference was. He finally asked. "What is different about our boats, Jean?"

Jean smiled. "Ah, Monsieur Richardson, our boats we build long and slim with a curve on the bottom. They do not haul so much freight. The design allows them to slide through the water like a canoe. Small wind and they move. These other boats are wide, flat bottomed; more like barges and haul more freight, only it takes much wind and many men to move them. It is not so good up the Missouri."

"Is it th' same with th' two Mississippi boats we have?"

Jean nodded in agreement. "It is the same. Mississippi boats are longer and wider, still the same. They are grown up Missouri keel boats, big brothers. They haul much freight going down the river to New Orleans. With smaller loads they come up the river riding on the wind; only sometimes with oars. Captain Ruechard says to me he passes other boats many times."

Jean toured him around, showing off the stacks of logs piled to dry, the overhead cutting racks where crews of men were sawing planks, the sail makers cutting and sewing heavy canvas into sails for the new boats, ending up at the boats themselves where carpenters were shaving planks and building the boats. Richardson paid special attention to the shape of the hulls, confirming what Jean had told him.

Madame Chadron came immediately from her office in the mercantile when Richardson arrived. She was wearing a grey dress with white lace trim around the neckline. She smiled happily. Richardson was surprised to see she wasn't wearing black; it was the first time since they met shortly after her husband's death. She held out her hand. "It is so nice to see you again, Mr. Richardson. Please come to my office, there is much for us to discuss."

"Thank yea, Madame Chadron, yea are looking very stylish in that new dress."

"How observant of you, Mr. Richardson," Madame smiled again. "It is hardly new; it predates the unfortunate death of my husband. At Christmas it was time to cease mourning; my children deserved better, so the black dresses are stored away."

Madame stopped beside a small table close to her office door where a young lady sat working on a ledger. "Mr. Richardson, may I introduce you to Josie, she helps me with many things and waits on lady customers when they require special attention. Josie, this is my business partner, Mr. James Richardson, who has just arrived down the Missouri."

The young lady looked up and blushed at the attention. "I am pleased to meet yea, Josie."

"Thank you, Mr. Richardson, I also am pleased."

"Josie, Mr. Richardson likes his coffee. When you have a moment, please bring a pot of coffee and two cups to my office."

"Right away, Madame, it will be there." Josie dropped her pencil and stood up as Madame ushered Richardson toward her office. He glanced closely at Josie as he passed.

Madame pointed at a chair and went around to the other side. Her desk was actually a table. "Possibly we should start with a review of the boat company and how business is progressing." She looked up and received a nod of agreement. "As you know, there are two segments to the business; hauling freight for a variety of customers and building boats for cost plus a fee. The account book is right here for you to look at." Madame picked up a book from the side of the table, opened it to the proper pages and turned it so he could look at the numbers.

When Josie arrived with coffee they were deeply engrossed in the numbers. Madame Chadron was explaining the various entries. It was midday when they finished the review and turned to talking about the future. "Mr. Richardson, now that we are Americans it would be wise …" His startled look stopped her. "You didn't know, Mr. Richardson?"

"Yea said we are Americans; I don't understand, Madame."

"My apology, Mr. Richardson, I assumed you had heard the news. Please let me explain. Mr. Thomas Jefferson, who was elected President of America in 1801, negotiated a treaty with France to purchase all lands west of the Mississippi. We have heard that he paid the enormous sum of fifteen million American dollars to France for what the French call Louisiana. The treaty became official this past winter on the twentieth day of December, 1803. The news that comes to us is that everyone who lives west of the Mississippi is now a citizen of the United States. So you see, Mr. Richardson, we are both now Americans, as are my children." The silence lasted several moments while he digested what she had said. He grinned. "What do you find humorous, Mr. Richardson?"

His grin turned into a wide smile. "Madame Chadron, I left Glasgow as a lad in 1794 with a dream of coming ta America. Now, ten years later, I have arrived."

She smiled. "Mr. Richardson, let me be the first person to say to you, welcome to America."

"Thank yea, Madame. Before yea surprised me yea were going ta tell me something."

"Yes, Mr. Richardson, what I was about to explain is that now with Louisiana Territory a part of the United States we will see the arrival of a large number of people coming from the east. Logically, they will come by the easiest route to travel which is down the Ohio River to the Mississippi, after which they will spread out along our rivers to take up land. The arrival of all these new people should result in a large increase in commerce along the rivers. The new people will require goods which will, in the main, come up river from New Orleans. In time, they will wish to sell their produce of varies types which must go down river. We should prepare, Mr. Richardson, by investing in additional keel boats to transport all this merchandise."

As always, he was amazed by her astuteness. For three years she had managed the Richardson Chadron Boat Company with a firm hand. She had been right. By having superior boats and crews which provided good service, the boats were kept busy hauling freight, and sometimes people, for satisfied customers. Three light, fast keel boats, including the one Captain Bouvier had just brought down the Missouri, worked upstream on the rivers. Two larger boats sailed between St. Louis and New Orleans on the Mississippi. Now Madame wanted to add additional boats. He mentally reviewed the facts. In three years they had recovered the cost of the five boats and accumulated a profit. If there was more business to be captured it was logical to do what Madame was suggesting. Richardson looked at her expectant face. "Yea ar' much better informed than I am, Madame. What is it yea ar' suggesting we do?"

"In my opinion, Mr. Richardson, the most immediate increase in freight will be south of here on the Mississippi. I should like to see us build two large keels to add to our capacity in that trade. After they go into service the demand for upriver shipping will be growing and we should build two more of the smaller keels for that trade."

Richardson ran a hand through his red hair. "We wull have nine boats ta man an' operate."

"That is correct, Mr. Richardson, provided we do not lose a boat to an accident on the rivers. We have been exceedingly lucky that in three years no accident has occurred."

"I agree; we have been fortunate." Richardson nodded his head thoughtfully, "I have several questions for yea. Firstly, what will be th' total investment fer th' four boats an' secondly how do we pay fer them? There are not sufficient funds to pay th' cost of four boats. We must find four new captains an' also good men ta crew th' boats. Have yea considered these matters?"

"Yes, Mr. Richardson, I have given careful thought to the questions you raise. First, let us consider the question of captains and crewmen. Two years ago we discussed and implemented a plan to set aside ten percent of the profit made by each boat to be divided among the crew of that boat. It has been very successful. The men are happy and few have left our employ. Our men have gained much experience. Each captain tells me he has men ready to become captains when we need them. In the shipyard there are many young men working on construction that wish to join a boat crew. Crews should not be a problem, Mr. Richardson."

"Thank yea, Madame."

"You asked about costs. So far, we have built five boats for our own use and have built an additional seven for customers. The consequence of all this activity is that our men have become much more efficient. They are building boats faster and for less cost than our first boat. My estimate is that large boats will cost 460 dollars each and smaller ones 380 dollars each. Our total investment for four boats will be 1680 American dollars."

Madame Chadron unfolded a sheet of paper and spread it on the desk. "We have sufficient funds on hand to pay for one boat and most of a second. On this paper is a projection of the funds that will be generated in the coming months which would be available to pay the remainder of the investment."

She handed the sheet of paper to him and sat back in her chair while he digested the numbers. Using one large finger to follow the numbers, he went down the page. It took a few minutes for him to sort it all out. "If I understand your projection of th' profits from th' existing boats, they will pay fer each new one being constructed. Is that correct?"

"Yes it is, Mr. Richardson. Of course, we should keep well in mind the fact that a boat may be lost or business may slow down temporarily, causing the funds generated to be less than my projection. If that should occur, we can adjust by delaying construction of a boat."

"Very impressive, Madame. I agree we should build these boats." Her happy smile was contagious and he grinned. "What other surprises do yea have fer me?"

The smile broadened. "Nothing immediately, Mr. Richardson. There is one other idea that I feel obliged to inform you of. Have you ever heard of steamboats, Mr. Richardson?"

That he was surprised was obvious and it delighted her. Richardson rubbed his chin and struggled to remember; 'there was something.' Suddenly, it came to him. "Madame, when I was working on th' docks in Glasgow helping ta prepare th' ship fer sailing th' men talked about a Mister James Watt who invented a steam engine an' it was being tried ta power a boat. There was much argument about it. Most men said it would never work."

"You have a good memory, Mr. Richardson. On behalf of Richardson Chadron Boat Company there has been correspondence with Mister Daniel French in Pittsburgh who is manufacturing high-pressure steam engines he claims can power a boat using a paddle wheel on the stern. A traveler who visited San Carlos last fall left behind a Pittsburgh newspaper which contained a detailed article about Mr. French and his engine. I wrote to him to make inquiries and recently received a reply. Would you care to read his letter?"

His amazed face pleased her. "Yes, of course, let me read th' letter."

Madame Chadron had neglected her merchandise business all day. She went to check with the staff while he digested the letter, knowing full well it would take him some time. She spent days herself trying to understand the notes and diagrams and did not feel she fully understood how it worked. If it did work she felt it would be a significant advancement. To think you could travel up a river with no oars or sails seemed like magic. All you needed was wood for a fire to make steam. She had been immediately intrigued by the article.

They were preparing to close the store for the day when Richardson emerged from the office. She asked, "What is your opinion of Mister French's amazing machine?"

"I do not know what ta think, Madame. Can we talk again tomorrow?"

"Of course, Mr. Richardson. In the morning, I shall come to the boatyard and we can inspect the work together. After that we can discuss Mr. French."

"Thank yea, Madame. I wull see yea in the morning." Richardson left the store to walk to the boatyard. As they watched him leave, Josie commented slyly, "He is such a big, fine looking man, Madame."

Madame Chadron turned her head to look at Josie. "Yes he is, Josie. Not handsome, although certainly large, strongly built and a good man. We are friends and business partners, Josie. Do not think otherwise."

In the bright hot sun of a warm morning Cabott guided them around the shipyard past stacks of logs arranged to dry and age in the air. Madame, wearing a plain dark grey dress and a sunbonnet that protected her head and provided shade for her eyes, let Cabott do the explaining. She knew every detail of the operation, but Cabott was the manager. Richardson looked at the piles of logs and asked, "Why so many logs, Jean, yea have never had such a large number before?"

"It is to age them longer, James." Jean pointed. "That smaller pile was cut two years ago and the logs are almost used up now. The large pile was cut last year and now we are bringing new logs that go in the pile closest to the water. We are preparing wood because Madame says more customers will come to order boats."

A horse was being used to tug logs from the river and tow them to the pile. James was interested in the harness on the horse and Jean explained. "The boot maker and blacksmith made this harness for us. See the large padded collar around the horse's neck? It allows the horse to push the collar with its shoulders and chest. The collar tugs the logs by the ropes tied to those iron rings on the sides of the collar. The work is easier for the horse and goes faster for us."

Cabott took them to see the progress on three boats being built for customers and explained the differences in them as compared to the company's boats. Captain Bouvier left his boat and walked over to join them. Richardson shook his hand and Madame Chadron greeted him. "Good morning, Monsieur Captain. All is well with the Lady Marie?"

Bouvier bowed slightly and replied in his quiet voice, "The Lady Marie is a fine boat. She handles well and glides through the water like an arrow in the air. Mr. Cabott and his men built me a fine boat."

"That is good news, Captain," Madame replied. "Your boat is full of Mr. Richardson's furs?"

"Yes it is, Madame. When Mr. Richardson is ready, we will sail for St. Louis to deliver his furs."

"Ah, yes Captain. There are several matters for me to discuss with Mr. Richardson. Perhaps Mr. Richardson will be prepared to leave tomorrow morning."

Richardson noted the way she gave an order without it sounding like an order. Bouvier bowed as before. "Of course, Madame. We have several minor repairs to make to the boat. Tomorrow morning will be ideal."

"Thank you, Captain. Your family, they are well?"

"Yes, Madame, everyone is well. The little ones grow like the weeds. My wife is very busy to care for them. I will excuse myself now and return to the boat."

Richardson shook the captain's hand again. "I will be ready at first light, Captain Bouvier."

Bouvier nodded. "We will have the Lady Marie ready before dark to sail at first light, Mr. Richardson."

When the tour was concluded they rode together in the carriage, which took them to the Chadron Mercantile. Seated in the office, they picked up the discussion of steamboats. "Do you not agree, Mr. Richardson, it would be like magic to travel up a river without need for a sail or oars?"

"Yes, it would, Madame, provided it works. I studied th' newspaper article an' Mister French's notes an' diagrams. It appears that his engine turns a crank which moves a lever ta turn th' paddle wheel which in turn moves th' boat. It seems simple enough." Richardson paused to rub his chin. "In th' newspaper it is mentioned that many of these steam engines have exploded."

"That is true, Mr. Richardson. In his notes, Mr. French talks about the problem of controlling the fire so not to make steam too fast. He claims to have invented something he calls a steam valve which prevents that from happening."

"Yes, I saw that, Madame. I do not understand how it works. Mr. French describes a large boat that will move many people an' freight at the same time. Should his engine explode all would be lost."

Madame frowned. "That is true and it would be a great worry to be responsible for such a tragedy."

"In many places our rivers are shallow an' there are sandbars to be avoided. That would be difficult with a large boat that needs several feet of water to float. This morning I awoke with a thought. Soon we will have nine keel boats hauling goods. Would it be possible ta build a smaller boat with Mister French's steam engine an' paddle wheel which could travel in shallow water with just a small crew ta run it? With ropes running back, it could tug the keel boats along the river."

"Why do you suggest that, Mr. Richardson? I do not understand."

"During the night I dreamed about a boat exploding like in th' newspaper. This morning I thought, if th' goods an' people were in keel boats they would be safe. Only th' boat with th' steam machine would be lost."

"A brilliant idea, Mr. Richardson." Madame waved her hands, smiling broadly. "Do you think it would work?"

He shrugged. "It is only an idea. Yea should correspond with Mister French an' ask him."

"That will be done immediately with an explanation of the shallow water and ask him if he can make plans for such a boat with one of his steam engines. I shall inform him that Richardson Chadron can build this boat he designs and ask about the cost of obtaining one of his engines. Thank you, Mr. Richardson, these are exciting times we live in, are they not?"

"Yes, Madame, they are." Richardson paused. "I have a list of goods ta take back wi' me to the trading post. Do yea have any other business to discuss before I take it to th' clerks?"

"No, Mr. Richardson. Perhaps there will be something when you return from St. Louis. The clerks will be pleased to help you. If there is anything you need help with, please come and see me."

Richardson went with his list to the long counter and discussed the windows, hinges, cast iron stoves and household items he was interested in purchasing. He preferred to purchase as many of these items from Madame Chadron's mercantile as possible. When he came to the ladies items on the list the male clerk suggested he talk to Josie. Richardson came to Josie's table and Madame Chadron watched him through the doorway of her office as he fidgeted nervously, attempting to talk to Josie. Madame arose from her seat and came to assist him. "Do you require assistance, Mr. Richardson?"

He looked at her, his face turning red. "I want ta order clothes for a lady."

"Of course, Mr. Richardson, what did you have in mind?"

"She will need dresses like yea wear. Like th' one yea wore yesterday. Could yea make them fer me?"

"We have ladies who sew for us. They will sew dresses for you. Would you care to look at material to choose the colors and patterns?" He shook his head no. "Fine, we will select material for you. Do you have measurements for the lady we can use to cut out the dresses so they fit properly?"

Madame almost laughed at the panic on his face. He stammered, "Measurements, I did…never thought, I don't know."

"Come, Mr. Richardson, tell me about the lady. How old is she, how tall is she, what color is her hair?"

He stared at her as he thought. "She is seventeen, slim as a willow tree an' as beautiful as a flower, with pure black hair that shines in th' sunlight. She is happy, curious an' loves to laugh. I want everything she will need, dresses..." his face turned red again, "things ta wear under th' dresses. I do not know these things."

"That is fine, Mr. Richardson. You have given us something to start with. Josie is also seventeen. Look at her and tell me how she compares in size to this lady of yours."

He went to stand beside Josie. "Madame, the height is close. Willow is a bit taller."

"Thank you, Mr. Richardson. Now come here and tell me how the width of Josie's shoulders compares."

He looked. "I think about the same."

"Very good, Mr. Richardson. Josie put your hands on your waist and hold your dress in. Now Mr. Richardson, what do you think?"

"I don't know, Madam, I'm not sure. I think, yes, I think Willow is smaller. She is very slim."

"Thank you, Mr. Richardson. Now the bodice, how would that compare?"

Richardson turned red again and refused to look. "I don't know, Madame, I have no idea."

"Come, Mr. Richardson, you are a big strong man. Surely you can look at Josie and tell me."

"No, I can't. It embarrasses me. I have never been around ladies."

The two ladies smiled at each other, enjoying his discomfort. "Fine, Mr. Richardson. Does the lady sew?" He nodded his head. "Very well, we will make the dresses so they can be adjusted to fit. How many dresses do you want us to make?"

"Two, an' extra cloth, so Willow can sew more dresses when she wants them. An' other things, thread, needles, scissors, everything she needs."

"Very well, Mr. Richardson, we will take care of this for you. May I ask, are you planning to be married?"

Suddenly, he was over his shyness and smiled broadly. "Willow and I are going ta be married as soon as I return ta the trading post."

"Congratulations, Mr. Richardson. Willow is a lovely name. How did you meet the lady?"

"I found her lost in an early winter blizzard an' returned her ta her home."

"How romantic, Mr. Richardson, just like a fairy tale. Will you bring her to San Carlos sometime so we can meet her?"

"Yes, Madame, I will bring her. Thank yea fer helping me. Now I will go ta th' shipyard."

He walked away and they watched him. Josie whispered, "He needs air after that experience." They laughed.

He stopped short of the door and came back to ask, "Those ladies who sew, would they make curtains ta fit our windows?"

"Yes, they will do that, Mr. Richardson. What size are the windows and how many?"

"Eight windows, each eighteen by eighteen inches."

Chapter 20

With the meat from a butchered buffalo wrapped in its own hide and tied to a pack saddle, Louis Chouart rode up to the McDonald farm and dismounted. The meat was unloaded before McDonald came from the cabin. At the inquiring look on McDonald's face, Louis explained, *"Monsieur Richardson,* he say Louis bring meat." Louis pointed. "There meat. Louis come again, soon cattle ready go south." Louis walked to the packhorse and came back with two cloth bags, one of coffee beans, the other white beans for cooking.

As Louis remounted his horse, McDonald told him, "Thank yea, Louis, fer bringing us food." Louis raised one hand and turned the horse away to return to the plains to get another buffalo. Late in the afternoon, he arrived at Reverend Christie's cabin with meat from a fat cow. Louis waited for Christie to speak. While he didn't understand everything that was said the last time he was there, Louis knew that Christie was a spirit man and therefore was someone to fear and respect.

Christie was always happy to have company. Most of his neighbors were too busy trying to survive to spend time visiting and he saw them only on Sundays. Christie waved. "Welcome, Louis, come an' sit awhile."

Louis didn't know what he was supposed to say, so he dismounted and started untying the meat. As small as he was, he lifted the meat to the ground with ease. He looked at Christie. "*Monsieur Richardson*, he say, Louis bring meat."

"Thank yea, Louis, tha' is very kind o' yea. Wull yea eat with me?"

Louis pondered that. There was enough daylight left for him to make a few miles and he was accustomed to eating just before dark. Louis hesitated; this was a spirit man who was not to be annoyed. He nodded his head. "Louis eat."

They cooked meat over a campfire and Louis decided the spirit man was hungry. He should have brought meat sooner. Louis did not understand these white men. They go hungry with food all around them. Why are they so different from Jar, the man the Sioux call Black Arrow? When the meat was ready, Louis took the buffalo tongue and carefully divided it before handing one half to Christie. Louis chewed methodically, enjoying the good taste of fresh meat while he wondered about Christie and McDonald. He did not understand them. They were important to Jar, so he would look after them. Louis kept his head turned away from the spirit man for fear the man would see into his mind through his eyes.

Louis used a patch of leather to pick up the coffee pot to fill his tin cup. He held out the pot and filled Christie's cup. They drank in silence. When Louis judged enough time had gone by he stood up. "Louis go now."

Christie looked up. "Thank yea fer coming an' bringing food. Yea ar' always welcome at maw fire."

Louis stowed his gear and mounted his horse. "Soon cattle ready go south. Louis come with horse for Christie."

"Thank yea, Louis. Take care of yea'self, do not worry, an' come when yea are ready."

Louis held up a hand and rode away, wondering if this spirit man could see into his soul. Christie said, 'take care of yourself.' No one had ever told Louis such a thing before. Many nights Louis stayed awake worrying about the great responsibility Jar gave him. He did not want to fail. How did the spirit man know?

Willow Flower rode her white horse around the corner of the hills and loped toward the trading post. Accompanied by Morning Sun Woman and her cousin Spotted Tail, she was coming to visit James; to talk to him, to see him, to be near him. It was more than two moons since he had given her the white horse.

Rene was alerted to the riders and came from the trading house to stand waiting as the horse climbed the gentle slope to the buildings. Willow watched the pen and saw the big roan horse, so James was here. Her heart soared with happiness. She looked everywhere, seeing Andre and the man with the evil eye, nowhere was James. Willow wondered. When the white horse stopped, Rene came to take the lead rope. Willow placed both hands on the horse's shoulders and jumped to the ground. "Ho, Rene, you like White Cloud?"

"White Cloud is fine horse, Willow Flower." He smiled. "Rene happy see Willow."

"Willow happy see Rene." Her head swiveled and Rene knew. "Where James?"

"James not here, Willow." Her face clouded. "He goes on big white man canoe to sell furs in St. Louis."

"Huh, Willow not like that. How long James go?"

Rene considered that. "Soon be two moons. One more moon he come back. Willow stay, talk to Rene."

Despite her disappointment, she managed a smile. "Willow like talk Rene. Rene show Willow more white man words."

Rene laughed. "We talk white man words. Soon Willow talk many words." Rene turned his attention to the other guests. "Welcome, Morning Sun Woman, you are healthy?"

"Morning Sun Woman healthy. Is good see, Rene."

"Welcome, Spotted Tail, Rene is happy to see you."

Spotted Tail nodded his head. "Good see, Rene."

Rene turned to Willow. "Take your mother and Spotted Tail to cabin. Rene put horses in the pen."

Willow shook her head. "Willow come. Rene have cawot?"

Rene held out his empty hands. "No carrots, Willow. All gone."

She shrugged. "No matter, Willow come see big horse." They unloaded the saddles and gear and together led the horses up the slope to the pen. Willow called. "Ho, big horse, come Willow." The roan lifted his head and came to get his ears scratched. He pushed her shoulder with his nose, making her laugh. Willow went to the hillside and pulled an armful of green grass to feed him. She teased him, giving him small handfuls. The roan ate each one and bobbed his head up and down before reaching for more. Willow liked it when he pushed her shoulder.

In the cabin, Rene rolled his bedding. Willow told him. "Rene, stay."

"No, Willow. Soon this cabin be Willow's teepee."

Willow nodded her head happily and looked around to survey what would be hers to look after. It seemed empty without James. She stamped her foot and announced. "Is strong floor." She was practicing her words. Willow went around the cabin naming various items and Rene only corrected her on a few of them. Her memory was good and she learned quickly. Willow stopped to look at James' bunk which was wider. She knew why and turned to Rene with a sly look on her face. "Why make bunk bigger? Willow no here." Rene laughed and she laughed with him.

Willow Flower stayed for two days. She cooked on the cast iron stove, washed the tin plates and carefully stacked them in their place on the shelf. Rene took her and Spotted Tail riding and stopped to show them the corner markers. Rene explained that James built those markers to tell other white men they could visit, camp over night, but must not stay inside the markers.

Willow walked through the garden and Rene told her what the plants were. Carrots, onions, potatoes, and of course she knew what corn was. The spring where they got drinking water was above the garden and Rene showed her the ditch that could bring water to the garden when the rain was slow coming. With help from Andre he showed her how the irrigation system worked and water ran between the rows of plants. Willow told herself, 'these white men very clever.'

The morning she was preparing to leave they drank coffee. Willow asked about the white man spirit man. Rene told her that James would be coming back soon and the spirit man would arrive not long after that. He told her about John McDonald who was coming with his wife to be the clerk for the trading post. Willow frowned, asking. "What white man woman's like?"

"Rene not see this woman. She is young. James says there be little one in fall." He smiled. "Willow, not worry. White woman learn much from Willow. Willow learn much from white woman."

Willow nodded. "Is good, be two womans."

Rene walked with her and held the horse while she mounted. He told her, "When Willow comes to live here, Rene make bridle for White Cloud like James has for roan."

Willow nodded her head. "Rene, is good." She turned her horse and loped after the other two. Rene watched her out of sight.

Richardson's business in St. Louis was wrapping up. Auguste Chouteau took the furs at a good price and assured him that the remainder that came on the second keel boat in the next month or so would get the same prices. Chouteau looked at the list of trade good to be sent north in 1805. He was surprised by the large increase in trade goods and Richardson explained that he was opening a second trading post; being careful not to divulge the location. People in St. Louis believed he was operating out of Yankton Landing and that was the way he wanted it to stay.

He enjoyed the haircuts and hot baths at the barber shop and outfitted himself with several sets of clothes. There was a pile of new books to take back for the winter to add to his growing library. That was one of the things he and Chouteau had in common, a love of reading and discussing books. In the piles of supplies were wide brimmed black leather hats for all the men and one for each of the two women which he hoped would fit. A sheet metal bathtub like the ones at the barber shop, a Spanish saddle for Willow and a pair of leather riding boots sized from one of her moccasins that he had taken when she wasn't looking. The stay in St. Louis lasted longer than he wanted because of the wait while the special items were being made.

Chouteau assured him the model 1794 Lancaster was still the best long gun available. Richardson ordered four hundred, with a supply of spare parts to make repairs when customers came in with broken guns. With all the other items it might be too large a load for two keel boats. He would worry about that next year.

Mrs. Ruechard was happy to see him again and fed him too well. Captain Ruechard had returned from New Orleans just four days before and they enjoyed a great visit, catching up on a whole year of activities. Henrie was happy working steady for the boat company as captain of a large keel boat. They talked about the Louisiana Purchase and Richardson listened closely to the news and opinions Henrie brought from New Orleans. Everything he heard supported Madame Chadron's conclusion that many new settlers would arrive in the next few years. Already there were more Americans from across the river moving into St. Louis. It was noticeable on the streets and in the taverns. The ones bringing families with them seemed like good steady men. There was also the riffraff who populated the taverns, drank, brawled, and caused trouble. Crime was increasing and Chouteau told him that for the first time the town was considering employing policemen to patrol the streets. Everywhere Richardson went he took his walking stick, belt knife, and pistol with him.

Chouteau took him in a buggy to visit their land holdings and talk to the tenant farmers. Much of the large acreage they owned was unoccupied. Soon, with the coming of settlers it should all be rented. They agreed not to sell land. It should rise in value every year and there would be a fortune to be made in the future. The first American authorities to arrive gave assurances that property, contracts, agreements and such that were registered with the Spanish would be recognized.

Finally, the day came to load the keel boat. Chouteau's men hauled all the sacks, barrels and crates to the river where the boat crew stowed them on the Lady Anne, being careful to distribute the weight to keep the boat balanced. The crew laughed and made jokes about the bathtub which was filled with merchandise. Why would anyone want a bathtub? Richardson smiled good-naturedly and made no reply; let them enjoy their jokes. Captain Ruechard came to smoke his pipe, chat with the crew and captain and watch the loading. When the boat finished loading he and Richardson walked home together to eat dinner.

Mrs. Ruechard put breakfast on the table before first light. They ate together and said their goodbyes. James Angus Richardson walked to the river in the first grey of day carrying a leather satchel, his long gun, a quiver full of black arrows, long bow and the walking stick. Few people were out at this time of day. Those that were, stayed away. He was bristling with weapons. Richardson was carrying four thousand dollars in gold coins to be added to the cache in Long Valley. Every year he extracted a large part of the profits from the fur trade to build future security for Rene and the family he hoped to raise.

Captain Josepha Burger stood waiting by the plank when

Richardson arrived. “Good morning, James. Are you ready to sail?”

“Yea fall oot o’ bed this morn, Joe?” They laughed and Joe followed him up the plank. “It wull be good to be moving agin, Captain Joe.”

Richardson stowed his gear in the cabin while the crew brought in the plank and the mooring ropes. The current pushed the keel boat away from the shore and they were moving. The sail was hoisted and men walked the runways with long poles to start the boat north. A good breeze filled the sail and the boat began to move against the current. If the breeze held, Captain Joe hoped to be near the Missouri before dark.

On the third day Richardson walked into the mercantile. Josie saw him and alerted Madame Chadron who came from her office. “Welcome back, Mr. Richardson.”

“Thank yea, Madame. It took longer than planned. Now th’ Lady Anne is ready ta load th’ goods yea have fer me.”

Madame raised her arm and a clerk came to her side. “Please send word to the stable and have them bring the wagon to take Mr. Richardson’s goods to the boatyard.” As the clerk hurried away, Madame turned back. “Come, Mr. Richardson to see what Josie has for your future wife.”

Josie displayed the dresses and explained how they could be adjusted by opening or taking in the seams. She explained how the lace trim around the neckline was held by buttons and would come off when the dress was washed. There was a sewing box with a hinged lid containing spools of thread, needles, pins, scissors, and a thimble. There were bolts of cloth to make more dresses and a package containing unmentionables.

Josie held up a bonnet. Madame explained, "Josie sewed a sunbonnet as a wedding present for your wife."

Richardson held the bonnet to examine it. "Thank yea, Josie, Willow will be very pleased."

Next Josie held up a well-padded package sewn into a cloth bag. Madame continued, "In this package is a hand mirror with a matching hairbrush and comb. It is a wedding present for Willow from me and my children."

"That is very considerate of yea, Madame." He looked at her. "Thank yea."

"You are welcome, Mr. Richardson." She looked at Josie.

"Come and see what the men at the shipyard made before these dresses are packed," Josie said. In the corner behind her table, she showed him a wooden chest made from polished oak. It had a curved lid on hinges and a clasp to hold it shut. On each end was a leather hoop by which the trunk could be picked up. Painted in blue on the lid were the words, 'Mrs. Willow Richardson.'

Richardson knelt on one knee to look closer. The craftsmanship was excellent. He opened the lid and peered inside. It was lined with heavy, blue cloth and across one end was a shallow removable box divided into three sections for smaller items. It reminded him of the sea chests sailors used to store personal items on sailing ships. He looked up at the ladies. "I don'na know what ta say. All this is so unexpected. Thank yea. Willow wull be so happy."

Josie laughed happily and Madame commented, "Come, Mr. Richardson, there are business details to discuss. Josie will pack the dresses and make the chest ready for shipping."

Their meeting went quickly and Richardson settled his account with gold coins. Madame Chadron was surprised at his suggestion. "When all th' Americans come, San Carlos will grow an' land will be in great demand. It may be wise fer us ta buy land around San Carlos."

Madame Chadron frowned. "Are you referring to farmland?"

"Yes, farmland, land ta build homes on, or land that may be located where businesses wull want ta be. We should be able ta buy at low prices right now an' in th' future it wull increase in value."

Madame looked thoughtful. "There have been very few sales of land in this area. Many people in San Carlos do not have title to land; they just moved in and settled. Some of the Spanish men have large blocks of land that the governor granted them title to."

"Perhaps, Madame, some o' them would be interested in selling. I have heard of hundred acre farms selling fer twenty cents an acre. Larger land holdings might be available at lower prices, say ten cents per acre. At a price like that, we could purchase 1,000 acres for one hundred dollars."

"What would we do with 1,000 acres, Mr. Richardson?"

"Keep it, Madame. When settlers arrive, not all wull come wi' money. We can rent them small farms fer a share of th' produce, which can be sold ta obtain a return on our investment. Over time th' value of land wull increase an' we should make a large profit."

Madame smiled and Richardson thought, 'She has a lovely smile, she should smile more, despite the large responsibility she has with businesses to operate and children to raise.' "My Mr. Richardson, you are shrewd. It seems to me that you may be correct and it would be a good investment. My funds are somewhat limited at the moment. How large an investment are you considering?"

Richardson placed a cloth sack on the desk. "There are two hundred gold dollars in this sack, yea take it an' see what can be purchased with it."

"I cannot afford to match that amount, Mr. Richardson."

"Madame, we have been partners fer three years an' yea always do more of th' work than I do. It is embarrassing ta me. Yea buy land with the money an' take a one fourth interest fer yourself. If yea care ta add funds of your own then increase your ownership in proportion. Yea will be doing me a favor."

"You are very generous, Mr. Richardson; I shall see what can be done."

"Thank yea, Madame. Next year possibly yea will require additional funds." They laughed together and he added, "Perhaps yea should hire a man ta represent us in land dealings, ta supervise th' tenants, an' do whatever else yea require. Pay his wages from th' two hundred dollars." He stood up to leave.

"You have a safe journey, Mr. Richardson."

With steady breezes, especially early in the day, the Lady Anne glided upriver at a steady pace. Sometimes, later in the day, the men manned the poles or the oars to keep the boat moving. Richardson always put his book away and joined the men. Six days out of San Carlos, they arrived at La Charrette, a riverside cluster of small log cabins inhabited by some twenty French speaking settlers and traders.

It being late in the day with no breeze, Captain Burger decided to stop for the night. The boat came in between two large trees where the bow end was tied first. The current swung the stern toward shore and the rear rope was pulled tight. A fire was started on a grassy spot between the trees and meat spitted to roast. Soon, two men drifted over to talk and an extra pot of coffee was put in the side of the fire. One of the men asked, "Who des keel?"

Captain Burger pointed at the name painted on the boat. "It is a Richardson Chadron boat. We haul freight for customers."

The man looked puzzled. "Chadron. Me tink old Chadron have died."

"You are right, Monsieur, Chadron died. His wife, Madame Chadron manages the boat company."

"Dis woman Chadron with de store?"

"Madame Chadron operates the mercantile in San Carlos. She is family to Auguste Chouteau."

"Ah." The man nodded his head. "Dis woman tough like Chouteau?"

"She is tough. Madame and Chouteau do much business together."

Richardson sat with his back to a large tree. He smiled at the conversation and turned to writing in his logbook to summarize the day. He checked and recorded the temperature. Sitting in shadow, he listened to the visitors tell a story of American army officers passing up the river in a giant keel boat that was overloaded, hard to control and was being pulled with ropes most of the way. He heard the man say, "Keel boat is much heavy for wind to move, des army mans no so smart. Tink dey has trouble."

When the other man began talking about the Spanish, Richardson's ears perked up. "Zee Spanish no like dos army man on river. Spanish mans plan trouble, say arrest." Richardson wondered if Madame's information was wrong; no Chouteau talked about the Louisiana Purchase and the changes that would happen in the years to come. In fact, they were already happening with an increase in the number of Americans arriving in St. Louis. Possibly the local Spanish Authorities hadn't received proper notification. Suddenly, he wondered if the Spanish Governor of Louisiana was hatching some plan of his own to take possession of a large part of the west. It was immense in size and no one knew for sure what was out there or how vast the area of land and mountains was.

Richardson, lost in his speculations, heard no more of the conversation at the fire. He wondered if his operation at the trading post was in danger. Finally, he decided that it was unlikely the Spanish would venture so far north. After one winter in that country they would run for the south as fast as they could. The Spanish were established in Mexico. If the governor was plotting, it would likely be to take lands adjoining or near Mexico. He would need supplies and trade routes and the Mississippi would be too dangerous for him. His trade would have to be south to Mexico or somewhere on the Gulf, far from this area.

The Bay Company, which didn't like anyone opposing them, was still there. They had ruled their vast territory for far too long and were accustomed to doing anything they chose. He had challenged them and must expect retaliation. The Bay was a far greater danger to the trading post than any threat from the Spanish.

The helmsman brought him meat and filled his tin cup with coffee. Jar thanked him and started eating. His thoughts turned to Willow. It was close to three months since he last saw her and he missed her terribly. What would she be doing? Probably helping to weed the corn; maybe riding the white mare. Damn he should have asked Rene to go and check on her, make sure she was alright. Jar chuckled softly to himself. Willow was with Morning Sun Woman and Red Thunder. They had raised her for seventeen years and would be looking after her. He was being foolish. For the first time, he told himself he was in love, not knowing what that was supposed to be like. He did know that he was only truly happy when Willow was with him. Her gentle laugh, the way she smiled, the way she wrinkled her nose and her habit of making small jokes at his expense. Willow loved the big roan horse, often going to talk to him and feed him carrots. It pleased him that she was so eager to learn to speak English and learn everything the white men did. The way her eyes flashed when something upset her, amused him. On a sudden thought he realized, 'I must work to drop my Scottish accent so Willow learns to speak good English.' He vowed he would correct his own speaking.

His mind went back to the blizzard, remembering the way she stood between him and Morning Sun Woman, ready with her knife to fight. She couldn't weigh much more than half of what he did and was a head shorter; still she had stood there ready. Willow was brave and a fighter.

They would be married soon. He hoped the preacher would be there when he arrived home. He wondered how Louis was making out; he should be starting south by now.

Louis was in camp on the south bank of the Pembina River. Since gathering up the white people the traveling had been slow. They couldn't ride at more than a steady walk and even then bounced in the saddles he provided. In one day he could have ridden as far as the little group came in four.

The Pembina was the first major hurdle on the trip. He got the people across and, while the woman complained to her husband about being wet, he left them to dry in the sun and turned his attention to the cattle. The cows wouldn't go into the water without the calves and the calves were frightened. That problem was finally solved when his two helpers rode into the water, each holding a calf in his arms. The cows immediately followed.

Every time they ate the spirit man prayed. Louis didn't understand why and it worried him. He, Louis Chouart, shot the buffalo, skinned it, and brought the meat to camp. Why did the spirit man thank his great spirit for the food? Strange what this white man did. Louis always took his meat to the far side of camp to eat at a safe distance from the white man, who if he wasn't praying, was talking.

Before dark, the three men filled a kettle with cut up meat, corn and onions for tomorrow. They would take turns tending it and the fire as it cooked all night. Louis threw in salt for flavor. He wiped his knife on one leg of his soiled deerskin pants and stirred the stew. He squatted there beside the kettle and considered how far there was to go. On his own he could cover the distance in ten, twelve days. At the pace of the last four days…Louis shrugged. He would speed them up. In his mind, he set a target of one moon to arrive.

Chapter 21

During the night it began to rain. The large drops hitting my face awakened me where I was sleeping atop the cabin. I moved into the cabin to settle against a bale to doze away the rest of the night, not expecting to sleep. It was surprising to awaken to the sound of feet and the sway of the boat as men moved around on a dull, grey morning with a heavy rain falling, driven on a west wind.

Captain Burger and the crew were securing the boat and using the canvas sail to erect an awning for shelter from the rain. I stood in the cockpit to watch. The bottom spar was raised a few feet above the cabin and tied with ropes to hold it down the middle of the back half of the boat. Quickly, the crew stretched the sail over the spar and tied it along the two sides of the boat, providing a steep, two-sided roof that shed rain efficiently.

After inspecting the work, Captain Burger came to where I was standing. "No sense wearing the men out trying to travel into the face of this storm. The boat can stay here until the storm blows itself out. A spot of rest will be good for all of us."

The crew dug out dried meat and everyone settled in sheltered corners to chew jerky, talk and rest. In the afternoon, the storm clouds moved away and the sun began peeking out. The wind moderated, but didn't stop. The boat got underway with the men walking the slatted pathways on the two sides of the boat, pushing with long poles. I took a turn at the poling. For days it was slow travelling and hard work in the hot sun. A tiring circle of walking to the front of the boat carrying the long pole, push on the river bottom with the pole and walk to the stern. Pick up the pole and start the cycle all over again. Finally, the wind switched to come out of the southwest and the sail was hoisted into place. The boat began to glide smoothly ahead and everyone on the boat heaved a sigh of relief.

Captain Burger knew the river and spent his time reading the water. From time to time, he shouted directions to the helmsman standing at the back of the cabin holding the end of the long steering oar. Sandbars, snags and floating debris needed to be avoided. When these obstacles were encountered it seemed go on mile after mile. After days of hard struggle, the boat passed the Platt flowing in from the west. Once clear of the mess of trees and logs the Platt was dumping into the Missouri, conditions improved. The wind became more favorable and the long, slim boat glided ahead with a full sail.

On July seventeenth, while passing up the east side of the Missouri, we sighted an overly large keel boat tied up to the west bank of the river. Captain Burger held his course and no one seemed to notice us. The crew speculated that the big boat must belong to the army men they were told of at La Charrette. There seemed to be no activity around the tied up boat and speculation started that the Spanish had caught up to and arrested the men. Burger looked at me, winked, and whispered, “The Spanish would not abandon the big keel boat and all it carries.”

Several days of good winds from the south and the keel boat glided into shore at Yankton Landing where it was tied up to two large trees. Pig Eye Parrant walked from the trees with a long gun in the crook of his left arm and waited for me to leap ashore. "How ar' yea, Pierre?"

"Pierre is fine, Mr. Richardson. We have wait nine days for de boat." Pierre shook the extended hand as Rene's two helpers came from the trees, each carrying a bale of furs. Jar greeted both with an extended hand. He was happy to be back.

"How be everything at th' post?"

Pierre turned his head to look with his good eye. "De garden she grows. Rene sends us with de furs. Now much room for Rene to walk in storehouse. Rene, he says it time to go Dubuque to fetch lead."

"Ha' th' new men arrived from Portage la Prairie?"

Pierre shook his head. "No man's come." They all saw the worried frown on Richardson's face as he turned to watch the gangplank being put in place for unloading. Pierre added, "De lady, Willow Flower, she come riding big white horse."

Jar turned back with a happy grin. "Is Willow at th' post?"

"No, no, she no there." Pierre shook his head vigorously. "She there two day. She talk Rene. Rene tell words. She point all time, say words."

The happy look on Jar's face pleased the men. "When was Willow there, Pierre?"

Pierre's long bony face with its pointed chin wrinkled up as he thought. "Pierre tink one moon back."

Richardson felt a surge of happiness, standing there thinking as the men went for more furs. This was the first news of Willow in over three months. She had come looking for him. Maybe Willow missed him as much as he missed her. He was tempted to take the roan and go straight to the village to see her, to hear all her new words. Willow was determined to learn to speak English; white man's words, as she called it. He smiled happily. She was curious about everything. He recalled her picking up a book entitled *Robinson Crusoe* he had left open, looking at it and questioning him. At first, she didn't believe him when he explained that it was words put there by a man named Daniel Defoe and that the words spoke to him, told him a story. Willow asked who Defoe was and when he told her he didn't know Defoe her eyes got large with amazement. When he added that Defoe wrote the words over eighty years before, they got into a long discussion as Willow tried to understand and he struggled to find ways to explain to her. With his finger, he followed the words as he read a sentence to her and Willow watched closely. Soon enough, Willow would be speaking English and he looked forward with anticipation to the day when she would want to learn to read his books. In his gear was a basic grammar book to use to help her get started.

He didn't want to change her; she was perfect as she was. He just wanted to marry her, bring her home and keep her with him. He rubbed his nose thoughtfully. Willow, with her avid curiosity, wouldn't be content; she wanted to know everything, to understand everything and there was so much in the white man's world that was new to her. Just wait until he took her to St. Louis and she saw all those white people speaking English, French, Spanish and often a mixture of the three. Willow would drive him crazy with her questions.

Suddenly, Jar became aware that fur bales were piling up, the crew was unloading the boat and he was just standing there. He hurried to the boat to gather his gear and bring it ashore, embarrassed to have the men see him standing still, lost in a dream world. Taking his gear to the camp, he picked up a bale of furs and carried it to the shore before returning for another. Daylight was waning by the time all the bales were stowed onboard. Captain Burger wasn't going to leave shore when darkness was almost upon him so the boat crew stayed for the night. With two men always on duty aboard the boat, the crew joined the fur traders to exchange news and cook the evening meal.

Just before darkness, Jar walked to the picket line where the horses were tied and talked to the roan, scratched his ears and patted his neck. It would be good to be back in the saddle after all this time away. He stood there with the horse until full darkness, enjoying the sounds and smells, getting a feel for the night, attuning his senses to the wilderness without the constant babble of voices as a distraction. Returning to the fire, Jar spitted meat on a stake and set it to cook, filled his cup with coffee and listened to the men in their discussions. Tomorrow, with the packhorses loaded, they would start for the trading post, two long days away. He hoped Louis would be there.

Long ago, the easiest route and the best camping places had been found and even the horses had the route memorized by now. Late on the second day, after two early starts, the trading post and its out buildings came into sight. Rene and Andre came out with long guns to watch them arrive. The fact that no one else was visible told Jar what he was worried about had occurred. Louis wasn't here.

Stopping the horses near the storehouse, they dismounted and

Jar walked to Rene, looking at him to see if he was healthy. Rene was doing the same. Rene stuck out his hand. "Good you back, Jar. Is long time."

Jar grinned. "Too long; how yea making it, Rene?"

Rene returned the grin. "Rene good. Hoe garden, eat, that all. You hungry?"

"I could eat. We pushed hard to get here. I will help get these packs inside an' we can eat an' talk afterwards."

"Rene make stew, Jar eat. Rene move packs." Rene knew it wouldn't be that way. Jar never shirked when there was work needing to be done; besides, the men would be hungry, too. All the trade goods and supplies were quickly moved inside, the door closed and Rene snapped the big lock in place. Andre helped the men take the horses to pasture. Rene and Jar walked to the cabin and lit the oil lamp. Rene stirred up the fire to warm the stew.

Andre arrived and they sat down to eat, mostly in silence, before rolling up in blankets to sleep—talking could wait till morning.

Over a plate of stew and steaming cups of coffee, Jar told them about his trip to St. Louis. It took a long time to explain about the United States buying all the land west of the Mississippi and everyone living here was now an American citizen. Citizenship was another long discussion as neither Rene nor Andre had any concept of what citizenship was. They were Métis; they had been born and lived all their lives on the land. It was home and now someone was telling them they were citizens with a right to be here. Of course they had a right to be here, this was where they lived. They never lived anywhere else. This was another strange idea the white man brought from far away.

Andre helped Jar move the items he brought for Willow into the cabin while Rene and the men organized the storehouse. They placed the oak chest at the end of the large bunk and left it for Willow to open. Jar explained, "The men in the boatyard made the chest fer Willow. Inside it are dresses an' ladies things that Madame Chadron sent ta Willow as a wedding present."

No way was he going to talk about the embarrassment of ordering the dresses. Let the men think that Madame did that. If she asked, he would explain to Willow.

Jar showed Andre the Spanish Saddle and boots for Willow. "The reason I was so long in St. Louis was because it took time for the cobbler ta make these things."

The two men found the curtains and examined them. "See these hoops here, Andre. They are ta put a rod through so the curtains can be moved. We need ta find straight branches ta make rods, sort of like ramrods in our long guns, so we can hang these curtains."

"Andre find rods. How many rods?" Jar held up eight fingers. Andre nodded and left.

Jar took his new books out of the satchel and arranged them on the shelf with his other books. There was more than enough reading to last the next year. It didn't matter; these were all good books which he could read over and over or sometimes just a few pages at a time. Often, he would remember something from a book and go back to read those pages again. His new shirts and pants went on a shelf all neatly folded. Jar hesitated over the black, wide-brimmed Spanish hats. He wanted Willow to have one that fit her and he didn't know which one it would be. He stuffed the hats back in the satchel with the iron strongbox and stored it under his bunk. After Willow got her hat he would give the others to the men.

The bathtub went against the wall behind the stove. It caused questions. The men wanted to know what it was. Rene turned away smiling when Jar explained it was for washing clothes. One of the men pointed and commented, "Much water in creek, wash clothes." Again, Jar explained that in the winter time the creek was frozen and Willow would be able to wash clothes inside the cabin. The tub was a great amusement to the men.

With the cabin arranged the way he wanted it, Jar went to see how Rene was making out sorting all the new trade goods. The trading house was full of trade goods ready for trappers when they came or for the few people who occasionally showed up wanting some item or to get a gun repaired.

Andre came back with a bundle of straight branches and all three men sat in the shade to peel the bark off and smooth the wood with knives. It was much like making arrows. When they started to put up curtains on the first window they discovered that the rod couldn't be put against the wall because the curtain wouldn't move. Rene volunteered to make spacers to nail on the walls to hold the rods.

After three days back, Jar told Andre, "Louis should be here by now. Yea better take a packhorse an' go look fer him. Tomorrow I'm going ta ride over to th' village ta take Willow her new saddle an' boots. Yea want ta come with me, Rene?"

Rene shook his head. "Andre go, better Rene stay."

Next morning, Andre saddled up. He was taking an extra riding horse and a packhorse with blankets and supplies to last him if he went all the way to la Portage to find Louis. Riding west to clear the hills, Andre continued to the northwest along the same route they used back in the spring.

Andre held a steady ground-eating pace and crossed the Parle River in midafternoon, kept on to the west branch of the Parle, and followed the river north until it turned east. From there he set a course across the prairies for the lakes at Big Stone and the Bois de Sioux River. He camped short of the lakes. Two hours into the morning, he came up to the lakes and searched for signs of a recent camp. Finding nothing, he followed the Sioux northwest, planning to use the campsite west of the big bend on the river if he didn't find Louis first.

In the west the sun was almost down and Andre estimated another mile and he would turn off for the campsite. Topping out on a slight rise, he saw smoke ahead and it was very close to the river. There was a camp and it could be anybody, friendly or not. He sat there considering and decided to change his saddle to the other horse. If he was forced to run it would be better on a fresh horse. Keeping to lower ground, when he could, he took his time approaching the camp. His first good view of the camp showed a number of horses and there were cattle. This must be Louis and his charges. Andre sighed and relaxed. He had been riding with the fear that something bad might have happened and he would never find the group, now he felt sure this was them.

Checking the priming on the long gun, he started toward the camp from a quarter mile out. Almost as soon as he moved from the low bushes where he had watched the camp, he saw men moving, spreading out. They were watching him. The man that walked out from the camp was short and Andre soon decided it was Louis. He remained cautious until he got closer before relaxing. It was Louis.

Pulling the horse up a few paces from Louis, Andre held up his hand. Louis grinned; he recognized the wide black hat almost as soon as he saw the rider. One thing he possessed was excellent eyesight.

Andre swung down and stuck out his hand. Louis came to shake it and they stood talking quietly. "It is good to see you, Louis. How has your trip been?"

Louis shrugged. "Trip not bad. Early day are slow. Calves not go fast. Now we move better."

"Good job, Louis. With no idea when you started out, I decided to look for you."

"Louis is happy see Andre. You come camp."

Together, they walked into the camp and Andre tied his horses before going to greet everyone—five people besides Louis and Louis was the youngest of the group. Sitting around the fire, he studied each of them to see how they were holding up and decided Christie and McDonald were toughened up to traveling and probably doing as well as could be expected. Mrs. McDonald was very obviously pregnant and Andre was sure she was uncomfortable. Andre waited to see if she complained.

Christie asked, "When did yea leave th' trading post ta come looking fer us?"

Andre watched Mrs. McDonald from the corner of his eye as he answered. "Started out early yesterday morning and rode two days. Five days, six at the most and you will be there."

Christie sighed. "It wull be a relief not ta spend every day on a horse. Th' lord has looked after us an' Louis has guided us with great care."

Andre saw the McDonalds look at each other and she smiled wanly at her husband. He decided to give her something good to look forward to. "Mrs. McDonald, a cabin just like Jar's is ready for you and John. Jar back from St. Louis a few days. He bring cast iron cook stove for cabin." Andre grinned. "Jar brings curtains for new windows."

She immediately perked up and Andre was happy he told her. Before she could say anything, Christie interrupted. "Are you calling Mr. Richardson, Jar?"

Andre laughed. "Yes. Jar are letters for names. All who knows him calls him Jar."

Christie murmured quietly to himself before looking up. "Ah see, James Angus Richardson, his initials spell Jar." Christie laughed happily.

John McDonald asked, "James ha' traveled ta St. Louis an' back since we last saw him?"

Andre nodded. "He takes furs to St. Louis to sell. Come back with goods for next season fur trading. Trading post full of goods, all furs gone."

"With a' that business ta tend ta he found time ta look fer curtains fer our windows?"

Andre nodded. "Jar bring curtains for cabin. Rene put windows in cabin now. You get there, everything ready."

Mrs. McDonald added, "Mr. Richardson is very kind." Andre

nodded in agreement.

Andre stayed with them for the first day. He didn't interfere, leaving all the decisions to Louis. When they stopped for the night, Andre estimated they had travelled twenty-five miles. In the morning, he told Louis he needed to get back to the trading post and rode away.

A scout brought word that Black Arrow was coming. Before Morning Sun Woman could caution her to remain demure Willow Flower ran to her horse and raced out of the village, scattering dogs and children from her path. Morning Sun Woman smiled. For days now Willow had gone to the river every morning to bathe and wash her hair. She kept her clothes clean and often her eyes strayed to the southern horizon. Black Arrow was always on Willow's mind. Morning Sun hoped the white man didn't wait any longer to marry Willow. She remembered Red Thunder coming to see her when she was fifteen summers.

White Cloud covered the trail in long loping strides with Willow straining to see him. Suddenly, there he was, coming around a corner in the path from behind a grove of poplar trees. Willow pulled White Cloud to a halt and waited, watching him ride toward her. As he got near she called, "Ho, white man, Willow is happy see James Richardson."

She was rewarded with a huge grin. They dismounted and grabbed each other. Willow got hugged so tight she was afraid her ribs would crack He held her a long time, not saying a word. She tried to lean back and couldn't. Finally, his arms relaxed and he held her shoulders in his hands to just look at her. She could see the hunger in his eyes, he wanted her. Her face showed a hint of a smile; she wanted him too. If he asked her to take off her dress right there, she would have a hard time saying no. He didn't ask and she knew he wouldn't. Rene told her.

When he spoke it was to ask, "Willow Flower is healthy?"

She nodded. "Long time James not comes talk Willow."

His face sobered. "Sorry about that, Willow. Every spring I go to St. Louis with the furs and bring back trade goods. Next spring Willow will go with me."

She knew all this. Rene had explained it to her. "Huh, Willow think James forget marry Willow."

He grabbed her again and she gasped for breath. Willow liked this. He was her man and she wanted to be close to him. She wished he would get the marrying over with, so she asked, "White man spirit man comes?"

James released her and stepped back. "Andre went to look for them. They should have been here by now. I want us to get married and to take Willow back to the trading post with me."

Willow prodded him. "No spirit man."

He looked at her helplessly. "If he doesn't come soon we will ask Red Thunder to marry us and the spirit man can marry us later."

Willow smiled. "Is good. Willow want marry James." She got another hug. They walked along the trail, leading the horses and talking. Neither were aware of the two scouts that trailed at a discrete distance and would report to Chief Red Thunder. In fact, they were only aware of each other until suddenly the village was there and the dogs ran at them barking.

Red Thunder and Morning Sun Woman were waiting. Everyone in the village was pretending not to watch. All were eager to see what was going on and hear any news. This strange white man that made Willow wait; a Sioux warrior would have taken her to his robes long ago. If it hadn't been for the Santee stories about Black Arrow they would have believed there was something wrong with him. Strange this white man. Black Arrow was also a strong medicine man with great powers to heal. Medicine men were often different.

Red Thunder saw how happy Willow Flower was. He stepped forward, his face expressionless, and put out his hand the way the white man did. Black Arrow came to grip it firmly. Red Thunder motioned at the fire and the robes that were spread and the men sat down cross-legged to go through the greetings and move on to talk. "Black Arrow not comes long time."

Jar nodded in agreement. "Black Arrow has been far down the Missouri to Saint Louis. Many days on white man canoe."

The silence lasted as Red Thunder considered this. "Ouis white man village like Sioux village?"

Jar took his time. "Many, many white men. More white men come every day from the east. Soon be white men everywhere."

Swinging his arm around to point at the village, Red Thunder stated, "Like Sioux village."

While Jar pondered, two elders came to join the circle. Red Thunder watched Black Arrow greet the elders courteously. Both were old, old friends and valued advisors and it pleased him that Willow's man knew how to behave properly. He watched Black Arrow form a circle with his hands and hold it up. "This Red Thunder Sioux village." The arms moved to form a large circle. "This St.

Louis white man village."

Red Thunder felt a sense of alarm. How many white men were there? He glanced at his old friends before asking, "Many white men Ouis village?"

Jar held up the first finger on his right hand. "This finger is how many Sioux live in Red Thunder's village." All three men nodded in agreement. Jar held up all the fingers on his left hand. "This how many white men in St. Louis village."

The chief fell silent. Now he was more than alarmed. He occasionally saw white men ever since he was a small boy and while they were interesting they presented no danger to the Sioux. The Sioux could sweep them away with one hand like swatting a mosquito and that would be the end of them. Now Black Arrow said there were many white men and more were coming. Red Thunder dreaded that life around him was going to change. He barely noticed when Willow Flower came to add sticks to the fire and sat on the robe beside Black Arrow. Normally, he would have glared at her for intruding on the men's circle, embarrassing him before the elders. Soon she would be Black Arrow's concern and he didn't seem to mind her being there. These white men were strange.

His thoughts were interrupted by an elder speaking. "Long ago a French trader told me that far east the white men are as many as the buffalo. I did not believe him."

The other elder asked, "How can that be? The buffalo are endless."

Chief Red Thunder turned his eyes to Jar. "Has Black Arrow seen all these white men? Is it true?"

Jar looked down at his hands and tried to think how to reply. In the end, the only thing he could do was tell the truth. His eyes looked at Red Thunder, the elders and back before he started. "Black Arrow was born far, far away in the east at a place called Scotland where there are many white men. So many white men there is not room for all of them on the land. Black Arrow knew there was no room for him, so when he was fourteen summers he left and came to Fort Garry. From there he came to the Mnisota River to build his life. Now, Black Arrow wishes to marry Willow Flower, the daughter of Chief Red Thunder and raise his family in the land of the Sioux. What the French trader said is true. Far to the east are more white men than there are buffalo on the great grasslands of the Sioux."

They looked at him in amazement, trying to understand the enormity of what he was saying. Willow never felt closer to him and reached to rest her hand on his arm. Chief Red Thunder seemed not to notice; he was lost in thought. What did all this mean for the Sioux? He needed time to think, to talk long with the elders and discuss every side of this issue. After a long silence, he looked around. Several of his people were gathered and sitting outside the circle listening. "Red Thunder thanks Black Arrow for telling us about Ouis village and the white men." He stood up to signal an end to the gathering. "Soon be time to eat. We will talk again."

Black Arrow stood up and reached a hand to help Willow to her feet. Everyone watching knew Willow Flower didn't need such help. He spoke quietly in Sioux to her. "Let's go to the horses, there is something to show you."

They walked away hand in hand, the way the people were accustomed to seeing them do. No one laughed behind their hands as they did before. He only took time to tie the horses before greeting the Chief; now, with the talking over, Jar uncovered the load on the packhorse. He handed a woolen saddle blanket to Willow and carried the Spanish saddle to White Cloud. "This saddle is for White Cloud so you can ride the same as me."

Willow ran her fingers over the leather and looked at him in surprise, not knowing what to say. James explained, "Before you put the saddle on you must smooth the horse's back hairs with your hand or White Cloud will get sores on her back. This is a saddle blanket to make White Cloud more comfortable. You put it on this way and lay the saddle on top. Hang the stirrup on the saddle horn so it is out of your way." Jar bent down and reached for the cinch. "Pull the cinch up snug and make sure it isn't twisted. After that, this leather strap goes through the iron ring like this and down and out this bottom ring. Now, you pull up to tighten the cinch and put the strap around again. Lift it up until you have it tight and fasten it to the ring by making a loop like this and putting the end through the loop. All that is left is to put the stirrup down."

"James brings saddle for Willow?"

Jar looked at her, smiling. "Yes, the saddle is for Willow. Should have told you before."

Willow's beaming smile was all the answer he needed. "Can Willow ride?"

Jar hugged her. "In a moment. There is something else you need to ride in the saddle." Her look of puzzlement pleased him. "Sit on the grass and I will show you." Jar hurried to the packhorse and came back with the leather boots. Willow's eyes grew large. "See these heels on the boots. They are so the boots won't slide through the stirrups and get your foot stuck. Give me your foot."

Willow watched him reach into the first boot and come out with a sock. Jar pulled it over her foot and up the leg before he pulled the boot on and did the same to her other foot. He helped her stand up and Willow hobbled around awkwardly in the strange feeling boots. She wrinkled her nose and concentrated on walking. Willow wasn't used to her heels being off the ground and felt like she was going downhill. She giggled. "Is not good walking."

"The boots are meant for riding. When you are used to them you will be able to walk."

Willow stopped and gave Jar a mischievous look. "Willow ride now?"

"Come on. I'll help you into the saddle." He lifted her, set her on the horse and went about adjusting the length of the stirrups to fit the length of her legs. He was acutely aware of all the leg showing as her deerskin dress was pulled up by the saddle. If Willow noticed his distraction she gave no indication. They started across the village at a walk. The people of the village looked in amazement at the white man equipment on White Cloud.

It is never easy to become accustomed to a large leather saddle when you are used to riding bareback, so they never got above a walk. They stopped to rest before starting back. Jar reached under his shirt, came out with her moccasin, and handed it to her. She looked at it in surprise. "Willow lose moc…Ho, James Richardson steal Willow moccasin!"

He laughed at her. "Needed your moccasin to get the boots made the right size to fit your feet."

"Huh, Willow think moccasin lost." She feigned a haughty look. "Now Willow find James steal moccasin. Willow think James Richardson much bad man."

They laughed together and started the horses back to the village where Morning Sun Woman was cooking. Many people came to look at the strange saddle and the black leather boots.

In the morning, when Jar stepped out of the teepee where he was sleeping, Willow was at the fire outside Morning Sun Women's teepee, with meat cooking. When she saw him she moved the coffee pot closer to the coals to boil. She looked up at him slyly. "Willow thinks white man sleep all day."

Jar laughed at her and went into the trees. When he came back Willow filled his cup and they sat side by side to eat. Now that Willow's man was taken care of, Morning Sun Woman allowed Chief Red Thunder to join them at the fire, where he ate in silence. Willow filled a cup for him. He hid his eyes to keep his happiness with Willow's man from showing. Finished eating, he looked at Jar. "Morning Sun say need meat. Black Arrow hunts with Red Thunder?"

"Thank you, Red Thunder. Black Arrow likes to hunt."

The chief grunted. "Good. We go before get hot." He stood up and went for his bow. Jar did the same. When the two men rode away Willow looked at her mother proudly; her man was being accepted.

Chapter 22

Jar took Willow riding to practice using her saddle. By midday she was getting comfortable at a walk and a lope. A trot caused her to bounce up and down until her backside was sore. They stopped on the bank of the Mnisota River to rest. Willow went to his horse and got her moccasins from the saddlebags. She pulled off her boots to rest her feet and put on the moccasins. They talked, held hands and watched the water flowing past.

Willow pointed at Jar's saddle. "Willow needs bags like James to carry goods."

"I made those saddlebags out west in the Black Hills when we were trapping. We will make a set to fit your saddle. Those were my first attempt, so we should be able to do a better job on yours."

"Is good. Willow make. James help Willow make."

They lazed around and finally he lay back on the grass and looked at the clouds floating overhead on a gentle breeze. There were long streaks of white, wispy clouds going past, looking much like cloth streamers he had seen blowing in the wind in St. Louis. He wondered why the clouds were separated like that. Willow lay with her head on his chest and soon she heard his even breathing. She felt happy. Her man was at peace, no worries to bother him.

Willow felt like a bath in the river after all the riding and besides her thighs hurt from rubbing on the saddle. The cool water would feel good on her legs. She debated with herself, 'How long would James sleep?' She giggled softly. If she went into the river and James woke up he would be embarrassed to find her with her dress off. Silly man! Soon they would be married and he would see her many times. Willow remembered seeing him. He hadn't known she was awake when he got up to add wood to the fire during the big storm. Ho, it was nice to have a secret from her man, just a little secret that could cause no harm. She decided not to bathe. She wouldn't cause him any discomfort. It would be a shame to disturb his peace and it was important he be able to relax.

Willow sat up and moved to sit with her back against a tree where she could watch him. As many times before she marveled at how large James was. The great width of his shoulders and the red hair she loved. The first time she saw that red hair it scared her, thinking he was some kind of devil come to torment her and Morning Sun Woman. Sioux did not have red hair. No one she had ever seen had red hair. It was an unheard of thing that was scary to a young girl of sixteen summers with her mother unconscious and no one to talk to. She had stayed on guard waiting for him to try some devilment. He did nothing to harm her, just those things needed to survive in the midst of a bad blizzard. Slowly, she had relaxed and come to trust him. The next morning when he left the shelter, Willow quickly whispered to Morning Sun Woman and they discussed this strange man, finally deciding he meant them no harm.

Now she could hardly wait to marry him, although it seemed to be taking forever. They could have been married many moons ago if he would have accepted that Chief Red Thunder could say the words. Instead, he insisted there be a white man spirit man also.

Willow worried about the spirit man. What would he be like? Would he scare her? Huh, her man would protect her and the spirit man better walk carefully or James would settle with him.

Willow lazed in the shade, waiting for James to finish his nap. Her eyes fell on the long gun that he always kept close. Willow thought it must be heavy. She wondered if she could make the long gun shoot. She knew how to use a bow and many times practiced against the boys when she was younger. Willow nodded her head. She was as good as most of the boys with a bow, why not with a long gun? She made up her mind. She would ask James to show her.

She waited patiently until his eyes opened and he sat up to look around. Willow hurried to sit beside him. She pointed at the Charleville. "James show Willow shoot long gun."

"You want to learn how to shoot the long gun?" She nodded her head. "That will be a good thing for you to know." Jar picked up the gun and looked out at the river. "See that log stuck in the sand? That will make a good target." He showed her the gun and explained how it worked. They found a place where she could lay down on the grass with the long gun resting on a fallen tree. Willow listened closely to the explanation on aiming at a target. She said she was ready and he warned her to hold the gun tight against her shoulder.

Jar smiled as he stood behind her and watched the rifle barrel moving around as Willow tried to aim at the log. Finally, she squeezed the trigger, the gun jumped, black smoke spewing from the muzzle. Jar watched the splash as the lead ball hit the water beyond the log. Willow missed on the high side.

He helped her up and she rubbed her shoulder where the gun hit her. Jar showed her how to load the gun and she tried again. This time she hit the sand in front of the log. Jar explained about keeping the bore of the barrel clean. Willow watched him run a patch of cloth up and down the barrel. This time Willow loaded the gun herself, got into position, and fired.

Jar admired her grit. Willow wouldn't give up, determined to hit the log and master the gun. She loaded and fired and after every third shot she cleaned the barrel. Jar worried about her shoulder. Willow didn't complain. He knelt on one knee to coach her. It didn't occur to them that the noise of the gun would attract attention, until a horse snorted and Jar looked over his shoulder. Chief Red Thunder and a line of Sioux warriors were sitting their horses on a slight rise in the ground, watching.

Willow was on her stomach preparing to shoot again, determined to hit the target. She dug her moccasin toes into the ground, pulled the gun tight to her shoulder, aimed carefully and slowly squeezed the trigger, just the way James kept telling her. The gun jumped, dust and bark flew from the log and Willow Flower leaped to her feet. She had done it, her shoulder hurt and her dear skin dress was grass stained. Willow threw her left arm in the air and yelled, "Ho, white man, Willow have killed log!" She was happy.

Willow spun in a circle and saw the line of horsemen watching. Suddenly she was quiet and came to stand beside James, embarrassed in front of all the warriors. Red Thunder lifted his leg over his horse's neck, dropped to the ground and paced toward them. He looked at the gun, glanced at his daughter and studied the log before turning to Jar. "Black Arrow say Willow Flower is fierce warrior like silver bear. Huh, warrior no eat log. Willow make much noise, worry whole village, no meat."

Jar saw the humor in Red Thunder's eyes. He was coming to know and understand this tough old warrior who carried responsibility for his whole village. The chief turned and walked away to his horse. Suddenly they were alone again. Jar wrapped his arms around Willow, held her tightly and told her how well she had done. Her hair smelled of black powder. Soon, her normal exuberance returned and she announced, "Willow go in river to wash, James no look."

He picked up the long gun and went to sit against a tree with his back to the river. Willow glanced at him, wondering if he would peek. She pulled the dress over her head and waded into the water to scrub her body with sand and wash her long black hair. She wished she had brought the bar of soap.

Jar cleaned the long gun, carefully loaded it again, and primed the powder pan. He sat with the gun across his legs and waited. Had Andre found Louis? This was the fourth day since Andre left the trading post. If he hadn't found Louis he would be nearing the Red by now. What could have happened? Maybe the calves took longer than estimated to develop strong legs or spring flooding held the group up. He just wished Louis would show up. He admitted to himself that it wasn't Louis he was waiting for, it was Reverend Christie. Maybe he was a fool to keep Willow waiting. No he wasn't. It would be difficult enough for Willow to find acceptance among whites. He wanted to give her every chance. A proper marriage with a wedding certificate would be a good start. It wouldn't be a problem here or along the river. Only in places like St. Louis where people were different. Sooner or later, white settlers would arrive in this area with all their prejudices, biases, and preconceived ideas of superiority.

Willow came and sat near him. Her hair was wet and she was combing it with her fingers, trying to get the tangles out. He watched her for a while before commenting. “Tomorrow it will be time for me to go back to the trading post.”

She stopped and turned her head to look at him. “James stay more days?”

Jar put his arm around her shoulders. “Sure would like to stay; only there is work that needs doing. James can’t be lying around sleeping in the sun all the time.”

Willow laughed at his joke before her face got serious. “Chief say words. Willow go trading post with James.” She saw the pain in his eyes causing her to regret pushing him, knowing full well he wanted her with all his heart. She tried to ease the pain. “Willow think spirit man come soon and Willow come trading post.” She smiled at him. “Thanks to James for showing Willow long gun. Ho, soon Willow shoot like James. Willow think time go village.”

They gathered the gear, tightened the cinches and rode back to the village. Chief Red Thunder was sitting at the fire in a circle with six elders. He looked up as Jar walked past and motioned to a buffalo robe across the fire. Jar sat down and crossed his legs with the long gun on his knees. They all watched him as he waited, knowing they were discussing something serious. Finally, the chief waved a hand at the circle and started.

“The elders much time talk about white mans in Ouis. White mans in east more than buffalo. Many white man worry elders. Chief asks Black Arrow what all white mans do to Sioux.”

Jar considered for a long time. “Black Arrow does not know what white men will do. Black Arrow can only tell chief what he thinks white men do." The chief nodded in agreement. "Black Arrow thinks first the Sioux will see more white men along the Missouri. They will come in the summer and disappear in the fall. Next summer they come again. Soon they will come an' build teepees." Several of the elders nodded their heads.

"Far to the east where all the white men live they have a new white man Chief. Black Arrow thinks soon Chief Jefferson will send army men to talk to Sioux. Black Arrow thinks they will come from the south up the Mississippi and Missouri."

An elder turned his sun-blackened and weathered face toward Jar. "What army men?"

"Army men is the name white men use for warriors." There was a shocked silence. They stared at him.

Chief Red Thunder asked, "Why Chief Jefferson send warriors? Chief want make war on Sioux."

Jar held out his hands, palms up. "No, not war. Black Arrow thinks Chief Jefferson send army men to scout the land and talk to Sioux."

An elder on the other side of the circle waved a hand. "Chief wants find Sioux villages, how many Sioux, after he send army, make war on Sioux."

Chief Red Thunder slowly nodded his head. "Is wise to scout an enemy first. Think Sioux must prepare. Chief Red Thunder will send scouts to tell all Sioux what Black Arrow says. Chief will send two scouts to ask Teton Sioux for council and to alert Dog Soldiers." After a time to consider, the elders advised their chief that they agreed.

Jar asked, "What are Dog Soldiers?"

Red Thunder acknowledged the question. "The Dog Soldiers of the Teton Sioux are the bravest warriors on the grasslands. They will not stop until all enemies killed in battle. Even the murderous Black Foot of the far west know not to bother the Dog Soldiers. They guard the villages and fight the battles for our cousins the Teton."

Morning Sun Woman added wood to the fire. The day was ending and soon it would be dark. Willow Flower helped her mother prepare the meat as the men waited to eat. Jar noticed Willow's hair was combed and braided; his eyes followed her as she moved around. Red Thunder noticed.

With the meat cooking, Willow came to sit beside him. Suddenly, they heard horses coming and turned their heads to look. It was Andre escorted by two Sioux scouts. Jar came to his feet and went to greet his friend with Willow following. Andre came down off his tired horse to shake Jar's hand. "Andre think Jar is here, so he come." His eyes shifted. "How is Willow Flower?"

"Willow is happy see Andre. Andre come fire, meat cook, soon eat." Andre hesitated, looking at his horses.

Jar slapped him on the shoulder. "Yea go with Willow. I will tether th' horses, yea look like yea could use a rest." Jar walked away, leading the horses to the edge of the trees behind the teepee where he was sleeping. He unsaddled Andre's horse and took the gear off the second horse. With the horses tethered, he made two trips to take gear to the teepee before walking back to the fire. As he approached in the darkness he could hear Willow talking. "James show Willow shoot long gun. Willow kill log far in river. Soon Willow shoot good like James." Jar stopped to listen.

Andre commented. "That good, Willow. Willow need long gun. Willow talk Rene."

Jar heard Willow chuckle. "No Rene, Willow talk James Richardson."

Andre laughed. "That will do it. Willow remember, Rene boss trading house. Rene tell Willow bring beaver."

"Ho, Willow can get beaver." She giggled. "Rene no say bring beaver. Rene say here good gun, Willow."

Andre agreed. "Yes, Rene get gun for Willow." Jar walked into the firelight and took his place between them.

"I was afraid Andre was going all th' way to la Portage."

"Didn't have to. Found Louis' camp at the big bend of Bois de Sioux. He be at post three, four days."

"Louis has everything with him?"

Andre used his fingers. "Louis have bull, two cows, two calves, one preacher man, one clerk, one wife, two men."

"That is good, Andre." Jar turned to Willow. "Did you understand that?"

Willow's face was split by a wide smile. "Spirit Man come four days."

"That is right, Willow. We need to talk to Red Thunder and make arrangements."

Willow looked puzzled. "What this arrangements?"

"We need to ask Red Thunder when James can marry Willow."

In rapid-fire Sioux, Willow addressed her father and explained; her hands moving as she talked. They talked back and forth. Jar listened carefully and as good as he was at speaking Sioux, the words were too fast for him. He caught a word here and there. Finally, Willow folded her hands in her lap and sat quietly. Chief Red Thunder watched Willow as he thought.

Willow Flower was his only daughter; none of the others lived. She was always different, full of energy, competitive and always wanting to learn. As a little girl, she would sneak close to hear when he talked to the elders. He pretended not to notice her. When the boys her age were being given bows she came to him asking for a bow. Together, they made a small bow with arrows and he taught her how to use it. Willow outshot many of the boys. He discussed this with Morning Sun Woman. No brave wanted a woman who could outshoot him. Other girls Willow's age married. No brave was bold enough to approach him about his daughter. When the white man came into their lives, coming with gifts for all of them, Red Thunder allowed Willow more freedom than was the custom in Sioux families. Willow walked with the white man, held his hand and went to visit him, with Morning Sun Woman along to keep a close eye on her, of course. This was unheard of and there was talk, which the elders reported to him. Now, Willow walked boldly into the circle when Black Arrow was there and sat beside him. This daughter broke many rules; it was time for her to marry, to have a husband to worry about her behavior. This white man who was a brave warrior and a great healer was like a timid rabbit around his daughter. Willow explained that the Rene man told her Black Arrow would not look on her until they were married; he would not sleep in the same teepee until they were married. Red Thunder knew the white man was wise; still, there were many things Red Thunder did not understand about him.

The Chief spoke to Jar. "My daughter say white man spirit man come four days. She say Black Arrow asks when he marry Willow Flower."

"Yes, Chief. Black Arrow wishes to marry Willow Flower as soon as Chief approves."

"Chief approves." He held up the fingers of one hand. "Red Thunder come trading post five days. Chief will bring Willow Flower, Morning Sun Woman and more. Chief will say words. Chief will hear spirit man. Willow Flower will stay in white man teepee of wood."

"Black Arrow says thanks to Chief Red Thunder. Black Arrow will keep Willow Flower forever and protect her."

Chief Red Thunder nodded his head and looked at Morning Sun Woman. She smiled at him. When he looked back, Black Arrow requested, "Black Arrow wishes to talk trade with Chief Red Thunder and the elders."

Despite his years of practice, the Chief couldn't hide his surprise. He looked at the circle of elders. They were all staring at Black Arrow. Wondering what this was about, he asked, "What Black Arrow trade?"

"Black Arrow and Rene have built the trading post and wooden teepees. Black Arrow has horses. Soon Black Arrow have wife. In seasons to come, Black Arrow and Willow Flower will have children. Chief Red Thunder has seen the trading post and the hills and valley where Black Arrow and Willow Flower will live. Black Arrow wishes to trade for the hills and valley so always there will be a home for Willow Flower and her children and their children."

The silence lasted, one elder pulled his robe closer around his shoulders, as they considered in silence. Jar knew that for the Sioux there was no concept of the white man's bent to own land. In their world, the whole tribe lived on the land and used it. It was unknown for individuals to claim they owned a piece of land. As long as the tribe could hold and defend an area it was theirs, for everyone in the tribe to use.

Finally, an elder asked, "Why Black Arrow want trade for Sioux land?

Jar pointed at his chest. "It is the custom of my people for a man to provide for the future of his family. Willow Flower will be my family; her children will be my family. By trading for the land it will be a place they can always come to. Black Arrow will be doing what his people have always done. This is something that Black Arrow has strong belief in for his family."

With the conversation going, another elder asked, "Morning Sun Woman is mother to Willow Flower. Is Morning Sun Woman Black Arrow family?"

"Morning Sun Woman will always be part of Black Arrow's family. As will Red Thunder, Willow's brother and Spotted Tail. All Willow Flower's family will be Black Arrow's family."

"They can come this land?"

"Always. Willow Flower's family will always be welcome."

The first elder came back. "What Black Arrow trade for this Sioux land?"

"Black Arrow will trade long guns, powder, ball molds, and lead."

"How many long guns Black Arrow trade?"

Before Jar could give an answer Red Thunder held up his hand. "No talk trade now. Chief and elders must talk long about this trade. Red Thunder come five days, talk trade with Black Arrow."

After a good sleep they saddled the horses and packed their gear for the ride south to the trading post. Willow watched them out of sight before hurrying to the teepee. There was sewing to do. When she rode White Cloud, James avoided looking at her long legs that became exposed when the saddle pulled her dress up. She had an idea. She didn't want James to be embarrassed.

Andre spotted Louis coming far in the distance, most of two miles away. He went to the cabin to tell Jar. Together, they walked to the trading house where Rene was. It was late on the third day so Louis did well getting here this soon. As a precaution, they spread out with long guns in hand and waited. Jar walked out a few steps to greet them.

Slowly, the caravan of horses and cattle came nearer, climbed the slope and came to a halt in front of Jar. He walked to Louis' horse and held his hand up. "Welcome, Louis. I am happy yer long trip is over."

Louis grinned, happy and proud to have done what Jar wanted. Rene and Andre came to talk to Louis while Jar went to welcome each of the others. Lastly, he went to Julia. "May I help yea down, Mrs. McDonald?"

"Thank yea, Mr. Richardson. It is a great relief tae finally be haur." She arranged her skirt and held his hand as she swung her right leg over the horse's rump. Jar put a hand on her back to steady her and eased her to the ground. "Thank yea, Mr. Richardson. It will be a great pleasure nae tae ride this horse agin tomorrow."

"Please come this way, Mrs. McDonald, we have your cabin ready for you. John come along noo and yea can get settled." Jar led them to the cabin and held the door open. It was set up just like his with a plank floor, four bunks, stove, table, and chairs. On the shelves were pots, tin plates and other utensils. Everything they needed except their personal possessions. John McDonald's first thought was, 'What a vast improvement over the rough cabin back on the little farm at Red River.'

While the McDonalds got acquainted with their new home, Jar took Reverend Christie to his own cabin. The men took the animals to the pen for the night. Christie was quick to notice the shelf of books, something unseen since arriving on the frontier.

There were now six men living in the bunkhouse. That was only until Andre left for the Yellowstone to build a trading post in Mandan country. Three of the men would go with him.

Normally, the men cooked in the bunkhouse and Rene in the cabin. Tonight Rene and Andre lit a campfire so everyone could roast meat, eat, and get to know each other. Mrs. McDonald was the only exception, choosing to lie down; the first time she hadn't slept on the ground in over a month. Louis came to Jar with coins in his hand. "Dis is left from Louis get supplies."

Jar looked at the three dollars for a moment. He put his arm around the boy's shoulders and told him, "Louis took on great responsibility an' did a good job of bringing everyone all th' way from la Portage. Not many men could ha' done as well. Yea keep th' coins, Louis, an' tomorrow Andre wull pay yea your wages."

Louis looked up at the big man in great surprise. He had bargained hard to save money for Jar and now he was being told to keep what was left over. He would have eight dollars that was all his own, along with his long gun, the horse and the other things Jar had given him. His fourteen summers had been one long struggle to survive. Now all this was his. Louis didn't know what to say. Jar patted his shoulder. "Let's see if th' meat is ready, Louis."

Eleven men sat in a circle around the fire as the day drew to a close and night came on. Christie sat on Jar's left with Louis on the other side. Jar started with Christie and introduced each man in turn, offering a few words about each. When he was finished Rene told the men, "In two day from now lady Willow come marry Jar. Tomorrow you must go hunt for meat to feed people. Must gather firewood, make ready. Andre take men to hunt. Need elk, buffalo, maybe some goose, turkey."

Andre grinned. "What Rene tell Jar do?"

"Him busy. Jar clean cabin, scrub floor. Make ready for Willow." The men enjoyed a good laugh at Jar's expense.

Andre added. "Willow shoot long gun good. Jar not make cabin clean Willow shoot." Jar laughed along with the men.

Pig Eye threw wood on the fire and sparks rose in the air as the coals were disturbed. The fire flared and cast long shadows of the men into the darkness behind them. John McDonald talked about the trip and related how Louis had handled river crossings, helped all of them adjust to travelling and found good camping places to spend the nights. Reverend Christie added his thoughts and praised Louis for the way he brought food for them prior to the trip. Louis was embarrassed. He felt like hiding behind the big man beside him. He had only done what Jar told him.

Christie came from the cabin and wandered around in the morning light, watching all the activity. The hunting party was busy saddling packhorses to carry meat back, checking guns, powder and shot. Rene and John were in the trading post preparing to list the inventory of trade goods. Christie spotted Jar and Louis lighting a fire in the horse pen so he decided to walk up the slope to see what was going on. On the way, he stopped to look at the large garden, thinking, 'So much better than anything Ah managed ta do.' Christie leaned on the rail fence and marveled at the long rows of carrots, onions, potatoes, beans, and corn, all being grown to supplement a diet heavy in meat. The rows of corn were taller than he was. Finally, he wandered over to the pen where a cow was tied to a stout post. He heard Jar say, "Louis, yea push th' cow over agin th' fence an' hang on ta her tail. I'll get th' iron."

Jar hurried to the fire and came back with a glowing, bright red branding iron. He placed the iron against the cow's left shoulder and held it there. The smell of burning hair drifted to Christie on the breeze. Not a good smell. The cow bellowed and tried to move away and the fence held her. Jar took the iron back to the fire and added a few sticks.

They untied the cow, now with a Bar R on her shoulder, took her out the other side of the pen and turned her loose in the valley. Christie watched them repeat the process until all the cattle and new horses were branded and out in the long grass of the valley. The only horse left unbranded was the one belonging to Christie.

It was hot, dusty work. The men were wet with sweat when it was over. Jar suggested, "Let us go an' sit in th' shade by th' creek ta cool off." A few minutes of sitting there and Jar pulled off his boots, stripped off his clothes and walked into the water to sit on a large rock. Bending far over, he scrubbed his red hair and splashed water over his body, his muscles rippling in the sunlight. After a few minutes, he walked out of the water and stood in the sun to dry off. "Tha' feels good. Tis no good feeling, being dirty an' sweaty." Jar put on his pants and pulled the cotton shirt over his head. Louis had never seen socks before and watched Jar stick his feet into the strange things before pulling on his boots.

Jar sat facing them and Christie asked, "Angus, tell me what is lady Willow's last name?"

Jar's eyes cooled and Christie wondered if he had said something wrong. "Willow's full name is Willow Flower. She be th' daughter of Chief Red Thunder of th' Yanktonai Sioux Indian nation."

Christie frowned. "She is not a Christian then."

"Willow would'na know what th' word means. She believes in th' same god yea do."

Christie was shocked. "How can that be?"

"Yea call god, God. Willow calls god th' Great Spirit an' she lives her life in accordance with what she believes is right." Jar softened the tone of his voice. "This be a far different land from th' place where yea grew up, Christie. Th' land where a person lives shapes their life an' the way they think. Th' Sioux have built a good life by adapting ta th' land they live on, a land that god created. Yea have experienced how poorly Europeans live in this land god made because they can'na see past how things ar' done back in th' old country. God is God. People everywhere have their own name fer him.

"Every summer I travel ta San Carlos an' St. Louis where th' people are mostly French an' Spanish. They believe in god an' build churches fer him. They both think their way is th' only way, just as yea do. The fact is that yea all believe in th' same god, yea just have different ways of doing it. Which one of yea is right?"

"Willow Flower believes in god, she calls him th' Great Spirit an' she fears doing anything ta disappoint him. I believe in god an' use both names."

Christie was astounded. A dissertation like this was the last thing he expected from anyone out here beyond the reach of civilization. That row of books flashed through his mind and he determined to take a look at what they were. This James Angus Richardson obviously went to school and he read books. He must also think about what he read and about the world around him. "Very interesting, Angus. Yea have given me much ta think about. Ah must say that Ah am looking forward ta meeting th' lady Willow. Have yea an' th' lady given thought ta what yea want at th' wedding?"

"We wish ta be married; as simple as that. We want ta be married in accordance with Sioux tradition an' in accordance with th' church. It is important ta me that th' marriage be recognized an' accepted by both native an' white people. Willow's people do not understand English an' yea wull no understand Sioux. When done, everyone will know that Willow an' I are properly married.

"White people are far more prejudiced an' unaccepting than th' Sioux are. It will no be easy fer Willow ta be accepted in white society. I want there never ta be any question that Willow is properly married." The voice hardened again. "She will be Mrs. Willow Richardson, I will be very proud of her an' will tolerate no discrimination toward her."

Chapter 23

The trading post was a beehive of activity. Willow Flower was expected to arrive today and tomorrow there would be a wedding. The day before the men had dug a pit fifty paces out in front of the trading post and lined the bottom with two layers of rocks. A huge fire was lit to heat the rocks and build a layer of hot coals. When the fire burned down, they put sides of buffalo and elk meat on the coals to roast and covered the meat with a thick mat of damp, green grass, added a layer of clay and lit another fire that would be kept burning all day.

Rene hung a large iron kettle on a tripod over a campfire to prepare one of his elk meat stews with new carrots, onions and potatoes from the garden. It would simmer and cook all day. Turkeys and geese were being plucked, cleaned and made ready for spitting.

Julia McDonald came to observe the preparations. It was her first time out of the cabin since arriving at the post. She was well rested, bathed, her hair washed and she was wearing a clean dress. Julia felt better than in many days. She smiled and talked as Jar walked her around, introducing her to the men. John came and took her to tour the trading post.

Jar's constant looking to the west for Willow amused the men. They smiled and looked at each other, but not one man made a comment. Rene was everywhere, checking and making suggestions. Rene was happy. After waiting years for Jar to find a wife, Willow came on the scene and Rene worried that Jar was moving too slow. Rene pushed, suggested, and argued; now it was about to happen.

Rene and Andre went to the cabin and rolled their bedding, gathered all their possessions and moved to the trading house, taking Reverend Miles Christie with them.

In mid-afternoon, Chief Red Thunder led a long line of horses and people around the western corner of the hills while Jar was sitting in the shade talking to Christie. Louis came to tell him the Sioux were coming. Jar hurried to the front of the cabin to watch as the long line of horses and travois came across the grasslands. Jar was both excited and surprised. He knew Red Thunder would bring his family for the wedding. He hadn't considered there would be this many people. They were still too far away to count, but he estimated there must be fifty or more.

As always, the men automatically moved to their defensive positions and watched. Jar stood in front of the cabin and Rene came to join him. Christie came with the McDonalds to stand nearby. Chief Red Thunder was dressed magnificently in a decorated deerskin hunting shirt with a long eagle feather headdress that circled his head and hung down his back, signifying a senior chief of the Sioux Indian federation.

Red Thunder rode right to Jar, amused as always that Black Arrow's eyes were only for Willow Flower, who was following him. As Red Thunder dismounted, Rene jabbed Black Arrow with an elbow. Black Arrow's eyes found the Chief and they both stepped forward to shake hands; that strange white man custom. "Welcome,

Chief Red Thunder, we are happy that you have come."

Keeping a stern countenance, Red Thunder replied, "Chief say five days, now five days." He turned to Rene who Willow said would be uncle to her and stuck out his hand again. "Rene is healthy?"

"Yes, Chief, Rene is healthy. Rene wishes Chief will come many times to visit, to talk." He got a nod as the chief looked past him so Rene turned to look at the three whites. In English, he told them, "This man is Chief Red Thunder of the great Sioux nation. He is the father of Willow Flower."

Back speaking in Sioux, Rene pointed at Christie. "Chief, this is the white man spirit man. His name is Miles Christie. He has come from Fort Garry to say white man words at the marriage." Christie couldn't understand what was said, but he heard his name. Red Thunder studied Christie carefully. So, this is what a spirit man looks like. The chief wondered if the spirit man possessed magical powers. He wasn't big like Black Arrow and there was no sign of weapons; the spirit man didn't seem scary. Satisfied, the chief stuck out his hand. The spirit man took it and his grip was firm, the words he said were a blur of noise. Rene interpreted. "Miles Christie says he is pleased to meet the great chief Red Thunder who Black Arrow speaks so highly of."

Chief Red Thunder nodded his head at Christie before switching his eyes to the McDonalds. Rene went through the ritual of introducing and explaining. The chief acknowledged Mrs. McDonald with a nod and didn't offer to shake hands with her. In his world women belonged in the teepee.

Morning Sun Woman was already on the ground as Jar hurried toward Willow Flower, still sitting on White Cloud. She waited in anticipation for him, wondering if he would notice her dress. She smiled when he remembered his manners and greeted her mother. "Welcome, Morning Sun Woman, you are healthy?"

"Morning Sun Woman is happy to see Black Arrow."

Jar nodded in agreement as he turned toward Willow Flower. He noted that she was wearing a new deerskin dress. His eyes were only for her, not the dress. Willow reached down to arrange the dress on his side of the horse and his eyes followed her hand. Jar's head tilted slightly sideways and a puzzled look crossed his face. Willow laughed happily. "James Richardson like Willow's dress?"

"It is very nice, Willow. Something is different. Your dress hangs to the top of your boots."

Morning Sun Woman came to stand beside Willow's leg. Willow took her foot out of the stirrup and her mother moved the skirt to show the leg. Willow's leg was enclosed in deerskin. It was part dress, part pants like Jar wore. Willow laughed again at his expression. "Willow surprise James?"

Jar looked up at her and grinned happily. "Yes, Willow surprise James. What have you done to your dress?"

"Ho, white man, you see." Willow put her boot back in the stirrup, swung her right leg over White Cloud's rump and dismounted. She stood there in front of him, wearing a normal looking, long, deerskin skirt; smiling at his puzzlement. Willow let him stare for a moment before bending down and parting the skirt. It opened, showing her leather encased legs. "Willow make dress for riding White Cloud. James likes."

"Yes, James likes." Suddenly, he understood. "You made the

skirt split part way up the front and back so the saddle doesn't pull the dress up when you ride. Very good, Willow! James likes." They laughed together and Morning Sun Woman smiled at their happiness.

Hand in hand, they went to greet Willow's relatives, after which Jar brought her to meet the new whites. Willow held her head high and looked them straight in the eye, especially the spirit man whom she didn't find all that scary. Willow found she was the same height as the white woman. When the introductions in a mixture of Sioux and English were completed, Willow turned to Rene. "Ho, Uncle Rene, you are healthy?"

Rene was pleased at being called uncle and smiled. "Rene is happy to see Willow Flower. Rene is happy Willow has come to live in Black Arrow's teepee." Willow smiled and they chatted on about White Cloud and all the preparations made for the marriage. Jar translated the Sioux words for Christie and the McDonalds. Julia McDonald commented, "Rene seems ta speak th' Sioux language very well."

Jar nodded. "Yes, he does, an' he ha' been teaching Willow ta speak English. Rene also speaks Cree, Mandan an' French."

It was amazing to the three Scots that these frontier men, never having been inside a schoolroom, were all conversant in several languages. Christie remembered the conversation about religion he had shared with Richardson. He decided it would not be wise to underestimate any of these people. Although these men dressed roughly and often looked unkempt, they were not dumb.

Rene invited Willow Flower to go to the trading house to see her ring. Jar dutifully told the whites what they were doing. He smiled when he added, "Rene ha' been fashioning a ring fer days an' refuses ta let me see it. He claims it is fer Willow an' I can see it at th' wedding."

They stood there and watched the flurry of activity as the Sioux erected teepees, set up camp and staked out their horses. It happened so quickly it was hard to believe. The Sioux were a mobile people who packed up and moved regularly in accordance with the demands of hunting and the changing seasons.

Willow and Rene returned from the trading post and Jar suggested, "Willow, come to the cabin and see what is new."

Willow shook her head. "Willow no go to teepee until Chief Red Thunder say Willow married."

Jar was stunned. Willow had visited the cabin many times before. Rene spoke to him in English. "Jar, Willow is following proper Sioux custom. Sioux families do not allow an unmarried daughter to be alone with a man who is not a member of the family. A Sioux girl does not go into a teepee with a man before the wedding. She goes to the teepee with her husband." Rene added in Sioux, "Everything changed when you asked Red Thunder for permission to marry Willow. You stopped being a family friend."

Jar sputtered. "I never meant…I just wanted Willow ta see th' gifts Madame Chadron sent fer her."

Willow's eyes lit up when she heard the word 'gifts.' She listened to Rene say, "Bring the chest outside the cabin. Willow can open it here."

Jar hurried into the cabin as Rene told Willow, "You wait here while Rene fetches Morning Sun Woman."

When they were all gathered, Jar took them to look at the oak chest. He explained to Willow and her mother that it was to store clothes. Willow put her finger on the words painted on the top of the chest. Jar explained, “It says Mrs. Willow Richardson. That tells everyone this chest belongs to Willow.”

Willow smiled at him. “Is good, James.”

“Open it, Willow, and see what is inside.” Jar helped her with the clasp and Willow lifted the lid to look. On top was a sunbonnet. Willow picked it up and looked at it curiously. Julia came and suggested, “May I help?” Jar translated.

Julia put the bonnet on Willow’s head and tied the long ribbons under her chin. The top of the bonnet stuck out over her eyes. Jar explained, “It is to protect your head and eyes from the sun on a hot day.”

Willow turned toward the afternoon sun. Yes, it did shade her eyes. She turned back. “Is good, James.” Next came the sewing box and the three ladies spent time sorting through all the contents. Using the scissors from the box, Willow cut open the package from Madame Chadron and gasped with delight when she saw the glass mirror set in its polished wood mount, with a handle for holding it. Willow looked at herself and laughed happily at the bonnet on her head. Julia showed her what the hairbrush was for and Willow went to Jar and brushed his red hair as she laughed at him.

When Willow picked up the package that held the unmentionables Jar took it from her hand and explained, “You can open this later,” and went to put it in the cabin. When he returned, Willow was holding up a dress. Julia held the waist in to Willow’s body and commented. “It should fit perfectly. My, what a nice dress, Willow,” Rene interpreted. The second dress got the same treatment. At the bottom of the chest were two bolts of dress material in different designs and colors. Julia exclaimed, “Oh, Willow, yea wull be able ta sew beautiful dresses whenever yea want.”

Willow was very excited and happy, still she remembered her manners. “Willow sew dress in winter. Julia sew dress.” Rene told Julia what Willow said and Willow saw Julia’s eye glisten with moisture. Julia came to hug her.

Rene told Willow. “That was very nice, what Willow did.”

Willow responded, “Willow, Julia two womans; are many mans. Willow, Julia talk, look after teepees, make dresses; mans work.”

Rene and Jar laughed. Julia heard her name and wondered. Jar put his arm around Willow’s shoulders and she let him hug her. Rene told Julia and the men what Willow said and they all laughed.

Julia told Jar, “Mr. Richardson, please tell Willow tha’ Ah am so very happy she is here. Tell her tha’ Ah hope we can be good friends.”

Jar translated for Willow and she asked what is this friend? When he explained, Willow smiled at Julia, pointed at her and said in English, “Julia, friend.”

Julia was caught off guard by the English words. After a moment, she pointed at Willow. “Willow, friend.” The women looked happily at each other.

“Mr. Richardson, ask Willow if I can help ta pack ‘er dresses back in th’ chest.”

The two women got busy folding the dresses and carefully packed them away. Morning Sun Woman stood close to watch.

With the camp established and his people settled, Red Thunder gathered the elders around a fire. He sent Spotted Tail to invite Black Arrow to talk trade. Richardson came with his map showing the valley, the hills around it and the markers erected at the corners. He estimated that the two mile by seven mile block outlined on the map contained about nine thousand acres. Assuming a value of five cents per acre it was worth 450 American dollars. Richardson felt this was fair since President Jefferson had paid much less to the French for the Louisiana Territory. Of course, this was a white man's way of looking at land. The Sioux might have an entirely different perception of the value.

On a trade basis, a Lancaster long gun went for thirteen beaver, making the value of a gun seventy-eight dollars delivered out here deep in the remote wilderness along the Missouri River. Jar figured five Lancasters would be a fair trade. Since obtaining title to the land was so important to him, he was prepared to go higher.

Richardson took a seat on the robe designated for him with Rene on his right and the Reverend Christie, who would be a witness, on the other side.

Chief Red Thunder didn't like the spirit man being at the council. He noticed that two of the elders were obviously uneasy. Was the spirit man there to work some kind of magic on the Sioux? He considered in silence before deciding that as in the past, Black Arrow could be trusted. Looking at Black Arrow, the Chief started the conversation. "Black Arrow asks Sioux to trade this Sioux land where he built his teepee of wood for long guns from trading post. Black Arrow tells chief and elders that white men do this to protect families. When the sun rises, Willow Flower will be Black Arrow family. Willow Flower is Sioux. Elders talk long about this strange thing Black Arrow asks. Elders say Black Arrow, Willow Flower and Uncle Rene can live here long time, no need trade. Black Arrow also tells elders this trade is much important to him. Elders have talked of this. Elders tell Chief that if trade is much important to Black Arrow he must trade this many beaver in long guns for Sioux land." Red Thunder held up both fists and flashed the fingers five times.

Rene used English to speak to Jar. "Elders want fifty beaver in guns." Rene held up four fingers, knowing the elders were watching. "Four long guns trade fifty-two beaver. What Jar think?"

Jar's head swiveled to face Rene. "I want ta be fair, Rene. It be important fer when white settlers start arriving that we hav' a signed deed ta go wi' this map."

Rene shrugged. "What Jar think is fair?"

Jar held up five fingers. "I want ta trade five long guns with powder an' lead for th' land. An', I will throw in five hunting knives fer goodwill if they agree ta put their marks on the deed."

Rene frowned. "Why Jar give more than Sioux ask for trade? Has Jar lost head?"

"I ha' no lost my head, Rene. I want ta be sure the trade is fair an' na' one can say I took advantage." Jar turned to Christie. "What do yea think, Miles?"

The Sioux watched closely as Black Arrow talked to the spirit man. They didn't understand the words, just watched the exchange carefully. Christie responded, "Angus, yea are offering ta pay more than th' Sioux ar' ask'n. Ah would say yea ar' being more than fair.

Yea need their marks. Yea could offer a knife fer each mark. Might Ah suggest something? Back in Scotland, when a mon can'na sign his name it is common ta put ink on 'is thumb an' press that ta th' paper."

"Thank yea, Miles." Jar smiled. "That be a good suggestion if th' Sioux will agree." He turned back to face the chief who was waiting, expecting the spirit man had suggested some argument about the trade. Jar looked around the circle at the chief and five elders watching him. He now knew how to handle the knives. Jar held up the map so the Sioux could see it.

"Chief Red Thunder, this is the picture Black Arrow made showing the Sioux lands he wishes to trade for. Red Thunder has seen the markers that Black Arrow and Rene built to show the corners of the lands." Red Thunder nodded his head in agreement. "These white man words below the picture tell other white men about this trade. Black Arrow will need Red Thunder and the elders to make a thumb mark beside the words. If Red Thunder and the elders agree, Black Arrow will trade to the Sioux five long guns with powder and lead and six knives like Black Arrow and Rene use."

Red Thunder struggled to hide his surprise. Black Arrow was offering more than was asked. That was no way to trade. He turned his eyes to Rene. "Uncle Rene tell chief why Black Arrow says more for trade."

Rene's hands were resting on the knees of his crossed legs. He raised one hand and held up four fingers. "Chief Red Thunder asks four long guns. Black Arrow thinks that not fair. Black Arrow say will trade five long guns." Rene added his thumb to the fingers.

Six pairs of eyes looked at Black Arrow. This white man was

different, he made many surprises. The silence lasted as the Sioux tried to fathom what went on in Black Arrow's head. Red Thunder's voice took on an edge as he looked back at Rene. "Black Arrow say six knives. Sioux not ask for knives. Why Black Arrow do this?"

Rene used his hands as he replied. "Black Arrow ask chief and elders to make mark on white man picture. Spirit Man say Black Arrow give knife to each elder as he make mark. Knife is trade for mark. Spirit Man say Black Arrow must be fair."

Now, the eyes all looked at Miles Christie, who didn't know why he was the focus of attention. He found the long silent pauses that were normal in Sioux deliberations to be unsettling. Neither Angus nor Rene seemed bothered, so he sat quietly and waited.

Finally, Red Thunder inquired, "Do the elders agree to this trade?" He looked at each elder in turn and received a nod of agreement. He turned his head to Black Arrow. "Sioux agree to trade. Sioux will make mark on white man picture."

They gathered around the Chief's fire to spend the evening eating and talking. Rene and his men uncovered the roasting pit and placed the meat on planks laid across logs to form low working tables. The meat was carved and everyone came to eat their fill. Afterwards, Willow Flower sat with Morning Sun Woman and other women of her extended family. She watched James sitting across the fire beside Red Thunder, the Spirit Man, and the McDonalds. Rene came and went as he made sure everyone was eating. The men of her family were scattered around the chief and the white men.

Julia was the lone woman in the crowd of men. Willow knew the men of her family didn't approve of her being there. At a time like this, they expected the women to stay on their side of the fire. This was another way in which James was different. He treated women the same as men. Willow used her hands to cover her face to hide the smile these thoughts caused her. James was full of surprises, which she loved. Even Red Thunder was coming to accept the way her man was. Tonight they would feast and she must remain apart from James as was the accepted custom. In the morning, she would be married, she would wear the ring Rene made for her and her life would change. At the thought of being with James, Willow felt a tingle of excitement in her stomach like it was full of small birds flying around. Tomorrow, she would have her own teepee to supervise and many new things to learn. Willow knew all that was necessary to live as a Sioux. Soon, she would master all the strange white man customs.

Willow watched Rene come out of the darkness and take a place on the ground beside the McDonalds. Julia spoke to Rene, who smiled and looked across the fire at Willow before replying. Rene stood up and held out his hand to help Julia to her feet. Julia held his arm and Willow watched them start walking carefully through the crowd of men. Suddenly, she realized Rene was bringing Julia to visit her. Willow moved sideways to make room on the buffalo robe, between her and Morning Sun Woman.

Rene stopped in front of Willow and asked, "Mrs. McDonald would like to sit with you Willow. Is that okay?"

Willow patted the robe and replied, "Julia, come."

Julia smiled at the English words. "Thank yea, Willow. Ah was most uncomfortable being th' only lady in midst of all those men." As Julia knelt to seat herself, Rene translated the words for Willow.

Willow touched Julia's arm. "Julia stay," for which she received a smile. Willow looked up. "Uncle Rene, stay?"

"No, Willow. All the men would laugh at Rene, think him a woman."

"Ho, Rene no woman. Willow think Uncle Rene much strong, no mans laugh. Rene go, Willow talk words with Julia, make much joke about mans."

Julia and Rene both understood her halting English and her attempt at humor. Rene told her, "Willow not make jokes about men." He turned away laughing and went to sit near Jar. Julia and Willow struggled to talk in slow, halting English. All the time Willow frequently glanced at James, wishing she could be close to him.

Willow and Morning Sun Woman went to the stream to bathe while it was still dark. Before first light, Willow was back in the teepee where she used the comb James had given her to remove the tangles from her long black hair. Morning Sun Woman waited patiently for her to finish before beginning to carefully plait Willow's hair in two long braids.

Red Thunder watched from his robes, thinking of the past seventeen summers. This daughter was different almost from the start. As soon as she could walk she would come toddling to where he was and sit beside him. When the elders sat around his fire to discuss serious matters she would come, sometimes sitting looking up at him, at other times staring at the old men in the circle, always listening. Morning Sun Woman often came for her and took her to the teepee or to where the women were working. Soon, Willow would return. As she grew older and was no longer a baby it was less tolerable. Often the elders frowned at her presence. When Red Thunder told her to stay away she would sit nearby to listen, so in the end, what difference did it make? The men resorted to ignoring her.

Willow was competitive with everyone, always wanting to learn. She was always asking why. The day came when in the safety of the teepee she raised the subjects being discussed and commented on the decisions. He was shocked at how much she understood. Slowly, he came to respect her observations. Willow knew more about the day to day running and planning of the Yanktonai than most of the men.

As a result, he allowed her more freedom than other Sioux families did their daughters. To cover up, he growled at her in front of others. At fourteen summers other girls were marrying and no brave showed real interest in Willow. By sixteen summers he was discussing with Morning Sun Woman serious issues on how to find a husband for their daughter. When the white man came into their lives, Willow quickly decided this Black Arrow was the man for her. She began her campaign to show him she would make a good wife.

Morning Sun Woman kept him informed of everything Willow did. Again Willow crossed the lines of proper conduct, going to visit at the trading post and walking around the village holding his hand. Always, of course, with someone from the family watching. Black Arrow brought her presents and in the spring the big horse they named White Cloud. That horse was the envy of everyone in the village. The people understood that Black Arrow would ask for Willow to be his wife. Now the marriage was about to happen and Red Thunder was pleased. Willow would be married and having such a man join the family would enhance his standing with all the Sioux chiefs and elders.

It was daylight and time for him to prepare for the ceremony. Throwing back the robes, Red Thunder stood and pulled a hunting shirt over his head, stuck his feet into moccasins and ducked through the teepee flap to face the day. First, he would wash at the stream, then the marriage, followed by the morning meal.

Starting the fire was Morning Sun Woman's duty. Since she was busy with Willow Flower, the men of the family gathered wood, lit the fire and arranged the buffalo robes. There was a place for Red Thunder and two elders on one side of the fire facing the rising sun and a robe for Willow and Black Arrow opposite them. Red Thunder changed into his ceremonial clothes, put on the eagle feather headdress and brought the deerskin case containing the pipe. Standing on the central robe, he looked around at the people gathered. All seemed to be there. He instructed Spotted Tail, "Tell Uncle Rene that all is ready for Black Arrow."

Rene watched Spotted Tail come up the slope to where he stood in front of the cabin along with the people from the trading post. "Chief Red Thunder sends word that all is ready for Black Arrow."

"Thank you, Spotted Tail. Rene will tell Black Arrow. Will you walk with us?"

"Spotted Tail will walk with Rene." He nodded his head, pleased at the unexpected honor of accompanying Black Arrow to the marriage. James Richardson came from the cabin for his wedding day wearing grey wool pants over his leather boots. He also wore a blue cotton shirt under the shining white deerskin hunting shirt he was given while trading three years before. Around his neck he wore the bear claw necklace from the Black Hills. Behind his belt was a hunting knife and pistol as befitted a warrior. The gathered Sioux watched the procession walk down the slope led by Black Arrow who was flanked by Rene and Spotted Tail, with the other whites following. Rene would interpret the Sioux words for those who didn't know the language.

Spotted Tail showed Black Arrow where he was to stand and went to rap on the flap of the teepee, before holding it open. Willow Flower ducked through the opening and stood up, looking for James, who was staring at her. She smiled as he looked at her black hair, glistening in the morning light. Willow was wearing the deerskin dress and moccasins she and Morning Sun Woman had spent many days sewing and decorating with quills and hollow bird bones.

Morning Sun Woman guided Willow to her place beside Black Arrow and stood behind them, still the ever-vigilant mother guarding her daughter, although now it was only ceremonial to demonstrate to all present that the family had kept their daughter pure.

Red Thunder waved everyone down and took his seat. He removed the carved stone pipe from its leather case and cut tobacco to pack the bowl. With great dignity, he offered the pipe to the four directions and to the sky before taking a taper from the fire to light the tobacco. When the pipe was drawing nicely, he blew smoke to the Great Spirit in the sky. Red Thunder handed the pipe to the elder on his right, who was his oldest brother.

The elder offered the pipe, puffed and blew smoke to the sky. Pointing the pipe stem at Willow Flower, he asked, "Does Willow Flower of the Yanktonai Sioux, daughter of Morning Sun Woman and Chief Red Thunder, wish to marry this white man?"

"Yes, Uncle, Willow Flower wishes to marry James Richardson."

Red Thunder took the pipe and passed it to the other elder sitting on his left facing Black Arrow. After going through the same pipe ritual, the elder looked for several moments at the white man. "Black Arrow asked Red Thunder for his daughter Willow Flower to be his wife. Does Black Arrow wish to marry Willow Flower?"

"Yes, Grandfather, Black Arrow wishes to marry Willow Flower."

"Will Black Arrow be a good husband, protect and provide for Willow Flower and her children?"

"Yes, Grandfather, Black Arrow will do all he can to protect Willow Flower and her children."

The old elder watched for a moment before handing the pipe to Red Thunder who placed it carefully on its covering before standing and holding his hands up to the sky. "Red Thunder asks the Great Spirit to guide this woman that she may always be a good wife to her husband, keep her teepee clean and be blessed with many children. Red Thunder asks that the Great Spirit guide this warrior's arrows so there will always be meat for the teepee and skins for clothing."

Red Thunder lowered his hands and held them out toward the couple. "Red Thunder tells all Yanktonia that Black Arrow and Willow Flower are married and from now, shall live as one."

Willow, who had sat demurely with her hands folded in her lap through the ceremony, was suddenly smiling and turned her head to look at James. He held out his hand to help her stand. He moved to hug her and Willow shook her head. "Spirit man say words." That stopped him.

Rene came with Christie and Mrs. McDonald. They stood together in a row with Rene beside James and Julia beside Willow, facing Reverend Miles Christie who was wearing a long, deep blue robe and a black hat, with a white collar around his neck. Andre walked to Red Thunder and asked if he could sit beside him and Morning Sun Woman to tell them what the spirit man said. Red Thunder nodded his head and pointed at a place on the buffalo robe for Andre to sit.

Andre decided not to translate the actual words, but rather to explain what was being said. "The Spirit man is praying to the Great Spirit for guidance of today's wedding and for a happy marriage."

Red Thunder nodded as he watched the white man spirit man.

"Now he is telling Black Arrow and Willow Flower that marriage is a blessing from the Great Spirit who is everywhere. They must work together to make a happy marriage and must always look after each other and their children.

"The spirit man tells Black Arrow to hold Willow Flower's hand and he asks Willow if she wishes to marry this man." They waited for Rene to translate the words for Willow and saw her smile as she replied, "Willow wishes marry James Richardson."

"Black Arrow is being asked if he wishes to marry Willow Flower," and they heard the answer. "Now the spirit man is asking Rene for the ring which Black Arrow must put on Willow Flower's finger."

They all watched as Rene handed the ring to Black Arrow who turned toward Willow and slid the ring onto the finger of her left hand. Both bent their heads to look at the ring before looking up at each other and grinning happily.

Andre looked at Red Thunder. "The spirit man is asking the Great Spirit to bless this marriage, to give them many seasons together and many children." Red Thunder thought it was not really different from what the Sioux do. Many children would make him happy. "Ah, the spirit man is telling them they are now married and are husband and wife."

Red Thunder watched Black Arrow reach out to shake hands with the spirit man and was shocked to see Willow do the same. He was amazed when the spirit man took Willow's hand and patted it with his other hand. These white men were very strange. Black Arrow put his arms around Willow and held her close. When he released her, Uncle Rene put his arm around her shoulders and talked to her. Willow turned to Julia and the women hugged before excitedly looking at the ring on Willow's finger. Red Thunder didn't understand these strange customs; there was much to learn about the white men. The good thing was that his daughter was married. His thoughts were interrupted when Andre said, "Andre must go to say congratulations to Black Arrow and Willow. Will Red Thunder and Morning Sun Woman come with Andre?"

Morning Sun didn't wait for Red Thunder to agree; she stood up and started around the fire. Red Thunder looked at her as he got to his feet. The men followed. Everyone wanted to see this thing called a ring that Black Arrow had put on Willow Flower's finger.

The women began warming food left from the night before and people gathered around to eat and talk about the two weddings. Such a thing was never heard of—a Sioux wedding and a white man wedding, both for the same people.

When the eating and talking were over, the men carried Willow's possessions to the cabin, leaving them on the table and chairs. It was midday when Black Arrow and Willow Flower walked up the slope to the cabin, went in and closed the door. Willow stood inside the door looking around at her teepee made of wood. It was clean and orderly. Now it was her home. As soon as she put her things in their proper places everything would be good. Her eyes moved to the large bunk where James slept before she turned to look at him. James held out his arms and she moved easily to him to be hugged. He didn't crush her like he usually did, just held her tightly in his strong arms.

Willow put her head on his chest and her right ear could feel and hear James' heart beating. For the first time, she put her arms around his waist and hugged him. Suddenly, she felt nervous. This was the day she had waited for. Now she didn't feel so sure of herself, a feeling she wasn't accustomed to. Willow's mind raced as she tried to understand what was wrong, what was bothering her. This day would be talked about for a long time by the Sioux. Two weddings to get the daughter of Chief Red Thunder married. There was nothing like that in the oral histories handed down from generation to generation. Deep in her thoughts, she almost missed the soft voice. "Are you happy, Willow Flower?"

Willow nodded her head against James' chest. "Willow happy."

"Is something bothering you?" Willow heard the concern in his voice.

Willow let loose of his waist and he let her go. She stepped back to look up at him. "James and Willow ride horses in valley, make camp."

It wasn't what James expected, thinking she was nervous

about being alone with him. "You want to pack up our gear and go camping?"

Willow nodded her head yes, her eyes looking overly large. James studied her for a moment before conceding. "If you want to camp in the valley, we will do it. Why Willow? We have everything here in the cabin."

James understood as soon as Willow told him. "Much peoples here."